Fourteen

The Army Cadets

C.R. Cummings

Also By
CHRISTOPHER CUMMINGS

The Boy and the Battleship
The Green Idol of Kanaka Creek
Ross River Fever
Train to Kuranda
The Mudskipper Cup
Davey Jones's Locker
**Fourteen*
Air Cadet
Below Bartle Frere
Bowling Green Bay
Airship Over Atherton
Cockatoo
The Cadet Corporal
Stannary Hills
Coast of Cape York
Kylie and the Kelly Gang
Beyond the Barrier Reef
Behind Mt. Baldy
The Cadet Sergeant Major
Cooktown Christmas
Secret in the Clouds
Mischief at Mingela
The Word of God
The Cadet Under-Officer
Through the Devil's Eye
Barbara in the Bush
Barbara and the Smiley People
Barbara at her Best
Barbara's Bivouac

Fourteen

The Army Cadets

C.R. Cummings

This edition Published 2021 by DoctorZed Publishing

DoctorZed Publishing books may be ordered through booksellers or by contacting:

DoctorZed Publishing
10 Vista Ave
Skye, South Australia 5072
www.doctorzed.com

ISBN: 978-0-6453427-9-6 (hc)
ISBN: 978-0-6453427-8-9 (sc)
ISBN: 978-0-6453427-7-2 (ebk)

National Library of Australia Cataloguing-in-Publication entry

Author: Cummings, C. R., author.

Title: Fourteen/ Christopher Cummings.

ISBN: 9780645342796 (hardcover)

Series: Cummings, C. R. The army cadets.

Target Audience: For young adults.

Subjects: Adventure stories, Australian.

Military cadets--Queensland--Fiction.

Cover image © Kuritafsheen | Dreamstime.com
Cover design © Scott Zarcinas

Printed in Australia, UK & USA

DoctorZed Publishing rev. date: 11/11/2021

Dedication

This book is dedicated to the Warrant Officers of the Australian Army, Especially those posted as Company Sergeant Majors and Regimental Sergeant Majors, for they are the steel core of the army, the rock on which the foundations of victory and success are built.
In particular the author would like to gratefully thank and acknowledge, with respect and admiration, the following:

Warrant Officer Class 2 Vic Holley
(ARA Cadre 4 Cadet Battalion 1961-63)

Warrant Officer Class 2 F. J. Baggaley
(Ex Grenadier Guards & ARA Cadre 4 Cadet Battalion-Charters Towers 1961- 63; later RSM 49RQR)

Warrant Officer Class 2 Jim Neil
(CSM Admin/Support Company,31st Battalion, Royal Queensland Regiment 1974-75)

Warrant Officer Class 2 Alan Bruce
(CSM 31 Independent Rifle Company, Royal Queensland Regiment 1980-81)

Warrant Officer Class 1 Digby Lawrence
(CSM Officer Cadet Training Unit, 11 Training Group 1981-1983)

Warrant Officer Class 1 Ashley Barker
(Cadet CSM 130 Regional Cadet Unit Heatley 1990, and later CUO and OOC of 130ACU; Army RSM North Queensland AAC Brigade 2016-2018)

Warrant Officer Class 2 Collyn (George) Thorogood
(ARA OPSWO, HQ NQLD AAC BDE 2020-2021)

Lieutenant (AAC) David Willmett Conspicuous Service Medal
(Regular soldier for 25 years & CSM 6RAR & RMC; and Officer of Cadets in 130 Army Cadet Unit 2001 to 2021) whose knowledge, skill and instructional flair has provided expert training and confidence to many hundreds of young people in the Australian Army Cadets.

Chapter 1

GRAHAM

Cairns, North Queensland. A cool morning in August.

Graham Kirk, 14 years old, sat on the Esplanade staring out to sea. It was 8:15 in the morning and the sunlight sparkled off the water to light up his sun-tanned and freckled face.

Graham was a big lad for his age, solid and strong. He had clear blue eyes and mousy fair hair, a straight nose and determined jaw. Good looking, and he knew it. But for all that he sat brooding over the fact that his life seemed to be a miserable mess, particularly his love life.

Why can't I get a girlfriend? he pondered unhappily.

For a moment he catalogued the girls he had tried to develop relationships with over the last few years: Cindy, Glenys, Rowena, Desley Desmond, Jennifer. It was so frustrating! Graham was at that age where he had discovered that not only did he really like girls, but his body was feeling the full force of puberty. At times this seemed quite beyond his control. It was intensely frustrating and lent a tinge of desperation to his search.

Not that Graham had ever experienced real sex. His experiences were limited to a few passionate fumbles and a lot of personal pleasuring. Even as he sat there, he was aroused. Muttering with frustration, he tried to will his body to stay under control. The fact that it often did not was bothering him a lot.

Over the last few weeks he had seemed to have no control at all, his body becoming frequently aroused, apparently at random. It just happened unbidden, often at the most embarrassing times. It was as though it had a mind of its own.

Oh, I wish I could get a girlfriend! he groaned.

Fantasies of what he and she might do added to his arousal. Then he made a wry face. Well, he did have a girl who loved him, and whom he was sure would let him do anything he wanted if he asked her: little Margaret.

"But she is only a kid. She is too young," he muttered.

Margaret was only 12 and in Year 7. She was his sister's best friend and had been his faithful admirer for years. Graham shook his head.

No. She is 'Jail bait', he thought, using an expression his father had used once when warning him of the perils in life. So too were many of the girls at his high school that he lusted over, but that was somehow different. They were his own age or older. *And they are big girls,* he told himself.

Images of several flitted across his mind and he smiled. *Very big some of them,* he thought, picturing the curves and prominent breasts of Loretta. She had recently become the unwitting target of his romantic hopes and he was determined to try his luck by asking her for a date. He had considered this for weeks but now resolved to put it to the test.

But the school holidays had intervened and that, coupled to the pre-occupation of Graham and his friends with sailing, had kept him from trying before, or so he told himself, to justify his lack of courage. The thought of sailing made Graham's face set in sterner lines. His eyes swept along the Esplanade to the left, towards the hospital. The tide was on the ebb, exposing a wide belt of black, glutinous mud. It was just out there that his friend Max had lost his leg to a shark attack three weeks earlier.

It had been a frightening experience and now Max seemed to have cut him off. So had Max's big sister, Cindy. That was a matter of some regret for Graham because Cindy had taught him some of his first real lessons in sex.

But it wasn't girls that had caused Graham to get up early and to make his way down to the Esplanade—it was ships. Ever since he could remember, Graham had wanted to be a sailor; a naval officer if he could, but if not, then captain of a merchant ship like his dad. His father was a Master Mariner and ship owner, so Graham had wide experience of what this entailed. The unpleasant reality of some of those experiences had not deterred him from his ambition.

But the previous November Graham had received a stunning blow. He had discovered that his left eye was defective, debarring him forever from achieving his cherished ambition. The shock had been so bad he had gone into a state of severe depression and had even seriously contemplated suicide. Feeling humiliated he had also left the Navy Cadets, which he had joined so full of hope a few months before.

But despite that blow to his hopes, it was a naval vessel he had come to see. And it was visible now, a grey painted destroyer, slipping silently in along the main shipping channel from the open sea. The sight of it caused all his dead hopes and dreams to rise from their bitter ashes. Even as his mind and eyes took in the details of the destroyer his emotions were torn by the misery of his loss. His mouth twisted into a bitter curl as his fondest daydream flitted across his consciousness.

For years Graham had fantasised about becoming the captain of just such a warship; powerful, sleek, and deadly; a grey hunter of the sea studded with guns, missiles, radars and radio aerials. In his imagination he had carried out a string of heroic feats and then brought his ship steaming into Cairns to a hero's welcome, to the adulation of his school friends, and particularly of the girls.

Now he watched the destroyer slip past along the shipping channel a kilometre offshore, the white uniforms of the crew plainly visible as they fell in for entering harbour. Even at that distance and against the backdrop of the jungle clad mountains across Trinity Inlet he could see a radar scanner rotating on the destroyer's mast. The sight of the ship caused a feeling of sick misery to well up. Tears prickled and his mouth puckered up.

He bit his lip and shook his head. A sigh that was almost a sob was torn from him. *I shouldn't have come,* he told himself. But the moment he had heard that the ship was coming in he had felt driven to make the effort to see it.

"I must be like one of those alcoholics who can't keep off the booze," he muttered.

For a moment he wondered if he was one of those people who like inflicting pain on themselves. Then he shook his head. No. It was just that the dream, and the interest in ships, had been so much a part of his life for so long that he found it very difficult to break with it.

That left him with the problem of what he could do as a career instead. "I'm no good at anything! What can I be?" he muttered as he watched the destroyer begin to vanish from view behind the buildings of The Pier. He could not imagine any other job that he might be interested in. Ordinary occupations all seemed to him to be dull and colourless.

As the stern of the destroyer slipped from view behind the buildings of the port Graham glanced at his watch: 08:35. He sighed. *Time I was moving. I will be late for school if I don't get a move on,* he thought. *If I am late, I will be in more trouble.*

It seemed to him that he had been in so much trouble recently that his whole life felt like one long struggle. For an instant the idea of ending it all again surfaced and a tear escaped. Feeling sick at heart and deeply depressed Graham stood up, then turned and started walking towards school.

As he walked, he brooded, turning over in his mind the twin problems of girls and his future. *How can I ask Ailsa? What do I say?* he wondered.

At that moment cries of distress attracted Graham's attention. Fifty paces further along the footpath he saw two young girls from St Monica's. They were being tormented by a group of four youths. The girls appeared to be a bit younger than his sister Kylie, 10 or 11 he guessed. Two of the youths were Aboriginal and another looked to be at least part indigenous, but the other one appeared to be white. They looked to be older than Graham, 15 to 17, and were not dressed in any school uniform.

The youths were teasing the girls and one of them had hold of one girl's school bag. The young girl was holding the bag while crying and asking him to let go. The other girl's school bag was already on the ground, its contents strewn around. The youths were also making exceedingly crude comments to the obviously upset girls.

Graham saw red. Having suffered badly from bullies himself he hated such people with a passion. First, he glanced around to see if there were any adults who could intervene. None were visible. At that point the footpath led along beside the concrete seawall through a narrow strip of park. Beyond that was a street with cars rushing in both directions. Graham looked towards the houses and holiday flats across the street but there was no-one in sight. His heart sank.

His rational mind told him he could just detour or turn and walk the other way. But he also knew that if he did, he would despise himself. Instead he kept on walking towards the group. By this time the largest of the youths had wrenched the bag off the little girl and had begun to search inside.

"Where ya money?" the youth demanded of the frightened little girl, who now dissolved in tears. She shook her head.

"I haven't got any. Please leave us alone."

"You lying little bitch! Where your money eh? You give it me or we take ya behind that shed an' we do ya!" the youth threatened, indicating a building at the nearby tennis courts.

The second girl tried to run away and was grabbed by one of the youths who twisted her arm up behind her back. She screamed and he slapped her hard. "Shut up bitch! Or we give ya somethin' ter scream about eh!"

Graham was now only 20 paces away. He felt very scared and sick at heart. *I could get a real bashing if I intervene,* he thought.

His heart began pounding and he could feel the surge as the adrenalin was released into his system. His vision seemed to narrow and focus only on the oldest youth. Summoning up his ebbing courage he studied the situation.

What tactics should I use? he wondered. He sensed that any attempt to parley would merely be futile. Surprise was his only advantage. *But how to win against four boys bigger than me?* he puzzled.

The only thing he could think of was to attack with such ferocity that he incapacitated a couple in the first few seconds. The seriousness of that, and the vague awareness of possible legal consequences, made his stomach turn over.

At that moment, the second little girl screamed again and this time the youth punched her. She fell as though stunned. The other girl, wide-eyed with fear, opened her mouth to scream as well. Another youth grabbed her by the throat and choked the sound off.

By then Graham was only a few paces them. "Let her go!" he yelled, anxiously aware that he might be provoking a bad situation for himself.

The youth turned his head and scowled at him. "Piss off and mind yer own business shit face!" he replied.

With his mouth now dry with fear and his heart hammering hard Graham shook his head. "Let them go I said," he croaked.

"Or what shit face? What you gunna do eh?" the youth retorted with a sneer.

Graham cast an anxious look around, aware that a second youth was moving towards his right side and that the third still had hold of the other girl's arm. The fourth was still searching the girl's school bag. *I'm in trouble here,* he thought, wishing now he had rushed in and delivered a few blows to incapacitate at least one of them.

"Bugger off!" snarled the big youth.

He let go of the girl and shoved at Graham with both hands. Graham tried to stand his ground but was pushed backwards. As he did the second youth sprang in and punched at the side of his head. Graham had been expecting something like that and was able to doge, but the punch still connected. Half stunned Graham staggered sideways.

The big youth jeered and stepped closer, his fists half raised. Determined to go down fighting Graham suddenly sprang forward, anger and resolve combining. With the heel of his hand he hit the big youth hard on the bottom of his nose. The youth screamed in pain and sprang back, falling on his back as his hands went flying to his face. The youth holding the other girl let go and jumped back in alarm but the closer one beside Graham began raining punches onto the side of his head and shoulder. Even as he turned to face him Graham noted that the youth had yellowish whites to his eyes and was missing two front teeth.

The two met with a wild exchange of punches. Graham landed several but was hit twice in the face. With his head ringing he sprang sideways to avoid an attack by the fourth youth. The two little girls stood as though mesmerised.

"Run you girls, run!" Graham shouted.

Then he was struck hard from behind and hands grabbed at him. He tried to twist free, but the sweaty hands gripped him. A boot thudded into his thigh.

To his intense relief Graham saw the two girls start running. But he also saw the first youth he had struck scramble to his feet, his face an ugly mask of rage, blood trickling from his nose.

I'm for it now! Graham thought.

Fear changed to panic. He struggled desperately and lashed out hard at the youth beside him. A blow struck the side of his head with vicious force. Waves of red and black blurred his vision. He knew he could be fighting for his life and hoped the youths didn't have knives.

For an instant Graham broke free. A throat appeared in his vision and he slammed a right into it, taking the youth hard on the Adam's apple. Then an arm went around his own throat from behind and he was struck by a rain of blows to his face and body by two other youths. Fear lent Graham strength. He sensed that if he went down he was done for.

They will kick me to death!

Fear was turning to terror now. The youths were screaming murder and hammered at him from all sides. Graham could smell their rancid body odour, plus the stench of alcohol. Later he decided they must have been half-drunk.

Otherwise I would be dead!

Suddenly, the youth holding his busted nose, and who was kicking at Graham, was knocked down. A figure appeared on the edge of Graham's vision and the oldest youth took one look and fled. A man dressed in dark green T-shirt and shorts crossed Graham's front and the arm suddenly released his windpipe.

It was all over in an instant. As Graham stood there gasping for breath and trying to focus his eyes, the four youths scattered in obvious panic and fled across the park. The man chased them for a few paces then stopped, fists on hips. There was obviously no chance of catching the youths, so the man turned and came back to Graham, who was now doubled over with pain.

"You okay, son?" the man asked.

Graham looked up and nodded. The man looked to be in his forties and was dressed for jogging: green T-shirt, shorts and runners. He had a hard, square face with a small mouth set in a grim line. Not the sort of face Graham would argue with. The man was obviously very fit: barrel chest, muscles rippling in his arms and sturdy legs. His grey hair was cut very short in a 'crew cut' style. Just visible around his neck was a chain with a metal tag on it. This showed a number and name.

Army dog tags? Graham wondered.

"I'll be okay," he gasped in reply. "They only hit me a few times."

The man grunted. "Not good tactics that young fella, one against four. You're damned lucky they didn't really do you over."

"I thought they were going to," Graham replied with a wry grin. With a wince of pain he straightened up. "Thanks for saving me."

"My pleasure. Pity I didn't get time to land a few more hits. It's time those troublemakers were cleared out of this park."

"They should clear them right away from here, the mongrels!" Graham added angrily, rubbing at his sore face.

The man gave a wry grin. "That's probably what they say about us." He turned and looked at the retreating youths and added, "That is one of those issues Australia still has to come to terms with. We need to resolve it."

Graham shrugged and dabbed at his split lip. "They probably don't even come from here," he said. "They probably come from one of the remote communities."

"Yeah, well, let's be fair. They resent the way they've been treated the last hundred years or so and somehow we need to make things right."

"I suppose so," Graham agreed. "But them continually doing the wrong thing isn't solving anything either. It isn't earning them any respect."

"Respect. That's a good choice of words," the man said. "We all need that, and those kids need it a lot. At the moment they are just reacting out of resentment to a long list of grievances. It's justice and respect they want."

Graham nodded but then felt dizzy. The man looked closely at him. "Now, are you sure you are alright?" he asked.

"Yes sir," Graham replied; that 'sir' being added because the man looked like he was that sort of person.

The man grunted. "Good. Now, if you don't mind, give me a hand."

The man bent down and began picking up the scattered possessions of the girls, thrusting them into one of the school bags. Graham did as he was asked and helped. When they had collected everything, the man said, "Right, let's see these little girls safely to school."

Graham looked around and saw that the two girls were standing across the street with two middle aged women. "I should be going, sir. I'll be late for school myself otherwise."

"I think you'd better come with me," the man said in tones which did not brook argument. Then he held out his hand. "I'm Kevin Howley. I'm a Warrant Officer in the Regular Army. What's your name?"

"Graham. Graham Kirk... er sir." Graham replied taking the man's hand and feeling quite self-conscious about it.

Regular army! He thought, almost in awe.

Warrant Officer Howley nodded. "Pleased to meet you. That was a gutsy thing to do son. I saw you go to their aid when you could have just gone the other way. Now come on. Don't worry about school. We can square that, I'm sure."

Graham bit his lip with anxiety but followed Warrant Officer Howley across the street. At their approach the two little girls looked anxious.

Warrant Officer Howley explained to the two women who he was and what had happened, "I was just doing my morning PT run when I saw those lads attacking these two girls," he explained. "Now girls, if you are willing, we will walk you to school. If you don't like that we will telephone the police."

The mention of the police made the little girls look even more anxious. The pretty one with black hair said they would go with them and even gave Graham a shy smile.

It was two blocks to St Monica's school. During the walk Warrant Officer Howley chatted to Graham as though nothing had happened, asking about his life. He explained that he was a Company Sergeant Major with the 51st Battalion, the Far North Queensland Regiment.

"That is the local Army Reserve unit. We are a regional surveillance unit with sub-units all across northern Queensland." Then he said, "You must go to the same school as my girl, Amelia."

Amelia? Graham nodded. "I'm in 9B. There's a new girl called Amelia who sits behind me," he replied.

"That's her. Amelia Howley."

"We call her Millie," Graham replied.

Millie! Fancy her dad being a sergeant major in the army! he thought.

Up till now Graham had hardly taken any notice of her. She was a plain, slightly dumpy girl who had joined the class at the start of the term. Brown eyes, brown hair bobbed at the shoulder, very quiet and shy.

Warrant Officer Howley chuckled at the nickname. "What else!"

After a few minutes' walk they arrived at St Monica's. Graham had never been in the school grounds and did not want to go in even now. It was a Catholic girl's school. He was an Anglican and had been brought up with some reservations about Catholics. But even more he was intimidated by all those females! The yard was full of girls who all turned to stare as the group made its way up the path to the office. Graham felt very self-conscious and knew he was blushing as the girls were obviously discussing them.

Inside the office was no better because groups of girls kept walking past, all curious to know what was going on. Only on the ringing of the bell for morning classes did this end. Warrant Officer Howley quickly explained the situation to the lady behind the office counter and they were shown into an interview room and the two little girls whisked off by a Sister and a lady teacher.

Glancing up at a wall clock Graham noted that it was 9:00. *I'm late now,* he noted unhappily. *Oh well, I've been in trouble so much recently that once more won't matter,* he thought bitterly.

He resigned himself to more misery. To add to his unhappiness he was now starting to feel the pain from where he had been punched and kicked.

To his surprise two nice ladies came in with coffee and biscuits and ice compresses. One of them began to tenderly wipe his face with a warm cloth. "You are going to have a couple of good bruises I'm sorry," she said.

Graham blushed as he realised they were treating him as a wounded hero. The other lady smiled at him and held an ice pack to the side of his head. The incident was discussed and the ladies were indignant.

"There have been reports of a gang of youths giving the girls trouble, but this is the first time they have actually attacked any. It is a real worry," she said.

The door opened and a severely dressed lady came into the room, followed by two policemen. The lady was introduced as the Principal. Graham looked up at the police and felt his spirits sink. He recognised the long, thin one with the pimply face: Constable O'Neil. They had clashed only a few weeks before on several occasions while the sailing races with the Navy Cadets were being run.

Constable O'Neil recognised him at once. A look of surprise crossed his face, "You! I didn't think you were that sort of bad egg Kirk."

"I'm not sir," Graham replied, hotly aware that the others in the room were giving him curious looks because the policeman obviously knew him.

"So what happened?"

The story then had to be told in detail. To his embarrassment and relief Warrant Officer Howley supported Graham's story. "I saw it all. Very bravely done I thought," he added.

Everyone in the room nodded and Graham felt even more embarrassed. He was also worried. "Please sir, will you explain to my school why I am late?"

Constable O'Neil smiled and nodded. "Be glad to. It's a pleasure to be congratulating you instead of kicking your silly bum. Come on. I'll give you a lift in the car."

Graham blushed again. He didn't want these people, and especially Warrant Officer Howley, to know that he had been in trouble with the police. After being thanked again by the principal for saving her students Graham was led out to the police car. On the footpath Warrant Officer Howley shook his hand and said goodbye then jogged off along the footpath. Graham was told to get in the police car. That made him blush too as he was sure everyone seeing him would think he was in trouble.

This feeling was reinforced when they arrived at his own school a few minutes later. As the police car pulled up outside Graham could see student's faces peering through the windows. To his heated mind it seemed as though the whole school was staring at him. He and Constable O'Neil went in the front entrance and up the stairs to the front office. Even before the policemen could speak, Mr Fitzgerald, the Deputy Principal (and Graham's much feared nemesis) appeared from his office.

Mr Fitz's face instantly took on a grim cast. "What the devil has Kirk been up to this time?" he growled at Constable O'Neil.

"Being a knight in shining armour I'm glad to say," Constable O'Neil replied. Graham blushed again at the description. The story was outlined and Constable O'Neil gave him a real build up. "A real little hero I'd say."

Mr Fitz listened and slowly relaxed his face to a semblance of a smile. "Well that makes a change. Now, are you alright young Kirk? Do you want to see a doctor? I'll phone your mother if you want."

"Oh no sir! I'm alright. I only got hit a few times," Graham replied anxiously. If there was one thing he did not want, it was his mother being told!

"You are sure? Alright then. Well, you gentlemen had better come in and give the principal a full report if you wouldn't mind."

Mr Fitz ushered them all into the principal's office. Grey-headed old Mr Croswell stood up and shook hands with the constables. Graham liked Mr Croswell, considering him to be a real gentleman, but he felt very self-conscious sitting in his office. He had only ever been there when he had been in trouble before.

By the time the story had been retold and Graham again congratulated it was morning break. The babble of a thousand students leaving their classrooms filled the air. Graham was told he could go while the principal and the police sat to discuss measures to stop the gang problem which was developing, one that was doubly complicated because of the racial aspect which made it politically very sensitive.

Graham first visited the toilet and washed his face. He had a real bruise on the left side of his head which was very tender to touch. Other bruises showed on his arms and right thigh.

Could have been worse, he mused. Satisfied his appearance was satisfactory he went outside.

The first person he saw was Loretta. Loretta! She stood under B Block. *God, she's beautiful!* Graham thought.

Without realising what he was doing he walked towards her, his eyes drinking in her beauty: Long blonde hair, pert little upturned nose, bright blue eyes, a lovely shapely body, and a pair of prominent breasts that jutted out in a way that made his teenage boy's mouth go dry with lust just to observe.

For once Loretta was on her own. Normally she was with a group of other girls. Graham looked around. Hundreds of students were surging out of classrooms and downstairs but they were just going about their normal affairs.

Now is a chance to ask Loretta for a date, Graham thought. He knew he was scared and that nettled him. *Go on you coward! You were game to fight four bullies. So prove you are a man and ask her!*

With a sudden surge of resolve he headed for her.

Chapter 2

NOTHING BUT TROUBLE

As Graham approached Loretta, she turned and looked at him. Her stare made his courage evaporate. For an instant he contemplated just saying hello or something. But stubborn pride held him to his course.

"Hello Loretta. You look beautiful today," he heard himself say.

She looked surprised, then embarrassed. "Thank you," she replied. But she said it in a neutral tone and her face gave him no encouragement.

Graham swallowed and wiped sweaty palms on his shorts. "I er... um... I wondered if... wondered if you would like to go out?"

"With you? On a date you mean?" she asked.

Graham nodded. His heart was thumping so hard his chest felt constricted. Even before she replied he sensed defeat, from the look in her eyes and her facial expression.

"Sorry, no thanks," she replied.

"Thanks anyway," Graham said.

He felt sick despair well up and knew he was burning with shame, hotly aware that he had made a fool of himself. He was about to turn away when he was suddenly pushed hard in the shoulder.

It was Larsen, a big, red-headed Year 11 boy. He pushed Graham again and growled, "Piss off Kirk, and stop bothering my girl."

Stung by the defeat and by the humiliation of being man-handled Graham's temper flared.

"I'll talk to who I like," he replied.

Larsen raised a fist in front of his face. "Clear out before I smash you," he threatened.

Stubbornly, Graham stood his ground and glared defiantly at the older boy. He knew he risked more than just a thrashing if he made an issue of it, but he was so fed up and angry that he no longer cared. Larsen was two years older, and a good head taller, with arms and legs proportionally longer.

The older boy placed his clenched fists on his hips. "Listen Kirk, keep away from Loretta or I'll beat you to pulp."

Graham swallowed and felt sick inside, but he was stung beyond endurance. Loretta had been the object of his lovesick adoration for weeks now.

"You don't own her! She can talk to however she likes," he replied.

"And she doesn't like you, you twerp! You are annoying her. She doesn't want you bothering her. So clear off!" Larsen replied.

Graham eyed the way the older boy flexed his muscles and it made him feel even more afraid. Larsen was a tough, with a bad reputation around the school for being a bully. Common sense and straight-out funk dictated that Graham obey. But somehow that stuck in his craw. And Loretta was watching!

If I back down now she will think I am a coward, he thought.

That idea hurt. So did the knowledge that he would despise himself as a weakling. His father's advice crossed his consciousness amidst the swirl of conflicting ideas, "If you back down when you believe you are right it will hurt for years. Better to fight and lose and at least save your self-respect. The bruises will only last a few days that way!"

Easy to say! It looked very different now, squaring up to a real situation. Graham licked his lips and shook his head. "She can tell me herself," he said defiantly.

"She asked me to get rid of you," Larsen snarled. "She's my girl, you moron. So piss off before I belt you."

Graham felt his self-control slipping. Somehow his vision seemed to narrow down just on Larsen. Black dots danced before his eyes, and he felt as though his chest was being squeezed. His heart rate increased and he knew he was breathing rapidly. Inside he felt as though he was turning to jelly, and he hoped the shaking of his knees was not obvious to the gathering crowd of spectators. Once again he shook his head.

"No."

Larsen's face registered both anger and disbelief and he stepped forward and shoved Graham hard with both hands. Graham staggered back but resisted and shoved back in return.

Larsen pushed him again and again Graham shoved back, his feet scrabbling for purchase on the loose gravel. That sparked even more anger and Larsen raised his fists.

"Okay idiot, cop this!" he snarled. He stepped forward, his right fist coming up in a sweeping uppercut.

Somehow Graham dodged the blow. He stepped sideways, terrified at the speed of the attack. His mind raced, trying to decide what best to do. And there was Larsen's exposed side and belly right in front of him. Before Graham realised what he was doing he stepped closer and swung his left in a short, hard jab into the older boy's stomach.

Larsen grunted sharply in pain. To Graham's astonished eyes Larsen's head appeared in front of him as he doubled forward.

I can hit that! Graham thought.

And he did, a smashing right cross which landed solidly on the older boy's jaw. It was an even greater surprise to see Larsen suddenly go down sideways to sprawl on the grit of the school yard.

For a moment a surge of exultation swept into Graham's brain as he saw his enemy go down, but this was replaced almost instantly by a sharp stab of pure fear as he saw the look of intense rage which transfused Larsen's face. Sickening reality burst on Graham's consciousness.

Oh bloody hell! Now I will really have to fight! he thought.

And he knew it would not just be a few punches and some pushing and shoving. Larsen had been humiliated in front of his girl. Stung by hurt pride he would now be twice as dangerous.

A rapid series of thoughts chased through Graham's brain. *I've done it now! Now he will really smash me! Run while you can!*

But he stubbornly stood his ground. Larsen swore and struggled to his feet. Graham saw a chance to step in and hit him again before he could get up but that didn't seem right, so he held back and allowed the bully to regain his feet. Too late to run now! He resigned himself to a battering.

Larsen wiped dirt from his face and rubbed his jaw. Red spots seemed to dance in his eyes- savage grey eyes Graham noted.

"You little toad! You'll pay for that!" Larsen swore again and came rushing in, fists flailing.

This time the punches came too fast to duck them all. Graham managed to avoid a couple but one smashed into his nose and sent him reeling. Another landed with numbing force on his mouth. He felt things snap and tasted blood. Then it was his turn to go staggering back.

Somehow, he managed to keep his feet and to dodge the next couple of punches. Blood welled inside his mouth and he tasted grit. *The mongrel has broken a tooth!* he thought.

And the pain was intense. More punches flailed in. Graham wore two on the left upper arm which left it feeling numb. Panic and flight were surfacing again as options.

He managed to block another punch with his arm, but that hurt too. To clear his breathing he spat out the broken tooth and a gobbet of blood and saliva. More blood ran down his chin. He was dimly aware of a ring of chanting, shouting students of both sexes. That hurt nearly as much.

Bugger it! I'll go down fighting! he determined.

He blocked another punch and suddenly there was another opening. Instead of stepping back he stepped forward and drove a hard left into Larsen's solar plexus. Again the bully doubled up and his chin appeared close in front of Graham's red-rimmed vision. In went his right.

Larsen tried to dodge and took the blow on the side of the head. It sent him staggering back. Graham took another pace forward. He now knew he had no option but to fight with all his might. He drew back his right to drive another blow into Larsen's face.

But the arm was gripped. There was shouting and screaming, and a man's voice bellowed in his ear, "That will do! Stop this fighting!"

It was Mr Page, the Senior Geography teacher. Mr Page was a big, athletic man. He held Graham's arm tightly. Graham noted the muscles cording in the teacher's arm and knew he could not break that grip.

Larsen had reeled back. Now, wild with humiliation, he seized his chance and dashed forward to slam a punch at Graham's face. It would have changed the shape of Graham's nose if he hadn't managed to twist his head away just in time. Instead it struck his chest and left him badly winded and with a stinging pain over his heart.

Larsen drew back to strike again, but Mr Page stepped between the two and blocked the blow with another muscular arm. Then Larsen was also gripped by another male teacher, Mr Conkey, Graham's History teacher.

Larsen shouted angrily and swore. "Let go of me! You can't touch me! I'll have you charged with assault."

"Go ahead!" Mr Page replied calmly. "Hit me and see what happens to you, boy. You'll need more than the police."

For an instant it looked as though Larsen would lash out at the teacher, but his eyes registered that Mr Page was not bluffing. With a wild glare in his eyes Larsen lowered his fist and snarled a few more threats.

"Take your hands off me! Teachers aren't allowed to touch students. I'll have you in court."

"Good idea. We can start the process right now. Both of you, to the office!" Mr Page commanded.

For a moment Graham stood to recover his breath. He trembled as a savage urge to lash out coursed through him. With an effort that left him breathing rapidly he controlled it. He bit his lip and turned away. Not the office! Twice in one morning!

The walk to the office was an ordeal in its own right. Mr Page walked beside Graham and Mr Conkey walked with Larsen behind them. They made their way between two lines of curious students. As he walked, Graham was torn between dread of what was to happen at the office, and awareness that he was the centre of attention.

He lifted his chin and strode defiantly along. *I don't care what they do!* he told himself in an attempt to lift his rapidly sinking spirits.

As he walked, he noted his friends: Peter, Stephen and Roger. Peter looked worried and shook his head. Stephen grinned and gave him a thumbs-up. Roger looked anxious.

There were girls there too. Graham met the curious gaze of Christine Sinclair. That made him feel a twinge of conscience. Christine had made it quite clear that she liked him, and he had so far rebuffed her hints in favour of his pursuit of Loretta.

At the main office Graham and Larsen were seated well apart and Mr Page went into the Deputy Principal's office. Mr Conkey stood between the two and cautioned them to say nothing. Graham eyed the office door anxiously. He had no desire to see Mr Fitzgerald again.

Larsen was called in first. Graham was told to sit on a seat outside and wait. Mr Conkey shook his head, then went on his way. Time then seemed to drag. From inside came the murmur of voices but Graham could not hear what was being said until Mr Fitz started to get angry. That did nothing to calm Graham. The longer he sat and waited the worse he felt.

As he sat there brooding over his probable fate, a few students walked past. Among them were Peter, Stephen, and Roger, but they knew better than to linger and talk to him. All they could do was give him signs of encouragement. Several girls also went past, including Christine and her friend Rosemary, another girl from his own class, but not Loretta.

Larsen appeared at the door followed by Mr Page who pointed inside. "In you go Kirk."

Larsen glared at Graham but said nothing as the two passed. With his heart beating anxiously Graham walked in. He felt physically sick by then, both from worry, and from his injuries. The sore tooth was the worst, but his arms and head felt like one huge mass of throbbing aches and bruises.

Waiting behind his desk was Mr Fitzgerald. He looked grim and did not invite Graham to sit.

"I don't believe this! Two fights in one day! Have you got a death wish Kirk?"

Graham stood and shook his head miserably. Mr Fitz pursed his lips. "Alright Kirk, tell me your version of what happened."

Graham had been thinking of how to word his defence but now that the moment had arrived, he shrugged. He wouldn't make up any stories or make excuses. He just told it as he saw it.

I don't care if I get expelled, he told himself. *I hate school!*

Mr Fitzgerald listened in silence. When Graham had finished, he pressed his lips into a thin line of disapproval.

"That is the third time this week you have been sent to the office, Kirk. You are becoming nothing but trouble! I don't know what's got into you, a Year 9 fighting with a Year 11, and Larsen at that! You are lucky he didn't splatter you all over the playground! And what a stupid thing to do after your good deed this morning!"

All Graham could do was nod. His head ached and his split lip throbbed. It had hurt to talk, and he had nothing much else to say in his own defence.

Mr Fitzgerald shook his head, "Fighting over a girl! And from all accounts she doesn't like you and is going out with Larsen. My advice to you is to leave her alone. Now, you need to get control of your temper before you end up in real trouble. To help you with that you will spend lunchtime in the 'Time Out' Room. If you don't like that then we will get your parents in and discuss a more suitable punishment. Which is it to be?"

That was an easy decision. Graham had no desire for his father to learn he had been in trouble again. It would mean a belting probably. Graham admired his father, but also feared him. Captain Kirk was a tough

Master Mariner who had a no-nonsense view of the world. Worse still he was currently home waiting for his ship to be loaded so retribution would be immediate.

"Time out sir."

"Right. Go to the Sick Room and clean yourself up, then sit outside till the bell goes. And don't continue your battle with Larsen; or you will have a more serious one with me!" Mr Fitzgerald replied.

Graham nodded and left the room. He felt relieved but still depressed. *Loretta doesn't like me!* he thought.

That hurt more than any of the punches. He shook his head sadly and wished he was away from the school and all the frustration and misery it represented.

* * *

When classes recommenced after morning tea, Graham made his way to the room where his next lesson was. This was History and Graham was not looking forward to it, partly because Mr Conkey was the teacher and partly because Loretta and her friends would be there.

Mr Conkey met Graham at the classroom door, raised his eyebrows and asked what had happened. Graham gave him a brief explanation. As he did, he was acutely aware that Loretta was just inside the room. When he looked in her direction, she turned her nose up and looked away. That caused a sharp stab of misery. He felt tears forming but managed to contain them. That would be just too shameful!

Mr Conkey was one of the few teachers Graham respected. He also liked the subjects he taught: History and Geography. But that hardly made school liveable. There were eight subjects, and most were nothing but absolute misery to him. Graham went into the classroom to his usual seat beside Stephen and sat down, hotly conscious of the curious stares. Stephen raised his eyebrows in interrogation but had the sense not to speak until the lesson was well under way.

Graham forced himself to settle to the work but after a while his attention wandered, and he began to alternately daydream and doodle. He stared out the windows at the distant, jungle-covered mountains which surround Cairns and wished he was hiking up one of them, free.

Hiking and bushwalking were now Graham's main interests. One result of carrying a pack up mountains every second weekend was that he had developed into a big, broad-shouldered lad. He was very fit compared to many of his contemporaries.

Stephen Bell, his long-time friend, was a member of the 'Hiking Team', along with Peter and Roger. Stephen was the same age but had dark hair, blue eyes, paler skin and freckles. He wore glasses and was not, to Graham's eyes, as handsome. That rankled somewhat as Stephen seemed to have great success with the girls. Graham suspected that Stephen's boasts about sexual experiences with several girls were true. As Graham had very few, this was a source of further irritation because it was something he badly wanted to try.

Stephen grinned at him and wrote a short note to which Graham made the even shorter reply that he was on 'Time Out'.

Stephen shrugged and grinned. "Never mind mate. Plenty more fish in the sea," he replied, alluding to Loretta. Graham just grunted and did not want to believe it. His pride was too badly hurt.

The next lesson was Maths B. On the way to the classroom Graham met Peter Bronsky, his other 'best mate'. Peter was the unquestioned 'brains' of their group, a fact accepted without rancour or jealousy by the others. He was the same height, with brown hair and brown eyes and was also very fit. Peter was in the other Year 9 'Academic' class, 9A, so they could only talk briefly on the veranda.

Three weeks before during the last of the sailing races there had been a fight with three Year 11 bullies. One of the Year 11 bullies, Burford, had fired a speargun at them and the spear had hit Peter, sticking through his right forearm. Graham now gestured to it. "How's the arm Pete?"

Peter grinned and held his arm up. A tiny pinkish scar was all that showed where the spear had gone through. "It's okay. I forget about it most of the time. What about you?"

During the fight Graham had been slashed by a knife across the front of his right shoulder and the cut had required six stitches. The stitches had been out for a week, but he was conscious of it now.

"I forgot about it," he confessed. Now it was tingling, and he wondered if the fights had somehow opened the wounds.

Peter pointed to his face. "You are getting a black eye there. What was the fight about?"

Graham started to tell him, but they were interrupted by their arrival at his classroom, where the teacher, Mr Ritter, was already impatiently waiting.

Mr Ritter looked up at them, his hawk-like face tightening into a scowl. "Hurry up you people! You are late. Kirk, you have been in enough trouble today. Don't sit next to Bell. Bronsky, you hurry up to your class."

Graham's spirits slumped. "Yes sir," he replied. He stood and looked around for a place to sit. The only empty seat was right in the back corner and next Amelia Howley.

Amelia Howley! Graham remembered his meeting that morning with her father and how surprised he had been to learn she was his daughter. Graham did not like her and did not want to sit there but Mr Ritter directed him to do so. Very self-consciously Graham walked to the seat and sat down, seething with dislike, for the school, for the teacher, the subject, and for Millie.

To his surprise she spoke to him as he worked at a Geometry problem. "Are you in trouble at the office?" she asked.

Graham turned and made a face. "Yes," he replied shortly.

For a moment their eyes met- hers were hazel he noted- he had never taken any notice before, and they were soft with sympathy. That aggravated him even more.

I don't want her feeling sorry for me! he thought angrily.

He turned back to his work and concentrated on it. She must have sensed his mood as she made no further attempt to speak to him.

While they worked Graham got another little shock. Glancing down he realised he could see a lot of Millie's thighs. In spite of his bad mood, he surreptitiously studied them while he worked.

Heavens! She has her dress pulled a long way up! he noted.

Now he became genuinely interested and made a careful study. To his surprise he saw that they were nice legs, tanned a golden, honey colour. They looked invitingly smooth and he felt a distinct stirring of interest. Millie appeared to be working and unaware of the fact that she had slid forward on her seat so that her skirt was pulled up. For the first time he gave her more than a cursory look.

She's no beauty, he decided, as he studied her covertly. She had an average face: brown hair bobbed just above the collar, brown eyes, ordinary mouth. *Nice boobs though,* he mused.

That got him more interested. Yes, she certainly filled out her blouse nicely. Then he shrugged. So what? She was the joke of the boys for being a 'frump' and a 'square'. He went back to studying the other girls in the class.

Apart from Glenys and her bitchy mate, Janet Ozgood, there were some real honeys. Top of the list, in his eyes, was Rowena. She had gleaming black hair which framed a heart shaped face. The sight of her made him go weak.

She'd never look at me, he sighed. *Too sophisticated and classy,* was his assessment. Then there was Ailsa. She set Graham's heart palpitating at any time. *But...?*

"Kirk! Get on with your work!"

The sharp reproof startled Graham. Nettled and frustrated he forced himself to focus on the work.

Lunch was next. Graham took his lunch and work materials and made his way sadly to the 'Time Out' room. What he disliked most about the punishment was that it deprived him of a chance to see any of the girls. As he sat in bitter silence, he brooded on this, wondering if he should try again with Loretta but knowing in his heart it was futile. Then he considered which other girl he might ask. For a minute he considered asking Glenys out, then made a face and shook his head. He had the previous year and had been badly used and deceived by her.

Memory of the rejections twisted inside him like a muscle in pain. His mouth curled into an angry scowl at the memory of those earlier defeats. His rational mind told him he was being a stubborn fool to persist, but he did not like to give up easily. So he sat and fantasised about how he might win Loretta's affection.

The afternoon lessons were more concentrated misery: Maths A with his mortal enemy, Mr Burgomeister; and Chemistry with Miss McLeod, a fat, humourless women who seemed to delight in picking on him. It was with a sigh of genuine relief that Graham heard the final bell. Stephen stood up and asked, "What are we doing this arvo Graham?"

"Dunno. What do you want to do?" Graham replied.

"Hadn't thought about it," Stephen replied. He turned and smiled at Yvonne as she passed and received a dazzling smile in return. *How does he do it?* Graham wondered.

"We could go over to Pete's," he suggested.

Stephen made a face and took his glasses off to polish them. "No go. It's Wednesday. He will be going to army cadets."

Graham nodded. He had forgotten. The school was one of the few in the region still to have a company of army cadets, largely because Mr Conkey, who was also an Officer of Cadets with the rank of captain, gave the time and effort to run it. The cadets trained part-time on Wednesday afternoons, plus a few weekends and longer camps.

The mention of the word 'cadets' touched that other very raw nerve: his great ambition to be a naval officer, to rise to command a sleek, grey destroyer. For years Graham had read everything he could about ships and navies. As well he had gained much practical experience by going to sea on his father's ships during the school holidays. As soon as he had turned 13 the previous August, he had joined the Navy Cadets, full of high hopes and determined to do as well as he could.

Then, after the adventure of the American warships, and his trip to America to see five real Battleships, he had taken a medical examination on the advice of the CO, just to check if his eyes were good enough. The result had been devastating. He had been informed that he would never be able to join the navy as a 'General List' officer because his left eye was defective. He might still be able to join in various technical categories but that was not his dream. He was hopeless at mathematics and science. It had been a stunning blow.

So upset had he been by the shattering revelation that he left the Navy Cadets. He felt a failure and a disgrace. The conviction that everyone was laughing and sniggering at him after all his boasting ate into his soul to such an extent he had attempted suicide the previous December. It had been a miserable time all round. Only good friends helping him had ensured he had come through the depression as well as he had.

Now the ugly monster of depression rose in his consciousness again. What would he do with himself? *Why do I exist at all?* he wondered. Life seemed to be a real burden. His mouth twisted into a bitter scowl at the thought of his failure.

Stephen nudged him, "Hey! Don't have a fit of the dejections. Come to town with me and we will chase some chicks."

"Aren't you going to cadets?" Graham asked.

Stephen shook his head. "Nah. Didn't bring my uniform. Don't want to go anyway," he replied.

"If you don't like it, why did you join?" Graham asked.

Stephen shrugged. "Had to. My old man made me."

"Weren't you in the Air Cadets?"

"Yeah. For a while," Stephen replied.

"Why did you leave?" Graham asked.

"Didn't like it," Stephen replied shortly.

From Stephen's manner, Graham sensed there was more to it than that, but he didn't press. Other kids who were Air Cadets had hinted that money had gone missing from the canteen. That saddened Graham.

He shook his head and started walking beside his friend.

Chapter 3

FRIENDS

Graham pressed his lips together but said nothing. Instead he followed Stephen down to the bike racks. On the way he noted Rowena riding off with Louise and again wondered what his chances might be. Then he shook his head.

No. They won't go out with me, he decided bitterly.

When he was in the company of girls like them, he knew he felt very inadequate. They were so beautiful, and acted so 'cool' and grown up.

The two boys made their way into the city, walking because Graham did not have his bike. Once there they dumped their school bags in the garden beds at the civic library.

As they started walking along the footpath Stephen nudged him. "Come on Grumps! Cheer up!" he said.

"Where are we going?" Graham asked.

"To check out the chicks," Stephen replied.

The idea certainly appealed to Graham, but Stephen's confident attitude made him feel a bit insecure and nervous. The pair strolled along, admiring the girls and discussing their 'finer points'. Stephen made what he considered to be witty and sexy comments about them, often within their hearing. This made Graham feel quite embarrassed, but he felt compelled to join in. Some of the girls were certainly very attractive and just looking at them made him feel strong stirrings and yearnings.

After a time they came to a newsagent. Stephen went in and Graham happily followed. It was a place they often visited and was where they usually purchased their comics and novels. Stephen began browsing the comic stand while Graham went to look at the books. These held his attention for ten minutes and he found several he thought he would like to buy.

Stephen caught this eye and called to him, "Hey Graham! Come and look at these."

Graham went around to where Stephen was flicking through a magazine. A glance set Graham's interest quickening. It was a glossy

'Girlie' magazine full of colour photos of naked and near naked females.

Stephen held up the magazine for him to see. "Look at the snuggle bumps on this one. Boy! Wouldn't they be fun to play with?"

Graham nodded in agreement but went red with embarrassment because the girl behind the counter was looking in their direction and could hear Stephen. Stephen seemed quite unconcerned by this and continued to slowly turn the pages and to make crude comments about what he would like to do to each of the models.

Some of the photos were completely revealing and Graham found them very arousing. To his consternation and added embarrassment he began to get an erection. This was a problem that had been bothering him a lot lately. It would just stiffen up at the most inconvenient times and he seemed to have almost no control over it.

To escape from the embarrassing situation he agreed with Stephen, then moved further along the aisle to pick up a magazine on aircraft. In his heart he really wanted to look at the nudes, but he was so ashamed of having such thoughts that he felt like running away. To his severe embarrassment, Stephen picked up another magazine and held it up for him to see.

"Cop the tits on this one!" Stephen called.

Graham glanced at the shop girl and noted her go red and purse her lips. That made him feel awful. He gave Stephen a sickly grin and moved even further along. He picked up another magazine, one on military modelling. He tried to focus on this, all the while uncomfortably aware that he was embarrassed. He began to flush with shame and knew he must be red in the face. To escape from the situation he moved along and selected a magazine on plastic kit models, even though he rarely constructed them. Burning with shame he paid for the magazine and walked outside.

To Graham's relief Stephen came out and joined him. "She is a horny looking chick," Stephen said, referring to the shop girl.

The two friends started walking along the footpath. "You didn't have to embarrass her," Graham muttered.

"Why not? They like it," Stephen replied.

Graham did not believe that, but felt he had to reply. He shook his head and said, "She didn't look happy." Then he wished he had said nothing.

Stephen snorted. "Crap! I'll bet she's a real goer," he replied, adding, "Or is it you that was embarrassed? Don't you like looking at naked women?"

That accusation made Graham go even redder. "I do so!" he replied indignantly.

Stephen reached inside his jacket and pulled out a magazine and opened it. "How about this one then?" He flicked it open so that several glossy photos of nude women were visible, both to Graham and to the other people walking along the street.

Graham was doubly appalled. It was instantly apparent that Stephen had stolen the magazine. He was also very embarrassed to be seen with that sort of magazine in a public street. These feelings were exacerbated when they were suddenly confronted by two girls from their own class who came out of a shop: Yvonne and Lorna. Yvonne was a slim and shapely girl with dark brown hair and hazel eyes. She had gone out with Stephen several times. Lorna was a sexy brunette with a broad bum and quite large breasts. She had been Stephen's girlfriend earlier in the year. Both girls lived in Kuranda and were waiting for parents to finish work.

Yvonne waved and walked over. "What are you boys doing?" she called.

To Graham's consternation, Stephen did not try to hide the magazine but instead held it out for her to look at.

"Bit of homework," he replied.

Yvonne glanced at the pictures, then turned up her nose and snorted. "Oh dream on! Don't be crude, Steve. Buy me a milkshake, please."

By then they were right near a corner milk bar, so Stephen steered them to a table. He tossed the magazine carelessly down so that it flopped open at a particularly revealing picture. Feeling very self-conscious and embarrassed Graham sat down quickly.

Stephen pulled out a chair for Lorna. "What would you like?" he asked the girls.

"A milk shake, please," Yvonne answered.

"I can give you plenty of what you enjoy any time you like," Stephen quipped.

Graham was shocked and flushed bright red. Yvonne just made a wry face and said, "Don't boast. Just get us a drink."

While Stephen was ordering the drinks, Yvonne turned to Graham and asked about the fight. He told her his version of it, all the while acutely conscious of the open magazine on the table in front of them. To his surprise and consternation, Lorna slid it round and looked at it.

"What a disgusting tart," she sniffed. But she turned the page and studied the next picture. Yvonne gestured to the magazine. "Do you like these Graham?" she asked.

That put him right on a spot. He did, but he didn't want to say so, lest they think him disgusting. "They're alright," he muttered.

At that moment Stephen returned. "Alright!" he cried as he placed four milkshakes on the table. "I reckon that blonde chick is real horny."

Lorna looked at him with interest. "Do you? What about you, Graham?" she asked.

Graham burned even more and could only nod. Stephen laughed and sat down. "Of course he does! Turn to the next page 'Y' and cop an eyeful of the sheila there."

Yvonne did so and Graham thought he could not get more embarrassed or aroused than he was, but he did. To his surprise the two girls studied the photo of a girl with huge watermelon-like boobs. "Oh poor girl! I'm glad mine aren't that big," Lorna said.

That comment drew Graham's eyes to Lorna's bodice, and he instantly blushed and tried to pretend he wasn't looking. It was thus a real relief to him when Lorna closed the magazine and said, "Thanks. I've seen enough. You boys can look at it later."

The conversation then shifted back to the fight. Graham did not wish to say that it had been about Loretta, but it became obvious the girls knew that anyway. They seemed to think that Larsen was a bully who deserved a smack on the nose, so Graham found himself the temporary focus of mild approval as a hero.

Stephen then produced a packet of cigarettes and offered them round. Yvonne and Lorna both accepted one. As Yvonne put it to her lips, Stephen pulled out a lighter and snapped it alight for her. Then he lit his own cigarette before offering the open packet to Graham.

"Want one?"

Graham shook his head and burned with shame at he thought of his friend thinking he was weak. "No thanks," he mumbled. For an excuse he looked at his watch. "I'd better get going. Mum will be wondering where I am."

Stephen's lip curled into a sneer. "You'd better not let her see what you are hiding in your shorts then," he said.

Graham had just stood up and was holding his model magazine in front to hide his aroused condition and was stunned and hurt. He had hoped Stephen had not noticed and certainly didn't want the girls to see it. Now he flushed with shame as the eyes of both girls swivelled to look.

"Thanks Steve!" he snapped in anger.

Stephen grinned. "You shouldn't look at naughty magazines if they make you all horny," he replied with a laugh.

Graham grunted and blushed, then met Lorna's eyes. She gave him a sympathetic smile and he managed a sickly grin in return before turning and hurrying off. Behind him he heard Stephen laugh but he did not look back. Feeling somewhat battered emotionally, as well as bruised in body, Graham strode off along the footpath.

* * *

It was a very confused and miserable boy that slowly made his way home. After retrieving his school bag, Graham walked along deep in thought. At the top of his worries was how his parents, and in particular his father, would react to him getting into trouble at school again. A month earlier Graham had felt he was making real progress in his relationship with his dad, particularly when he had helped them in the sailing races against the Navy Cadets. Now it all seemed to have turned sour.

Dad is always grumpy. And he never understands how I feel, Graham thought. *He never even takes the time just to talk to me.*

Still brooding over what might happen he arrived home. As soon as he walked in he was greeted by his big brother Alex, a Year 11. "Heard you got smacked about by Larsen today," Alex said.

"I got him a few times," Graham replied.

Alex laughed. "From the look of you he landed you a few beauties!"

Graham grimaced and moved to look in the mirror. To his consternation he saw that what Alex had said was true. He had a big bruise on the side of his face, a black left eye, and the split lip was puffed up with a scab clearly visible. He had been hoping that the results of the fight would not have been so obvious. To add to his distress he also noted that the front of his shirt was spotted with dry blood.

At that moment girl's voices came from the next room and in walked his little sister Kylie and her friend Margaret. That made Graham even more upset. The last person he wanted to see at that moment was Margaret. She was two years younger than him. She and Kylie were in the same class at school. For years Margaret had openly adored him, and he usually found this both annoying and embarrassing.

As he had said on several occasions: 'She follows me round like a faithful little puppy!' But what really bothered him was the fact that she was only in Year 7 and he didn't want the boys in his class calling him a 'cradle snatcher'.

That would be a real shame job! he thought.

To make matters worse he knew in his heart that he really liked Margaret, who was a lovely person.

Margaret was a short, fairly tubby little girl with a pleasant, open face covered with freckles. She had mousy fair hair and soft brown eyes which glowed with concern. But being only 12 she had no figure, her breasts being just tiny bumps. Compared to girls like Loretta she just didn't rate, a fact she was obviously unhappily aware of.

Kylie spoke first. "What happened to you? You look a wreck."

"Just a fight," Graham replied offhandedly.

Alex laughed and added, "He got smashed by that thug Larsen in my class."

"Why?" Kylie asked.

Graham didn't want to say but Alex provided that information. "He was trying to cut in on Larsen's girl. He won't do that again I reckon."

Graham blushed and felt uncomfortable when he noted the look of pain which crossed Margaret's face. Then he shrugged.

She can be as jealous as she likes, but it won't stop me picking my own girlfriend.

To avoid further conversation on the topic, Graham took himself off to the bathroom. After a shower and change of clothes he went downstairs, intending to avoid both Margaret and his mother. The house was an old 'Queenslander' built of weatherboard on high stumps. Underneath was a concrete floor divided into three areas. At the point where the back stairs went down was a largely open area containing the car port, laundry and a storeroom. Next to that was a closed in area about ten metres by twelve. This was the 'Ship Room'. By default this was largely Graham's private domain. The front section, under the front veranda, was given over to orchids and ferns.

The Ship Room was where Graham kept his ship models, and where the boys played various games with models. It was also where Graham liked to retreat to when he wanted to be alone. He went there now and sat in a corner out of sight of the door.

For a time he just sat, staring into space and brooding. Stephen was a thief! What should he do about it?

Stephen is a mate! I can't just drop him, he thought. It was an awful situation and thinking about it made Graham feel physically ill in the stomach. And girls! *What am I to do?* he agonised. Loretta seemed a lost hope. *What about Rowena? Or maybe some other girl?* he wondered. But who? Which one?

Margaret's voice broke into his thoughts. "I'm going home now Graham. I hope you are alright. See you again."

She smiled at him from the door. Seeing her there made Graham flush with shame. During the last few years he and Margaret had several times been in the bath together and had indulged in some fairly innocent exploration and touching. That memory now stirred resentment. In reply he just nodded and grunted. Kylie poked her head around the door and scowled at him. Margaret looked hurt but tried to keep her smile. She and Kylie left but Kylie returned a few minutes later, after seeing her off.

"There was no need to be rude to Margaret," she attacked.

"She's a pain!" Graham replied, stung by his own guilt.

"She is not! She's a very nice person, and she loves you."

"More fool her! I didn't ask her to. I wish she would go away," Graham snapped back.

"More fool you, you mean! You don't realise just how loyal and loving she is. She is nice and kind and better than you deserve," Kylie retorted angrily.

At that moment their mother called them from upstairs. "Stop bickering you children and come up and have your tea."

Reluctantly Graham stood up and made his way upstairs. As soon as he entered the dining room, his mother saw his bruises. A look of distress crossed her face.

"Oh dear! What have you been up to now? What happened to your face?"

"Nothing much. Just a fight," Graham replied, trying to sound offhand.

"Who with? Why? Did it happen at school?" his mother asked.

For a moment Graham was tempted to lie, to mention the fight on the esplanade and to gloss over the later one. But then he knew he would despise himself, so he shrugged.

"Just a bully named Larsen," he replied. He gave an abbreviated version of events and tried to minimise its importance.

His mother shook her head and pursed her lips. "Did you get sent to the office?" she asked.

Graham nodded. His mother again shook her head sadly. "I don't know what has come over you these last few weeks. You seem to be in trouble all the time. Just you wait till your father gets home!"

At that last threat Graham felt his stomach turn over. Then it turned over again as he heard the car drive into the carport. His father was home!

Captain Kirk joined them a few minutes later. He was a big, solid man who looked what he was: a tough ship's captain. Now he also looked very tired and after a perfunctory greeting he sat and quickly explained to Mrs Kirk the business troubles that had taken up his day. He owned three ships: a 500ton coastal freighter named *Malita;* an old ex-navy Landing Craft Tank named *Wewak;* and a salvage tug named *Bonthorpe*. Graham understood that things were going badly in the business, mostly because of competition from road transport as better roads were extended into the remote communities around Cape York Peninsula and the Gulf of Carpentaria, which were the main areas serviced by the ships.

As Captain Kirk started on his soup, he noted Graham's face. He stopped and asked, "What happened to you boy?"

"A fight dad," Graham answered meekly. His heart was now beating rapidly, and butterflies were fluttering in his stomach.

To his relief his father just grunted irritably and asked, "Did you win?"

"No, Dad. He was a Year 11, and the teachers broke it up."

"Are you in trouble again?"

"No... er... well... yes, Dad."

Captain Kirk's mouth compressed into a hard line. "You'd better get a grip on yourself, boy! You seem to be in trouble all the time these days. A bit of discipline is what you need." He turned to Mrs Kirk. "Maybe I should take him with me on this next voyage and knock a bit of sense into him?"

To Graham's relief his mother shook her head. "Oh no! He's missed enough school as it is."

"Maybe he should be packed off to boarding school? That would soon pull him into line," Captain Kirk suggested. Graham was appalled. That was the threat hanging over Alex, who was also in trouble a lot. To his immense relief his mother shook her head.

"We can talk about it later," she said firmly. "Now eat up before the food gets cold."

Graham felt a bit safer but knew he was on very shaky ground. Captain Kirk looked hard at him and pointed with his spoon.

"I'm off on Saturday. While I'm away you had better behave yourself or I'll give you a good thrashing when I get back. I don't care how big you think you are. So grow up and get control of yourself."

Graham could only nod. He felt scared and remembered previous beltings (rare, but all earned, he conceded) with the lawyer vine cane kept for that purpose. His father was wont to talk about how that would cure him of mischief, and then boast about how many times he had been caned himself when at school. After that the subject was dropped as a roast was placed on the table.

Graham tried to eat as quickly as he could so as to escape from the uncomfortable atmosphere, only to be rebuked for his poor table manners. Afterwards he had to do the washing up, which was his special duty. While he did this, he could hear his mother and father talking quietly but could not make out their actual words. But he was sure they were discussing him and that depressed him even more. After finishing the washing up, he walked back through the house towards his 'bedroom' (really the enclosed front veranda). As he passed through the lounge room, his father looked up from the TV.

"You done your homework yet?"

"Not yet."

"Then get it done and show me."

"Yes, Dad."

So Graham settled at his desk and unhappily applied himself to the hated maths. This took longer than he expected and then he had to endure half an hour of cross-examination on mathematics by his father, who, being a Master Mariner, was of course an expert. It was all a hateful ordeal from which he was at last released.

After that, Graham lay on his bed and read *Phantom* comics until bedtime. When the lights were out, he lay there thinking, wondering what to do, and then escaping into fantasies where he rescued maidens in distress from pirates or smugglers. This led to sexual fantasies which soon got him very aroused.

He drifted into a restless sleep with dreams in which he almost got to kiss a girl, but something always happened to stop it.

Chapter 4

SCHOOL

Graham was in Year 9. There were seven Year 9 classes, divided up according to the subjects they took. He and Stephen were in 9B. Peter was in 9A. They had to study eight subjects for the 'Junior' Certificate, plus a number of specialist subjects such as Physical Education and Music. For all but one subject Graham and Stephen were in the same class. That was when the class split into those who did Geography (Graham) and Art (Stephen).

Normally Graham and Stephen sat together in the third of four rows, over in the second line of desks from the left. Much of the time they were in the same room. Graham sat on the right. Directly in front of him sat Annette, a real 'Square Bear'. Next to her sat Rowena. On Graham's right sat Dawn and Rhonda. Behind him sat Rosemary and Ailsa. Max and Angus sat over against the windows to Stephen's left. In front of them sat Loretta and Ashlee and the two 'Brains': Nigel and Don. Yvonne and Lorna sat in the back row to the right of Rosemary, with Amelia Howley on her own in the right back corner. The classroom was in a timber building set on high concrete posts with an open, concrete floored area underneath.

That morning, as Graham entered the room and dumped his books on his usual desk, he saw that the arrangement had been changed. Louise was now sitting beside Helmut in the left rear. That was a severe jolt as he had been contemplating asking her out. He made a sour face and sat down to hide his disappointment.

Further changes followed. There were now two desks with only one person at them. This gave the teachers some flexibility in relocating people. Mr Burgomeister, the Maths A teacher, and the one Graham most feared and disliked, at once told him to move.

"You and Bell are a bad influence on each other. Kirk, you move to the front here." He indicated a seat next to Norman.

There was nothing for it. Graham moved, but he made no attempt to be friends with Norman and sat there filled with sullen resentment until the end of the period. The next lesson was Maths B. Before Mr Ritter arrived, Graham moved back next to Stephen. Luckily Mr Ritter did not change this, merely raising one eyebrow at Helmut and Louise.

The lesson began and Graham was soon in trouble. Stephen had drawn an animation along the edges of about 50 pages. This showed a man walking forward to mount a motorcycle. When the pages were flicked quickly the motorcycle appeared to race across the page and up a ramp. It became airborne, then crashed. Graham watched it and chuckled.

"That's good, Steve! Show us again."

Before Stephen could, Mr Ritter scowled at them. "Bell and Kirk! Get to work and stop that nonsense!"

Reluctantly, Graham bent to his work. After a few minutes, Stephen again distracted him, this time with a joke which made him snicker.

Mr Ritter arched an eyebrow at them, and said, "Kirk, Geometry is fun, not funny. Now settle to your work or I will keep you in."

That threat was effective. Graham worked, but he hated it. It all seemed so pointless. It was a relief to go to German, if only because the teacher, Miss See, was a very shapely young woman.

Morning break followed. As he left the room, Graham tried to pluck up the courage to speak to Loretta. Somehow, he could only stand and look at her, feeling quite paralysed by the fear of being rejected again. Instead, he made his way downstairs to where his friends normally sat. On the way there he passed Larsen. If he had seen him earlier, he would have gone another way, but it was too late by the time he saw him.

Larsen curled his lip into a sneer. "Get out of my way, Kirk, before I smash you again!"

Graham braced himself for another clash, but Larsen contented himself with a shove as he passed. Even so, it set Graham's heart thumping. Shaking his head, he walked on to where Roger sat. Roger was a chubby and cheerful person with brown eyes and brown hair.

"Thought you were in for another fight then," Roger said.

"So did I!" Graham replied as he seated himself.

"Where'd you get to yesterday afternoon?" Roger asked.

Graham flushed with guilt at the sudden rush of memories. "Downtown with Steve," he replied.

Roger nodded. "I phoned your place. I was hoping you would come over and see what I've added to the railway."

Roger was only a few months younger than Graham, but this was enough to put him a whole year behind at school, so he was only in Year 8, among the lowest of the low in the high school pecking order. He was also a rank lower in the scouts. The four friends were all in the same scout troop. All four had teamed up to build a large HO Scale model electric railway at Roger's. They had been working on this for over a year and were currently constructing the section which represented the Kuranda Range railway.

"What is it?" Graham asked, feeling guilty that he had been neglecting both Roger and the railway of late.

"A big area of rain forest. It covers a whole ridge and looks very good," Roger replied. He went on to describe how he had made the model forest using twigs around the edges and then covered it with cotton wool dyed in various shades of green.

While he was talking, Peter and Stephen joined them. Peter was very interested. "It's time we did a bit more work," he said. "We've hardly done anything these last couple of months."

"That's because we were too busy with model ships and sailing," Graham replied.

"Time we did another hike too," Peter added.

"Where to?" Graham asked.

That idea appealed to him as it was nearly four months since their last expedition, the four-day hike to Kuranda during the Easter Holidays. That had been a fairly traumatic event because of the madman nicknamed 'Tarzan' and it had severely strained relations within the group. There had then been the sailing competition against the navy cadets during the June-July holidays. So Graham was looking forward to another expedition. For the next ten minutes they discussed possible places to explore on a hike. Then the bell went and sent them in to classes again.

English with Mrs Ramsey was next. Graham sat beside Stephen and drew pictures of ships or scrutinized the girls. He found English easy and made no attempt to study, nor to read the set books. Chemistry with Miss McLeod took them to lunchtime.

This brought no relief to Graham as he then had to report to Mr Fitz to work in the 'Time Out' room. For the whole hour he sat listening to the sounds of a thousand luckier students having a good time. The noise fuelled his resentment and frustration and the work he found a real chore.

The afternoon was taken up by Physics, which he disliked intensely, partly because of the lady teacher, Miss Tate ('Tart' to the kids); then by History, which he found bearable. They were studying the American Revolution and Mr Conkey managed to make it reasonably interesting, partly because he had actually visited many of the sites and knew what he was talking about.

Still, it was a real relief to finish the day. The four friends then went to Roger's, which was only in the next block, to work on the railway. Afterwards, Graham made his way home and lay on his bed brooding. Whichever way he looked at it, life seemed to be just a battle, and one he was losing.

On Friday he reluctantly made his way to school, after seriously contemplating playing the 'wag'. Still, Friday wasn't so bad. It was the best day of the week. It started with Geography, which Graham enjoyed. This was followed by German, then Maths A. As usual, Graham found the Maths difficult and he ended up in trouble with Mr 'Buggermaster' for not working and for talking to Stephen.

Mr Burgomeister scowled at him. "I thought I told you two boys not to sit together," he said. "Kirk, you move. Go and sit down at the back."

That meant sitting next to Amelia. Graham made a face but did as he was told. To his surprise she beamed him a smile.

"You didn't tell me about the fight the other morning down on the Esplanade," she whispered when he was seated. Her eyes shone as she leaned over to speak to him.

Graham shrugged and blushed. "I didn't want to big note myself," he replied. "I'm in enough trouble as it is."

"Dad says you were very brave, to fight four boys bigger than you, and you didn't have to he says. You went to help two little girls."

Graham blushed with embarrassed pride and grunted a reply. He wanted to forget it and did not want to talk to her. He pretended to work at his maths. But once again he found himself unsettled and distracted by the sight of Amelia's thighs.

I wonder if she realises I can see so much? he thought. Then he shook his head. *Nah! She's too much of a 'square' to even know about such things. She is a real 'Goody Goody'.*

Period 5 was Physical Education, and they were learning lifesaving. The school had its own swimming pool, which was used all year round.

Even though it was winter, the class made their way down to the pool with the PE teacher, Mr Randal. Graham always enjoyed swimming, partly because he was a very good swimmer and found it easy; and partly because he got to see the girls in their bathing costumes.

But it could also be embarrassing. The boys went into their change room. Graham was not normally interested in boys but of late he had become very self-conscious about his penis and was curious to compare it with others to reassure himself he was normal. Part of the problem was that, whenever he thought about things like that, he seemed to develop an instant erection. That started to happen as soon as he began to undress.

To hide this, he tried to turn his back on the other boys and stood in the corner as he pulled on his bathers. Stephen, on the other hand, seemed to delight in prancing around in the nude, even though his body looked scrawny and hairy.

Holding his towel in front of him, Graham made his way outside to stand over beside the fence. Mr Randal was there already, and Graham could not help admiring the teacher's physique. He was tanned and fit. He was also very well endowed, a fact which was obvious by the Speedos he wore. That made Graham feel embarrassed and a bit angry as the girls could obviously see this.

The girls came out in ones and twos to stand with the boys: Ailsa in a white one-piece that set off her curves to perfection, or at least in Graham's eyes; Glenys in a green one-piece; Louise in a bikini with yellow dots on it; Rowena in a shimmering dark blue lycra one-piece; Amelia also in a dark blue one-piece, which showed what a thick waist she really had.

And what big boozies! Graham observed.

He wondered how he had never noticed before. Surreptitiously he admired her and was granted a glimpse down her cleavage when she bent forward to rub her leg.

Quite nice really, he decided.

Mr Randal strode along past the girls, rippling his muscles as he did. *Bloody show-off!* Graham thought.

The lesson was on floating, especially how to do a 'Survival Float', just bobbing almost submerged to conserve energy. Graham found it simple, although it reminded him of the time the previous year when he had needed to do it to actually save his life when he, Andrew Collins and

Ken and the injured floatplane pilot had ended up in the sea for 18 hours after a plane crash.

As he drifted slowly around the pool, Graham thought back to that event. At the time he had been ready to just give up and drown, and only Ken's words had needled him into making the effort to survive. That had been just after Graham had learned he could never be a naval officer and he had been very depressed. Suicide had been much on his mind.

As it is at the moment, he thought bitterly. Life seemed so empty and pointless.

An hour working in the 'Time Out' room at lunch time did nothing to ease his depression. As he worked, he tried to fantasise about how his life could be turned around. This resulted in him daydreaming about girls and his failure in that department sent him into an even blacker mood.

* * *

Friday after lunch was devoted to sport or hobbies. Graham was no sportsman so usually joined the craft and hobbies group, which was supervised by Mr Poschalk, a Manual Arts teacher. Stephen and Peter were also on the same group and they sat together working and talking quietly. Graham settled to constructing some tiny 1:240 scale model aircraft out of cardboard and balsa wood. These were for the war game he played with Peter and Alex in the Ship Room at home. Stephen was busy drawing a comic and Peter was making a leather belt.

As they worked, Graham asked, "What are we doing this weekend?"

"What do you want to do?" Stephen countered.

"Play Battleships?"

"When?" Peter asked.

"Have to be Saturday afternoon. I have to work on Saturday morning," Graham replied.

Peter shook his head. "And I have to go visiting relations on Saturday afternoon."

"Sunday after church then?" Graham suggested.

"Okay. What about going to the movies on Saturday night," Stephen asked.

"Sounds okay." Graham agreed. "I'll have to ask mum but I think she will let me."

Friday afternoon was Graham's favourite time of the week. Not only did it mark the end of hated school but his mother always purchased them chocolates and comics. In the evening was Scouts. At Scouts Graham relaxed and enjoyed himself. He was the 'Second' of the Crocodile Patrol. Stephen was 'Second' of the Kookaburras and Peter 'Second' of the Platypus Patrol. Roger was in the Crocodiles with Graham.

It was a pleasant evening at Scouts and Graham went home afterwards to sleep soundly. The week had quite worn him out.

Saturday morning was a time of some emotional tension and family storms. Graham's father was sailing on the tide at 11:00 and there was much packing and cleaning before then. Graham had to mow the lawn, clean out the guinea pig cage, wash Skip the dog (the family pet Fox Terrier), and make his bed. It all kept him busy till it was time to climb into the family car for the drive to the wharf.

At the wharf at Portsmith they climbed out of the car. Graham had no desire to go aboard the *Malita*. He thought he had had enough of ships. The sight of them only added to his pain. Luckily the family tradition was for quick, unemotional farewells. Captain Kirk kissed Mrs Kirk, then Kylie. He shook Alex's hand and then Graham's. As he did, he uttered a last warning:

"Now you behave yourself my boy. If there is any more trouble, then it is off to boarding school for you. And don't think I won't know. I will be talking to your mother on the phone every day."

"Yes, Dad."

Captain Kirk turned and went up the gangplank. This was pulled in and the mooring lines singled up. By the time Captain Kirk had reached the bridge the ship was held by only a single spring. A shouted command released this and the ship slid away from the wharf, moving rapidly within a few seconds under the combined effect of tide and engines. Within ten minutes she had vanished from sight around the end of Smiths Creek into the Inlet.

Graham breathed more easily. Life would be more liveable for the next few weeks at least. The family climbed back into the car and drove home. Lunch followed, an almost silent meal as each adjusted to the Captain's departure.

For Graham the afternoon dragged. Reading held his interest for a while, then he worked on a model ship before getting depressed and frustrated. After that he just moped around till dinner time. During dinner his mother asked if he wanted a lift to the movies.

"No thanks mum. Steve is coming over and we will ride our bikes thanks," he replied. The last thing he wanted was for his mother to drop him off and pick him up in the car.

"You be home early," she added.

"Yes, Mum."

Stephen arrived on his bike at 6:15pm. Graham dressed with care, hoping that some of the girls might be there. The two friends then rode to town and hid their bikes in a garden bed before going to the theatre. Once inside they settled down in a row near the back.

Soon after sitting down, Graham's wish was granted. Four girls came in together: Louise, Amelia, Karen, and Annette. Stephen called out and they waved but did not sit with them. Instead the girls settled in the row in front. This suited the boys fine as they could tease and toss Smarties over onto them. Stephen kept up a flow of witty innuendo, some of which made Graham blush, but which seemed to amuse the girls.

The movie began and Graham wracked his brain to try to come up with a plan to get to sit beside one of the girls: Karen for preference. But his schemes were all wrecked by Stephen. The first movie was the famous old horror story *Psycho* about a psychopathic murderer who crept into houses to kill women with a huge knife. There was the scene in which a girl was in the shower. The maniac came creeping into the house and then into the bathroom. Just when the entire audience, Graham included, was literally on the edge of their seats as the madman reached forward to slash the shower curtain Stephen reached over the back of the seat in front of him and grabbed Annette around the neck.

The resulting scream sent a thrill of terror around the theatre. Graham jumped in fright, as did almost everyone else in the theatre. Stephen got such a fright he let go instantly. Annette dissolved in tears. The other girls turned angrily.

Louise stood up and leaned over to hit at Stephen. "Stephen Bell, you are a bastard!" she shouted.

A powerful torch came on and pinned them in its beam. An usher arrived at the end of the row.

"What's going on? Is everything alright?" the man asked. A lady with another torch joined him.

"No it is not!" Louise cried. She quickly explained what had happened, to a backdrop of murder on the screen as the maniac slashed and stabbed at the poor woman.

"It was only a joke," Stephen replied defensively.

"I don't care. Out!" the usher ordered.

"Aw! Fair go!" Stephen tried.

"Out, I said!" the man bawled.

Stephen stood up and made his way along the row. Graham felt very self-conscious and was unsure what to do. The torch beams kept settling on him.

"What about you? Were you involved?" the man asked.

"No," Graham replied. But he felt very embarrassed.

His emotions went into turmoil as he watched Stephen being led out and decided he did not want to stay on his own. He stood up and made his way past the other patrons in the row, feeling all hot and bothered. Then he had to run the gauntlet of hostile stares from the theatre staff who had put Stephen on the footpath.

"Sorry about that, Steve," Graham said.

Stephen shrugged. "Not your fault. No sense of humour some people," he said.

He lashed out with his boot, kicking a rubbish bin so hard it fell out of its bracket and rolled noisily on the footpath. Graham was a bit nettled that Stephen did not say thanks for joining him. Stephen kicked at the bin again, causing it to skitter and clang into the gutter, emptying papers and rubbish all over the footpath.

Graham tugged at his sleeve. "Come on, let's get out of here before we get into trouble."

At that moment, the usher appeared in the doorway. "Oy! You bloody kids! What are you doing?"

"Run!" Stephen cried.

Without waiting for a response he fled. Graham hesitated, then followed, burning with shame as he did.

The man made no attempt to follow. Half a block further on, Stephen slowed down to a walk.

Graham joined him. "What do we do now?" he asked.

"Look around for some fun," Stephen replied.

So the two boys walked around the block. Stephen made a big thing of commenting on any of the girls they saw, which embarrassed both them and Graham. The pair wandered around the town for over an hour before meeting up with two other Year 9 boys from their school, Wally Dru and Derek White. Graham did not really like either, particularly Wally who was a bully and was always picking on Chris Walker, the smallest boy in their class and also a Navy Cadet.

"Want a fag?" Derek asked, offering an open packet of cigarettes.

"Thanks," Stephen replied, taking one. Graham shook his head.

Derek's lip curled. "What's wrong with you, Kirk? You a snivelling 'Goody goody' are ya?"

"My mum will smell it," Graham replied. "Then I will be in deep shit."

To his relief, White accepted this. He lit up and took a deep breath. "What ya's doin'?"

"Just muckin' around," Stephen replied.

He then described how they had been chucked out of the pictures. The others thought this was a great joke. They group began strolling around the main block again although the streets were fairly deserted by this.

"What'll we do?" White asked.

"What about trying to get some booze?" Dru suggested.

That worried Graham who did not like or trust him. Wally Dru and his brother had been in the gang that had gotten Stephen into all the trouble the previous year.

Stephen struck a match and lit another cigarette, then flicked the still burning match into a rubbish bin. "Dunno... hey! Watch this."

The match had gone out, but Stephen now lit another one and carefully placed it into the rubbish bin. Smoke began to billow out.

"Aw beauty!" cried Dru. "Come on. Let's set a few more on fire."

Graham wanted to distance himself from this but did not want to appear a coward. Reluctantly, he went with them as they walked quickly along the footpath in Abbott Street. On looking back he saw flames licking out of the rubbish bin they had first set alight.

"We had better get out of here fast," he said, noting a taxi driver looking at the fire as he cruised past.

"Nah! Let's watch," White said.

The others slowed and dawdled. Soon after there came the shriek of a siren and a fire engine appeared at the other end of the block where the plastic rubbish bin was now blazing high, the bin having caught fire as well.

"Bloody good!" Dru chortled. "Come on, let's find another and set the town ablaze!"

They set off around the corner towards the City Place. By now Graham was feeling very uneasy and wished he had some excuse to leave the group. To his relief the next rubbish bin they came to was empty, so the group wandered on towards the next. This was almost at the corner of the City Place. As they arrived, Dru began peering into the rubbish bin Graham noted a group of Aboriginal youths coming along Lake Street towards them.

The Aborigines were laughing and chiacking, and a couple appeared to be weaving with unsteady steps. Two more were bickering and exchanging teasing punches on each other's arms. Graham focused on them and he felt himself go cold with fear. They looked very much like the gang he had clashed with on the Esplanade.

"I think we might have a problem," he said to the others as Dru struck a match. Stephen glanced at the gang who were now only about 50 paces away.

"Who them? They won't bother us."

"I dunno. I reckon..." Graham began.

At that moment, Dru tossed a piece of burning paper into the bin and one of the youths shouted at them.

"Hey, you whiteys, get outa our territory or we bash ya, eh!"

At that Graham tugged at Stephen's sleeve. "Come on, let's split."

"Crap! Let's fight 'em," Stephen snarled.

To Graham's relief, White agreed with him. "No, they look pissed to me; and there are seven of them."

The debate ended abruptly as the bin flared into flame and smoke, simultaneous with a bottle being hurled by one of the youths. The bottle shattered on the footpath, spattering the friends with broken glass. The youths all let out a yell and started running towards them.

"Run!" Stephen cried. Graham needed no urging. He took to his heels.

Chapter 5

BRAVADO

The four friends stuck together and ran across past Hides Hotel and along the footpath of Shields Street. As they ran, Graham kept glancing back. The youths pursued them for about a hundred metres, then stopped and jeered, hurling insults and obscenities. These burned Graham's pride, but he felt there was nothing to be done about it. Near the end of the next block the group encountered a man and his girlfriend. They were walking along the footpath arm in arm and looked anxiously around. Ignoring the couple, Dru shouted some crude insults back at the youths. This made Graham ashamed to be with him as the woman was obviously disgusted.

At the corner of Grafton Street they slowed down. By then the youths had given up and were no longer following. Puffing and muttering comments about the youths the group came to a standstill.

Dru looked around. "Well, that was fun. Time for another rubbish bin I reckon," he suggested. He moved over to one and looked inside.

At that moment, Derek White called out, "Cops!"

Before Graham realised what was happening, Dru and Derek were running off across the road. A spotlight came on and lit up the street. Stephen started running as well and the beam caught him and followed him. A police car screeched to a halt next to Graham. One officer leapt out and sprinted after Stephen. Another policeman came over to Graham. The beam of a powerful torch was shone straight into Graham's eyes.

"Graham Kirk, eh? What are you doing here kid?" asked the policeman. It was Constable O'Neil. Graham stood as though paralysed. He had to swallow and lick his lips before he could reply.

"Nothing."

"Nothing eh? Then why did your mates bolt?"

"We were being chased by a mob of youths. They are just back there," Graham replied.

Constable O'Neil grunted disbelievingly. "Oh yeah! So turn out your pockets kid."

His stomach churning with anxiety Graham did as he was told. As he did, the other policeman came back, holding Stephen by the arm. "Caught the little toad," he said.

Stephen also had to empty his pockets. To Graham's relief he had nothing except a small pocketknife.

The other policeman, an older Senior Constable, asked, "What do you kids know about some rubbish bins being set on fire?"

"Nothing," Stephen replied. "We just came out of the pictures along there and were walking this way when we ran into that gang of youths." To support his story he produced the stubs of the theatre tickets.

Graham could only stand and admire his coolness and quick thinking. *I wish I could do that,* he thought.

The Senior Constable studied them. "So who were the two blokes with you?" he asked.

"Just two kids we go to school with," Stephen replied.

"Their names, smart alec!"

"Nigel Vincent and Gordon McDougal," Stephen lied.

The policeman wrote this down. "Okay you two, get out of this area. I don't want to see you around here anymore tonight. Go back to the pictures."

The police got into their car and drove off. Graham and Stephen did as they were told and walked back to the theatre. Once there they continued on to where they had hidden their bikes.

Stephen scowled. "Bloody pigs!" he grumbled. "They are always spoiling things." He punched savagely at a sign on the edge of the curb.

"What'll we do now?" Graham asked.

"Go home I suppose," Stephen replied. "If those cops find me again and tell my parents I have been up to mischief I will be grounded again for months." He swore and cursed at fate.

The two friends pedalled to Graham's home, muttering about the unfairness of life and of how parents were so unreasonable. When they reached Graham's house, he dismounted at the gate and asked:

"Will I see you tomorrow?"

"Nah! Not in the morning. We are going to visit rellies," Stephen replied. "I should be home in the afternoon."

"Might see you then, okay?"

"Sure. See ya."

Stephen mounted and rode off along the street. Graham wheeled his bike in and went upstairs. His mother was still awake and asked about the movie, so he told her about the horror scene (but not Stephen's part in it!).

"I didn't really enjoy it mum," he concluded.

"Would you like some Milo?" she asked.

"Yes, Mum."

For the next ten minutes they sat and drank Milo. Graham then changed and went to bed. Alex was still out, and his mother was worrying about him. Graham lay in bed and brooded. In the midst of his depression he switched to fantasising about girls and fell asleep in a very aroused but frustrated state.

Sunday morning meant church. Graham usually went every Sunday, had all his life. And he genuinely believed, in a non-fanatical, Anglican sort of way. Alex refused to come ("Load of bull!" was his comment). His mother did not insist. In church she and Kylie usually sat on Graham's right. On Graham's other side sat little Margaret. She had sat beside him for years, a fact that he increasingly resented.

And Loretta was there with her family, to remind him of his defeat; and over near the front was the lovely English girl, Jennifer Jervis, that he had thought the sun shone out of the previous month. It was all very frustrating!

All through the service Graham kept casting wistful glances at Loretta and Jennifer. *Now why can't I get a girlfriend like them?* he wondered.

That thought led him to a depressing inventory of what he saw to be his many faults and failings. Not for the first time he prayed earnestly for guidance as to what he should do with his life. But, as always, he ended the service feeling calmer and more at peace with himself.

After the service, he joined the others at morning tea in the church hall. Margaret stood with Kylie and talked happily away, and he tried to be polite and act normal. Margaret chatted brightly to him, smiling and trying to be friendly. His main response was to think what a little girl she was. Roger was also there, but Graham did not really want to talk to him.

Roger asked, "What are you doing this afternoon?"

"Going over to Stephen's," Graham replied.

"Can you come over to work on the railway for a while?"

Graham was about to retort that playing trains was for little boys, but noted the anxious look on Roger's face and bit back the comment. Roger was okay. In fact he was a good friend. Besides, he had nothing else to do.

"Okay," he agreed. "What about now, before lunch?"

Roger nodded happily. Graham went and asked his mother if it was okay. She was happy to say yes as he knew she considered Roger a suitable friend. The look which crossed Margaret's face as she overheard this suggested she wasn't so happy.

She must have been planning to come to my place, he deduced. The thought made him feel both relieved and guilty.

He and Roger walked to Roger's house and retired to the train room. Roger's home was a lovely old high-set Queenslander which was kept in immaculate condition. The downstairs area had a concrete floor and was enclosed to provide a carport, laundry, storeroom and the 'Train Room'. This was a space 9 metres long and 3 metres wide. Most of this space was taken up by the timber framework of their partially completed railway model. As well there was a workbench, an old table, four rickety chairs and two cupboards that had seen better days.

The model had been under construction for over a year now but was still only about a quarter complete. It had originally begun as Roger's electric train set, a simple HO scale oval track with British *Hornby* rolling stock. Graham, Stephen and Peter had combined their efforts to build one big layout.

Roger's dad had actually done the hard work of carpentering. He had constructed a solid framework of 4" X 2" timbers. The base was 6 metres long and 3 metres wide but so far only a strip about one metre wide had been completed. This represented the coastal plain of North Queensland and included a small port, mangrove swamp (complete with a plastic crocodile as befitted the Crocodile Patrol), a town, some sugar farms, and a space where they intended to build a model sugar mill.

This section was raised half a metre off the floor. A double track main line ran the length of the base, curving at each end in under the coastal mountains. Under the mountains were a return loop and a maze of sidings which were partly hidden from view by the work now in progress, the landscaping of the jungle covered mountains. The main line allowed them to realistically run big Express passenger trains and heavy goods trains, which were 'just passing through'.

The model was based on the era of steam trains. This was the personal choice of all except Peter, who preferred diesels. It had been Graham who had convinced them of adapting British and American rolling stock (the only types that could be purchased in the local hobby shops) to look like authentic Queensland period rolling stock.

The mountain line was based on the Cairns to Kuranda railway, although the tiny town at the top of the range had been named 'Fairyland'. The landscaping was more than half done and included many patches of rain forest. There were also 7 tunnels and four bridges, including one across the face of famous Stoney Creek Falls. Four of the tunnels were complete but the other three were just cardboard lightly glued in place.

Roger was adding more cladding to the mountainside up near the Barron Falls. Graham settled down to helping him. First Roger tacked a layer of thin chicken wire netting over the rough framework. The sharp edges were snipped off with wire cutters. Calico was nailed over this. Then old newspapers were soaked in water and turned into *papier mache* which was laid on as a layer. Roger had already done some of this the previous day and it was now dry. Once Graham was busy, Roger mixed Plaster of Paris and spread it over the dry area.

Graham found it very relaxing to become absorbed in creative work with his hands and he worked happily, talking from time to time, but also remembering. Every horrifying and embarrassing detail of the Kuranda adventure was replayed in his mind as he worked, particularly when he was directed to prepare the steep cliffs above the Devils Cauldron where the final tragedy had been played out. He had come so close to death then he had resigned himself to it, only to see the mad rapist plunge to his doom instead. He shuddered at the memory of the sound the man's body had made when it had crashed through the treetops far below.

By lunch time the plaster was nearly dry. Roger suggested Graham stay to lunch, which he happily agreed to. This was such a normal event that Mrs Dunning had already prepared lunch for both of them anyway.

Afterwards, Roger marked off part of the plaster with a black felt pen. "These areas are going to be bare rock. The rest will be covered with trees and jungle," he explained.

The boys continued with the landscaping, Roger sculpting rock cliff faces by adding more wet plaster. Later this would be painted to make it look realistic.

By 2pm the boys had completed all of the covering right up to the top of the mountains and even some of the inland slope leading to the Tablelands area behind them. No track had been laid there yet but the framework was in place. At present the line ended at Fairyland. The engines had to travel back down in reverse. The boys had to accept that as there was insufficient room for either a Y-junction or a turntable. One was planned for the end of the line at Timbertop.

By then Graham had a headache from all the close work and was feeling a bit stiff in the back. With a jolt he remembered he had told Stephen he was coming over.

"I'd better be going Roger. I'll see you at school tomorrow."

"Yeah, okay," Roger replied brightly, but Graham sensed that he wished Graham was staying longer.

I suppose he gets a bit lonely, he mused.

Graham walked quickly home. Alex was out and so was Kylie. His mother was lying down sleeping. As quickly and quietly as he could Graham changed into old shorts and shirt, grabbed a pullover in case it got colder, and wheeled his bike out.

Stephen lived in Whitfield, and it took Graham about half an hour to ride there. On arrival he saw three other bikes on the lawn. For a moment he hesitated, wondering if he would be welcome. Summoning up the courage he knocked.

Stephen peered through a side louvre. "Oh it's you. Come in mate," he said.

At the rear of the house in the laundry were Derek White, Wally Dru, and his brother with glasses, Ernie. As soon as Graham walked in, he got a shock. The place reeked of cigarette smoke, which he had expected, but there was also alcohol.

"Have a drink, Kirky!" Ernie called.

"What ya got?" Graham asked cautiously.

"Rum 'n some jungle juice wot we made from Vodka and softdrink," Ernie replied.

Graham sat down, shaking his head at the offer of a cigarette. "Where's your mum and dad Steve?" he asked.

"At some flower show in Innisfail," Stephen replied, taking up a glass and sipping from it.

Even from three metres away Graham could smell the rum. Graham had extensive second-hand experience of alcohol. His father and his business associates drank like… well, like old sailors. The results had left Graham less than impressed and he had a strong dislike of beer and drunks, particularly as his dad seemed to be very belligerent and give him an even harder time after he had been drinking. Over the years, Graham and Alex had surreptitiously tasted and tested most of the bottles in their father's collection so he was familiar with the taste of rum and vodka.

He did not really want to drink but could not think of a reasonable excuse to say no. *They will think I'm a real wimp if I don't drink with them,* he thought.

Reluctantly, but pretending to be keen, he accepted a rum and coke from Stephen. Even before he sipped it he could tell it was strong. The fumes rose to make him gag. But he could see that the others were watching closely, and he knew he was being tested.

Bracing himself he quaffed a good mouthful and tried to grin. In this he was partly successful, but then he coughed and his eyes watered. The others laughed unmercifully. All Graham could do was laugh with them and play along.

"Pshaw! By Cripes, that's a nice strong brew!" he said.

To prove he was also strong he took another mouthful before he had fully recovered. Again he coughed and spluttered and the spirit burned down his throat. The fumes seared along his sinuses, and he found tears streaming down his cheeks and he gasped for breath.

"Cor, bloody strong all right!" he gasped, pretending to enjoy it.

The others hooted with laughter again and Ernie raised his glass and drank with him, in a signal that he had been accepted as a drinking partner.

After that, things rapidly deteriorated. Graham finished one glass and was handed another. By then his head was spinning. They began to sing dirty ditties and tell crude jokes.

Derek said, "What about showing us that porn video ya got, Steve?"

Stephen nodded agreement. "Yeah, righto. But no smoking in the house. The oldies would smell it right away."

Glasses were refilled, cigarettes puffed to a finish and the boys followed Stephen through into the lounge room. Graham felt embarrassed but took another sip and settled himself in an armchair. Stephen went into his room and appeared with a DVD which he placed in the TV. It was pure X-rated pornography showing, in the most graphic detail, a man having sex with two women.

Graham was both repelled and fascinated. He was also strongly aroused. He found this very embarrassing as he did not want the other boys to know it. They appeared to have no such inhibitions. Ernie in particular kept gripping himself and stroking the front of his trousers.

"This is bloody good, Steve. Did you get it through one of those mail order catalogues?" Dru asked.

"Nah. Mum might have found it in the post. She would have wanted to know what it was. I bought it off a bloke," Stephen replied.

Graham took another gulp of his drink and shook his head, both in disbelief at what the three people on the screen were doing, and at what Stephen was saying.

Derek pressed the front of his trousers. "Oooh this is makin' me randy!"

To which they all agreed. Graham certainly felt that way. At that the boys began to discuss their last sex. There was no way Graham was going to admit he had never done it so he lied when Derek asked him who it was with.

"My cousin from down south," he said. At that he blushed fiercely. To hide his confusion he drained his glass and refilled it from the bottles on the coffee table beside him. He settled back to watch the video, while listening to the lurid exploits of Ernie and Dru with a girl named Sonya in Year 10. He was sure they were exaggerating but suspected some of it was true, if only from the rumours he had heard about the Dru brothers. They were in the gang Stephen had got involved with earlier in the year and were real juvenile delinquents.

Suddenly Dru bumped over a glass. Rum and coke surged across the table and onto the carpet. At that Stephen sat up with a jerk. He looked very red in the face and glassy eyed but from the look which crossed his face Graham knew he was scared.

"Bloody hell! Quick! Mop it up" he cried.

The group tried, somewhat ineffectually. Stephen went to the kitchen and brought back a sponge and knelt to mop up the wet patch. As he stood up, he looked at the wall clock.

"Holy Moses! Look at the time. My oldies will be home any minute. Come on you guys. We gotta clean up and you'd better be gone before they get here. If they catch us drinking, I'm done for. I'll be grounded for so long I'll finish school first."

Ernie and Dru jeered at this, but Derek and Graham both supported Stephen. Graham liked Stephen's parents and did not want to antagonise them. The TV was turned off and Stephen hid his DVD again. With some difficulty they collected all the bottles and hid them. Graham finished his own drink in two gulps and rounded up the glasses and rinsed them. As he tried to wipe one, he dropped it. The glass smashed on the floor. He bent to try to clean up the pieces and suddenly found himself falling. He sprawled hard on the kitchen tiles.

Ernie jeered, "Ah, you're pissed, you weakling!"

Stephen looked down, horrified. "Bloody hell!" he groaned. "You've cut yourself. Come on you guys. Either sober up and help or piss off."

Dru straightened up. "Don't tell me ter piss orf!" he snarled angrily, lurching across the room.

Suddenly he gripped the kitchen table, then vomited. Graham rolled clear just in time. He stared at the blood dripping from the heel of his left hand in disbelief. It didn't hurt but he knew they had a problem. Somehow, he couldn't get his eyes to focus but he managed to reach the sink and wash the blood away. A handkerchief was hastily wrapped around the hand.

Stephen meanwhile helped Dru out the door and onto the lawn. "Take him home please Ernie, quick! Before my parents come home."

Muttering and swearing Ernie did as he was told. Stephen shoved bottles into their bag and carried it out to the bikes. Then he came back. "Come on Graham, you go too please."

Graham pointed to the floor. "We gotta clean that first."

A look of desperation crossed Stephen's face. "I'll do it. Come on, go please. You are drunk. My parents will smell it the moment they walk in. Go please!"

Aware that he was still seeping blood, Graham gripped the handkerchief and walked unsteadily to the front of the house. Derek came with him carrying more bottles in a bag. Stephen ushered them out to their bikes and urged them to go. By this time he was sweating with anxiety. Graham found he was sweating too, even though it was cold outside. As he bent to pick up his bike, he felt nausea swill in his stomach. He shook his head and muttered.

"I... I think I'm gunna be sick," he said.

"Not here! Get going please," Stephen pleaded, pushing Graham towards the front.

Unable to clip his helmet on, Graham left it hanging on the handlebars and then swore and adjusted the blood-soaked bandage.

"Go Graham! Go!" Steve pleaded.

Reluctantly Graham mounted his bike. He could see Derek and the Dru brothers further along the street. A car turned into the street down at the corner. A white car. *Stephen's parents?* he wondered. He didn't wait to find out but climbed unsteadily aboard and started pedalling.

It wasn't the parents. The car drove past and Graham tried to relax. But he was having trouble with his focus and his vision seemed to swirl. The world looked very funny and he laughed, then found himself lying on the grass verge of the road.

"Shit, I am pissed!" he laughed.

He picked himself up, aware that a lady was frowning disapproval at him over a garden fence. *Got to get away before Steve's oldies come home!* Graham told himself. With that single-minded aim he again mounted his bike and wobbled off along the street. He reached the corner and chortled with glee at the achievement.

After narrowly being missed by a car he swerved across the road and set off along it. A few minutes later he was weaving along the side of McManus Street feeling very lightheaded and pleased with himself. Suddenly he lost control at a pothole. Down he went, landing hard on the roadway. A car screeched to a halt. A man hopped out and anxiously helped him to sit up.

"You alright, kid?" he asked.

"Too... too bloody... hic!... hic! bloody right," Graham said.

He started to laugh. The man muttered something and went away. Graham remounted his bike, aware that he was having difficulty and that he had an audience. Off he went again.

He made it to the Pease Street roundabout with only three close shaves. Here he had to choose and got flustered. The end result was another crash. More cars stopped and worried drivers ran to help. Their anxiety quickly turned to anger as they realised his condition.

"Get off the road and walk you stupid kid!" one man snarled.

"Get stuffed!" Graham replied.

He tried to stand and found himself reeling. He gripped his bike for support, but it was no good. Over he went again, landing hard on the gravel beside the road. A vehicle pulled up beside him and he saw mud-caked brown leather boots and camouflage pattern trousers. He looked up, trying to focus his eyes.

It was Warrant Officer Howley. A flush of shame coursed through Graham. He knew he must be a spectacle and struggled to get to his feet. Warrant Officer Howley knelt to help, his face showing curiosity and puzzlement.

"Are you okay, lad? Don't I know you?" he asked.

"I... I.. " Graham began.

He felt the world spin and knew he was falling again, in spite of the helping hand. As he sprawled in the dust, another car pulled up. Shiny black leather boots and dark blue trousers appeared in Graham's blurred vision.

"Oh no! The cops!"

Chapter 6

ONE THING AFTER ANOTHER

It was Constable O'Neil and his mate. Graham tried once more to stand. With difficulty he got half up, then lost his balance. As he staggered, he reached out for support. Warrant Officer Howley grabbed him and held onto him. Graham steadied himself and tried to focus his eyes on the policeman's face. Anger he could detect.

"What the bloody hell's going on here?" Constable O'Neil rapped.

Warrant Officer Howley answered, "This kid just fell off his bike. I pulled up to help him. I reckon he's drunk, or on drugs."

Even in his drunken stupor Graham was aware enough to be both scared and appalled. "N... not .d… d... drugs," he gasped.

Constable O'Neil gave him a look of distaste and turned to Warrant Officer Howley. "We've met, I think?"

"Yes, last week down at St Monica's after those youths attacked two little girls. Warrant Officer Howley. I was just on my way home from the depot when I saw this boy on the road. In fact, I think he's the same kid who fought off that gang."

"He is," Constable O'Neil confirmed. "Graham Kirk. What have you been up to? Are you sick or have you been drinking?"

Graham felt his spirits droop and wretchedness well up in their place. *No point in lying,* he thought. *They must be able to smell the rum. Besides, they will test me with their 'Breathalyzer' thing.*

So he said, "Drunk sir."

"Drunk! In the middle of a Sunday afternoon!" Constable O'Neil said.

He took out his notebook. Graham met Warrant Officer Howley's eye and looked away, thoroughly ashamed of himself. Suddenly he broke into a cold sweat. Nausea welled up from deep in his stomach. He gasped for breath. "I... I... I think... I'm gunna be sick," he managed to say.

Then he spewed. Warrant Officer Howley held him so he did not fall flat on his face. His stomach heaved again, and the horrible hot liquid spurted out of his nostril as well as from his mouth. The acrid stench of bile made him retch a third time. The disgusting taste of stomach acids caught in the back of his throat. He stood bent over, dribbling vomit and bile into the mess at his feet. With an effort he wiped his mouth and straightened up.

Shock and shame surged within Graham in equal amounts. Cars were driving past and people gaping and pointing at him, and he knew he was in deep trouble. After a few more heavy breaths, Graham managed to stand and look at the men.

Constable O'Neil shook his head sadly. "Yes, you have been drinking, and too much, too fast from the look of it," he said in a voice heavy with sarcasm.

Graham knew there was no point in denying it. "Yes sir," he whispered. His stomach moved again, and he prepared to spew again but the spasm passed. He broke into a sweat again, but this time as much from fear. With an effort he focused his eyes.

"Drunk in charge of a vehicle, eh?" Constable O'Neil said.

"It's only a bloody bike!" Graham replied.

"Don't you get stroppy with me boy! The Traffic Act applies equally to bicycles. And where is your safety helmet?"

"Oh Christ!" groaned Graham, partly because he felt awful and knew he was going to vomit again. He bent over and heaved until he was dry retching. That hurt. So did his knees and hands, and he discovered they were gravel-rashed and bleeding.

"You finished puking?" Constable O'Neil asked unsympathetically.

"Yes sir," Graham replied. He stood unsteadily, wishing they would just get it over so he could flop down.

"Then get in the car. And if you throw up in there you will clean the bloody thing. Got it?"

"Yes sir."

Graham was bundled into the back of the car and had a seat belt buckled around him. Then he slid sideways and lay sprawled across the back seat. He found the world revolving and he knew he was seeing double. He was aware that Warrant Officer Howley and the policeman were talking but could not make out what they were saying. After a time the car started up. Graham tried to raise himself up to see where he was going. Worry about his fate began to dominate over his wretchedness.

To start with he thought he was going to be taken to the police station and that made him feel sick again. *Now dad will find out,* he thought miserably. That would mean grief in big heaps. *Boarding school!* he thought bitterly. Tears of self-pity began to form.

Instead, the police drove him home. This was only a few blocks. As they pulled up outside his house Graham glanced at the neighbour's house and groaned again. Bloody nosey old Mrs Foley was peering out of her front window.

Bloody old cow! he thought.

Now it would be all over the neighbourhood in a flash. In an attempt to counteract the probable rumours Graham tried to stand and walk normally but almost at once tripped over the gutter and went sprawling. He saw his mother's anxious face as she came running through the front gate.

"Oh dear! Is he hurt?" she cried.

"No Mrs Kirk, drunk," Constable O'Neil replied.

A look of horror, quickly replaced by hurt, appeared on Graham's mother's face. She gripped Graham's arm as he stood up. "Oh you have hurt yourself!" she said.

"Only gravel rash ma'am," Constable O'Neil replied.

Graham tried to speak but felt his stomach heave again and he lurched to the front fence and leaned on it. But there was nothing much left to bring up, just a few dribbles of bile. He found himself gasping and sweating. Alex's amused face swam into focus.

Their mother called, "Alex, get Graham's bike please."

Graham shook his head in an attempt to clear it. His mother led him through the gate and upstairs. The two policemen followed. He was sent into the bathroom to clean up while they explained the circumstances to his mother. Quickly Graham washed his cut and minor abrasions and then stuck Band Aids on the cut hand and his skinned knees and elbows. While he did his mind boiled with anxiety about possible consequences.

Boarding school probably, he thought bitterly.

When Graham came out, he felt wretched. He seated himself in the lounge room. His mother shook her head anxiously. She was obviously ashamed.

"Oh Graham! What have you been up to? I thought you were at Roger's. You weren't, were you?"

"No, Mum."

"Where were you?" she pressed.

Graham shook his head. “Won’t say. I’m not going to get anyone else into trouble,” he muttered stubbornly.

Constable O’Neil pursed his lips. “You’d better say something, kid,” he rasped. “Who gave you the alcohol?”

Graham shook his head again and pressed his lips together, a difficult feat as he found it hard to get enough air through his nostrils.

Constable O’Neil glared at him, “Won’t talk, eh? Did your mate Bell give you the drink?”

Graham’s mind raced. Had Stephen handed him the drink? No, it had been Dru. He shook his head again, “No he did not. It was someone else.”

“Who?”

“Not saying.”

“Did you buy it at a hotel?”

Graham shook his head, surprised at the notion. He was years underage and would never have dared to go near a licensed premises.

“No sir,” he replied.

Both police tried a few more questions but Graham still refused to answer. By this time he was feeling giddy and badly wanted to lie down. He heard his mother say, “Oh I wish his father was here! He is getting more out of hand all the time. I am so worried.”

“A firm hand is what he needs for sure,” Constable O’Neil replied. “Because if he keeps going down this track he is going to end up in real strife. Okay young Kirk, this is an official caution. Do you understand?”

“Yes sir.”

Constable O’Neil met his eye and nodded grimly, then formally warned him not to consume alcohol while underage; and not to break the state road laws. “Now wake up to yourself kid!” he concluded, snapping his notebook shut.

The two police then left. Graham bit his lip and met his mother’s eye. She had been crying.

“Oh Graham!” she said. “Where did you go? You might have told me. And who were you with?”

“Not now, Mum,” Graham snapped.

He felt unsteady but also ashamed and angry. He pushed himself to his feet and lurched through to his bed and flopped onto it. His mother left him, but Alex came past and snickered.

“Silly little bugger! Getting pissed on the main road on Sunday afternoon."

"Piss off Alex!" Graham snapped.

Then he groaned as the effort sent a stab of pain through his head. He rolled over to face the wall and tried to sleep. He did eventually, but not before he had experienced some awful sensations as his senses swirled and his vision continually lost focus.

His mother left him alone once he was asleep and he woke in the middle of the night with a ghastly taste in his mouth and a throbbing headache. He blundered through the house to the toilet and then returned miserably to his bed. Hunger gnawed at him, but he did not dare raid the fridge. Instead he went back to bed and lay there brooding until he drifted off to sleep.

When he woke on Monday morning Graham felt very shaky. He still had the headache and horrible taste in his mouth, and he felt thoroughly ashamed of himself. It took an effort to get out of bed and go to face the family at the breakfast table.

His mother looked very pale and strained. Kylie appeared worried but sympathetic. Alex just grinned. Graham met their eyes defiantly and sat down. He ate in silence, ignoring Alex's jibes.

Afterwards his mother called him aside. "Are you going to school?"

"Yes, Mum," he answered. *What else would I do?* he thought in surprise.

"Please don't do anything like that again," she asked.

"No, Mum. Sorry mum."

Graham made his way to school, still with a throbbing headache and eyes that seemed to be very sensitive to the strong sunlight. Stephen was the first of his friends he met. Graham made a face and asked, "Did you get it all cleaned up in time?"

Stephen nodded. "Yeah. No problems," he replied. "Mum and dad didn't get home till nearly six. You okay? You look a bit the worse for wear."

Graham made another face and related the meeting with the police. Stephen just laughed. "Grief happens!" was his comment.

Graham was not amused, but the arrival of Peter ended that discussion. Soon after that the bell sent them off to lessons. Geography was first. Graham didn't mind. He sat quietly and drew maps, but all the while his head throbbed and he just wanted to lie down. During the change of lessons he mentioned this to Stephen.

"Go to the sick room then," Stephen suggested.

Graham nodded and stood up. Stephen did likewise and they went out the door. "Where are you going?" Graham asked.

"Me? I'm going to skip the next class. It is only old Mrs Ramsey, and she never checks the roll," Stephen replied.

"What are you going to do?" Graham asked.

"Just going down the oval for a lie down. I feel a bit crook too," Stephen replied.

Graham knew he should go to the sick room but somehow he ended up walking down to the oval with Stephen. They found a corner behind a big tree which was out of sight of the PE classes on the oval. Both lay down. For a while they talked but Graham was so exhausted that he slipped into a deep sleep.

He awoke some time later to find his head still ached. His mouth tasted foul and he had ants crawling on him.

A voice penetrated his slumber. "Hello, the dead have risen!"

Graham opened his eyes, then squinted against the glare. It was Dru. Next to him sat Derek White. Both were smoking. There was no sign of Stephen. Graham struggled into a sitting position and groaned.

"Where's Steve?"

"Gone to Maths," Derek replied.

Maths! Graham shook his head, something he instantly regretted as pain lanced through it. "Maths! Christ! What time is it?"

Derek told him. Graham groaned again. He was late for Maths A, and Old Buggermaster always checked the roll!

Dru laughed. "Stop worryin'. Here, have a drag on this. You'll feel better."

He held out a burning cigarette. The whiff of marijuana reached Graham's nostrils. He shook his head. "No thanks. I'm in enough strife already."

Dru shrugged, then sneered and said, "Hear ya got busted by the cops."

Graham nodded and rubbed his forehead. Then Dru needled him some more. "Tough! Ya shouldn't be ridin' if ya can't hold ya grog. You must be piss weak if ya can't ride a bloody bike after only a coupla rums."

"Get stuffed!" Graham snapped.

Quickly he rolled over and stood up, then walked away. *I don't want to be found with people who are smoking marijuana,* he thought. Dru and Derek both laughed and jeered. He ignored them and strode off towards the sick room, brooding over the fact that Stephen had not woken him.

The Sick Room will be the best alibi, he decided.

He reported to the office. The office girl looked pointedly at her watch. Graham blushed but said, "I was in the toilet. I don't feel well."

"Do you need a doctor, or need to go home?" she asked.

"No."

She took Graham's name and logged him into the Sick Room. Once there he thankfully subsided onto the couch, ignoring two Year 8 boys on other couches. Almost at once the bell went. Graham badly wanted to get up and leave as it was morning break, but he did not think it would look right so he lay there.

A few minutes later Mr Burgomeister appeared in the doorway. "Ah, there you are Kirk. I wondered where you were. What is wrong with you?"

"Headache sir, and upset stomach," Graham replied.

Mr Burgomeister grunted and walked away. Graham lay back and closed his eyes, hatred seething within him. Minutes dragged past, long, boring minutes. Graham yearned to be free and slipped into a daydream. The bell for classes went. He debated whether to go or not.

Mr Fitz arrived and settled the issue. "If you don't need a doctor and aren't sick enough to go home then go back to class," he ordered.

Graham did as he was told. The lesson was German. He knocked at the door and Miss See told him to sit. He slid into his seat next to Stephen.

"Thanks a bundle, Steve, leaving me like that!" he hissed.

"Keep your hair on! You were sound asleep. Anyway, I told old Buggerlugs you were at the Sick Room. He's too lazy to check," Stephen replied.

"Pig's bum! He came and looked. Lucky I woke up and went there," Graham replied.

At that Miss See intervened, ordering them to stop talking and to get on with their work. Graham politely agreed. She was a beautiful young woman just out of university, and he greatly admired her and had no wish to cause her trouble.

The day dragged on, Physics, lunch, Music, then Maths B. Maths

B brought Mr Ritter. He was in a savage mood and began a vendetta on homework. Needless to say neither Graham nor Stephen had done theirs, along with a dozen others.

Mr Ritter looked grim and shook his head. “Then you can all stay in till it is done. If you don’t like that then get your parents in to see me.”

When the final bell went Mr Ritter stood at the door to check each student’s work as they left. Then he stood on the veranda talking to Mr Holden while a dozen students settled to the chore.

After a few minutes, Stephen muttered, “Bugger this. Let’s sneak out. Ritter won’t notice.”

Graham wasn’t so sure. “How?” he asked.

Stephen pointed behind them. The back wall of the room was really a sliding divider which could be moved aside to make one large room out of two. The centre panel was often unlocked and, at that moment, was slightly ajar. Nor was there a class in the next room.

Graham studied the layout, then nodded. “Okay, you go first.”

They packed their bags and checked that Mr Ritter was not looking. Stephen then slid off his seat onto the floor and started crawling along the aisle between the rows of desks. Graham slid off and followed him. Angus and Vincent grinned down at them and made smart and unhelpful comments.

“Shut up you two!” Graham growled.

Stephen reached the divider and slowly started to pull the panel wider to allow room to slip through. At that moment, Mr Ritter came back into the room. Graham could just see the teacher’s shoes under the desks. His heart was already beating fast but now he broke into a sweat.

He’s spotted the divider moving! he thought.

At that moment, Stephen crawled through into the next room. Mr Ritter moved at once. He strode back to the door and along the veranda outside the room and went in the door of the next room. Instantly Graham saw his opening.

Ritter has left his position at the door. Now’s my chance! he thought.

As soon as he heard Mr Ritter say, “What do you think you are up to, Bell?” Graham stood up, ran to the front of the room and out of the door. Beyond were the stairs. He went down them in three leaps and raced off under the building.

Made it! he mentally whooped, exhilarated by the small triumph.

He fled out of the side gate and ran along the footpath. Only after he had covered half a block and was winded did he slow down to a walk. Free! He walked slowly home looking at the distant mountains, wishing he was up there.

As soon as he reached home, Graham settled to afternoon tea then lay on his bed. As he lay there, he brooded on all the things that had gone wrong. It seemed to be just one thing after another. Frustration and anger gave way to depression as he contemplated what would probably happen the next day. The apparent failure of all his hopes and the pointlessness of life made him miserable and irritable.

His mother noticed this as at teatime when he picked at his food and asked what was wrong. Graham shrugged and said, "Nothing." To his relief, she didn't press the issue and he was able to escape to the privacy of the veranda. He took himself to bed early and pretended to read.

Sleep claimed him but did not refresh him. He tossed and turned and had a nightmare in which he was being chased by some sort of dark spirit from which he could not escape because his limbs would not move. He woke feeling tired and irritable.

By the time he reached school Graham was in a state of morose surliness. This was aggravated by being told his name was on the morning notices, along with Stephen's: Report to the Deputy Principal.

Mr Fitz was in an angry mood, "Running out of a detention like that! What the devil do you young tearaways think you are on about?"

Graham could only shake his head. He knew it had been foolish. Mr Fitz blasted them both then pronounced 'Time Out'. "And I shall inform your parents. Now get back to class."

Graham walked back to class in a mood of savage hostility at the whole world. Everything seemed to be going wrong. *It all seems so pointless! I wish I was dead!* he thought.

The morning dragged by: English, a double Chemistry, then morning tea. As soon as the teacher released them Graham left the laboratory. Stephen headed for the tuck shop and Graham made his way to their usual spot. On the way he met Peter coming in the other direction. He was carrying a large cardboard poster.

Peter smiled a greeting. "Hi Graham! Heard you had a spot of bother with old 'Rhomboid' Ritter," he called cheerfully.

Graham scowled. Peter's happiness aggravated him even more. Easy for him to talk! He was brainy and could do his schoolwork in his sleep! He gave Peter a brief description of the incident.

Peter laughed. "I know. Stephen told me. He was a bit stroppy that he got caught and had to stay in an extra half hour."

"Good! Serves him right!" Graham snapped. He was not too happy with Stephen at that moment. "What's that you've got?" he asked.

Peter unrolled the poster. "A recruiting poster for the Army Cadets. Captain Conkey just gave it to me to pin up on the main noticeboard. We are doing a big recruiting drive to bring the unit up to strength for Annual Camp in September."

Graham glanced at the poster and shrugged. Peter looked at him and asked, "Why don't you join? It's a lot of fun."

Graham curled his lip. "No thanks. Not me. There are enough people telling me what to do already without a lot of little Hitlers shouting orders at me."

"It's not like that," Peter persisted. "We do lots of camps. There's one coming up in a few weeks."

"No."

"Suit yourself," Peter replied equably.

Whistling happily he walked away. Graham went and sat in their favourite spot and waited till Stephen joined him.

"Bugger!" Stephen said good-naturedly. "You got away and I got caught."

They both laughed and recounted the incident. It then had to be retold for Roger's benefit. He shook his head sadly. "You guys will get into real strife one day."

Geography was next. Graham worked quietly and the period passed without incident. So did Physics, although Stephen kept making crude innuendos at everything Miss 'Tart' said. Lunch time meant 'Time Out' and was a real drag. Manual Arts was alright, enlivened by an attempt to overheat a soldering iron while the teacher wasn't looking.

Last period was again Maths B. And once again half the class had not done their homework. Knowing what was coming, Stephen whispered to Graham, "I've got a better plan. When he says those who haven't done their homework can leave, we hide under the desk. That way he won't notice we are still here, and while his back is turned, we sneak out."

Graham shook his head. "You are crazy! We will get hung if we get caught again."

"What's wrong, no guts?" Stephen taunted.

That stung. Graham bit back a retort and went red. At that moment, Mr Ritter said, "Those people who have done their homework can show me and leave."

Twenty people stood up. Stephen scooped his books into his bag and slid off his seat and crouched under the desk. "Come on scaredy cat!" he hissed.

Graham swallowed and slid down to join him. His heart began to beat rapidly and he knew he was perspiring, even though it was quite cool. From across the aisle Angus grinned down at him.

The students who had done their homework formed a line at the door so Mr Ritter could check them individually. This was his normal procedure and was the basis of Stephen's plan. After several minutes the line at the door was gone but Mr Ritter remained standing there. Graham could see his shoes and wondered if the teacher had noticed their absence. Their classmates all knew they were there, but none gave any hint as they sat and worked.

Time began to drag. Still Mr Ritter stood at the door. Once he walked into the room. Graham's pulse rate shot up and his mouth went dry but the teacher stopped at his desk. For a minute or so he stood there and then he turned and went back to the door. Minutes dragged by. Several students finished the work and left. The room began to look very empty.

Mr Ritter then began to talk to 'Old Jock', the senior maths teacher, a much feared, but much respected teacher who had taught at the school for thirty years.

Stephen nudged Graham's ribs. "Now's our chance," he whispered. Cautiously he crawled back along the aisle to the divider. He tried to open it. "No luck. It is locked," he hissed in annoyance.

"How can we escape then?" Graham asked.

The situation was starting to look ridiculous. Instead of getting away they were trapped in uncomfortable circumstances.

"Out the window?" Stephen suggested.

Graham glanced up at the open shutter-type window. "Okay."

Stephen was on his right and the window on their left. He pointed. "You go first this time," he insisted.

Graham nodded. He risked a peek over the desks from behind

Angus. Mr Ritter's back was visible but Old Jock could not see them. Graham stood up and walked the two paces to the window. Looking out gave him an unpleasant shock. The classroom was on the first floor, and it looked a long way down.

Stephen nudged him from behind. "Go on! Get going, quick!" he urged.

Nothing for it. Graham wasn't game to admit he was scared. He leaned out to check there was no-one below, then threw his bag down. It landed with a thud on the lawn of the quadrangle. Another look around showed no sign of any other teacher over in the main building. Graham put his leg over the sill and slid out. That was the easy bit. He reached down till his left shoe was firmly resting on the metal cap of one of the concrete posts, then slid the rest of his body out, hanging on tightly with both hands to the windowsill.

He bent his knees to get his head clear of the window frame and looked down to pick his spot. It did look a long way down and he felt scared. He licked his lips and breathed in deeply, trying to summon the courage to jump.

Stephen had moved into the next window and tossed his port out. "Go on!" he urged. "Jump! It's only one floor. Land like a paratrooper; knees bent. You shouldn't break anything."

Graham licked his lips and looked down again to pick his landing spot. What he saw made his heart stop.

A grim-faced Mr Fitz stood there, hands on hips, glaring up at him. "What the devil are you up to, Kirk? Get back inside at once!"

"Yes sir."

With his heart sinking into his boots Graham climbed back in the window. Stephen made a face and shrugged. There was nothing for it. They were caught again.

Chapter 7

OUTBURST

Mr Fitz came upstairs carrying their bags. He explained the situation to Mr Ritter, who gave the two boys a withering glance. They were then marched off to the office and again severely lectured. Mr Fitz was very angry.

"You pair are headed for hell in a handcart at fantastic speed. What the devil is driving you, eh? Stop this stupidity before you really come to grief."

He glared angrily at them then went on, "Now, Kirk. Mr Burgomeister tells me you skipped Maths yesterday and were allegedly in the Sick Room. According to the office records you only arrived five minutes before the end of the period. Where were you?"

"At the toilet, sir. I did not feel well," Graham replied, blushing at the lie.

"So what do you know about the graffiti in the toilets?"

Graham felt as though the ground had suddenly opened beneath his feet, exposing a pit full of fire. He broke into a cold sweat. He shook his head.

"I don't know anything sir. I didn't see any graffiti."

Mr Fitz gave him a withering stare which clearly indicated he did not believe him. "Well, you two can have another punishment. This time it will be two detentions in the 'Time Out' room at lunch time. That will be today and tomorrow. And you will also do the homework Mr Burgomeister set for the class. Kirk, you get the work off Bell. Now wait while I write your parents a note."

The two stood and waited until the Deputy had penned notes to their parents. These were placed in sealed envelopes. As Mr Fitz handed the envelopes to them, he growled, "Make sure they get them. I expect a reply. Now get going."

Outside the two commiserated with each other before making their way home. As soon as he got home, Graham handed his mother the note. When she saw what it was a look of pain crossed her face. She sat and read it, looking sorry and thoughtful. After a few minutes, she shook her head sadly.

"I don't know what to do anymore, Graham. You seem hell bent on getting into trouble. I know your father thinks you should be allowed to make your own decisions, but I wonder."

Graham bit his lip. He vividly remembered his father lecturing him and Alex the previous year after one of their escapades. "Do what you bloody like!" his father had shouted at them. "But you take the consequences. If you choose to do the wrong thing, then you can pay for it. And you have to live with yourself afterwards, so let your conscience be your guide."

Captain Kirk had glared at them through eyes red-rimmed from lack of sleep and salt spray (he had just battled down the coast into the teeth of a storm for four days). "And another thing, if the coppers pick you up and clap you in the watchhouse, then you can bloody well stay there. I won't be coming along to bail you out. Now wake up to yourselves!"

Graham left his mother to brood while he went down to the Ship Room to do the same thing. He stayed there till teatime then watched TV. For most of the evening he sat and drew pictures. Art was something he was good at, and he had been slowly drawing a long story in comic book form for several years. It was a pleasant escape fantasy.

Once again he slept badly. This time the nightmare was different. He dreamt that he was at school but had somehow lost his pants and was in deep trouble. Mr Fitz was after him and he managed to escape by blowing Mr Fitz up with a 100-litre drum full of Nitro-glycerine. Mr Fitz had exploded in a spray of black sludge. Then Graham had found Constable O'Neil chasing him to arrest him for murder. He woke shaking and exhausted.

Over breakfast his mother asked him to try to stay out of trouble during the day. She handed him a note to give to Mr Fitz. "I shall be talking to your father today as well. Maybe you should go to sea with him for a while," she suggested.

A voyage with 'Captain Bligh'! Graham was appalled. "It will be okay, Mum," he assured her. He hurried off to school before she could pursue the subject.

On arrival at school, Graham was immediately put in a bad mood. Larsen pushed him as he came through the main entrance.

“Outa my way ya little shit!” Larsen ordered.

Graham boiled with anger but restrained himself. They were just near the deputy’s office. He went up and gave his mother’s note to Mr Fitz, then went looking for his friends. Before he found them, he got another jolt. As he walked along, he saw Glenys and Janet Ozgood talking. Janet looked up and saw him, then said something to Glenys. She glanced in his direction and curled her lip. That really burned. Graham walked past seething with hurt pride and resentment.

Dru and Derek were the next to stir him up. Graham met them in the toilet when he hurried in to have a quick leak before classes. Inside he found Dru and Derek. Both were smoking and the reek of marijuana was strong in the air. In their hands were oil based felt pens and they were scrawling obscene insults about Mr Burgomeister on the wall. Seeing this brought Mr Fitz’s question about graffiti to mind.

Dru looked over his shoulder and saw Graham. “Well here he is, the drunken bike rider!”

Graham gave a weak grin and tried to pretend it was a joke. He went to the urinal and unzipped his fly. To his embarrassed surprise, Dru came over and peered down at him as he started.

Dru curled his lip and jeered. “That’s not very big, Kirky. You won’t give the girls much of a thrill with that,” he said.

Graham flamed with shame but had now started peeing and couldn’t stop. “It’s not how big it is that counts. It’s how you use it,” he retorted, using a comment he had overheard.

Dru laughed and sneered. “What would you know about it! You wouldn’t have the guts to do it, even if you could find some ugly bag desperate enough to want you.”

“Get stuffed!” Graham cried angrily.

He managed to stop peeing and put his penis away just before Dru thumped him. He stepped away from the urinal and shoved back, a red mist of anger making his vision hazy. Even so, he was aware that Dru was looking odd, that his face looked slack and his eyes bright. A caution at the back of his mind warned him that fighting someone high on drugs might not be a good idea.

The two started to shove and spar at each other. Derek stepped between them. “Stop it you two. Come on Dru, let’s get out of here before anyone spots our artwork.”

He grabbed Dru and led him away. Graham stood and watched, breathing heavily and wildly angry at the insults. Several Year 10 boys came in and looked at him curiously, then noted the graffiti and ran off laughing to tell their mates. Graham returned to the urinal to finish relieving himself. While he did, more boys crowded in to study the graffiti. Graham ignored them and went off to find his friends.

The bell went before he managed that. He swore angrily, not feeling in the mood for schoolwork. Worse still, the lesson was Maths A: Mr Burgomeister. Trouble erupted almost at once. As soon as the teacher entered the room he looked around. His gaze settled on Graham and his eyes narrowed.

"Ah! Master Kirk. He who is sick. Show me the homework Mr Fitzgerald said you were to do. You too, Bell."

Graham shook his head in dismay and irritation. He had completely forgotten to do it. He felt anger rising. Stephen had done his.

What's the use? Graham thought.

Mr Burgomeister proceeded to lecture him on what a failure he would be unless he 'pulled his socks up'. "You are on the road to nowhere, you stupid boy!"

"I don't care!" Graham replied, frustration and misery welling up.

"Don't you talk back to me like that boy!" Mr Burgomeister snapped. "You will stay in at lunch time and do the work."

"I'm already on detention," Graham shouted.

"Don't shout at me boy."

"Leave me alone!" Graham cried.

A red rage engulfed him. What was the point of anything? Hatred of the teacher, of school, of himself, all boiled up.

Mr Burgomeister glared at him, "You had better get a grip on yourself boy, or I send you to the office. Now get on with your work and no backchat."

Graham sat and looked down. He could hardly see for the tears which were forming and that scalded his already injured pride. In an attempt to calm himself he gripped the desk and shook his head.

Mr Burgomeister walked angrily towards him, "Why are you shaking your head? Do you defy me? Do as I say! Get on with your work or else!"

"Or else what!" Graham shouted. He sprang to his feet, knocking over his chair. His vision was all blurred and he had to gulp to get any air.

"Sit down boy! Don't you shout at me!"

Graham stared at the hated red face with its jowls, double chins and hairy nostrils. Without thinking he raised his clenched fists, "Leave me alone!"

The teacher's face went very white, then suffused with rage and turned red. "You threaten me! Office! Get to the office!" he screamed.

Stephen was on his feet beside him. He grabbed Graham by his left arm and began tugging him towards the door. Through a mist of rage and tears, Graham realised he had made another terrible mistake. He stumbled towards the door and fled sobbing out along the veranda.

Stephen came with him and stopped him from running out the front entrance. "No good running, mate. Old Buggermaster will be sending a note to the office right now. If you run it will just make things worse."

Graham knew he was right, but he was so torn up it took him a few minutes to calm down. For a while he sat under the school and cried. Stephen sat with him and talked to calm him down.

"You okay, mate? What's wrong?" he asked.

Graham shook his head. How could he explain? "You go back to class. I'll be alright now," he said after a while. He stood up and headed for the office. Stephen went with him.

Mr Fitz knew all about it. "Ah! There you are, Kirk. Sit there. What are you doing here, Bell? Are you in trouble too?"

"No sir. Just helping Graham," Stephen replied.

"Then get back to class."

Stephen did as he was told, and Graham slumped down on a seat. Mr Fitz went into the principal's office. Minutes dragged by. The bell went and classes changed. Mr Burgomeister arrived, cast a venomous glance at Graham and went into the principal's office as well. He emerged ten minutes later with a look of grim satisfaction and stalked off to his next lesson. Mr Fitz appeared and beckoned Graham. Feeling totally defeated he walked into the office. The Principal, Mr Croswell was there and indicated that Graham should stand on the matt in front of his desk. Mr Fitzgerald stood to one side.

It was an unpleasant interview. Graham made no attempt to deny the accusations that he had threatened a teacher. He just stood there as though stunned, sunk in a deep pit of depression. None of it seemed to matter. The future looked so black he just wanted to get it over with.

At length Mr Croswell pronounced judgement. "This cannot go unpunished. We have been very lenient with you in the past. This time I think it will mean a week's suspension. Now, that means calling in your parents. And if there is another incident then we will be looking at expulsion. Do you understand that?"

"Yes sir," Graham whispered. He was shivering and battling to hold back the tears.

"All right. That will be all for the moment. When your parents are here, we will continue the discussion. Now, until you have calmed down you are to go to the 'Time Out' room and work there. Go and collect your bag and go there now," Mr Croswell said.

Mr Fitz spoke up as Graham stood up, "And you'd better get a grip on yourself boy. If you keep up this behaviour pattern you will end up a petty crim with no future. What you need is some self-discipline because if you don't learn to control yourself then you can be sure the authorities will!"

Future! Graham thought grimly as he left the room. *What future? I may as well kill myself now and get it over!*

For the next three hours he sat in the 'Time Out' room engulfed in a haze of misery. Most of the time he was the only student there. A bored teacher sat at the front supervising. Again, Graham went over all his options and considered running away or suicide. When the teacher wasn't looking, he shed silent tears. The self-pity was like a physical force which surged within him.

At the end of the lunch break, Mr Conkey appeared at the door. "I hear you've been in trouble, Graham."

"Yes sir. Sorry sir."

"You'd better come to class and get some work done. There is no future in sitting here brooding," Mr Conkey said.

"Fitz... I mean Mr Fitzgerald told me to stay here sir till my mum could come in," Graham replied.

"I know. I've spoken to him. They haven't been able to contact your mother yet. So come with me."

"Yes sir."

Reluctantly, Graham walked with Mr Conkey to class. During the lesson, which was Geography, Graham sat on his own and worked. It was map drawing and interpretation and he could do that easily. Mr Conkey did not bother him and he was happy to be left alone, well aware that he was the object of speculative gossip among the other students.

Last period was Maths B with Mr Ritter, again in B7. Stephen rejoined the class after Art. As soon as he saw Graham, his face lit up. He came and sat next to him in their usual seat.

"What's going to happen?" he asked.

"Suspension probably, with expulsion if I muck up again," Graham replied. He managed to hold back the bitter tears.

Mr Ritter arrived and surveyed the class. His gaze settled on Graham and Stephen. "Ah! The escapees! Well, we won't have any more of that nonsense, will we?"

"No sir," Stephen replied. Graham was so choked up he couldn't speak. Instead he shook his head. Mr Ritter walked over to their desk. "Good. So show me your homework for today."

Graham bit his lip and felt Stephen grip his arm. It helped steady him. *Bloody homework!* He had not done it.

"I have... haven't done it sir," he managed to croak.

"Oh well. You can stay in again and finish it," Mr Ritter replied grimly.

He's pushing me, Graham thought. *He wants me to react so that the school can chuck me out.*

It was a sobering and chilling thought. Feeling close to desperation, he gripped his chair and willed himself to nod and say nothing although savage rebellion and hatred flamed in his heart.

Somehow, he got through the lesson without getting into further trouble. At the end of the forty minutes Mr Ritter checked who had done their homework. Six others including Stephen, Angus McDougal, and Vincent were kept in. This time Mr Ritter walked up and down inside the room. Graham was gripped by a sullen rage but forced himself to work.

While Graham and the others worked at completing their detention the school's army cadet unit formed up outside on the grass quadrangle. The sound of their talking, then of the shouted orders carried clearly up into the room.

Stephen put his hand up. "Please sir, can I go? I am supposed to be at Cadets."

"No, Bell. You can be late and make your own explanations. You have chosen this course of action, now pay for it," Mr Ritter replied.

At that moment, the cadet sergeant major bellowed loudly, "Companeee... On... parade!"

Mr Ritter stopped beside Graham and pointed towards the window. "That's what you need, Kirk, a bit of army discipline. If you don't get your life together, that's probably the only job you'll be able to get, the army."

Graham gritted his teeth and did not answer. *That'll be the bloody day!* he thought savagely. Then another thought crossed his mind: *The French Foreign Legion is the army I will join.*

He started to fantasise over this as a possible escape from all his misery. Mr Ritter walked on to check Vincent's work. At that moment, another voice came from outside: Warrant Officer Howley's. Graham felt a flush of shame, which fuelled his resentment.

As the cadets came marching off parade to go to their training lessons, Mr Ritter finally said they could go. Stephen fled at once to go and change into his uniform.

"My mum and dad have been checking up. I better be at Cadets today or I will be in real trouble," he explained.

Graham packed his port and walked slowly down the steps. A platoon of cadets went marching past. To his surprise, he saw that the cadet sergeant calling the step was a girl; and not just any girl, but Anastasia, a Year 11 who was generally reckoned to be the hottest and most desirable sort in the whole school. Graham waited till they had passed, then walked through under the building on the way to the front entrance.

As he did, he saw Warrant Officer Howley coming the other way. Warrant Officer Howley looked at him with a quizzical eye.

"Hello. Young Kirk, isn't it?" he said.

He stopped, so Graham felt compelled to do as well, although all he wanted to do was leave. "Yes sir," Graham said. He blushed with shame at the humiliating memory of their last meeting. "Sorry about the other day sir. I... I... I've never done anything like that before," he blurted out.

Warrant Officer Howley raised an eyebrow. "Not a habitual drunk then? So what's the matter; things getting you down a bit?"

Graham nodded. He felt misery welling up and tears started to prickle in his eyes. That would be the worst humiliation. He battled against that. At that moment, Mr Conkey joined them. He was now dressed in his captain's uniform.

"Hello there, Graham. What do you want?" he asked.

"Just talking to Warrant Officer Howley, sir."

"Oh! I didn't know you two knew each other. I was hoping you had come to join," Captain Conkey replied.

Graham shook his head. "We... we've met sir."

To his added embarrassment, Warrant Officer Howley said, "It's a pity he doesn't want to join. He's just the sort you want, brave as a lion."

Captain Conkey nodded. "Yes, he's a good kid basically, although he's in a spot of bother at the moment," he replied.

Graham wanted to walk away but could not think of any way to end the conversation without being blatantly rude.

Warrant Officer Howley looked at him. "Hmm. Yes, I know a bit of it. What's the problem?" he asked.

Captain Conkey outlined the morning's incident with Mr Burgomeister. Warrant Officer Howley looked thoughtful and rubbed his chin. Then he said, "I see. Are you in a hurry, young Kirk? Would you mind waiting a few minutes?"

Graham shrugged in surprise. "No sir. I don't mind."

"Thanks. Would you mind sitting there while I speak to Captain Conkey?" Warrant Officer Howley asked.

Graham nodded and moved to a seat against the wall while Warrant Officer Howley led Captain Conkey into the room which doubled as Q Store and office for the cadet unit. Graham was worried, but also curious. They were obviously talking about him. He bit his lip and hoped he wasn't in trouble for something else.

As he sat there feeling anxious and depressed, cadets came and went to the second room, the 'armoury' where the plastic Drill Purpose rifles were stored. Another teacher was there in uniform, Mr Hamilton. With him were three Year 11s that Graham knew. All were sergeants: Neville Strutton, Mike Masters (a champion sportsman and hero of the school), and Alistair Macalistair (who was a 'Rover' in Graham's Scout Troop). They looked at him curiously but left him alone.

Later, two Year 12 boys: Garth Grant and Alan Broughton, wearing the rank badges of Cadet Under-Officers, came to the office door. Graham knew both by name. Garth Grant was the School Captain and heart throb of half the girls. Alan was Graham's House Captain in Cook House and was also a Rover in the Scouts. They stood chatting cheerfully with another teacher in uniform, Mr Maclaren, one of the science teachers. From time to time they also glanced at Graham making him feel self-conscious. After a while he began thinking he might leave.

Just as his resolution was crystallising, Captain Conkey and Warrant Officer Howley came out of the office and walked across to him. Graham stood as they approached.

Captain Conkey said, "I've been on the phone to the principal, Graham. He tells me he is considering suspending you from school. That's getting pretty serious. The next step is expulsion; and that is the start of the road to nowhere in life. You've obviously got some problems at the moment. Would you care to talk about it?"

Graham pressed his lips together and cursed the fact that his eyes began to prickle again as self-pity and misery surged within him. He did not want to talk but found himself telling them all about his great ambition to be a naval officer and how his eyes were not good enough. At that he felt the first tear trickle out and he turned away, desperately ashamed of himself. To his mortification, he began to sob.

Warrant Officer Howley moved to stand between him and the cadets at the Q Store. He put a hand on Graham's shoulder. "It's okay, son. Take it easy. We understand that. But it isn't the end of the world. Lots of people go through life blind and still enjoy it and live fulfilling lives. So snap out of your self-pity. Captain Conkey has a proposition to put to you."

Graham wiped his tears and took several deep breaths as he struggled to master his emotions. He knew that what Warrant Officer Howley had said was true, but that just fuelled his lack of self-esteem. But the comment about snapping out of his self-pity really bit hard. He looked at Captain Conkey.

Captain Conkey waited till he was calm, then said, "I'm going to ask you to join the Army Cadets. In return I'm going to ask the principal to drop the suspension. What do you say?"

Chapter 8

HARD CHOICES

Graham stared at Captain Conkey in appalled surprise. *Join the Army Cadets! Me!*

"Why sir?" he asked.

"Because I believe it will be a good experience that will help you," Captain Conkey replied.

Graham's mind raced. He was horrified at the idea and tried to think of an answer that would get him off this most unexpected hook. "But... but I'm not sure if I could stand taking orders, sir. I'm always in trouble," he replied.

"You thought you could be a naval officer. That is a very exacting profession where you have to obey orders," Captain Conkey pointed out.

That was true, but Graham did not want to admit it. "I'm not sure, sir. I will have to ask my mother," he replied. His dilemma was that the idea of Army Cadets did not appeal but the thought of escaping the suspension did.

Captain Conkey nodded. "You do that. I will get you the enrolment forms to take home," he replied.

He turned and walked back to the cadet office. Graham stood beside Warrant Officer Howley feeling uncertain and embarrassed. For something to say he asked, "What do you think I should do, sir?"

Warrant Officer Howley looked him squarely in the eyes. "Join. Take the opportunity. Captain Conkey thinks you are a good kid who is worth an effort to save," he replied.

That made Graham even more flustered and embarrassed. Another thought came to him. "But if my eye isn't any good, I won't be able to join the army either, so what's the point?"

Warrant Officer Howley chuckled. "The army isn't quite as fussy. A cynic would say that all you need to be fit for the army is a head, a body, two arms, and two legs so that you resemble a figure target at three hundred metres. Seriously though, the Cadets are not part of the army and joining them doesn't involve you in any obligation to ever serve in the army. The main aim of the Cadets is character development; to turn out good citizens."

Captain Conkey returned and passed him a plastic document holder containing pieces of paper. "The enrolment forms: Parent Details, Health Declaration, and Application. Bring them back tomorrow when you come with your mother to see the principal."

Graham could only nod. He felt confused. Part of him was grateful for the chance and part of him was resentful, feeling that he was being forced. Captain Conkey then said he had work to do and turned to go.

Warrant Officer Howley looked Graham in the eye. "Captain Conkey must have a high opinion of you to make that effort. The honourable thing you should do is return the favour and take the opportunity being offered. That's my advice. Anyway, good luck. I hope to see you in the future doing well." With that he also turned and walked away.

Graham walked slowly home, resentfully turning over the options in his mind. *I'm being press-ganged into this,* he thought. But he could not see any easy way out, other than accepting the suspension. *And that could mean boarding school,* he thought unhappily.

As soon as he arrived home, Graham found that his mother knew about his threat to Mr Burgomeister. She was very upset, more than he could ever remember. Kylie was worried and puzzled, knowing only that Graham was in trouble again and obviously concerned on his behalf.

Alex also knew about the incident from school rumour. He teased Graham at once, "I hear you've been a naughty boy, little brother, calling old Buggermaster names. Boarding school for you boy if they expel you."

"I'm only going to be suspended for a week," Graham replied testily.

Alex smirked. "You should have thumped the grumpy old prick," he said.

Mrs Kirk bridled angrily. "Alex! Don't you dare use such filthy language in your sister's hearing, and no talk like that in this house. And you get those sorts of ideas out of your head. You are liable to end up in boarding school as well, or worse, if you keep on the way you are. Now you two get out and leave us for a while."

Alex and Kylie left the room. Graham swallowed anxiously. Boarding school! Was that to be his fate? His mother faced him and demanded to know what had happened. Graham recounted the whole incident, feeling slightly foolish as he did. In retrospect it did not sound much to get steamed up over. The only way to justify it was to say that Mr Burgomeister had been victimising and intimidating him. Graham couldn't bring himself to lie. In his heart he knew the problem was his behaviour, not the teacher's.

When he finished, he plucked up the courage to ask, "Have you told dad?"

"Yes, I have! We spoke on the radio as soon as I got the phone call from the school," his mother replied.

Graham felt his heart sink. "What did he say mum?"

"He thinks you should be shipped off to boarding school," his mother replied. "And I'm inclined to agree with that."

Graham's hopes sank even lower. Into his mind came fearsome visions of what he had heard about boarding schools from friends and relations. He knew some kids loved it but sensed he would hate the experience.

I would have to leave all my model ships. And my friends are here. And they probably wouldn't allow me to go hiking, and there are no girls at the school they are considering.

It would mean a complete change in lifestyle, and he viewed the prospect with dismay, seeing it as a prison sentence. He made a face to show how he felt, then put the cadet enrolment forms on the table.

"What's this?" his mother asked sharply, reaching for her glasses.

"Enrolment forms for the Army Cadets. Captain... I mean Mr Conkey, gave them to me after school. He wants me to join and asked me to get you to speak to him." He explained the meeting and what had been said.

His mother listened, then said, "And you say that Captain Conkey has spoken to the principal about this?"

"Yes, Mum." Graham felt his spirits rise fractionally and realised he was now pinning a lot on being allowed to join.

"Do you know his phone number?" his mother asked.

Graham nodded. "It is written there," he said, pointing to the top document. She looked very thoughtful for a minute then said, "You are grounded. Don't leave the house please. Now leave me alone for a while."

Graham went to his bed and lay on it. Kylie came and sat beside him and asked what had happened. He gave her the story then had to retell it for Alex. As he talked, he was aware that his mother was on the phone but could not hear what she was saying.

It was a miserable night. All Graham could do was brood (after doing his homework!). For hours he lay and considered his options. With a sigh he realised that all he had was a range of hard choices to make; the hardest being to change his outlook on life.

* * *

When he awoke on the following morning, Graham felt calm but depressed. For a while he lay and pondered the coming ordeal. To his annoyance, he had butterflies in the stomach and he knew he was scared.

Oh well, better get it over with! he told himself.

He rose and went to the bathroom. After a shower he dressed in school uniform and went to the kitchen.

Both Alex and Kylie were agog with morbid curiosity. At their mother's insistence, they stopped talking about Graham's possible fate and were hurried off to get ready for school. Graham sat and ate in silence, too ashamed to look at his mother most of the time. Only as he finished eating did he meet her eye and she came and held him.

"How do you feel?" she asked.

"I'll be okay," he replied.

To his immense comfort and embarrassment, she hugged him tight. "Good. Now, remember this, I still love you and will, regardless of what happens. Now let's get ready."

At that Graham felt tears well up and he bit his lip and tried to hold them back. He did not want to show weakness again. As soon as they were all ready and Alex had set off for school, Graham joined his mother and Kylie in the car. Kylie gave him a sympathetic smile and that helped. Mrs Kirk then drove to the high school. As they parked outside, Graham felt his stomach turn over. For a moment he wanted to just run away, and he found he was trembling all over as he got out of the car.

As they went into the main entrance, Graham knew he was the object of gossip from the students who saw him. He noted Peter in the distance. Peter gave a grin and a thumbs-up. Graham could only nod. His mother gave Kylie a hug and a kiss and sent her off.

At the office, Graham and his mother were met by a stony-faced Mr Fitzgerald who showed them through to a conference room. There was then a harrowing delay of half an hour during which the bell went and

First Period began. Then the door opened and in came the principal, plus Mr Fitzgerald and Mrs Brown (the Deputy Principal for Senior School), followed by Mr Conkey. His appearance surprised Graham but also cheered him.

The principal seated them around a table and sorted a sheaf of papers. After a delay which set Graham's heart palpitating with anxiety,y Mr Croswell cleared his throat and began, "This morning's meeting is to consider what action to take in relation to Graham's behaviour. In this we are primarily concerned with his threat to Mr Burgomeister. There are also the other incidents where school rules have been infringed recently."

He paused, then nodded to Mr Fitzgerald who read from a list in front of him, "These are what Graham has been in trouble at the office for within the last month: disobeying a teacher, skipping classes, fighting, back-answering teachers on three occasions, kept in for not doing homework, suspected of writing graffiti on the toilet wall; and most serious of all, threatening physical violence to a teacher."

"I didn't do the graffiti!" Graham cried.

"Be silent boy!" Mr Fitzgerald thundered. "Your name was mentioned. Other students saw you in the toilets when it was done yesterday. If it wasn't you, then who was it?"

Images of Dru and Derek and then of Year 10 boys peeking in to look flooded his mind and he broke into a cold sweat. It certainly looked bad. But he wasn't going to dob.

"It wasn't me, sir. I can't prove it, but I did not do it," he said firmly.

"Who did then? Yesterday's effort about Mr Burgomeister, I mean."

Graham hung his head. It would be easy to name Dru and Derek, but they would just deny it. *And then they will make my life hell!* he thought. The knowledge that he was scared made him despise himself even more.

His lips twisted into a bitter smile. "I can't prove it, sir."

The principal then asked whether Graham had any defence to the other cases. Again, Graham shook his head. He had done them alright.

Mr Croswell said, "The question now is, what is the appropriate course of action to be taken. There must clearly be some corrective consequences and an apology to Mr Burgomeister. But we must also develop a plan of action to help prevent similar occurrences in future."

There was a moment of silence. Then Mr Conkey said, "May I propose we proceed along the lines that we have discussed?"

Mr Croswell nodded. "Yes, I agree with your plan. How do you feel about that, Mrs Kirk?"

"Oh yes. Please try it. I think it is a good idea and I am grateful to you for proposing it."

"What does your husband think of the idea?" Mr Croswell asked.

"He is in favour of trying it. His exact words were a bit more forceful, to the effect that a few years in the er... in the bloody army, would do the little bu ...er do Graham, good," Mrs Kirk replied. She looked very anxious and twisted a handkerchief in her fingers. Then she sighed. "Oh, I wish his father was here more often!"

Mr Fitzgerald grunted agreement. "Yes, at the risk of being labelled sexist and old fashioned there are times when a boy needs a dad."

Mr Croswell looked at each in turn. "Are we in agreement then?"

They all said yes. Graham was mystified as well as worried, although he could sense that the outcome was not going to be as drastic as he had feared.

Mr Croswell turned to Mr Conkey, "You explain please, Mr Conkey."

Mr Conkey looked Graham in the eye. "This is the plan. You are going to make some promises and change your ways. In return you will not be suspended and will get some help. The first condition is that you are to join the Army Cadets. The second is that you will promise me personally that you will not misbehave at Cadets. You will apologise to Mr Burgomeister. You are to stop causing trouble at school and your homework is to be done under supervision."

He paused while Graham absorbed this then went on, "Now I know that is a pretty tall order. I personally don't expect you to change everything overnight. But I do expect you to try, and that there will be continual small changes for the good. Actually, I think you will manage this quite well once you calm down because I think you are basically a good kid and I know you have a good brain. Now, what do you say?"

Graham bit his lip and felt emotions surge within him, both pleasure at the good things said about him and resentment at the seemingly hard conditions. Through his mind flitted the options; leaving him with the conclusion that he had only hard choices to make. For a few fleeting seconds concepts like suicide and running away flitted across his mind. Then he took a deep breath.

"Yes sir. I accept."

"Good. Now, one of the documents includes a Code of Conduct. It lists the rules and when you sign it you are agreeing to obey them. But you will also promise to me that you will not misbehave at Cadets. This is a personal promise, on your honour as a man, not just a vague perhaps. You understand?" Mr Conkey said.

Graham nodded. The appeal to his honour touched something deep inside him. "Yes sir. I promise."

Mr Conkey went on, "If I give a lawful order, it will be obeyed, or the whole agreement is cancelled and you get suspended. Is that clear?"

"Yes sir."

Graham's mother gave a little gasp of relief. The meeting then shifted to administrative matters. Graham's mother produced the enrolment forms and signed them. Graham was required to read the Code of Conduct and sign it. These were handed to Captain Conkey, who smiled and said, "Good. You can report to the Q Store to get issued this afternoon. And get all the camping equipment. You will be needing it this weekend."

Graham looked surprised. "This weekend, sir?"

"Yes. You are going into the mountains," Captain Conkey replied.

Graham looked at his mother who nodded. "That's right. You won't be going anywhere else this weekend. On your father's orders you are grounded until I can convince him your behaviour has improved. If you slip, then it is boarding school. We mean it."

Graham bit his lip. Life certainly looked grimmer. He was nettled to have his freedom taken away; especially on the weekend. He had been hoping to meet some of the girls at the pictures or at the pool on Saturday. But he was also curious about what was to happen.

"But where am I going, sir? I didn't know the Cadets had a camp this weekend." Graham said. Neither Peter nor Stephen had mentioned one.

"They haven't. It is a reconnaissance by the staff for an exercise we are planning. Your mother tells me you are a great hiker, so you can join us. I will give you the details later."

With that Graham had to be content. The meeting was concluded and Graham went down to the car with his mother. She had tears in her eyes. "Oh Graham, I'm so pleased. Now do try. Mr Conkey has really put himself out to help you."

"Yes, Mum. Thanks."

Mrs Kirk got into her car and drove off. For a few minutes Graham stood on the footpath contemplating what he had got himself into. Army Cadets! It was certainly not something he had thought he would ever be involved with. Life was certainly full of unexpected twists!

But life also went on and had to be lived. Graham turned and headed for his classroom. It was Period 3 by then: German. On arrival at the room he noted the curious stares from his classmates and wondered how to explain things. Miss See told him to sit and indicated work to be done. Graham moved to his usual seat next to Stephen, who raised one eyebrow. After opening his books and waiting till the teacher was busy, Graham described the meeting and its outcomes.

Stephen nodded. "Army Cadets, eh! Well, it could have been worse. Be better than getting shipped off to boarding school." Then he grinned. "Maybe we can have some fun in the Cadets. They do a couple of alright things."

During morning break, Graham met with his friends and again described the meeting and its outcomes. Peter broke into a smile and said, "That's great! You will really like Cadets Graham. You should do really well."

Graham hoped so. Secretly he had reservations about it though. *I don't seem to be very good at anything much,* he mused.

English and Chemistry filled in the time till lunch. During these lessons Graham sat and reflected on his decision, wondering if he had made the wrong choice. The things he had agreed to seemed to make his life very restricted. Niggling doubt and natural rebelliousness made him restless.

Lunch was spent in the 'Time Out' room. He was given extra work to do and settled to it most unwillingly, irritated that he had allowed himself to be talked into accepting this as part of the price. History was next and that meant Mr (Captain) Conkey. Graham felt quite mixed reactions when he went to the room. Part of him was grateful for the help Captain Conkey had given him. But he was also embarrassed and felt that somehow he had been outmanoeuvred.

The lesson went easily enough, and Captain Conkey made no special references to Graham and did not check his work or ask him any questions. He just met his eyes from time to time and gave a little nod of satisfaction. At the end of the lesson he reminded Graham to go to the Q Store as soon as school ended. That was after Physics. The last lesson passed in a blur. Graham felt a mounting apprehension mingled with interest that he was annoyed to acknowledge. He really wanted to feel he was being persecuted and coerced.

When the last bell went Graham walked downstairs and stood outside the Cadet Q Store with Stephen. His nervousness increased with every minute and he began to wish he had not committed himself.

Me, an army cadet! he marvelled. It did not seem possible.

A few minutes later, the Officer of Cadets who was the unit Quartermaster came along with a set of keys. This was Lieutenant Hamish Hamilton, a young man with a moustache. He was dressed in his civilian work clothes.

"Hello. Graham Kirk, is it? Welcome to Cadets," he said as he opened the door. "Okay, in you come. And you keep your hands in your pockets and don't steal everything, Bell."

Stephen gave a cheeky grin. "But sir, you said that cadets shouldn't put their hands in their pockets! It looks slovenly and unmilitary you said."

"Don't be a smart ar… er smart alec, Bell. Just do what you are told," Lt Hamilton replied.

Stephen grinned again and pushed Graham in ahead of him. The room smelt of some sort of oil and was chock-a-block with shelving laden with clothing, boxes and bundles. Peter joined them and leaned in the doorway cracking jokes. Two other students arrived: Nev Strutton, the Year 11 boy who was the Company Quartermaster Sergeant, and Vince Brooke, a surly Year 10 who was the Corporal Storeman. Both set to work at the direction of the QM to lay out a full issue.

Graham was interested in spite of himself. He was also amazed at the pile of gear they built up on the counter: Boots, camouflage shirts and trousers, socks, a cloth hat, a Hat, Khaki, Fur Felt (Slouch hat he thought it was called), chinstrap for same, puggaree (ditto), badge (ditto), kitbag, pack, web belt (Black) and web belt (Pistol), ammunition pouches, water bottles and carriers, cup canteen, straps suspenders, Field Pack Combat Small (Bum Pack they called it), mess tins, Knife Fork and Spoon set (Called by its acronym, KFS set); sleeping bag, field jacket, pullover, hexamine stove, even a nylon rope. Graham quickly began to be bewildered and annoyed by all the jargon.

Twenty minutes later he was back outside the Q Store, having signed for what looked like a mountain of kit. The Q staff closed the Q Store and left. Graham began sorting the gear and stowing it in the pack and kit bag, helped by Peter and Stephen. As they worked Captain Conkey came down the stairs from his staffroom.

"Good. I hope you have everything Graham. You will need it on the weekend remember. It is good of you to help Graham you two."

Stephen nodded and smiled. "Can Graham be in the same section as me sir?"

Captain Conkey shook his head. "I don't think that would be a good idea. You two tend to spark each other off into mischief. Besides, we try to keep the sections and platoons roughly equal by adding new recruits evenly as they join."

He opened a folder and consulted it. Graham was a bit peeved that he couldn't be in the same section as Stephen or Peter, but only a bit. Deep down he sensed that Captain Conkey was right; that it would be easier for him to keep out of trouble on his own.

Capt Conkey took out a pencil and made a note in the folder. "I will put you in Number Two Platoon Graham. That is commanded by CUO Garth Grant. Sgt Masters is the platoon sergeant. You will be in Number Four Section. Got that? Four Section. The section commander is Corporal Elwyn Grenfell. Do you know him?"

Graham nodded. He dimly knew who Grenfell was, a good looking, fair haired, stocky Year 10. Capt Conkey then looked down at the litter of gear. "Will you two help Graham to get that all organised please?"

"Yes sir. No problem," Peter assured him.

"Good. Thank you. Now Graham, here is a list of things you will need for the weekend. I know you have done a fair bit of camping and hiking with the Scouts so none of it should come as a surprise." He handed Graham the list and then told him he would be picked up at home at 0830hrs on Saturday morning.

Graham scanned the list and saw that it was all standard hiking stuff. "Where are we going, sir?" he asked.

"I won't say, and you are going to promise not to tell these two afterwards," Captain Conkey replied.

Graham resented that but was also intrigued. "Yes sir," he replied.

Peter grinned, and Stephen said, "Oh sir, we can be trusted."

Captain Conkey grunted. "Huh! It's for an exercise and we want to keep the location secret so that you enjoy it more," he commented. When he was sure Graham had all the information, Capt Conkey said goodbye and walked off.

Stephen was curious. "What's all this about the weekend?"

"I have to go bush with Mister... I mean Captain Conkey and Warrant Officer Howley. They are doing some sort of reconnaissance for an exercise. What's an exercise?" Graham answered.

Peter answered, "It is a field activity where we practice various drills or manoeuvres," he explained.

"Like a war game?" Graham asked.

Peter looked annoyed. "We usually have cadets acting as the opposing force, but we don't call training exercises that."

"Opposing force? Do you mean enemy?" Graham asked.

Peter nodded. "Yes, but cadets don't use that word and we don't train to be soldiers. We only touch the edge of the tactics stuff."

Stephen agreed. "Yeah, but why are you going?" Stephen pressed.

"I think it is to keep me out of mischief during the weekend," Graham replied.

"Take some rum in your water bottle," Stephen said with a grin.

Peter shook his head and glared at Stephen. "Stop giving bad advice, Steve!" he snapped. Then he looked thoughtful. He said, "They probably want to test you out, to see what you are worth."

That was a sobering thought. And, as it turned out, was not far off the mark.

Chapter 9

ARMY CADET

Graham struggled home with his newly issued kit, helped by Peter and Stephen. On arrival he had to explain the whole story to Alex and Kylie. While Graham talked his friends assembled his webbing. Alex, who had been a cadet for a year, helped with this. From his hiking experience Graham knew how to put most of it together. The hardest thing he found was to roll the cold weather sleeping bag up so that it would fit into the bottom compartment of his big pack.

Alex explained how. "Line it up so that the end is inside the pack, then kneel on it and keep your weight on it as you roll it up," he advised.

Peter held up the new boots. "I hope these fit you well, Graham, if you are going bush this weekend."

Graham held out his hand. "Give them to me. I'll put them on now and start breaking them in."

Kylie's eyebrows went up with interest. "Where are you going this weekend?" she asked.

"Don't know. Somewhere with Capt Conkey."

Alex laughed. "This is the army brother. They work on the 'mushroom principle': keep 'em in the dark and feed 'em on bullshit."

Graham grinned but wasn't really amused. After all, Alex had only reached the rank of Cadet in nearly two years and then been discharged. *Plenty of kids of his age are corporals or sergeants*, Graham thought. There were times when he really disliked his big brother.

Later that night, Graham tried on a uniform. He did this in private as he did not want Alex jeering at him. When he had finished, he stood in front of the full-length mirror in his mother's room to see how it looked. He was amazed how different he felt. In spite of his resentment at the situation, he realised he was even a bit proud (although he did not want to admit that, even to himself). What impressed him the most was the thought that he looked good in the uniform. He experimented with getting the correct angle for the slouch hat.

While he was testing various rakish angles, his mother came in. She stopped at the door and let out a little cry, though whether of dismay or surprise Graham could not tell. She made him stand back, then turn around. Then she nodded with apparent satisfaction.

"I hate to say it about a son, but I think it suits you," she said. Then her eyes went moist, and she stepped forward and hugged him. "Oh Graham! I hope it all works out for you. Please take this opportunity and try hard."

Graham was embarrassed and managed to free himself. "I will, Mum. It will be alright," he replied.

That night in bed he began to fantasise about being a soldier, battling off hundreds of enemy soldiers (and rescuing a beautiful girl who was suitably grateful!).

Friday slid past in excited anticipation. Despite his irritation at losing his freedom for the weekend, Graham had to admit he was looking forward to it, even if it was with some apprehension. School went by with no real incidents, other than his apology to Mr Burgomeister. After school he packed the food his mother had purchased for the weekend. Then he lay and read comics.

He was allowed to go to Scouts, but his mother drove him and picked him up. It was made very clear to him that he was under observation and was on probation. Boarding school still loomed large in the background.

His mother woke him from a deep sleep at 0600hrs the next morning. Graham had been enjoying a dream in which he had been kissing Ailsa and was hoping to go further. To struggle out of his warm bed into the cold did not amuse him. He dressed in uniform and went to have breakfast. Alex and Kylie were still in bed, but his mother had prepared a full cooked breakfast.

"You need a solid meal if you are going to be working hard," she explained.

Just before 0830hrs, two army Land Rovers pulled up out front. One was driven by Lt Hamilton and the other by Warrant Officer Howley. Lt Maclaren sat in front beside Lt Hamilton and Capt Conkey beside Warrant Officer Howley. All were in field uniform. Graham carried his gear down and loaded it into the back of Warrant Officer Howley's vehicle.

"Good morning, Cadet Kirk. Get in the back," Warrant Officer Howley said.

Graham did as he was told, mildly annoyed at the abrupt dropping of his given name. As soon as he was seated, the vehicles drove off. Capt Conkey turned and passed back two maps: Cairns 1:50 000 and Tinaroo 1:50 000.

"I know you can read these because you have been in the Scouts. Map read as we go and keep track of where we are. I want to see how good you are."

"Yes sir," Graham replied as he took the folded maps.

It was a challenge but one he relished as he considered himself to be a very good navigator. Quickly he located his position on the Cairns map. He was very familiar with it so had no trouble doing this. Then he sat and moved his thumb along the red line that represented the main highway as they drove along it. From time to time, Capt Conkey turned and asked where they were. Each time Graham was able to show him exactly and Capt Conkey nodded approval.

Capt Conkey also had a map open and was also following their route. The first part, up the Kuranda Range to Kuranda, was very familiar to Graham. Passing through the area sparked a strong flow of memories and not a few pangs for the lost love of Deslie. It was also cold, and Graham was glad the back of the vehicle was closed in. After Kuranda they went west along the Kennedy Highway.

As they passed Davies Creek, Graham was interested to overhear Capt Conkey and Warrant Officer Howley discussing the Lamb Range. This huge mass of rugged, jungle-covered mountains was 'terra incognita' to Graham. He had often studied it on the map but none of the hikes or expeditions he and his friends had been on had ever been into it. All he had ever done was what they were doing now, driving around it at a distance along the main roads.

They went on along the Kennedy Highway into open country to Mareeba, then turned south and drove towards Atherton. All this was familiar territory to Graham. Even when they turned off at Tolga and drove to Tinaroo, it was to pass through places he had often been to before. Only after Tinaroo did they enter new territory. As the vehicle ground up the slope on the far side of the huge concrete dam, Capt Conkey checked that Graham had their location accurately.

The two vehicles drove along the Danbulla Drive, the gravel forestry road which skirted the north shore of the vast lake impounded behind the dam. Graham loved travelling and exploring so he peered out eagerly, noting all the changes of scenery and keeping track of their progress on the map. Signposted creeks like Kauri Creek helped him to do this.

A hundred metres beyond Robsons Creek, they stopped at a side road. The adults climbed out to stretch themselves and to check the map. Graham climbed down as well. The air was cool and fresh and he breathed it deeply. Graham felt very self-conscious standing there in his new uniform, the only teenager with a group of adults.

Capt Conkey indicated his map. "Well Cadet Kirk, where are we?"

Graham had his finger on the spot. He pointed to it on the map. Capt Conkey grunted approval. "Not bad. In fact the road has been re-aligned just here, but you are only a hundred metres out. See how the road lines up?"

He indicated the changes on the map.

Graham nodded and Capt Conkey pointed to the vehicle. "Good! Now get in."

Graham did as he was told, silently seething with rebellion. His anger made it difficult to concentrate on the map reading but he noted that they had turned up the side road which climbed continually up into the Lamb Range, winding through thick jungle. His interest in the country pushed other emotions out of his consciousness.

After about half an hour, they stopped and parked beside the gravel road. An overgrown timber road went off to the right into the rain forest. Graham could see they were high up but had lost track of their exact position and had to admit this when asked. They all dismounted and Capt Conkey pointed to a jungle covered peak a few hundred metres to the east and considerably higher.

"That is Mt Edith. We are climbing it. Bring your basic webbing."

The group set off at a brisk walk. Graham was then peeved to find that he could hardly keep up with the adults. He had considered them to be decrepit old fogies and it galled to find he was puffing and panting and had difficulty keeping pace with tubby old Capt Conkey who was in his forties.

A narrow foot track wound up the slope through thick rain forest. As they neared the top, Capt Conkey stopped and drew Warrant Officer Howley's attention to a hole beside the track. It was half full of leaf litter and dirt.

"Old weapon pit. Dug during World War Two. Many of the troops who fought in New Guinea against the Japanese did their jungle training here before going overseas."

Warrant Officer Howley studied the hole with professional interest then looked along the slope. "Should be another one just along there. Yes, there it is."

Graham looked and saw the faint depression. He was amazed that Capt Conkey knew so much about these things and also at his own interest. It was fascinating to actually see something dug by real soldiers all those years ago. Even if it was just a shallow hole full of dead leaves it was still a real link to those legendary men who had battled the Japanese on the Kokoda Trail and Shaggy Ridge. (He knew a bit about that from stories his grandfather had told, and now felt slightly ashamed that he did not know more).

They plodded on to the top, the older men now puffing hard. Once there they scrambled up onto a huge boulder which protruded from the treetops. Graham was thrilled and amazed.

"What a view! You can see for ever!" he cried.

Capt Conkey grinned. "I thought you might like it. Look, you can just make out the sea near Trinity Inlet. That is Cape Grafton, and there is May Peak. Go right and you can see Walshs Pyramid near Gordonvale. That is the Little Mulgrave Valley down below us. Off to the south is Bartle Frere, highest mountain in Queensland."

Graham stood enthralled. The view was certainly worth the climb. But it was also dangerous. One slip and he would be pitched over the edge of a steep drop into the jungle, so Capt Conkey made sure they all stood well back. After ten minutes admiring the view and discussing radio reception possibilities, they all slid back to ground level and set off back down the mountain. As they went, Capt Conkey pointed to a square hole beside the track.

"Either a company CP or mortar pit," he said.

As they made their way back down the track, Graham peered into the rainforest and tried to imagine what it must have been like to be a soldier in such an environment. It was certainly something to think about.

I wonder if I would be good enough? he worried.

By overhearing snatches of conversation, Graham now learned that Warrant Officer Howley had done several tours of duty in Southeast Asia and in Afghanistan. He had even taken part in active operations against guerrillas in both East Timor and Makasang. Graham eyed the man with new respect. He had actually been shot at, and shot back!

They climbed back into the vehicles and drove on for a couple of kilometres, winding downhill. At a creek crossing where an old vehicle track came in from the right, they stopped and got out. A long discussion followed about where they were. This led to the conclusion that the road had been realigned since the map was made.

Capt Conkey explained to Graham, "There is a road which comes in from the north along Davies Creek past the Davies Creek Falls and then comes over that mountain to the north of us, Mt Tiptree. The map shows a road coming all the way to here, but the Forestry people don't think it ever existed. We'd like to know. That means some walking. Grab your webbing and make sure you have lunch."

The vehicles were driven up the side road and locked. A hundred metres in the old road was blocked by a fallen tree. Beyond that the old road was overgrown but the earthworks were very obvious. The group set off along it on foot. What followed was four hours of pure pleasure for Graham, of plotting old timber tracks, of seeing ferns and palms and stinging tree, of a crystal-clear creek flowing swiftly past (Emerald Creek he was told).

This is real exploring, he thought.

It was wonderful, in spite of the cold, the 'Wait-a-while' vines, the thorn bushes, the snagging vines and the leeches. He saw a goanna, a red-bellied black snake, several small rodent-like animals, white cockatoos, huge butterflies. It was fascinating.

After three hours, Capt Conkey stopped them. By then they were hard up against the bottom of a steep slope. "This is no good. We haven't found a road going the way we want. The road on the map certainly exists here on these lower slopes, but only seems to go to that old camp area back there."

Lt Hamilton agreed, "No sign of any road going up that slope at all. I think we have missed it, if it exists."

Capt Conkey studied his map. "We will have to try from the other side and see how much of that exists. Let's get back to the vehicles and drive around to Davies Creek."

The group spent an hour making its way back along the old tracks to the vehicles. By then it was 1500hrs and the air was already getting cool. They climbed into the vehicles and continued along the road which followed the valley of Emerald Creek for ten kilometres, winding along the side of the mountain. The high ground on the left was Mt Haig Graham noted. The road emerged from rainforest into more open country forested with magnificent tall, white-trunked trees. It then turned sharply left over a ridge, down a switchback and through several kilometres of open forest to a road junction. From here the road wound down the west side of the mountain with magnificent long views out to the north and west.

Capt Conkey pointed through the windscreen. "That is Mareeba in the distance," he said,

Graham looked and saw the afternoon sun glinted on distant roofs. Twenty kilometres away at least, Graham measured off his map. He did not want to openly admit it, but he realised he was enjoying the trip immensely.

They drove down into rough hills clothed in savannah woodland. Several side roads came in and they passed three poor looking farms before coming onto bitumen on Tinaroo Creek Road. This led them to the Kennedy Highway near Mareeba. Here they turned right and headed back towards Cairns. After ten kilometres they slowed and turned right again onto the Davies Creek Road. This was bitumen for a few kilometres, then rough gravel with many corrugations.

After ten minutes, they reached the Davies Creek National Park. There was another stop while they looked around. The adults looked at the toilet and camping facilities. Graham went to look at the delightful rock pools and rapids where the creek flowed down over large sheets of black granite.

I must bring the hiking team here one day, he decided.

They drove on, winding up a rough, steep, narrow road past the Davies Creek Falls and across a small concrete bridge. As they wound around the hillsides, Capt Conkey pointed to a steep, rocky mountain top to the front.

"That huge rock up there is called Kahlpahlim Rock. It is part of Lambs Head."

Graham nodded. "I know, sir. I see Lambs Head every day when I walk home from school. We are going to climb it one day."

Capt Conkey nodded. "Good idea. I will show you a photo of me on top many years ago, way back when I was a Cadet Warrant Officer."

That was another fascinating insight. Capt Conkey had once been a soldier who had also been to war. But before that he had been a cadet. Graham was curious to know more but was too shy to ask.

The road levelled out in a pleasantly forested valley: She-Oaks and Eucalypts. At a small clearing the vehicles were parked.

Capt Conkey climbed out. "We will camp here. Unload and start collecting some firewood while there is still light," he instructed.

Graham was surprised to see that his watch read 1800hrs. Already the sun had gone behind the mountains to the west. A chill started to nip at fingers and ears. He unloaded his pack and webbing, hauled out a jacket and set to work collecting wood.

The evening that followed stayed in his memory for the rest of his days. The adults sat around the fire and talked. Graham sat with them but kept back and said very little. After cooking his tea on a hexamine stove, he was content to listen. Warrant Officer Howley kept watch to check he knew how to use the stove. When he saw that Graham was quite capable of looking after himself, he nodded and grunted approval.

The talk ranged across cadets and army, much of it being humorous reminiscences about the funny incidents that had occurred over the years. To Graham it was a revelation of another world, of a way of life that held these men under its spell. He listened avidly to the accounts of real action, of ambushes and attacks in the jungle, mostly with some very funny incident mixed in among the horrible things.

What really struck Graham was how Warrant Officer Howley radiated self-confidence; and how the man despised weaklings who could not 'hack it' when things got tough, who let down their mates.

"And it's not when the bullets start to fly," Warrant Officer Howley added. "It is when sheer bloody endurance is needed, to stay alert on cold wet nights when you are sentry and your mates' lives depend on it; or when you have to keep marching up some mongrel bloody mountain in the mud and rain to help another section that is in trouble; or when you are just bored rigid and nothing happens for weeks on end. That is what really sorts blokes out."

When Graham lay down to sleep, he had plenty to think about. It was a cold night, but he loved camping out and the army cold weather sleeping bag kept him snug and warm so that he slept soundly.

* * *

In the morning they were up at 0600hrs and set about their morning routine. While the coffee was heating, he saw Warrant Officer Howley shaving, using hot water in a Cup Canteen. Graham was surprised. He had just packed his mess gear away and was sipping his coffee when Warrant Officer Howley came over and peered closely at his face.

"Have you washed your face this morning?"

Graham swallowed with resentment. "No," he replied.

"No what?"

"No... sir."

"Do so. And I think it is time you started shaving. A good soldier shaves before first parade every day," Warrant Officer Howley went on.

Shave! Graham was amazed. He had not thought about it. He rubbed his chin and decided it did feel bristly. But would his mother allow it?

"I haven't got a razo,r sir. And I don't know if I am allowed to start by my parents," Graham replied.

"You can use my spare one. No lather though. You will have to use soap. Watch how Capt Conkey does it. And don't worry about permission. I will square that away. It is one of the Cadet Regulations. And it is time you started; you have to begin sometime," Warrant Officer Howley replied.

"Yes… sir," Graham answered.

Warrant Officer Howley looked grim. "So unpack your stove and a mess tin or Cup Canteen and heat some water and shave now. You now have the honour of wearing the army's uniform and you will not disgrace it by looking like an unemployed layabout. As I said, a good soldier shaves every morning. It is good for your pride and morale. No matter how bad life gets or how many things go wrong, start the day by doing your personal grooming. You will feel better. Understand?"

"Yes sir."

So Graham shaved himself for the first time and felt very grown up. He hoped it wasn't too obvious that he was secretly very pleased.

By 0800hrs they were ready to move. Both vehicles were driven on along the road south along the valley until they reached a small concrete bridge. Just beyond this the road deteriorated dramatically so the vehicles were parked.

"We walk from here," Capt Conkey explained.

Graham collected his webbing and climbed out. Lt Hamilton and Lt Maclaren turned the vehicles. Lt Maclaren set off to drive back around to the Mt Haig area where they had been the previous day. Lt Hamilton was to wait for three hours as a safety vehicle, then follow. Capt Conkey, Warrant Officer Howley and Graham were to walk over Mt Tiptree.

Graham noted both Capt Conkey and Warrant Officer Howley take broom handles out of their vehicles to use as walking sticks. Graham was inclined to scoff at that idea, thinking them only suitable for old men but after slipping a number of times on muddy slopes he wished he had one. Capt Conkey pointed out that the real jungle veterans of the war in New Guinea all had walking sticks to assist them.

It was a most enjoyable walk. For the first couple of kilometres the road was clear and easy to follow. A fork to the left marked the start of a network of old timber tracks which led around to Lambs Head. They took the right fork and went on. The road rapidly deteriorated to an overgrown earthwork with hundreds of fallen logs blocking it, large tracts of prickly Wild Raspberry which they had to cut their way through, and occasional clumps of 'wait-a-while'.

Several side-tracks led in and each was carefully plotted on the map. It became very obvious to Graham that both Capt Conkey and Warrant Officer Howley were very competent navigators. Graham tramped along enjoying the exploring and the jungle. The road led steadily uphill for six kilometres. From time to time they got glimpses out through gaps in the thick foliage. Mostly this showed line after line of jungle covered ridges but once they were granted an impressive clear view of Kahlpahlim Rock back across the valley behind them.

I must climb that one day, Graham decided.

After another half hour, Capt Conkey called a halt. "Fifteen minutes. I need a toilet break," he said.

So do I, Graham thought.

He had been feeling uncomfortable for some time. So when Capt Conkey went on ahead Graham turned and went back down the track, and straight into another situation.

Only 50 paces back around the bend, just as he was looking for a good spot to relieve himself, he met a snake. It had not been there a minute before when the group had walked along this section of road, but it was now, a metre of shiny black reptile. And it had heard him and instantly coiled itself and raised its head.

Graham froze. To his dismay he found he felt paralysed. While his mind registered that the snake was a red-bellied black and tried to tell him that its bite probably wouldn't be fatal he could not seem to make his muscles respond. Shocked and afraid, he stood and stared, noting the sheen of its scales and the brilliant scarlet of its underbelly.

How long he stood there, staring in horror at those tiny black eyes and that forked tongue that kept flicking in and out, he was not aware. It was his body that helped break the spell. To his shame a thunderous fart escaped. It was so loud it caused the snake to hiss and start to sway its head from side to side.

For a few embarrassed seconds, Graham feared he had actually soiled himself and he glanced down to see if he had wet himself. His mind noted that he hadn't, but then he looked back at the snake and took a deep breath. To his enormous relief, he realised his muscles were now flexing and that he could move.

That snake is too far away to bite me, he thought, estimating the reptile's probable striking distance.

Taking another deep breath, he consciously mustered his courage and then slowly moved his right foot back. The snake flattened and looked like it was about to strike, but then it stopped and its tongue flickered.

Easing his chest and taking another breath, Graham moved his left foot back. The snake did not move, except that flickering forked tongue. So Graham took another step back. Still no movement. Another step and then the snake did move, and with horrifying speed. It suddenly went flat and slid off through dead leaves and grass. There a flicker of movement at the edge of the road and then it was gone.

Graham was aghast. *I could not have run away in time,* he thought, now thoroughly ashamed at having frozen up.

And then he knew he had another challenge to face. His body was urgently informing him that he did need to do a crap, and that meant dropping his trousers and squatting in a most vulnerable pose.

It took another conscious effort to get moving and then he hurried on for 25 paces past where he had last seen the snake before deciding on a suitable place. Placing his webbing aside he again looked carefully around. Quickly he scraped a shallow hole with the heel of his boot, all the while looking anxiously in all directions.

Then he undid his trousers and slid them down and then his underpants. By this time he was almost hyperventilating with anxiety, his eyes flicking in all directions. But his body was insistent, and he made himself squat. It was an embarrassing few minutes before he was able to finish and then stand up and pull his clothing up.

Quickly he dressed and then used his boot to scrape soil over the hole. Scooping up his webbing he hurried back along the track. It took an effort just to walk past where he had encountered the snake. A glance at his watch told him that he had been gone the whole 15 minutes and he was dismayed.

Surely I didn't freeze up for ten minutes? he worried. Fearing that the adults would have noticed he boiled with upset and anticipatory embarrassment.

But the others were busy studying the map and discussing the possible route and did not even glance at him. Then Capt Conkey just glanced at Graham, nodded and started to walk.

On the crest of the mountain there was some to-ing and fro-ing along old tracks till Capt Conkey decided which was the right one. To get through the tangle of vines they snipped a path with secateurs.

"This is what real jungle soldiers use," Warrant Officer Howley explained. "All this macho stuff about machetes you see in the movies is all baloney. Machetes make too much noise and you go too slow. Garden secateurs allow you to silently snip the few vines that are actually catching at your gear, and you can then just slip quietly through the jungle."

He proceeded to demonstrate and Graham was impressed in spite of himself. It was very apparent these men knew what they were about. Even more impressive was Capt Conkey's navigation. Following a compass course when the timber tracks petered out on the crest line, he led them down a long, steep ridge and came out on the old track they had explored the previous day, within 50 paces of where they had turned back.

After scouting around and deciding that the road marked on the map did not in fact exist, the trio walked back along the old timber track beside Emerald Creek to where the two vehicles waited. The consensus was that the route was feasible.

As they discussed this Capt Conkey turned to Graham and said,

"I am asking you not to talk about where we have been with anyone, Graham. If we use it for an exercise, we want it to be a secret. Will you promise me that?"

"Yes sir."

"Fine. Now, let's get home."

They climbed into the vehicles and drove for four hours to get back to Cairns. It was a tired but happy Graham who was dropped off at his home late in the afternoon.

Chapter 10

PEER PRESSURE

As soon as Graham got home, Alex questioned him. "Where did you go then?"

"Can't say. Sorry," Graham replied.

"Poop! I'm your brother. Now spit it out you little wart," Alex insisted.

Graham shook his head. "No. Captain Conkey made me promise not to tell."

"Give or I'll thump ya!" Alex threatened.

But to Graham's relief he didn't. Instead he gave up and went away muttering angrily.

Exactly the same treatment came Graham's way as soon as he got to school. Peter asked but happily nodded and dropped the subject when Graham explained that Captain Conkey wanted the trip kept a secret.

Not so Stephen. He persisted until Graham snapped at him in annoyance to let the subject drop.

Stephen scowled. "Okay, okay! Keep your shirt on!" he retorted.

Period 1 was Geography with Mr (Captain) Conkey. He made no reference to the trip but gave Graham a smile of welcome. Graham returned the smile and felt a warm glow of fellowship and embarrassment. He also marvelled that Captain Conkey could look so relaxed and fresh.

He must be a fit old coot! he decided.

Stephen resumed the probing questions during English, but Graham just shook his head. Derek White, who was also a 2nd Year cadet, was next. He met Graham at morning break near the tuck shop.

"G'day Kirky. Heard ya was out campin' with the officers on the weekend. Where'd ya go?"

"Sorry, I can't say," Graham replied, maintaining a good-natured smile with an effort.

"Why not?" Derek asked.

"Because Captain Conkey asked me not to say. He wants to use the area for an exercise."

"Oh yeah? Are you snivelling for a stripe already then?" Derek said. The jibe stung but Graham could not think of any rebuttal.

During class, Stephen tried several more times to get him to say where they had been. Graham became annoyed but held his temper. He also made an attempt to work and not to talk or get into trouble. Boarding school still loomed large. A period of History with Captain Conkey did not help, as that made Graham relive every incident from the weekend.

At lunch time Graham encountered Larsen as he went downstairs. Larsen was with two of his Year 11 cronies. He sneered and said, "Hear ya joined the stupid bloody cadets, Kirk. That'd suit a gutless creep like you."

Graham compressed his lips and made no reply. He tried to push past but Larsen blocked his path.

"Don't you just ignore me, you little turd."

With a sigh Graham stopped and stepped back, raising his clenched fists as he did. Boarding school was one thing; being continually insulted and bullied was another.

If that is the price I have to pay, well, so be it, he thought grimly.

At that moment, two other boys appeared at the top of the steps: Year 12s, Garth Grant and Allan Broughton. Grant took in the situation at a glance.

"Leave Kirk alone, Larsen," he commanded.

Larsen curled his lip but stepped aside. "There'll be other times," he sneered.

"I wouldn't advise it," Grant said frostily, pausing to meet Larsen's eye. "If I hear you are bullying the younger kids, I will see you are dealt with. Come on Kirk, come with us."

Graham did as he was told, but unwillingly. As they walked down the stairs, he snapped, "I can fight my own battles!"

Grant eyed him coolly and nodded. "I don't doubt you can. But I happen to know you will be expelled if you get into any more trouble. So leave it to us."

"You don't have to."

"No, I probably don't. But you are now one of my platoon, and I look after my cadets. So, if you need help, then let me know," Grant replied.

That reply left Graham with mixed emotions. He grunted his thanks and went to join his friends. They had observed him walking with the two

CUOs, and Derek called out as he joined them, "Hobnobbing with the officers again, eh? You must really be grovelling for promotion."

"Get stuffed!" Graham flared angrily.

Derek and Dru both laughed, and so did Stephen. Dru took up the teasing. "Heard you were camping with the officers all weekend. What did they want you along for?"

Derek answered this at once, "He must be their bum boy, why else?"

This caused some cruel laughter and made Graham blush angrily. "It wasn't like that!"

"Oh yeah? So what was it like?" Derek taunted.

Graham pursed his lips and decided not to react. He sat down and deflected more questions about where they had gone on the reconnaissance. It seemed later that the whole day had gone on that way, and he was relieved to get home in the afternoon.

* * *

Tuesday was easier. Most of his friends dropped the teasing and questions but there were several comments such as, "Bending over for the officers to get ahead." These were usually delivered with leering innuendo. Graham burned with mortification but could not think of any policy to counteract the rumours.

I wish I hadn't allowed myself to get forced into joining! he thought savagely.

Wednesday brought a different form of the same challenge to his self-control. Wednesday meant attending a Cadet 'Home Training' parade. Graham had never attended a training parade and it was with very mixed feelings that he packed the uniform in a carry bag in the morning. He also had to endure more teasing about the weekend, with barbed and malicious comments such as: 'crawler', 'brown noser', 'boot licker' and the like. These fuelled Graham's resentment and made him surly and truculent.

Thus, when classes finished and it was time to go to Cadets, he was in no mood to do so. It was Peter who persuaded him to go. He saw Graham walking away and called out to him, "Come on Graham. Come and change."

"I don't want to. I hate Cadets," Graham replied angrily.

Peter nodded sympathetically. "Probably, but do you really have any choice at the moment?"

"Yeah. I can go to boarding school," Graham replied.

Again Peter nodded. "Yes, you can. But I would like you to stay here. You are my mate, and we do lots of things together. Who will I go hiking with, eh?"

Graham hadn't thought of it like that, and the direct appeal was hard to counter. He was very touched but also embarrassed. To hide it he gruffly assented to go and change into uniform. That was an emotional experience he hadn't gambled on either. The boys changed in an annex to their toilet and the place was crowded and noisy as 50 boys all shed school clothes and put on their army uniforms. Graham pulled off his shirt and buttoned on the camouflage shirt in its place. All the while he kept glancing around.

Most of the others he knew, some quite well. Thankfully they paid him little heed as they dressed. He did up the shirt, then took off his school shorts and pulled on the long trousers. Tugging on the thick woollen socks and boots he found harder. He still wasn't used to them and by then most of the others had finished and were hurrying out. Graham fumbled with the bootlaces and then settled the slouch hat on his head, thrust his school clothes into the bag and followed.

He was just in time to join his platoon before the parade began. Sgt Masters yelled at him to hurry up, then pointed where he was to stand, in the middle rank near the end. Feeling very self-conscious as the new recruit he moved into place and glanced nervously at those on either side of him. On his left was a boy named Morris from 9D who just nodded. On his right was a very attractive blue-eyed blonde from 9A, Gwen Copeland. She gave him a smile of welcome which helped to offset the sneer offered to him by Crane from 9C, who stood in front on his right.

Lance Corporal Bannister, from 9A, who stood in the rear file, whispered to him what to do when the Company Sergeant Major, Warwick Grey, stood out front and shouted the command, "On parade!"

It was familiar enough to Graham from his brief experience in the Navy Cadets: come to attention, march forward fifteen paces, halt, left turn, stand at ease. Some of the drill movements were slightly different but he coped without being obviously wrong. Once on the parade ground, the company was called to attention and 'Right Dressed' then stood 'At ease'. Sgt Masters called the roll and reported to the CSM.

Once that was done, the officers got involved. Lt Hamilton took over the parade and posted the officers. Graham watched all this with a mixture of interest and resentment. He noted that CUO Grant looked very good in uniform (Handsome was the word he would have used except he did not want to be accused of being gay, even to himself). CUO Grant saluted and marched on to take over from Sgt Masters. The CUO and sergeant exchanged salutes and then Sgt Masters made a verbal report. The pair then saluted again and stepped around each other to the left. CUO Grant took up his position three paces in front of the platoon and Sgt Masters marched around to the rear of the platoon.

Capt Conkey took over the parade and detailed what each platoon was to do. The CUOs obviously already knew this as they called out the sergeants on being told to 'Carry on with training'. First there was an inspection. Sgt Masters called them to the 'Open order', then stood the ranks not being inspected 'At ease'. He then followed CUO Grant along, noting in his notebook which cadets were incorrectly dressed. Graham was in trouble at once. He had not bothered to clean his boots after the weekend, and they were still scuffed and caked with mud.

CUO Grant noted this and said, "Have your boots cleaned next Wednesday, Cadet Kirk."

"Yes... sir," Graham replied.

He blushed angrily, his annoyance fuelled by several sniggers from other cadets. After the inspection Sgt Masters took over and marched the platoon off to the oval. Graham had no trouble marching or keeping in step and was annoyed with himself for feeling a sense of belonging as a result of such a simple collective activity.

At the oval the platoon split into section groups. Cpl Grenfell took over 4 Section. After standing them at ease he snapped, "Stand still! That was 'ease', not 'easy'."

The sharp rebuke caused Graham to bristle, even though it wasn't specifically directed at them.

Bloody little Hitler, he thought resentfully.

Cpl Grenfell continued, "Now, during this lesson you are going to learn some fieldcraft. We are doing 'Day movement', that is the various crawls used for stalking."

At that Cadet Crane turned to Graham. "You'll be good at that Kirk, crawling I mean."

The implied insult caused Grahams to flame with anger and embarrassment. "Get stuffed, Crane!" he snapped back.

Cpl Grenfell at once stepped forward. "That'll do! Stop that sort of talk! Now be silent during the lesson. That's you Cadet Crane. And you keep quiet too Cadet Kirk."

The injustice rankled. "But he just called me names!"

"Corporal. You call me corporal. Now be quiet so I can get on with the lesson," Cpl Grenfell grated. He glared at both and then held Graham's eye. "I've been warned about you Cadet Kirk, so don't give me any trouble."

The implied 'or else' hung in the air and Graham seethed but he managed to bite back a sharp retort and then stood silent and resentful.

Cpl Grenfell stepped back and said to the squad, "Now, let's get on with the lesson. You are learning how to move during the day in the field. You will need to know these for the next bivouac in a few weeks," he explained.

That further annoyed Graham. *Not me!* he thought.

He didn't really want to go camping again with cadets. His mood transmitted itself to Cpl Grenfell who gave him several warning glances. When it came to practicing the crawls, Graham made only a half-hearted attempt. As he did, he made several sarcastic comments in an attempt to be funny.

This drew Cpl Grenfell's wrath instantly. "Stop being a smart-arse, Cadet Kirk. You might be the officer's pet, but you can shut up and get on with it."

This jibe added to Graham's dislike. He glared at Cpl Grenfell but saw that CUO Grant was watching from nearby so made no reply.

The second period was First Aid, how to deal with bleeding. Graham found this boring as he already had a St John Ambulance Certificate from the Scouts. Instead he sat and made smart comments until Sgt Masters snapped at him to cut out the wisecracks.

"Do as you are told Kirk, or we will chuck you out on your ear. We don't need troublemakers!" he snapped.

That burned but Graham bit his lip and shut up. Into his mind came his promise to Captain Conkey to behave at Cadets.

After the dismissal parade, Graham walked home. As he walked, he could see Lambs Head in the mountains. *I must climb it one day,* he thought, then resumed mulling over his reactions to his first cadet training parade. He couldn't decide whether he had enjoyed it or not.

That evening he had to talk to his father on the radio-telephone. He made much of having joined the Cadets. His father obviously approved.

"Just what you bloody need!" he commented.

"Am I still grounded?" Graham asked.

There was a pause, then his father replied, "No, not if you are keeping out of trouble and doing your homework. Now put your mother back on please."

Relief at having his grounding lifted cheered Graham enormously. He was in such a good mood he did his homework without fuss, his mother sitting nearby to check. Things seemed to be on the up. He went to bed that night feeling happier than he had for a long time.

* * *

On Thursday Graham went to school quite happily. Before classes, he talked to his friends and felt even better as the teasing seemed to have stopped. The peculiar activities of a kid named Paul in Year 8 had taken over as a new topic of conversation.

Period 1 was Maths A. Graham did not tempt fate by sitting beside Stephen. He had several seats to choose from but opted for obscurity at the back, even if that meant sitting next to Amelia. As he walked back towards her, she looked up and gave him a smile. That made him feel better.

She's not a dog at all. In fact she's quite pretty, he decided. *And heavens! Isn't she showing a lot of leg!*

Once again, his eyes were drawn to her thighs, which were almost completely exposed as her dress was pulled right up. She appeared not to notice this, and Graham did not draw her attention to it. Instead he took frequent opportunities to glance down.

As he seated himself, Amelia said, "My dad tells me you have joined the Cadets."

"Yeah, that's right. I had to, or go to boarding school," Graham replied.

"That's what I get threatened with, only it will be a convent in my case," Amelia replied, her face dimpling into a mischievous grin. She then asked, "Do you like Cadets?"

Graham shrugged. Aware that all his comments might be carried straight to Warrant Officer Howley, he said, "It's okay. I think I'll like the bush work."

At that moment, Mr Burgomeister arrived and the conversation ended. The lesson proceeded with Graham not in trouble for a change. He even earned grudging approval for having done his homework (and getting it right!).

Later, his curiosity prompted him to ask Amelia, "How come you aren't a cadet?"

Amelia made a face. "Dad would like me to join but I don't think I'd like it. Besides, you have to promise to behave yourself at Cadets and I'm not sure I could."

The implications of that left Graham's mind in ferment. *Is she a naughty girl then?* he wondered. *Is she living proof of Stephen's oft quoted dictum that it was the ones you don't think will do it that do?* It was certainly food for thought. But no, surely not?

The rest of the day slipped by easily. So did Friday. Once again Graham made an effort to work and to keep out of trouble. That threat of grounding was what was bothering him most directly now. He had hopes for the weekend, but wasn't quite sure what they might involve. He just knew he wanted to go to the movies with Stephen on Saturday night.

I might meet a girl, he thought hopefully.

In Period 5 Graham got another surprise from Amelia during PE. The lesson was on lifesaving. After changing into his bathers, Graham made his way outside to stand over beside the fence.

As before, the girls came out in ones and twos to stand with the boys: Ailsa in her white one-piece; Glenys in a green one-piece; Louise in a bikini with yellow dots on it; Rowena in a shimmering green lycra one-piece; Amelia in the dark blue one-piece.

Once again, Graham was surprised just how large her breasts were. He surreptitiously admired her and was granted a glimpse down her cleavage when she bent forward to rub her leg.

Quite nice really, he decided.

Mr Randal ordered them to pair off. This produced a problem. There should have been 14 boys and 14 girls but one of each was absent.

"Max is still in hospital, sir," Glenn offered as explanation.

Dawn was also absent. That meant a boy would have to pair off with a girl. Mr Randal pointed and said, "Kirk, you team up with Amelia."

This produced snickers from some of the boys, causing Graham to blush. He didn't want to but did not feel the rebellion would be worth it. *Randal can be a hard bastard,* he thought.

Reluctantly, he moved to the end of the line and stood next to Amelia. She gave him a brief smile which he resented and did not return.

The lesson was on recovering people who were drowning. Mr Randal demonstrated, using Wayne as the victim. The activity involved one of each pair to swim out to the middle of the pool, then the second person swimming over to pull them to the bank, lift them out and place them in the 'Recovery' position.

"You can tow them by the chin, by the hair, or by an arm across their chest and under their armpit," Mr Randal explained. "Now off you go."

That raised a problem. Who was to go first? Amelia solved this by saying she would and by diving in. As soon as she reached the middle, Graham dived in. Being winter, the water was icy and quite took his breath away. A dozen strokes had him beside Amelia.

"Turn around so I can tow you," he ordered.

She did as she was told and he reached forward and gripped her hair, all the while treading water.

"Not by the hair! That hurts," Amelia called.

Unwillingly, Graham moved closer and reached forward to grip her under the chin. Her skin felt cool and smooth, and their legs bumped together as they both trod water. Graham was extremely conscious she was a female and tried not to touch her. In spite of that, as he began swimming, her body bumped against his. She trailed behind on her back while he did a side stroke. His male body responded to the touching, and he almost instantly became aroused.

At the bank he had to take both her hands and hold them together on the side of the pool, then climb out while stopping her from slipping under. Because he was aroused, he did not want to get out but could not think of any plausible excuse not to. Reluctantly he climbed out and knelt on the side, partly to keep his grip on her but mostly to hide his front.

The next thing he had to do was turn her around, then lift her out and lay her on the concrete apron. As he lifted her, he glanced down and was horrified to see his arousal was very obvious. To add to his dismay, he saw that she was looking up and knew, from the way her eyes dilated, that she could see his state.

Graham became so flustered he almost let her slip in again. With a quick heave he lifted her and rolled her on her side.

As he did, Mr Randal came along. "Further over," he called.

Graham knew that, but to roll her more on her front meant squashing her left breast and he was afraid to do that.

To his surprise, Amelia nodded. "It's okay. You won't hurt me," she said.

Very aware of the way her breasts were bulging in the swimsuit, Graham gently rolled her half onto her front. Fascinated, he wondered just what happened to a breast when it was squashed like that and that kept his body aroused.

The next part of the procedure, moving her right leg to act as a brace, made this worse as he had to grip her ankle and upper leg. His arousal grew.

Go down! he thought frantically. *Go down!* But no matter how hard he willed it wouldn't. To hide it he crouched low over her.

Next, he had to touch her throat to check the pulse and then open her mouth to clear the airways. *Nice throat,* he noticed. She felt nice to touch and that aroused him even more.

When he had finished, he remained crouching. Amelia rolled over and sat up, to sit close beside him.

"Your turn," she said.

Graham nodded and did a quick dive. He swam out and trod water, all the while willing his body to return to normal. Instead, it became even more stubbornly aroused. Amelia didn't help. She stood on the bank, then leaned over to do a dive, allowing him a glimpse down her front. She swam over to him and put her arm around his shoulders and across his chest. That caused their bodies to bump and rub together, keeping him excited. She started towing, her hip under the small of his back and her arm across his chest.

At the bank she turned him with some difficulty as he was a head taller than her. In the process their legs kept bumping and rubbing together. She did not seem to mind and even pressed her bosom against him as she held him up. She then climbed out and knelt on the side above him.

To lift him she had to swing up and down three times, hauling him out on the third lift. To Graham's dismay, she had to heave very hard to drag him over the edge. Burning with embarrassment, Graham lay on his front on the concrete and hoped she would just leave him that way. Instead she gripped his shoulders with surprisingly strong fingers and rolled him on his side. Then her hands slid down his leg and moved it into the correct position. As she did, he noted that her expression varied from obvious interest to apparent sympathy. It was all very embarrassing.

They were then told to have another practice. Graham did not want to move but had to stand up to dive in. He fervently hoped no-one was looking. As he reached Amelia, she reached out and touched him.

"I'm sorry. I hope I didn't hurt you then," she said.

Graham wasn't sure what she was alluding to so just grunted. "Turn around."

She did so, then said, "You can try the same way I used."

That meant putting an arm over the top of her chest to grip her under the armpit. Graham's mind raced. Did she really want that? Was she really innocent? Or did she actually want him to?

He was flustered and could only shake his head and say, "Oh! Oh I couldn't do that. I might... might accidentally touch your... er... you... I. er... could get into trouble."

"It will be alright," Amelia replied.

But Graham couldn't bring himself to do it. Instead he again gripped her under the chin and towed her to shore. As quickly as he could he climbed out, bent over, and pulled her out, then placed her in the recovery position.

Amelia then rescued him again. Then Mr Randal ordered them all to come and stand in a group while he showed them another technique. Graham stood up and held his hands in front to hide his aroused state as he walked over. Once there, he tried to stay at the back of the group. To his annoyance, Amelia came and stood so close beside him that her bare thigh touched against his leg. This was like an electric shock and kept him aroused.

Graham tried to move away but Glenn was beside him. Amelia moved closer and even put her hand on his arm, ostensibly to steady herself.

Is she doing that deliberately? he wondered. *Does she know what effect she is causing?*

He could not decide and remained hot and flustered until it was time to return to the dressing room to change. That raised another problem: How to change without his condition being noticed by the other boys? If they did Graham knew that would be a real 'shame job'.

They will tease me unmercifully if they became aware, he thought. As he walked back to the change room, he tried unsuccessfully to will his body to relax. In the end he had to go into one of the toilet cubicles to change on the pretext of going to the toilet.

He found it a relief to go to lunch, then to the 'Time Out' room. At least that allowed him to get his body back to normal.

Friday after lunch was hobbies. As the friends worked Stephen shattered Graham's composure by saying, "Have you got the hots for Amelia Graham?"

"No. She's a dog!" Graham replied.

Stephen smirked. "So why did you have a prong like the bowsprit of the good ship *Venus* at swimming?" he replied.

Graham flushed hotly and tried to deny it. Stephen laughed and said, "Boy! Look at you! Talk about guilt!"

Graham knew he was blushing furiously and went even redder. "She kept bumping against me," he muttered.

"I'm not surprised the way it was sticking out," Stephen laughed.

Graham was appalled. Had it been that obvious? Who else had noticed? "It was nothing," he insisted.

"I hope she thinks it's something. She's got her sights on you, mate," Stephen replied.

"Oh, she has not!"

Stephen shrugged. "She has. You'll see."

To change the subject, Graham asked, "Never mind that. What are we doing this weekend?"

"What do you want to do?" Stephen countered.

"Play Battleships?"

"When?" Peter asked.

"Have to be Saturday afternoon. I have to work on Saturday morning," Graham replied.

Peter shook his head. "And I have to go visiting rellies on Saturday afternoon."

"Sunday after church then?" Graham suggested.

Stephen looked at Peter and nodded. "Okay. What about going to the movies on Saturday night?" he asked.

"Sounds okay," Graham agreed. "I'll have to ask mum, but I think she will let me."

Stephen nodded again. "I'll ask some of the girls too," he added.

He did not elaborate, and Graham was too embarrassed to ask which ones but the notion sent his hopes soaring.

At last the bell went and the week was over. It had been a tiring time and Graham was glad to go home and lie down, to read comics and eat chocolates. Scouts was fun as well. Once again, his mother drove him there and picked him up afterwards. The main development was to arrange to meet Stephen again the next day.

The major fly in the ointment, as Graham drifted off to sleep, was that he still did not have a girlfriend; and he knew from his physical state that he badly desired one. Images of several girls floated as erotic fantasies in his mind.

Maybe tomorrow? he thought.

Chapter 11

MILLIE

On Saturday morning Graham slept in. His mother let him stay in till nearly 9am before digging him out for breakfast. After that, he had to do his chores: mow the lawn, wash the dog, clean the guineapig cage, and sweep out the Ship Room. After that he had to sit and do his homework. 'No homework, no play,' was the rule his father had imposed. Graham grumbled but settled to the hated task.

As arranged, Stephen came over after lunch and the boys talked and read comics for while. After an hour of this, Stephen tossed the comic he was reading aside and said, "I'm bored. Let's do something else."

"What?" Graham asked.

"How about a swim?" Stephen suggested.

"Be a bit cold, won't it?" Graham replied.

Stephen shrugged. "I've heard that some of the girls might be there," he said.

Graham liked that idea. Images of curvy girls in their bathers flitted through his mind. "What will you do for bathers?"

"I've got them on under my shorts," Stephen explained.

When she was asked, Graham's mother had no objection, so Graham changed into his bathers and collected his towel and bicycle. The two boys set out on bikes for the swimming pool at North Cairns. It was 2:30pm by the time they arrived. As soon as they had passed through the entrance, Graham was happy he had come. Several of their classmates were there. They waved them to come over to where they were settled on towels behind a garden bed near the back fence.

Even as he walked towards them, Graham could feel his interest quicken as he could see lots of bare skin. Three girls lay face down in their swimsuits: Rhonda, Rosemary, and, to his surprise, Amelia. Three boys sat beside them: Wayne, Walshy and Angus.

Graham stood for a moment and eyed the girls hungrily, while pretending to be not the slightest bit interested. Rosemary and Rhonda both wore bikinis. Amelia wore the same dark blue one-piece she had worn at the school pool. She lay on her front so that her breasts bulged out either side. The sight of all that bare skin had an instant effect on Graham. He spread his towel and sat down with them, uncomfortably aware that he was fast becoming aroused.

To maintain his pretence of not being interested, he looked around to see who else was there and noted several of the Year 11s and Year 12s from school. These included the lovely Margarita, heart throb of half the school (the male half!). She was being ducked and chased by three of the senior boys and their shrieks and laughter quickly roused Graham's jealousy. He badly wanted to take part in such activities, to be accepted, to be happy.

As they sat there, Graham was surprised to see Amelia lift herself up on her elbows so that half of her breasts were exposed. He had to battle with himself not to goggle.

"Hello Graham. How are you?" she asked.

"Fine," Graham answered, breaking into a cold sweat of anxiety as he stiffened up. *If she lifts herself another centimetre, I will be able to see everything!* he thought.

He tried not to stare but desire surged in him. He badly wanted to see all of her charms. To avoid people thinking he was perving, he forced himself to look away and to talk to the others but his eyes seemed to be dragged back every few seconds.

To his relief, and frustration, Amelia lay back down again so that all he could see was the smooth skin of her back and the bulge of her right breast.

Stephen was no help. "Come on you lot, swim time!" he called.

The other boys agreed and stood up, so Graham stood up and started walking without waiting for the others. He did not mind that because he thought he looked good in his bathers. As soon as he reached the pool, he dived in. That was a shock, as the water was cold. It took his breath away.

He swam back to the side and looked back at the others. All were now walking towards him across the lawn except Amelia. She stood up and walked towards him. Graham licked lips, which had gone suddenly dry.

Gosh, she's attractive, he thought.

There was much splashing and giggling as the group entered the water. Amelia came and sat on the side beside Graham. She bent forward to test the water. This presented an eyeful of cleavage to the watching boys and Graham thirsted for more. He badly wanted to splash her and pull her in but did not dare. Stephen had no such scruples. He slapped the water and showered her with drops. She squealed but obviously enjoyed the attention. Then Stephen added to Graham's jealousy by grabbing her ankle. While making half-hearted shrieks to stop it she was pulled in.

Graham felt anger surge and recognised that he did not want Stephen doing that. Even as he tried to decide what to do about it Amelia rose spluttering and swam over to him.

"Save me, Graham, save me!" she cried.

She moved in close against him so that their arms and bodies touched. Seeing this, Stephen stopped his attack and shifted his attention to Rhonda. Graham did not know what to do so he just stood there in the shallows smiling. Amelia stayed with him until a game of 'Tiggy' was voted.

To Graham's further surprise, Amelia was a very good swimmer. She was able to escape most of the boys. When Graham was 'in' he concentrated on catching her and it took him all his efforts and skill to finally tip her foot as she swam away. The game kept them all occupied for twenty minutes and was followed by a few minutes of gossip and water fighting.

As he stood up, Amelia called to him, "Help me out, please."

Graham turned and leant down to take her hand. In doing so he realised he could see straight down her cleavage and was amazed how strongly his emotions and body reacted. She smiled and appeared not to notice where his eyes were focused.

Up on the side she kept hold of his hand and said, "Thanks. You can stop staring now."

"Oh! Oh I... er... I," stammered Graham in confusion. "I'm sorry. I didn't mean to."

To his relief, Amelia's face crinkled into an impish grin and she squeezed his hand. "That's alright. I don't mind you looking."

Graham couldn't believe his ears. Flustered he let her hand go and walked quickly back to his towel. He flopped down on this, hoping no-one else had noticed, to be met by Stephen's smirk. Amelia walked with him and again down.

She is so desirable! Graham thought in mild astonishment.

With something of a shock, he realised he wanted her and became instantly jealous when Stephen began talking to her. He was relieved when Stephen and Rhonda wandered off to the kiosk. Hoping Amelia would not mind, Graham lay down on his towel beside her, his head turned so that he could see her the whole time. To his relief, she didn't seem to mind as she smiled and chatted happily to him.

Graham was also hotly aware that Rosemary was also lying close beside him. Both girls were face down, but it was still very pleasant to look at. He lay and tried to make happy small talk.

Stephen and Rhonda returned with ice creams and chocolates. There were a few minutes of good-natured horseplay before the group settled down again.

Ten minutes passed before Wayne suggested another swim. Walshy and Angus seconded this. Graham walked with Amelia to the edge of the pool.

To his confusion, she said, "You are nice. I like you."

Graham didn't know what to say. A mixture of delight and fear swamped his emotions. He licked his lips and looked into her eyes to try to determine if she was joking or teasing him. At last he managed to stammer, "I like you too."

There was an embarrassed silence, broken by Stephen swimming up and asking if they would play another game. They agreed to this, but Graham spent most of his time watching Amelia and trying to be with her as they splashed around the pool.

At the end of the game, the group climbed out and returned to their towels. This time Amelia remained sitting and talked. Rosemary interrupted them by saying, "We'd better be going, Millie. It is nearly five and we need to get a wriggle on if we are going to get to the movies on time."

Stephen at once asked, "Are you both going to the movies?"

Rosemary nodded and indicated Rhonda as well. "We all are, and so are Louise and a couple of others."

Stephen grinned and casually asked, "Can we come?"

Graham was impressed. *I would love to have the courage to ask that,* he thought. But he also sensed that he was jealous of Stephen's easy style. Equally he was glad Stephen had asked.

"We might be going with someone," Rosemary replied.

"But you aren't," Stephen guessed. He cast a quizzical glance at Wayne, Glenn and Angus who all shook their heads.

Graham felt his heart leap. Perhaps there was a chance! He heard himself say, "Where are you going?"

Amelia met his eyes and told him. Then she smiled and said, "You can come if you like."

"He will if you keep on like that," Stephen quipped.

Graham blushed fiercely. Amelia poked her tongue at Stephen, and said, "Don't be crude, Stephen Bell. You might not be invited otherwise."

But he was. Rosemary indicated it would be alright. Then another thought struck Graham; a very forbidding thought. "Do I have to ask your dad?" he asked Amelia.

The idea of asking the burly Warrant Officer did not appeal. *He will guess at once what I am interested in,* he thought.

To his relief, Amelia shook his head. "No. Dad's away on a silly weekend bivouac. We have arranged to go in a group so you could just meet us there."

That puzzled Graham. "I thought your dad was a regular soldier."

"He is, but he is posted as an instructor to an Army Reserve unit, you know, 'Weekend Warriors'," she replied.

"How are you getting there?" Graham asked.

"Mum will drive us, and pick us up afterwards," Amelia replied.

That dashed one of Graham's rapidly rising hopes, but he still wanted to go very much. It seemed too good to be true.

* * *

As Graham rode home alone (Stephen lived in the other direction), he sang softly to himself and shook his head in disbelief.

A girl says she wants me to go out with her!

Luckily, his mother made no objection. He told her he was going with Stephen and did not mention the girls although he suspected Kylie was suspicious. After a hurried tea he made a special effort over his toilet, worrying about bad breath and pimples and body odour. Then he dressed in a long-sleeved shirt, long trousers and shoes. His mother reminded him to take a pullover in case it got cold.

Graham walked as it was only a few kilometres and he did not want his bicycle pinched while he was in the movies. In the end he miscalculated the time and had to jog, which caused him to perspire, again raising his anxiety about body odour. When he reached the movie theatre Stephen and the girls were already there. So were Wayne and Glenn, and Glenn was holding Rhonda's hand.

As soon as he saw Amelia, Graham began to get excited. She wore a plain yellow cotton skirt and white cotton blouse but she looked very fresh and pretty. Rosemary was wearing a pair of shorts with a bib arrangement over a white sweater. This outlined her large boobs in a very provocative way. Rhonda was dressed in a sweater and jeans.

As soon as he had seen there were three other boys and only three girls, Graham had become very worried, hoping he would be able to sit beside Amelia. To his relief, she smiled at him and came over to stand beside him. To Graham's surprise Stephen was the odd one out. He stood and pretended everything was fine but Graham could sense he was badly put out. For an instant Graham experienced a surge of malicious glee. Then the worry returned: who would sit next to whom?

To Graham's relief Wayne put his arm around Rosemary's waist and Glenn kept hold of Rhonda's hand.

Even as they went into the theatre Graham could not believe it was happening as Amelia walked beside him and even touched his arm a few times. She stopped him at an empty row near the back on the right, then led the way in. Graham followed, with Rosemary next, then Wayne, Rhonda, Glenn and Stephen on the end. Amelia went half way along the row and sat down. There were no other patrons in the rows in front or behind them.

Couldn't be better, Graham thought.

No sooner had the lights dimmed and the movie begun than Amelia leaned over against him. Their arms touched and Graham felt the electricity course through his body.

Heavens! he thought. *I might even get a kiss tonight!*

By this time his heart was pounding fast and his mouth had gone dry. With wondrous delight he smelt Amelia's scent as she leaned against him. Her hair brushed his cheek and he wondered what to do next. She seemed to be willing for a bit of a pash. Graham had often heard boys discuss what they did to girls at the movies, and how things were done, but he was very inexperienced, and scared.

I'd better not go too fast or I will frighten her off, he decided. So for a while he did nothing but watch the movie, although he was acutely aware of Amelia's every move.

Out of the corner of his eye he saw her move her arm onto the armrest. *Should I try to hold her hand?* he wondered.

For a few minutes he steeled himself to pluck up the courage. Then he moved his own hand up to touch hers, ready to instantly pluck it away if she objected.

To his relief, and delight she eagerly grasped his, after a few moments of fumbling. Graham thought he could not be happier, till he became aware that she was turning her head to look at him. He looked at her and their eyes met. In the flickering light from the movie they seemed to be very large and shiny. Her face appeared to be rounder and softer than he remembered, and her lips were slightly parted.

Without realising what he was doing, he leaned across and kissed her. Their lips met in an inexperienced clash of teeth and dryness. Graham had to release himself and lick his lips before trying again. The feel and scent of her swamped his senses. Now he did think he was in heaven as they kissed and kissed. He had no idea how long they went on for, but he knew he was enjoying it very much.

They kissed again and this time Graham released her hand and put his arm around her shoulders. That cost him some sweat and measure of courage, but it was amply rewarded as she snuggled against him and pressed her face into his neck. Delightful and stimulating girl scents made his senses swim.

When they stopped kissing again Graham glanced around, partly to see what the others were doing, and partly to see if they had noticed. He very much wanted Stephen to see that he could also win with the girls. Wayne was engaged in a passionate embrace with Rosemary.

Seeing that got Graham's imagination going. He could feel Amelia's left breast pressing against his upper arm and he had a deep urge to caress it. *I wonder what she will do if I try?*

But knowing there could be dire consequences if she objected, he wasn't game to push his luck, so he contented himself with continuing to kiss. During this, Amelia half turned in her seat and placed her right arm across his front and around his neck. He put his left up to her shoulder and held her firmly to him. It felt just wonderful.

When they eased apart after the next kiss, Amelia leaned her head on his shoulder and her right hand slipped down his chest and onto the front of his trousers. To Graham it was as though a hot iron had been placed there. He could feel her touch burning through the cloth.

Has she done that without realising, or...?

He could not decide but knew he had never been so aroused and that her arm was pressing right on it. He badly wanted her to do some of the things his mates had talked about, but he did not dare even suggest them. Instead he kissed her again.

At this she moved her hand back to his neck, to his instant regret. After a while he realised his own left forearm was touching her right breast. Greatly daring he allowed it to press more firmly against her. To his relief, she made no objection and did not try to move it. Rather, she pressed harder against him and kissed him even more passionately. Graham was astounded.

Heavens! She is a hot little number, for a square bear!

By now his blood was pounding in surges that made a sound like heavy surf on a beach. His fingers seemed to tingle in anticipation. Oh, he wanted to touch her!

After another round of passionate kissing he decided he would try it. Very slowly he inched his hand down from her shoulder. She kept on kissing but gave a little sigh as his fingers gently brushed around the curve of her bosom. Seeing that she did not stop him, Graham became bolder. He had at least done this before and knew how to do it. With a firm but gentle grip he slid his hand up her side and on to her breast. She stopped kissing for a moment, then eased her face back. He could feel her rapid breathing and sensed that she was aroused. Then she reached up with her own hand and gently removed his.

Graham had expected that and was not disappointed. He had achieved his initial aim. *I'd better ease up now,* he thought. He sensed that she was not offended and thought he might get another opportunity. It came sooner than he expected.

She nuzzled at his cheek and whispered in his ear, "Not here."

For a moment Graham could not believe what he had heard. As the implications exploded in his consciousness, he became almost a quivering mass of anticipation. "Where then?" he asked.

"Let's go outside somewhere," she replied.

Chapter 12

EMOTIONAL STORMS

Graham was astounded. A girl wanted to go outside with him! To have a real pash!

She might be going to let me do things! he thought incredulously. But how to go about it? What to say to the others?

"What will we tell the others?" he whispered.

"Nothing. What's the time?" Amelia replied. She gripped his wrist and turned it so that she could read his watch in the dim light. "Eight thirty. We have to be back by nine thirty. That gives us an hour. Come on."

By now Graham was on fire both emotionally and physically. Worry about what the others might think almost made him chicken out, but when Amelia stood up he did likewise. She led the way out to the end of the row past the others.

Glenn looked up as they moved past. "Where are you two off to?" he asked with a laugh.

Amelia sniffed. "Never you mind," she replied.

Graham said nothing. He was so dry in the mouth he did not want to speak anyway.

Stephen smirked. "Don't do anything we wouldn't do," he said.

Graham glanced at him in passing and thought he detected a sneer. *He's jealous!* he decided.

Outside in the bright lights of the foyer, Graham walked close behind Amelia. She slowed down and took his hand as they reached the front entrance.

"Where will we go?" she asked.

Graham was intrigued by the look on her face. She seemed to glow and her eyes were wider than seemed natural. His mind now grappled with the problem of a suitable place.

"Munro Martin Park I suppose. It's only a couple of blocks," he said.

They turned in that direction and started walking. Outside in the lights on the footpath Graham felt very self-conscious. To him it seemed that every person on the street was staring at him. A mixture of anticipatory guilt and shame caused him to burn. But the lust was strong in him, and he set himself to keep going.

They walked quickly, aware that they had to be back before Amelia's mother arrived to take her home. It was pleasantly cool outside, and Graham plucked up the courage to put his arm around Amelia's shoulders. She gave a murmur of pleasure and snuggled closer, her arm around his waist.

After ten minutes' walk they arrived at Monro Martin Park. It wasn't an ideal venue, but Graham could not think of anywhere else. He fervently hoped there were no drunks there. To complicate matters the park was well lit, with only small pools of shadows in the larger garden beds. Where to go? He began to get anxious as they walked along the path to the small monument in the centre of the park.

The darkest place appeared to be under the trees in a garden bed off the main path. Graham steered Amelia towards this and they halted in the shadows. It was still very light, but Graham was getting impatient and fierce desire was coursing through his veins.

"This will have to do," he said.

He had been hoping for a seat but none was visible, so he dropped his pullover and turned Amelia to face him. To his delighted surprise her arms went around his neck and she pressed herself against him and kissed him passionately.

To Graham it was heaven. He gripped her waist and returned her kisses. She appeared not to notice, or not to mind, his hardness as she pressed herself against him. For the next ten minutes they clung together, repeatedly kissing while their hands gently roamed each other's backs and sides.

After a while Graham became more adventurous in his exploring. *After all, she had said 'not here' in the theatre. That must mean she wants me to do things,* he reasoned.

Risking a rebuff and a slap, he summoned up the courage to gently use one hand to caress her. To his relief, she did not move his hand away or object. In fact she sighed and moved so that he could. That sent Graham's hopes soaring. He pressed himself hard against her.

"Oooh, that feels good!" she murmured.

That encouraged Graham even more. He began to gently explore and fondle. Amelia responded with murmurs of pleasure and by squirming. Her breathing became rapid, and her eyes went wide and soft and he sensed she was very aroused. So was he and for the next ten minutes they clung together and engaged in passionate kissing and exploration.

Graham could feel her heart beating as well as his own and he knew she was very aroused as well. That was scary and made his fingers tremble even more.

After a few passionate minutes they drew apart. To Graham her face appeared to be glowing with wonder and desire, which frightened and encouraged him. She put her nose up to his cheek, then kissed him and said, "Oh you are sweet. You are so gentle." Then she leaned back.

Graham took this as a cue to act and kissed her again. Blood pounded in his ears and he pulled her firmly against him and kissed her fiercely.

"Oh that feels so good!" he cried.

In a state of wonder he held her tight and slowly caressed. "This is wonderful! I could do this all night," he murmured.

Amelia gave a sigh and pressed against him, to kiss him again. She said, "I'm tired of standing. Let's lie down."

Graham was astounded. He was also frightened. This was getting a bit too serious much too fast! But Amelia suited her actions to her words. She released him and stepped back. Then she knelt and arranged their pullovers on the leaf litter of the garden bed.

Graham stood and watched this, his heart pounding, wondering fearfully if things might get out of control. He badly wanted to try things; but he knew he was only a kid.

She is underage. We could get into terrible trouble, he thought. Fear began to battle with desire. *What will I do if that is what she wants?* he asked himself. But he knew.

If he got the chance, he would do it and damn the consequences. In a flash of revelation he suddenly understood something his father had said to him, "A standing prick has no conscience."

Too right! Graham thought. He licked his lips and flexed his fingers in anticipation as Amelia lay down on the pullovers.

Anxiety made Graham cautious now. Instead of lying on her he knelt beside her and then lay half on her. They kissed again and she clearly liked his touch, and he was tempted to try more but could not summon up the courage. That would really be playing with fire!

After a few more minutes she put her arms around him and drew him down on top of her. Graham worried that he was too heavy and said so. She shook her head.

"You feel really nice. Lie right on top of me."

Graham was amazed but by now was in the grip of urgent desire, so he lowered himself onto her. She kissed him again and he knew he was losing control.

By now they were both panting. Graham started to get the urge to go further and drew back to study her face. He saw it was suffused with passion and he recognised it for what it was.

She is turned on and wants it! he thought.

For a moment he raised himself and swallowed to moisten his throat as fear and desire had made it dry. He was panting rapidly and could feel strong surges of desire. Holding himself up on his elbow,s he pressed hard against her. As he did, she moaned softly and he studied her face to try gauge whether it was from pain or pleasure. He began trying to summon up the courage to go further.

At that moment, there was a sound behind Graham. He froze in fear and glanced quickly over his shoulder. It was someone walking along the main path only 20 metres away. And not just someone, it was Stephen. Graham hardly dared to breathe. Had Stephen seen them? Did he know they were there?

It was quickly apparent that he did as he sat down on the pedestal of the monument, just visible to them but with his back towards them.

"Stephen," Graham breathed in Amelia's ear. He felt a wave of coldness sweep over him and prickles of sweat broke out. His desire began to ebb.

"What does he want?" Amelia groaned in annoyance.

A horrible thought struck Graham. "The movies might be over."

"Oh shit!" Amelia gasped, shocking Graham. "What's the time?"

Graham let go of her and held his watch up to the light. "Nine forty-five," he said.

"Oh no! We'd better run!" Amelia cried.

Graham rolled off her and she sprang up. There followed a minute of rapid dusting to remove leaves and dirt. Amelia hastily adjusted her dress and hair. Graham looked down and saw that the knees and front of his white trousers were quite grubby.

Oh no! It will be very obvious what we have been doing, he thought.

A wave of anxiety almost amounting to nausea welled up. He burned with shame in anticipation. His desire ebbed away, and he worried about what his mother might say.

"Let's go!" Amelia said.

She walked quickly along the path with Graham hurrying beside her. As they reached the monument Stephen stood up.

"I thought you two would never finish," he said.

Graham wanted to explain that they hadn't been doing anything but bit it back. Stephen had seen them and wouldn't believe it. Besides, it was good for his reputation as a man.

Stephen fell into step with them. Amelia looked anxiously at him. "Has my mum arrived yet?"

"Hadn't when I left. The movie was still going. It doesn't finish till ten," he replied.

"We might make it. Oh, let's run!" Amelia cried.

She broke into a trot. The boys did likewise. But they only ran for about 50 metres, to the edge of the park, then slowed to a fast walk.

"Please don't say anything," Amelia said to Stephen. "Not to anyone."

"I won't," Stephen replied. "But the others saw you go out and you've been gone a long time."

Amelia pursed her lips and kept walking. By now Graham was scared as well as being worried. For a moment he contemplated not going back with Amelia. But this seemed so fundamentally gutless that he kept walking with her. He began to prepare himself for an ordeal.

He need not have bothered. They made it back to the theatre with five minutes to spare. There was no sign of Amelia's mother, so the trio stood on the footpath talking.

"You boys had better not be seen with me," Amelia suggested.

"Too right!" Stephen agreed. "Particularly you, Graham. You look like you've been crawling around the garden."

Graham glanced down and was horrified to see that the knees and front of his trousers were streaked with green grass stains and patches of dirt. Worse still, there were wet patches. He wished the floor would just open up and swallow him.

Looking anxiously at Amelia, he moistened his lips. "Can I see you tomorrow?" he managed to ask. He badly wanted to be alone with her again.

Amelia shook her head. "Sorry. I'd like to, but I have to go with mum to look at flowers at Orchid Valley. Go on, get going. I'll see you on Monday."

Graham nodded unhappily, then turned and walked off along the street with Stephen. The friends headed back the way they had come, towards the park.

Stephen chuckled. "Well, you are a dark horse! Was it good?"

Graham was in no mood to discuss something so personal, and so important. It had been so exhilarating and wonderful that he did not want to cheapen it by sordid boy talk. His emotions were in turmoil. Worse still he was fearfully frustrated but there was nothing he could do about that with Stephen there. So he walked along in a steadily worsening mood until they reached Roger's, where Stephen had left his bicycle.

On the way they walked back through Munro Martin Park and as they passed the monument Graham looked and noted how well lit the area was where he and Amelia had been lying.

Stephen must have been able to see everything! I wonder how long he was there? he thought. But he did not dare ask.

On arrival at Roger's, Stephen was disposed to talk, but Graham gruffly told him he didn't feel well and said goodnight. Quickly, and in some pain, he walked the rest of the way home, all the while torn by conflicting emotions: relief at not going too far, regret at not doing it, ecstasy at the memory of Amelia's wonderful smooth skin, happiness at having a girl like him. He became aroused again at the memories.

He was also worried about how he would explain or hide the stains on his trousers when he got home. To his relief, the house was in darkness when he got home so he was able to undress, hide the trousers under his bed, then give himself relief. It was a very perplexed but happy boy who dropped off to sleep that night.

* * *

In the morning, as he joined the others in the kitchen, his mother immediately, but inadvertently, put him on the spot.

"How was the movie dear?" she asked.

The movie! Graham's mind raced and he knew he was starting to blush. He could not even remember what it was called and had missed most of it anyway. He gave a non-committal answer, very aware that Kylie was listening intently.

She's suspicious, he thought, and blushed even more.

Kylie twisted the knife by adding, "They say it's a very good movie. Did that scene where the man comes back from supposedly being dead really scare you?"

"Yeah... yes it did," Graham said. He knew he was starting to sweat.

Kylie laughed and then sneered. "You didn't go to the movies at all! That movie doesn't have a scene like that in it."

"Has so!" Graham replied. Guilt began to swamp his emotions.

"Has not! I saw it last week," Kylie replied.

Graham felt utterly wretched. He was saved from a further inquisition by his mother who gave him an odd look before saying, "Stop arguing and hurry up you two. We will be late for church as it is."

Church! Graham was no religious fanatic but there was enough fear of hell fire to make him sweat when he sat in the pew beside Kylie and his mother. As usual little Margaret sat on his other side, making him feel even more guilty.

Well, for once I've got some sins to confess! he thought unhappily.

The thought that he might be damned by his 'sinful desires of the flesh' made him deeply worried. This was exacerbated when, by thinking about his sins, he began to get aroused. That added an extra level of concern, and he bit his lip as he wrestled with his conscience and his body. But the body refused to be commanded. Hot memories of Amelia's warm delights got him fully aroused.

It was a very anxious boy who made his way out to Communion. As he made the sign of the cross and then received Communion he flushed with shame. In his mind he writhed with real concern that God might be watching and judging him too. Walking back along the aisle afterwards was worse as he was sure everyone was looking, and he interpreted every glance as censure. He almost promised to behave himself and to never do it again.

Luckily, by the time the service was finished, he had restored himself to normality. He joined the others at morning tea. Margaret stood with Kylie and talked happily away, and he tried to respond and act normal.

Graham's main response was to think what a little girl she was. Roger was also there but Graham did not really want to talk to him.

"What are you doing this afternoon?" Roger asked.

"Nothing. Homework I suppose," Graham replied.

"Come over and we will work on the railway then," Roger suggested.

Graham thought rapidly. He had been hoping to see Millie again but had not made any arrangement to do so. He was unable to think of any reason why he should not go to Roger's. Besides, he had no wish to hurt Roger's feelings.

"Okay," he agreed.

Then it was home in the family car. Once there, Graham remembered his dirty trousers. That made him break into a sweat of anxiety again. *I'd better clean them before mum finds them,* he thought.

So he waited till Kylie and his mother were busy then hastily retrieved the trousers from under his bed and scuttled down the front steps with them under his arm. He made his way around to the back and went to the laundry.

But how to get the stains out? Graham studied the various containers of soap, whiteners, fabric softeners and so on till he found one labelled as a 'Stain remover- Whiter than White!'

That's the stuff, he thought with relief. He hesitated to use the washing machine. *They will hear that.* So he began filling a tub, then poured some of the blue liquid onto the stains and began to rub them.

"What are you doing Graham?" asked his mother.

Graham jumped with a guilty start. "Washing mum," he answered lamely.

"I can see that. What's the problem?" she asked. She came forward and took the trousers from his trembling fingers.

"I... I fell over on a garden bed," Graham explained lamely. As he did so, he blushed fiercely, both with guilt and at the shame of trying to lie to his mother.

She gave him an odd look, then took them off him and said, "I'll worry about these. Now you be more careful next time."

"Yes, Mum."

Graham felt wretched. He was sure his guilt was written all over his face. His emotions in turmoil he handed her the trousers and fled to the Ship Room.

Chapter 13

PLAYING WITH FIRE

On Monday morning Graham went to school with very mixed emotions. Part of him could hardly wait to see Amelia. The rest was worried about what the other boys in his class would say about him going with her, because of her reputation for being such a frumpy and unexciting thing.

Stephen had obviously spread the story because as soon as he arrived, Vincent, the class clown, said, "How's tricks? I've heard you've been teaching them to your new pet dog."

It took a moment for the insult to sink in. Anger and shame both flamed. "She's not a dog! Say that again and I'll smash your face in," Graham grated.

He raised his fists and stepped forward. It was instantly apparent that his reputation for fighting was well established because Vincent immediately retreated.

"Okay, okay, only a joke. Keep your hair on," he said.

Graham wasn't amused, and he went on his way wondering if he should be friends with Amelia. But then the memories of those glorious moments of pleasure swirled in his brain and he knew he wanted her, and badly.

Peter and Roger joined him, and they discussed what they had done on the weekend until the bell went, allowing no chance for Graham to go looking for Amelia. But he saw her as soon as he went up the stairs to the first lesson. By then his stomach was all aflutter with nerves. What if she regretted what they had done? What if she did not want to see him again?

It was instantly apparent that he had nothing to worry about. She gave him a big smile and came over to talk to him, to the undisguised interest of the other girls, who did a bit of behind-the-hand whispering.

First lesson was Geography. Normally Graham would have sat next to Angus because Stephen was at Art, but without even discussing it he went and sat beside Amelia. She gave him a smile which set his heart bounding, then touched his knee under the desk with hers, which gave him instant arousal. When Mr Conkey arrived to teach the lesson, he saw them and raised his eyebrows but said nothing.

That lesson proceeded without any problems except for Graham's physical concerns. When he had to get up to go to the next lesson, he was able to hold his school bag in front and managed to arrive at the next room without attracting unwelcome attention.

The lesson was English. As he walked into the room, Graham paused. A decision was required. Normally he sat beside Stephen, and he was already seated at their usual desk. Amelia walked to her usual desk in the back, right-hand corner. Graham only hesitated for a moment, then walked past Stephen to sit beside her.

Once again, she rewarded him with a smile and touched his leg, setting him on fire again. Maths A followed, luckily in the same room; and because old 'Buggermaster' had told him not to sit beside Stephen, he remained where he was.

After morning break, Graham hurried to German. Once again, he sat next to Amelia and, to his astonishment, he became as aroused as ever. Physics followed and only then did his desire subside. This was a relief as Graham then had to make his way to the detention room. Thus he got no chance to really be alone with Amelia all day.

During Music he sat beside her and managed to whisper, "What are you doing after school?"

She gave him a sympathetic look and replied, "I'm sorry. I have to go home and do my homework."

Graham wanted to ask her when he could see her again, but the teacher told him to keep quiet and to pay attention. Maths B followed and once more Graham sat beside Amelia. When Mr Ritter noted this, he arched one eyebrow but did not tell him to move. Graham forced himself to work and managed to keep out of trouble.

When school was over Graham turned to Amelia, his heart beating breathlessly and said, "See you tomorrow."

She smiled and nodded, "Yes please."

Graham wanted to stand and talk to her, but she said goodbye and hurried off.

Stephen joined him as he watched her go. "Boy, you've got it bad. Do you reckon you'll win?"

Graham instantly flamed, with resentment at the implication that sex was his motive; and with guilt, because he knew that was what he ardently desired.

"It's not like that. I like her," he replied.

Disbelief showed on Stephen's face. "Oh yeah! You following the old principle of not wasting time on the pretty ones but going for the 'Plain Janes' because they are liable to be more grateful and more likely to do it?" he replied.

That hurt! Graham pressed his lips together but said nothing. Instead he followed Stephen down to the bike racks. On the way he noted Ailsa riding off with Rowena and wondered. They were the beautiful ones. Then he shook his head.

No. They wouldn't go out with me, he decided bitterly.

"What are you doing this arvo?" Stephen asked.

Graham shrugged. "Nothing special. What did you have in mind?"

"I'm going to town. There's something I want to get," Stephen replied. Having nothing better to do Graham agreed to go with him.

The two boys made their way into the city, walking because Graham did not have his bike. As before, they dumped their school bags in the garden beds at the council library and Stephen placed his bike in an alleyway.

"Where are we going?" Graham asked.

"The chemists," Stephen replied.

"Chemists!" Graham replied in surprise. "Are you sick?"

Stephen shook his head. "Nope, and I don't want to catch any diseases."

"What do you mean?"

"I want to buy some frangers," Stephen answered with a grin.

Once again Graham was astonished. *Condoms! What on earth does Steve need them for?* he thought, then blushed at his own stupidity. His mind raced. Who was the girl?

"Are you on to a sure thing?" he asked.

Stephen grinned again, "Reckon so."

"Who?"

"Fair go mate! A gentleman never tells," Stephen replied.

Poor Graham. Now his mind was really in turmoil. He had never had sex, but of late he had become so driven by urges that the thought of 'doing it' with a girl had become one of his obsessions.

If only! I wonder if... I wonder if Amelia will let me do it? he pondered.

The idea bothered him intensely, and he knew that at back of it was the lurking fear that, if and when the great moment arrived, he might not be able to perform.

The fear of being sexually inadequate haunted him, even as his body went out of control and he started to get another involuntary erection while he walked along the street. It was very embarrassing. All he could do was try to conceal it with his hands and hope nobody noticed.

When they reached the Chemist shop, he was in such a state of arousal that he was sure it must be glaringly obvious to everyone on the street. To hide it he turned to look in the window and held his hands across his front. Stephen went into the shop and Graham stopped on the footpath, burning with embarrassment.

"Hey, come in with me," Stephen called. He had re-appeared in the doorway.

Graham broke into a cold sweat. "I'd rather not," he replied lamely.

"Why not? Ain't you game?" Stephen asked with a hint of a sneer.

That hurt. Graham groped for a suitable answer. "Just don't want to," he replied.

Stephen jerked his head towards the shop. "Rosemary's in there. She works here after school."

That made Graham even more concerned. "I don't want her to think that's all I want. She might tell Millie," he muttered.

Stephen chuckled. "From the way you two were carrying on Saturday night I'd recommend that condoms are what you need," he replied with a grin.

Graham blushed hotly. "But... but we can't ask Rosemary! She will be so embarrassed. Can't we go to some other shop," he said. He felt very uncomfortable at the idea of mentioning condoms to a girl, particularly one who was in his class.

Stephen shook his head and grinned. "It'll give her a real thrill," he replied.

Graham wasn't so sure. He had no desire to embarrass Rosemary. Stephen snorted at this idea and persisted, "Come on. Anyway, I need you to attract her attention."

"Why?"

"You'll see. Come on. Just keep her talking."

So saying Stephen turned and went back into the shop. Reluctantly Graham followed. He felt very ill-at-ease. Chemist shops were such female places, all baby things and female staff and lady shoppers.

There were two female counter staff. One was Rosemary. The other was an efficient looking lady in her thirties. The woman raised her eyebrows. "What can I do for you boys?"

Stephen pointed to Rosemary. "We just want to talk to Rosy. She's in our class."

The woman pursed her lips but moved away. Rosemary saw them and gave them both a shy smile. "Hi. What can I do for you?" she asked.

"Lots that I can think of," Stephen replied, with deliberate double meaning.

Rosemary blushed but she still smiled. Her eyes met Graham's and he blushed even more. "Don't be rude, Stephen," she chided, but her voice had no bite in it.

"We want a couple of packets of condoms," Stephen said.

A blush mounted Rosemary's neck and lower face. She glanced quickly sideways to see if the lady had heard. Graham felt himself blushing as well and knew he must be bright red. He wished he hadn't come and just wanted to get out of there. He watched her hands flutter nervously and felt sorry for her. She pointed.

"They are over there, on that rack."

"Thanks. Graham, you talk to Rosemary while I choose," Stephen replied.

He went over to the rack and began searching the products on it. Graham was left looking at Rosemary, burning with shame and very aware that he was still very aroused. He felt completely tongue tied and had no idea what to say.

"Sorry," he muttered. "I didn't mean to upset you."

To his relief, Rosemary smiled and replied, "You haven't. It's that Stephen. He is very direct."

"Yes." It was all he could mumble.

Stephen returned with two boxes of condoms and placed them on the counter. Rosemary went red again and quickly slid them into a paper bag. Graham was acutely aware of the older woman working further along the counter. To his relief, she went into a back room. Stephen laid money on the counter.

"I hope these are good," Stephen said. "I wouldn't want an accident. Are they any good, Rosy?"

Rosemary went even redder. So did Graham, whose heart was now beating very fast. This was getting pretty serious. Condoms were adult stuff and he and Millie were only 14.

Rosemary pursed her lips. "I wouldn't know. I've never tried them."

"Do you use a different brand?" Stephen asked, pretending to misunderstand her.

"No! I've never used one," she replied hotly.

"That's taking a risk," Stephen said, still pretending to misunderstand her. "Particularly with horny devils like Graham around."

Rosemary went even redder, but to Graham's surprise she didn't bite Stephen's head off. Her facial expressions puzzled Graham. Was she excited? Or interested? Her eyes met his, then went back to Stephen's. Graham felt his temper beginning to slip.

Rosemary replied coolly, "No thanks. I haven't even seen one, so I'm not sure what you are talking about."

"We will soon teach you," Stephen said. "Graham here would love to show you what it's like."

At that Graham reacted. "Steve! That's enough," he said.

Rosemary nodded. "Don't be disgusting, Stephen," she added, but she still didn't sound angry.

Again her eyes flicked to meet Graham's. Another flush of embarrassment flooded through him.

At that moment, the lady shop assistant returned. With her was a middle-aged man, the chemist. Stephen grinned and took the package and his change.

"Oh well, keep it in mind. See you then."

With that he turned and walked out. Graham gave Rosemary a worried smile and hurried after him, aflame with shame and lust. Out on the footpath Stephen burst out laughing.

"She liked that. I reckon she will be in it with a bit of smooth talking," he said.

"Don't be crude Steve," Graham snapped.

He was ashamed of his behaviour, and of his innocence. He had never seen a condom, and Stephen had two packets in his hand. That set his mind speculating.

Trying to sound gruff and off-hand he asked, “Can I buy some of them off you?”

Stephen grinned again. “Sure. Here, have a packet.” He reached inside his shirt and took out another packet. As he did, Graham noticed at least two more packets. “Five finger discounts,” Stephen added.

Graham was appalled. Stephen had stolen them! He was shocked. Worse, he felt used. Now he understood what Stephen had meant by wanting him to keep her talking. As the full realisation of what had actually happened in the shop sank in Graham found he was shaking with shock. He glanced behind him in case they were being followed.

“Steve! You shouldn’t have,” he said.

Stephen laughed again. “Why not? The shopkeeper’s got plenty of money. Don’t worry about it.”

“But it’s stealing!” Graham replied. He was genuinely upset.

“Don’t be such a wuss! Here, do you want them or not?”

He held out the packet. Graham felt a hot feeling of genuine pain. He didn’t want to be involved in theft; but he badly wanted some condoms. Feeling sick at heart he took the proffered packet and slipped it into his pocket. A feeling of shame swept over him as he knew that he had been a weakling for not doing the right thing.

At least my stiffie has gone down! he consoled himself. But he suspected that fear had been the main reason for that, which was another cause for concern.

The pair walked on around the main block, Stephen openly ogling at girls and making comments of a sexual nature which both excited and frightened Graham. He wasn’t really enjoying himself but didn’t know what to say to get Stephen to stop.

If I do, he might not be my friend, he thought.

That was another anxiety. Of late he seemed to have drifted away from his friends.

* * *

All in all, it was a relief when they set off home. They walked together, Stephen wheeling his bike, until they were back near the high school. There Graham turned left and went his own way, feeling very mixed up and depressed.

He walked past Roger's house, but he did not feel like going in and was glad that Roger did not see him. Once home he went down to the Ship Room and opened the packet of condoms. After carefully reading everything on the packet he took one out and felt it. It was in a silvery plastic envelope and felt soft. Very curious about the whole process he tore the packet open, though not without some difficulty.

Inside was the rolled-up rubber sheath. The first thing Graham noted was a distinct rubbery smell which he decided instantly he did not like. Then he felt the sticky lubricant on the rubber and wrinkled his nose with distaste. But he was very aroused and badly wanted to know how they worked so he spent the next half hour finding out.

As he did, all the sarcastic comments he had heard about using condoms; such as 'like having a shower with a raincoat on' flitted through his mind. As he had never had sex at all he couldn't comment, but he decided that if getting sex depended on wearing one then he would. In his own mind having sex had become a major priority, but he didn't want complications like pregnancies or loathsome diseases.

Afterwards he felt mildly disgusted. He shook his head. This growing up wasn't necessarily all that enjoyable.

I suppose when the time comes, I won't care, he decided.

The next problem was how to dispose of the used condom. The rubbish bin, with it wrapped in old newspaper was the solution. Then he had the problem of where to hide the condoms so that Alex, or Kylie, or (heaven forbid!) his mother, would not find them. In the end he put them in his school bag. That night he had several long fantasies about having sex with Amelia and became very aroused. In spite of that, he still had a dream full of sex where he could never quite get to do it.

On Tuesday at school, Graham got a rude shock. As soon as he sat down next to Amelia, all keen for more thrills, she looked at him anxiously and asked, "Do you really like me Graham?"

Graham was surprised. "Yes, I do," he replied.

"You aren't just saying that?"

"No, why should I?" Graham asked.

Amelia looked very anxious. "You aren't just pretending to like me hoping for sex, are you?" she asked.

That put Graham on a real spot. Up till now he hadn't really considered whether he and Amelia were suited as a pair, or what type of person she was.

"No," he replied, but felt guilty and wondered if that was the truth.

"But you are hoping to have sex with me?" she asked, more as a statement than a question.

Graham was, but did not want to admit it. He hesitated, trying to find a diplomatic answer, then decided to tell the truth.

"Yes," he said, blushing fiercely and feeling slightly sick.

"Is that why you bought the condoms the yesterday?"

That rocked him. *Rosemary must have told her,* he deduced.

"No. Stephen bought them," Graham answered.

"Did you get any?"

Graham nodded. "Yes," he answered lamely.

To his relief, Amelia smiled. She squeezed his arm. "It's alright. I know I've been really forward, so I don't blame you if you jumped to that sort of conclusion. But I do want you to like me as a person too."

Too? Did that mean she wanted sex as well? Graham did not dare ask. Amelia then surprised him again.

"Did you bring them with you?"

"The... the condoms?" he asked, almost choking on the word.

"Yes."

"Yes, I did."

"Can I see one? I've never seen one before."

Graham was amazed, and excited. He nodded. "They are in my bag. I'll get one at the end of the lesson."

The thought of how he might show Amelia the condom carried him through Maths A in a haze of fantasy. He just shrugged of Mr Burgomeister's sarcastic comments. But even though he collected a condom during the period change Graham could only slip it into his pocket because Maths B was next, and Mr Ritter was on to him all the time to check homework and to make sure he worked.

Nor was German any better. It was not till English in Period 4 that he found himself seated safely in the back corner beside Amelia. It only took them a few minutes to start playing around. This time Graham took the initiative and not only gently pressed against her but then, greatly daring, lightly caressed her leg. Her head came round sharply and for a moment he was afraid he had made a serious mistake.

But then she smiled and murmured, "Naughty boy!" in a way that told him she was not offended. Encouraged by that he did some more stroking. Her reaction was obvious pleasure, so he became bolder. In return she leaned over and pressed against his arm.

By then Graham was in the grip of what he dimly recognised as lust. A niggling little voice at the back of his mind kept saying 'Stop!' but he knew he was loving the thrill and the dare of it all and kept on. But Mrs Ramsey ended that by organising them to move into groups to prepare debate topics. Graham was allocated to a different debating team from Amelia and could only curse his luck and grit his teeth in frustration.

Chemistry was next but again no chance offered itself. Throughout the lesson, Graham kept watching Amelia and thinking about what might happen. This kept him aroused and very much on edge. From time to time Amelia met his eyes and made a face to indicate she was not happy either. Driven by his urgent desire a plan formed in Graham's mind to try to get Amelia somewhere private at lunchtime. He went over the school plan in his mind to work out the best locations.

The best place Graham could think of was in the Manual Arts storeroom behind the stacks of sawn timber. When the suggestion was put to her, Amelia indicated she was willing and they both headed off there as soon as the bell went. As he walked, his thoughts were a riot of speculation about what 'it' would be like.

By the time they arrived at the storeroom, Graham was very aroused, breathing very fast, sweating; and extremely scared. Five minutes later he was very annoyed and frustrated. Stephen had followed them with Rosemary. Just as Graham was about to embrace Amelia to give her a passionate kiss, Stephen poked his head around the door.

"What ya's doing?" Stephen asked, pretending all innocence.

"Piss off Steve!" Graham grated angrily.

"Oh don't be like that, mate! Can't we watch?" Stephen replied. He led Rosemary into the room.

Graham flushed with guilt and gulped air to calm his seething anger. Then his annoyance found voice.

"Yes, you might learn how to do it!" he snapped.

That verbal barb went home, judging by the look on Stephen's face. But before any more action could develop one of the Manual Arts teachers appeared from among a line of lathes.

"What are you kids doing in here? Get out! You aren't supposed to be in here without a teacher," he growled.

They fled out to the playground and ended up sitting in a row under the trees down at the oval.

"Thank you very much!" Graham snapped.

Stephen waved a hand airily and replied, "So you should. If we hadn't arrived, you would have been caught in the act."

"We would not!" Amelia snapped. "Don't be disgusting."

"Suit yourself," Stephen replied. "Want a smoke?"

He produced a packet of cigarettes even though the teacher on playground duty in that area was only 20 paces away. Graham shook his head. He didn't like smoking but even more he disliked the emotional pressure he was now put under.

Stephen persisted. "What's wrong? Aren't you game?"

"No I'm not!" Graham cried. "I'm in enough trouble already, and if I smoke mum will smell it and I'll be sent to boarding school."

To his relief, Stephen accepted this. He then offered the girls a smoke. Rosemary accepted but Amelia shook her head and Stephen did not press the issue. As soon as the teacher's back was turned, the cigarettes were lit and then smoked by being held in the hand. Graham wished Stephen would go away so he could talk to Amelia privately, but he refused to take the hint.

It was a very annoyed and frustrated boy that went back into the next lesson!

No sooner had they sat down than Amelia touched his leg with her knee. Graham was in such a state of anticipation that he became instantly aroused. As before, he was glad he was sitting and at the back of the room. His condition was exacerbated when she leaned over and her left breast pressed gently against his bare arm. He glanced down at it and felt a surge of intense desire.

"Am I bothering you?" she whispered, noting his eyes and rapid breathing.

"No. I love it," Graham replied in a hoarse croak.

That made her smile and press against him harder. The touch on his thigh was like a burning brand. He started to lose focus on where he was, with the fairly inevitable result that the teacher, Mrs Ramsey, noted his inattention.

"Graham! Graham Kirk!"

Graham woke with a start. "Yes... yes miss?"

"Answer the question. What does the poet mean by this passage?" Mrs Ramsey asked.

Answer! Graham had absolutely no idea. For a few moments he stammered and then shook his head.

"Sorry Miss, I don't know."

"You need to pay more attention. Now focus on the work," the teacher snapped.

That earned another smirk from Stephen. Graham slumped back in his seat, burning with embarrassment as Rosemary whispered to Christine behind her hand. No sooner had he settled than Amelia put her hand on his arm.

"Have you got a horn?" she asked.

Graham was astonished and even more embarrassed. "Can you tell?" he whispered anxiously.

Amelia nodded and smiled. "Yes."

"Sorry. I don't mean to offend you. It... it's just that I can't seem to control it anymore. It just pops up whenever it wants," he explained. He knew he was beetroot red and felt as though his skin was burning.

Amelia smiled. "I'm not offended. It's perfectly natural. I get horny a lot too," she replied.

That set Graham's mind spinning of in rapid speculation. He was surprised at her directness. He swallowed and felt his heart rate increase noticeably.

Then Amelia surprised him even more. "Do you want to have sex with me?" she asked.

Graham was astounded, and scared. For a few moments he gaped and struggled to find the right answer. He looked into her eyes and felt he was being consumed by them. They were large and questioning and he noted that her skin had gone pale, and her freckles were really standing out.

"Oh, er... er… yes," he croaked."

"You can if you want to," Amelia said.

Her eyes now seemed to draw him in and he felt a sensation of such intensity he was momentarily powerless.

"Oh, er… I'd like to. But I... we could get into terrible trouble."

"No you won't. I won't tell," she replied.

Graham stared at her in near disbelief. After all these years of drought, the flood! He found he was torn between surging lust and bowel-watering fear.

Amelia squeezed him again and he felt his resolve weakening. She whispered, "I'd like you to," she said.

That simple statement left him speechless. He was humbled and conversely filled with a very special feeling of being chosen. Even so Graham found the situation hard to believe. But he was now in the grip of an emotional storm and could feel a rising urge to act. He licked his lips and nodded.

"Where? When?" he croaked.

Chapter 14

A REAL THRILL

Graham looked around the room. He broke into a sweat of anxiety and then his eyes again met Amelia's. They were wide with interest and her mouth was slightly open. Her breath was coming in short pants. So was Graham's. He was fearfully excited and very, very scared.

If I get caught, I will be in terrible trouble, he thought.

Amelia leaned over and pressed her breast against his arm. "Please."

Graham swallowed and bit his lip. His hands felt sweaty. "But I could get taken to court," he muttered.

"I won't tell," Amelia whispered.

Graham was astounded. His imagination boggled. What she was asking was very serious. But he badly wanted to.

"What about after school?" he asked.

Amelia shook her head and made a face. "No chance. Mum picks me up and I'm not allowed out," she replied.

"When then?" Graham said. He knew his resistance was crumbling and broke into a cold sweat.

"Have to be next weekend," she said. "I will try to organise a party or the movies or something and we can slip away like we did the other night."

That notion of slipping away and all it implied got Graham's heart beating even faster and he was again assailed by alternate waves of desire and anxiety.

"Who else will you invite?" he queried.

Amelia shrugged, "Rosy, Louise, maybe Judy; and Stephen and a couple of the boys."

Graham nodded, his imagination conjuring up another session in the park. "That will be good?"

"Will you be allowed out?" Amelia asked.

Graham nodded. "Yes, I think so."

He was certain his mother would not say no. And with the promise of such delights he decided he would just defy her if he needed to.

Perhaps she isn't a virgin? he speculated.

That would be a great relief if it came to sex because he was having agonies of conscience over being the one to take away a girl's virginity. Such thoughts got him so aroused that his vision seemed to blur in and out of focus and he found he was breathing very fast.

Amelia added to this by gently hugging him. And then, to his regret, the bell rang. Amelia gave him a mischievous smile and picked up her books.

"Oh well, Domestic Science for me. I will see you in Geography," she said.

Graham could only nod and sit there feeling intensely frustrated. He stayed that way all through German, his emotions in a turbulent boil. The classwork barely held his attention. The only good thing about German, he decided, was Miss See, the very attractive female teacher in her twenties.

I will never need to know any of this stuff! he thought. Much later, he would look back at this moment and realise how little did he know what the future had in store!

Chemistry was next. His mind now a fever of hope and fear he met up with Amelia outside the Laboratory. But in the laboratory, he sat at his usual place next to Stephen rather than next to her. The formidable Miss McLeod was not the person to take any risks with.

Graham spent the next two periods in a state of absolute excitement. His arousal came and went, and he had wild fantasies about what he and Amelia might do. Part of his mind did not believe what she had said.

Is she just teasing me? Surely, she didn't mean she wanted to actually do it? he thought.

During morning break he went with her to the tuck shop, then sat beside her and talked. They could not get any real privacy, but he was able to speak freely.

"You are sure you want to?" he asked.

"Yes. You aren't scared, are you?" Amelia replied.

Graham swallowed and nodded. "Yes. I don't want to get into trouble," Graham replied.

"Don't worry about that. I won't tell," she replied. Then she shocked him even more by saying, "It's alright. I'm not a virgin."

Graham stared at her in amazement, relief and prurient curiosity alike surging across his jumbled thoughts. He found he could not decide what to say. Curiosity about who with and when and so on flitted across his mind but he thought they would not be tactful questions.

She smiled at his obvious flustering and shook her head. "It was last year, in Year 8. Lots of Year 8 girls try it out then, just to see what it's like. It was at my old school in Sydney. Some of my friends did it and they liked it and I was curious. So I tried it."

"Did you like it?" Graham croaked.

"Yeah,

Graham nodded and was left speechless. She noted this and then laned closer. "You haven't done it have you?" she stated.

Graham could only shake his head and stare into those mesmerizing eyes. "No," he managed to croak.

"It'll be good," she promised. Then she shocked him even more. "Have you ever seen people do it?"

Again Graham shook his head. Amelia raised her eyebrows. "Not even on those sex videos?" she queried.

"Oh yeah," Graham croaked, nodding and feeling very embarrassed.

"So it will be alright," she replied.

The next lesson was Geography. Graham sat beside Amelia again, but he would not do anything in Mr Conkey's class. He always walked around the room continually, checking their work. So Graham and Amelia sat touching each other but keeping busy with class work. But the whole time Graham was aroused and his mind was filled with churning speculation and fantasies.

I might be going to get to actually do it! he thought. But when, and where?

At the end of the lesson, after Mr Conkey had walked out, Graham nudged her, "Are you sure you want to be alone with me?" he whispered, aware that Stephen had walked in and was looking towards them.

"Yes, I do!" Amelia replied with an emphatic nod.

Her eyes gleamed and she showed her teeth. Graham almost kissed her there and then but the teacher, Miss Tate, entered at that moment.

While he struggled with the schoolwork Graham's imagination explored possible secret meetings with Amelia. That got him very aroused and hopeful. But it also got him very worried.

If we go too far and I get caught I won't just be in trouble at school, he thought fearfully. *It will the police and angry parents and going to court.*

Then another thought took hold and he tried to push it out, but couldn't. The words 'Wrath of God' flitted across his mind, and he became even more anxious.

During the remainder of the lesson, Graham was in turmoil. He was elated, and scared. His hopes of getting a girl to have even a little bit of sex with him were rapidly coming true; and now he began to feel pressured and scared. It was frighteningly real, and he wasn't sure it was all going a bit too fast. He had an uneasy feeling that things were getting out of his control.

At least the afternoon was easier. They had Manual Arts straight after lunch and there was no chance of any mischief standing up in the workshop. Last period was Maths B and Graham was too afraid of Mr Ritter to try anything during his classes. What he really wanted to do was get to meet Amelia out of school, but once again she reminded him she was being picked up by her mother.

He asked, "Does she always pick you up? Haven't I seen you ride a bike?"

"Yes, you have. No, she doesn't always."

"Could I walk you home tomorrow?" he asked hopefully.

She looked doubtful "I don't know. If dad saw us, he'd skin me alive. He thinks I'm far too young to be having anything to do with boys."

And so you are, Graham mentally agreed, but, hypocrite that he was, he badly wanted to have lots to do with her.

So he walked home in a mixture of happiness and frustration. After making a perfunctory effort to do his homework he lay on his bed, reading a book and fantasising.

* *

With the prospect of more delights ahead, Graham was early to school the next morning. But Amelia was not there when he arrived, and he found himself talking to Peter and Stephen.

"When are we going on another hike?" Peter asked.

Graham shrugged. At the moment all he could think about was how to get Amelia on her own.

Peter persisted. "What about next weekend, or the weekend after that?"

Stephen answered first. "I'm still not allowed to go on hikes. The only camping I'll be allowed to do is with the Cadets."

Peter made a face. "The next bivouac isn't for two weeks. Surely something can be organised. What about you Graham?"

Again Graham shrugged. "I'll think about it."

Stephen grinned. "All you are thinking about is how to get into Millie's pants!" he teased.

The jibe was too true to be funny. Graham blushed and angrily denied it. Stephen just laughed and Peter wanted to know who Millie was. Stephen told him. Graham sat stony faced and then walked off in a bad mood to see if she had arrived at school.

That set the tone for the day. Period One was Maths A with 'Buggermaster' and Graham did not dare to try anything. German followed and they were grouped on chairs at the front of the room to watch a video, so no opportunity presented itself. Manual Arts was next, under the eagle-eyed supervision of Mr Duncan. It was a very frustrated Graham who went out to morning tea.

English was next. Amelia indicated she still liked him by sitting next to him and by pressing against him. Several times she put her hand on his leg and he became very aroused. The urge was so strong upon him that he fairly itched to touch her, to do something! But he did not dare, fear of the consequences if she objected strong in him. But then he was in trouble- for not working and for not having even read the 'Set Book' so as to be able to give sensible answers to questions.

There was no opportunity in Chemistry either, partly because Stephen and Rosemary were put with them to make up a group and then they had to stand around a bench and, in Graham's case, pretend to do experiments. All he could do was cast meaningful glances at Amelia, and from time to time nudge or bump gently against her. To his delight, she returned the favours, pressing her bosom against him and getting him all hot again.

Miss McLeod's movements ended that. She came and stood between Graham and Amelia and supervised their next experiment. All Graham could do was take part and cast the occasional glance at Amelia while hoping his arousal wasn't too obvious. Then a glance showed that Stephen was smirking at him and when the teacher wasn't looking he even gave him a wink! Hot shame engulfed Graham. Embarrassed he moved away and pretended to work.

To Graham's annoyance, Miss McLeod stayed with them and no further opportunity to flirt arose during that lesson. Then it was lunch, and detention for Graham to do that homework he had neglected. That made him even more annoyed, and he sat in the 'Time-Out' room in a state of anger and frustration.

Geography did no good either as Mr Conkey kept walking around the room checking their work as they drew maps of Europe. Mr Conkey was in his army uniform, which reminded Graham that it was Wednesday afternoon- which meant Army Cadets.

Maths B followed, and with it more trouble. Graham had not done his Maths B homework properly and Mr Ritter was not the teacher to overlook this.

"You can stay in and finish it," he instructed. "And don't bother to bring it to me until it is correct. And that applies to you others who haven't done it as well. That is you Bell, and you McDougal, and you pair of clowns down the back."

"Please sir, I have to go to Cadets," Graham said.

Mr Ritter looked at him with a surprised expression. "Yes, I'd heard that. Sorry, you must finish your homework."

To his own amazement, Graham felt deeply worried at being late for Cadets. He settled to working as fast as he could. But not fast enough to make up all the backlog!

Thus, when the final bell went Graham found himself moved to sit beside Stephen, who also appealed unsuccessfully that he would be late for Cadets.

"Too bad, Bell. You can explain that to the sergeant major, the same as Kirk. Work comes first. Now get on with it."

Seeing no option, the boys settled to work. It took half an hour to get the task completed and during the last fifteen minutes of this they could hear, and partly see, the cadet unit having its administrative parade.

"We are going to be late," Graham said to Stephen, who was still in school uniform.

"Don't care," Stephen replied. "I wasn't going anyway."

"What were you going to do?"

"Go downtown. There's something I want," Stephen replied.

"Won't you get into trouble?" Graham asked anxiously.

Stephen curled his lip and shook his head. "Nah! If I only miss a few parades the officers won't report to mum and dad. It's only when you miss three or four parades in a row that they send a letter home to your parents."

"Don't take risks, Steve," Graham replied.

"Stop worrying. Besides, you are the one who's taking the risks," Stephen replied.

Graham blushed. "What do you mean?" he asked, although he thought he had a pretty good idea.

And he was right. Stephen grinned and said, "Playing around with Millie. Hear that bloke out there shouting the orders? That's Warrant Officer Howley, her 'Old Man'. Tough as nails, regular army type. If he found out he'd de-knacker you before you even knew what was happening."

Graham blushed and tried to deny he had done anything, but that just made Stephen grin even more. Another shouted command made Graham glance out the window. Warrant Officer Howley was striding along beside the platoons as they stood in lines. He was dressed in camouflage uniform, slouch hat and boots and certainly looked every inch a soldier. Watching him snap at a platoon of cadets caused Graham's resentment of authority to rise. Warrant Officer Howley was everything he hated: an authoritarian bully. But he also looked tough; not a man to take foolish risks with. A feeling of uneasiness curdled in Graham's stomach.

Ten minutes later, the two boys took their work to the staff room where Mr Ritter waited. To Graham's relief, he had completed the task satisfactorily and he and Stephen were allowed to go.

As the two boys went down the stairs, Stephen grabbed Graham's sleeve. "This way, quick! I don't want the Officers to see me."

Graham looked towards the cadets with a mixture of interest and hostility. They were just marching off the grass quadrangle they used as a parade ground. He could see 2 Platoon and felt a twinge of guilt, knowing he should be marching in the ranks with the others.

"I'm going to get changed into uniform," he said.

"Suit yourself. Just don't dob me in," Stephen said.

He then turned and walked off around the next building. Graham hesitated, then walked over to where 2 Platoon would have to pass. As they did Sgt Masters saw Graham.

"You coming to cadets, Cadet Kirk?" he asked.

"Yes sergeant. I got kept in. I'll just change into uniform."

"You are late, so hurry up! We will be down at the oval," Sgt Masters replied.

Feeling quite resentful Graham did as he was told. It took ten minutes to change, have a drink and walk to the oval. He was torn between going slow out of rebelliousness and fear of being in more trouble if he was too late. But when he arrived there, he was thrilled to see that the cadets were being issued with weapons from the back of a truck. Warrant Officer Howley and an army corporal were there.

Warrant Officer Howley! Graham thought, his guilty conscience pricking him. *I hope he doesn't learn what Millie and I have been up to!*

Feeling slightly uneasy, Graham moved forward to join the others. A glance showed Graham that the weapons were Steyr rifles. He felt a surge of interest and was glad that he had decided not to go with Stephen. Hoping his lateness would not be punished he reported to Sgt Masters. To his relief, Sgt Masters just nodded and told him to stand in line with the others.

Five minutes later, Graham was handed a Steyr and moved to join his section. Another army corporal, wearing webbing and bush hat, was there and he took over the squad from Cpl Grenfell, who fell in to join the lesson.

For Graham it was a revelation. The regular army corporal was a very good instructor. His voice had a real snap of command in it and he obviously knew what he was talking about. He talked them through safety precautions and then practiced them over and over till they got it right.

"Trigger fingers!" he said repeatedly. "The sign of a good, well-trained soldier, one who is safe to be with, is one who keeps his trigger finger straight and off the trigger; until such time as he is about to fire the weapon. Got that?"

"Yes corporal," they chorused.

"Good. Then let's practice it again. Straighten those fingers and keep them off that trigger. Now, let's go on with the 'Degrees of weapon readiness'. Watch as I demonstrate the 'Load'."

Graham went to copy the movement. The corporal saw this and snapped, "I said watch! Don't do anything. Wait till I tell you. During weapons lessons never do anything until you are told. Now stand still and if you do nothing else in life, watch the demonstrations. Now watch!"

Graham flamed red with embarrassment and shame. This was only partly eased when the corporal snapped at another cadet, "Stop waving that bloody rifle around! Hold it still and keep it pointing away from other people. Remember your muzzle awareness. We are teaching safe weapon handling here. I tell you, when you are on active service don't worry too much about the enemy. It's the bloody idiots in your own army with loaded guns who are more of a danger! Now keep the damned things still."

And so the lesson went on. Graham was thrilled to be learning to handle a real army rifle and he paid close attention. After that first stinging rebuke he tried his hardest to do everything right and burned with shame when he forgot to apply the safety catch after one practice. All the time his mind took in the feel and smell of the rifle. He had never associated rifles with smell before but now realised the oil used to stop them rusting gave them a very distinctive odour. He also discovered that handling such a well-designed combination of plastic and steel was a pleasing tactile experience.

The weapon training went on for both periods. At the end of that time Graham felt he had really learned something. He wished the training would go on longer and kept handling the rifle as long as he could.

As he stood in line to hand the rifle back, Warrant Officer Howley came along and spoke to him, "Well son, how did you like that?"

"Great sir! It is a really good weapon. It sort of feels right."

Warrant Officer Howley chuckled. "Too right it does. It is a damn good rifle, better than the old SLRs I used in Makasang. You can actually hit things with this. Mind you, it doesn't have quite the same stopping power at longer ranges."

Graham was interested in the technical details and wished he knew more so that he could contribute intelligently to the conversation. Instead all he could do was nod and agree. As he handed the rifle back, he asked, "When do we get to train with them again?"

"When do we get to train with them again, *sir*," Warrant Officer Howley replied.

"Sir?" Graham was puzzled.

"You call warrant officers sir or ma'am," Warrant Officer Howley said in a firm voice.

For a moment Graham flamed with a mixture of resentment and embarrassment. Then he took a deep breath. "When do we get to train with the rifles again, sir?" he forced himself to say.

"Annual Camp in September," Warrant Officer Howley replied. "You will be put through the whole training program so that you can fire them later in the year."

That was interesting news to Graham. Despite his antagonism, he felt a flicker of interest in going to the Annual Camp, now only a month away. He took his place in the ranks and talked enthusiastically about the rifle to the other cadets. By now it was obvious they had already accepted him as part of the section, and he felt no stigma at being only a new recruit. Gwen Copeland in particular was friendly to him.

On the dismissal parade Graham felt much better. Life was going well for a change. He went home feeling very happy. At home he stayed in his uniform till bath time. After tea he settled to do his homework without having to be prompted. Not only was he happy but did not want to be grounded.

Hopes of being alone with Amelia fuelled his efforts.

Chapter 15

IN TROUBLE AGAIN

On Thursday at school Graham got a rude shock. As soon as he sat down next to Amelia, all keen for more thrills, she looked at him anxiously and asked, "Do you really like me, Graham?"

Graham was surprised. "Yes, I do," he replied.

"You aren't just saying that?"

"No, I really like you," Graham replied. He was tempted to say he loved her but did not. Then he voiced his anxious hopes. "Do you... do you still want to... to do it?"

Amelia nodded. "Yes, I really do. I... I... need it," she added, which was another lesson in life for Graham.

That sent Graham's hopes soaring again, and he glanced around to check if they would be overheard.

"When?" he croaked, his lust surging along with is hopes.

"What about the weekend?" Amelia replied. "I am allowed to go to the movies on Saturday night with a group of girls. Same as last time."

"What about that party tomorrow night?" Graham asked. Now that his hopes were up, he felt driven to act as soon as possible.

Amelia nodded. "Yes, there's a chance we could go to a party at Christine's tomorrow night," she said.

"What sort of party?" Graham asked, his mind racing with options.

Friday night meant Scouts, but he was losing interest in them. *If I ask mum if I can go to a party, she will want to know all the details,* he thought. From that came the germ of an idea that made him squirm with shame. *I could tell her I am going to Scouts and go to the party instead.*

Amelia shrugged. "Her big brother's birthday, I think. He's in Year 11."

"Will we be allowed to come?" Graham queried, now assailed with doubts about he might be received as an uninvited Year 9 at a Year 11 gathering.

"I'll ask," Amelia replied. "I know a couple of the girls in our class are going."

They left it at that and continued on to the classroom, Graham's imagination fantasising about what might happen on Friday night. First after lunch was Physics. By then Graham was a-tingle with frustrated lust. As soon as the lesson was well underway, both pressed on each other under the desk.

Greatly daring, Graham lightly stroked her leg through her skirt and when she just purred with pleasure he got bolder. After a few minutes he had took courage and pushed her skirt up her leg. He was then able to slide his hand around and down onto the warm, silken smooth skin of her inner thigh. She responded by pressing against him and placing her hand on his leg.

Suddenly Graham sensed something was wrong. He glanced up over Amelia's head, and froze in shock. Miss Tate was standing in the aisle beside Amelia and was staring down at him, her lips set in grim disapproval.

Graham stared at Miss Tate aghast. A wave of absolute fear surged through him. It was like being doused in ice water. She was standing hands on hips and watching. Amelia also looked up and let out a little cry, instantly withdrawing her hand.

Done for! Graham thought in panic. *Caught in the act!*

He opened his mouth, but no sound came. Despite his shock he had the presence of mind to move his hand.

Miss Tate leaned over, putting her face close to theirs. "Get on with your work you two. And I'll see you both at the end of the lesson," she hissed.

Graham could only nod and cringe. He felt he was shrivelling in his seat. It took a moment for him to realise that the teacher had not flown into a rage or put on a big scene. For a long minute they both stared up at the teacher, hearts pounding and gripped by mounting panic. Dread of the awful consequences which must follow swamped Graham's consciousness.

It won't be boarding school, it will be Lotus Glen Prison! he thought in horror.

But then Miss Tate turned her back and began snapping at Rosemary and Christine, "And you two stop talking and get on with your work as well!"

The teacher stood next to Amelia with her back to them and snapped at several other students around the room, including Stephen who was craning to see what was going on.

Graham sat as though stunned. *What will happen next?* he fretted, his stomach churning with anxiety.

His mind raced, hastily examining various awful options. What would he say to Mr Fitz? To the Principal? To his mother? And worse still, to his father? It was enough to make him sick just contemplating it. But still Miss Tate did not order them both to the office; and there was no outburst of the sort Graham expected. Instead the teacher walked slowly back along the aisle checking other people's books and telling them to get on with their work.

At the front, Miss Tate turned and met his eye. Her face betrayed no emotion. Graham was still panting with anxiety, but he was puzzled too.

Maybe she doesn't want to make a big scene in the class which might embarrass people, he decided. *So she will send us to the office at the end of the lesson.*

That was even worse. They had to sit and work, knowing that the sword was hanging over their necks. By the time the lesson finished, Graham was so sick he thought he was going to throw up and Amelia was sobbing quietly.

As soon as the bell went Miss Tate called out, "Graham and Amelia, stay there and finish that exercise. The others may go."

The class filed out, Stephen and Rosemary giving them anxious and curious glances as they went. Graham just wished the floor would open up so he could drop through. When everyone was gone Miss Tate came walking slowly along the aisle towards them, every footstep distinct. She halted facing them, hands on hips and shook her head.

There was a moment of silence, then she said, "What's the matter with you two? Can't you find a quiet corner at lunch time to do that?"

Graham was shocked. For a minute he tried to make sense of what she was saying. She went on, "For heaven's sake! Don't you realise how much trouble you could be in? Organise your lives to do your loving in private. If any of the others had seen that, I would have had no option but to report you to the office. Do you know what that would mean?"

"Yes miss," Graham croaked.

"Yes miss!" she mimicked. "Police! And Juvenile court! And angry and ashamed parents! Don't be so stupid!"

Graham cringed under the lash of her tongue, but managed to look her in the eye. She went on, "Are you two lovers?"

"No miss," they both chorused.

Miss Tate shook her head. "Well, the way you are carrying on you soon will be! I hope you know what you are doing."

"Yes miss."

"I hope you are planning on taking some precautions. Are you on the pill, Amelia?"

Amelia sobbed and shook her head. "No miss. My mum and dad would kill me if I tried that."

"They are more liable to kill you if you get pregnant!" Miss Tate snapped. "Have you got any condoms?"

Graham nodded and burned with embarrassment. Miss Tate met his eye again. He was just starting to grasp the fact that perhaps she wasn't going to send them to the office.

"Well, that's something. Now, for heaven's sake kids, be careful and don't be silly. And don't you dare put me on a spot like that again. Don't do dumb things in my classroom."

"No miss," they replied.

"Now get going," she said.

Graham sat and gaped. Then he swallowed and asked, "Aren't you going to send us to the office, miss?"

Miss Tate shook her head. "No, not if you will promise not to say anything about this to any other students."

"No miss!" Graham couldn't believe his ears. He had expected being called a disgusting, filthy little boy. He could not understand. "But... but...?"

"You are wondering why not?" Miss Tate asked. "Because I doubt if it would make you into better people. All it would do would be to destroy both of you. Poor Amelia would have her reputation ruined and her parent's upset, and you would be in even more trouble, Graham. And it would not help either of you. So let's leave it at that. Now get going."

The pair fled. They had History with Mr Conkey next, but they took several minutes to recover. Neither could believe their luck and said so. Graham felt weak in the legs and wanted to sit down.

Amelia recovered first. "That was close!" she said, wiping tears from her cheeks.

"Close! I thought my goose was cooked," Graham replied.

"I wonder why she didn't send us to the office?" Amelia said.

Graham thought he could answer that. "I think what she said is what she believes. And I don't think she was shocked. From what I've heard, her nickname isn't 'Miss Tart' for nothing."

"Oh that's a bit unkind," Amelia defended.

"Not from what Alex has told me. He reckons he's seen her drunk and half undressed downtown with a couple of men," Graham replied.

Amelia's eyes lit up with interest. "Do you think that is likely?"

"Yes, I do. Steve and I saw her down near the wharf a few weeks ago. She was pissed as a parrot and being groped by two Yankee sailors and all she was doing was giggling."

Amelia's eyes widened and her mouth opened in scandalized interest. She obviously wanted to talk, but Graham grabbed her arm.

"Come on. We'd better get to History or we will be in more trouble."

As it was Mr Conkey asked where they'd been.

"Miss Tate wanted to speak to us, sir," Graham replied.

He saw no point in not stating the truth. Mr Conkey accepted this and told them to sit and start work. As they walked to their seats Graham met Stephen's eye. Stephen smirked knowingly, which annoyed him. Then he met Rosemary's eye. Hers were alive with curiosity but Amelia said nothing. For the next half hour Graham just sat and concentrated in work, with some speculation about the reprieve they had just been granted. He half expected Miss Tate to change her mind and for him and Amelia to be summoned to the office. But nothing happened.

After the last bell went, Graham asked Amelia, "When can we meet again? I want to be with you."

"Not tonight," Amelia replied. "But I will ask Christine if we can come to her brother's party tomorrow night. And if I ask Rosemary, we might be able to meet at the pictures again like we did last Saturday night."

Graham's hopes soared. "I'd like that. Please ask her."

So it was agreed. Amelia went off and Graham left quickly so as not to have to talk to Stephen. He walked directly home and spent the next few hours walking his dog and pondering the day's events.

Friday was the inter-house Sports Carnival. Graham had contemplated wagging school with Amelia but decided this was not a good plan.

They always make a careful check of the roll, he thought gloomily.

Still, something might be possible. Besides, he always enjoyed Sports Day because all the girls ran around in short sports dresses.

Amelia certainly had a short sports dress. The moment he saw her, Graham felt his pulses race.

She looks really horny, he thought noting that her dress was so short it barely covered her.

Better still, she beamed at him and he felt as though the sun had come out again. He began to get aroused. This had the potential to be quite embarrassing and he was hotly conscious that a condom rested snugly in his back pocket.

But Amelia was in a different house, so they were separated for the first hour while there were roll calls, nominations, and movement to the oval. Once the carnival was under way, Graham sought Amelia out; only to find her sitting with Lorna and Stephen. Graham hid his irritation and sat down with them. For a while they talked and watched.

Then Graham said quietly, “Why don’t we go somewhere more private?”

Amelia nodded. “Good idea. Where?”

To Graham’s annoyance Stephen said, “We could go back up to the school somewhere.”

Lorna shook her head. “Too many teachers watching,” she pointed out.

Graham looked around. A thousand students were walking around, running, jumping, throwing discus, shot put and javelins.

“Nobody will notice us in this crowd,” he said.

“Yeah, but where can we go?” Stephen asked.

“Behind the swimming pool?” Graham suggested.

“Good idea. Let’s go,” Stephen agreed.

He stood up and pulled Lorna to her feet. Graham was reluctant to get up because he was aroused but he stood up and started walking with the others. They sauntered along and Graham used all his willpower to keep his body under some sort of control. Avoiding the teachers watching for people sneaking away took a bit of doing, but by waiting till they were busy with another band of would-be escapees, the friends managed to slip behind the sports shed and then off behind the first of the Manual Arts buildings.

By a circuitous route they arrived at the back of the swimming pool. This was an area of trees and gardens about five metres broad by fifty long. Beyond were the school fence and then a street with houses beyond it. Finding a shady spot on the grassy bank they seated themselves. Graham sat on the mound facing the street. Stephen sat beside him with Lorna on his left. Amelia spread a towel in front of Graham and sat on that.

They began chatting but all the while Graham felt his body responding to Amelia's nearness and he silently wished Stephen and Lorna to the devil. *I wish they'd go somewhere else,* he thought in frustration.

Stephen produced cigarettes. Again Graham declined. So did Amelia, but Lorna took one and lit up. Some Year 8 boys appeared but were told bluntly by Stephen to "Bugger off, or else!" They did and the four settled down to tell jokes and talk.

A few minutes later, two more Year 8s appeared. It was Willy Williams, the school's 'Mad Scientist' and a black-haired girl. Stephen quickly hid his cigarette.

"Bugger off Willy, find somewhere else," he called.

Willy and the girl both blushed and looked embarrassed but did so.

Stephen steered the conversation around to sex and told some very crude jokes, which made Graham blush, but at which Amelia giggled. All the time he kept wishing the others would leave and he thought, from her facial expressions and eyes, that Amelia wanted that as well.

"What are you people up to?" boomed a voice.

Graham looked along to the end of the pool and felt his heart skip a beat. *Oh no! Mr Fitz!*

The deputy principal came striding towards them with a face like thunder. Graham felt the sour bile of nausea swirl in his stomach and hung his head. Mr Fitz stopped and stood facing them, hands on hips.

"I asked what you were doing here?" he rasped.

"Just talking, sir," Stephen replied.

"Smoking you mean!" Mr Fitz snapped. "Stand up and open your hands."

The others scrambled to their feet. Reluctantly Graham did so, trying to hide his aroused condition as he did. Mr Fitz's eyes flickered to meet his and his lips compressed into a thin line. Shame coursed through Graham. But Mr Fitz then looked down at Stephen's hand. This was closed up but a wisp of smoke curled up from between his fingers.

Mr Fitz's face became even grimmer. "As I said, smoking. Where's yours, Kirk?"

"I don't smoke sir," Graham replied.

Stephen nodded. "That's right, sir," he added.

Mr Fitz turned to Amelia. "What's your name, girlie?"

"Howley, sir. Amelia Howley," Amelia replied.

"Oh yes. I remember. I know your father. He is Warrant Officer Howley who helps with the Army Cadets. Well, he won't be impressed to find that you have joined the smokers lurking at the back of the dunny!"

Graham resented that insinuation but knew it was true. He stood unhappily trying to think of what to say while Amelia insisted she was not a smoker and was only talking.

At that Graham spoke up. "That's not true, sir. She wasn't doing anything wrong," he put in.

"Speak when you are spoken to boy!" Mr Fitz thundered.

Graham swallowed and went red, partly from indignation and partly from embarrassment. Mr Fitz then asked each in turn if Amelia had been smoking. They all said no.

Mr Fitz nodded, then said; "Even so, you all know you should be down on the oval watching the sports, not hiding here behind the pool. Bell, you and Lorna go to the office and wait for me. You other two, get back to the oval!"

"Yes sir!" they chorused.

Graham felt sorry for Stephen and Lorna but did as he was told, relieved to be off the hook once again. By this time his arousal had quite gone, shrivelled by fear, and he was able to walk normally.

Once they were back at the sports, Graham sat beside Amelia and asked if she had asked Christine about her brother's party tonight.

Amelia nodded. "Yes, I have. She says we are welcome. Will you be able to come?"

"I'll be there," Graham replied, fierce desire surging in him. "What about you?"

Amelia nodded but looked thoughtful. "I think so. Dad will be away at some Army Reserve weekend thing and mum is usually okay."

"Where does Chrissie live?" Graham asked.

Amelia told him and Graham nodded. Luckily it was not far from the school. In his mind he began to plan how to get there instead of going to

Scouts. He asked, "What about the movies tomorrow night? Have you arranged to go with Lorna tomorrow night?"

"Yes, Saturday night. Can you make it?" Amelia replied.

"I'll be there," Graham replied.

He did not know if his mother would give him permission; but what he was sure of was that he was going to meet Amelia, come hell or high water. So he arranged times and places. Amelia agreed to meet him and gave him a winning smile. Graham felt his heart leap with hope.

If tonight isn't the big night, then it might be Saturday night, he thought.

After lunch, Stephen and Lorna returned from the office. Graham raised his eyebrows. "What happened?"

"Aw nothing much. Bloody Old Fitz just gave us lunch time detention next week."

"What you doing Saturday night?" Graham asked.

"Nothing, why?"

Graham outlined his plan. Stephen turned to Lorna. "Okay if I come too?" he asked.

"Sure. The more the merrier," Lorna replied.

Chapter 16

COURAGE?

Graham could hardly contain himself for the rest of the day. What was consuming his mental efforts was plotting how to get out of Scouts so he could go to the party. What he was sure of was that he did not want to ask his mother.

There will be too many questions that I can't answer. She will just say no, he decided.

As soon as school finished, Graham started to put his plan into action, but not without frequent niggles of guilt at planning to deceive his mother. Luckily, she wasn't home so he was able to quickly pack some suitable party clothes, thanking his lucky stars it was going to be a very casual party. Then he leapt on his bike with the bag of clothes and pedalled fast the four blocks to the old cemetery near the Scout Den. His plan was to hide them there and later change.

But even that simple task caused him some emotional grief. As he placed his bike in the long grass of the overgrown cemetery, he looked around, his guilty thoughts making him feel that every person was watching him. Nobody appeared to be, but he still blushed with shame as a car went past.

He then experienced another mild twinge of guilt as he passed his great, great grandfather's tombstone. It was in the first row of headstones, the Kirk's being among the very earliest British pioneers in the district.

Do ghosts know what we do? Graham wondered. But his lustful desire was stronger than any such concern, so he shrugged and continued on.

Then a much stronger fear delayed him. The grass was long and there were lots of weeds. *There will be snakes,* he thought, pausing before moving his foot forward.

Three years before, while playing in a vacant allotment in McManus Street with his friend Victor, he had been bitten by a snake. Now that memory flooded back to momentarily paralyse him. The reptile had been an indeterminate brown and had left two obvious puncture marks on the side of his bare foot. He had walked out to Victor's and then carried out the First Aid as he had been taught in Scouts while Victor had phoned for an ambulance. There had been a rush to hospital and a night in their care, but no obvious symptoms. The hospital tests concluded that the snake had not injected any venom. But the psychological trauma of the event still lingered.

He had planned to hide the clothes well away from the road but now opted to just put them behind the next big tombstone. His other notion of bringing Amelia there as a private place he now rejected.

She will probably be freaked out, he thought.

A dozen silly jokes about sex in cemeteries also flitted across his mind to confirm that decision. Still staring fearfully into the long grass as he moved each foot, he made his way back out to where his bicycle lay on the mowed verge near the railway crossing. Still feeling shame at his actions possibly being noted from the houses across the street he hopped on his bike and hurried home.

Back at home he acted cool and innocent, but still felt very anxious and ashamed. After having afternoon tea he lay on his bed and read *The Phantom* and ate the chocolate his mother handed him when she arrived home.

Forcing a smile and thanking her caused him another wash of shame. But now he was determined. *If I don't turn up Millie might think I am a coward and I might not get the opportunity again,* he reasoned, dimly fretting that he might actually be a coward.

That night he was allowed to go to Scouts on his bike. That pleased Graham even more as it made it easier to carry out his plan. *I don't even have to go to the Scout Den,* he thought.

That had been one of the holes in his plan as he had pictured himself being dropped off by his mother from her car and immediately meeting other people who would know he had arrived there.

By the time he came to have a shower and get into his Scout uniform Graham was almost shaking with emotion. He was perspiring and felt sure that his mother or Kylie would notice. He was also almost continually aroused as hopeful fantasies flitted across his mind. With an effort he forced himself to act relaxed, and as he went down the stairs to get his bike he gave a very nonchalant, "See ya!"

Phew! That was a bit stressful, he thought.

But he was sure he had carried off that part of the plan alright. But now the tension began to build again. Going to a party at a strange house now loomed as an even bigger challenge.

But first the cemetery in the dark! Even that turned out to be a test of courage. On arriving at the Groves Street end of the cemetery, Graham stopped and hopped off his bike to look around. He did not want to be seen by a person going to Scouts. The lighted Scout Den was only a hundred metres away across the railway line.

Seeing no-one, he turned his attention to the cemetery. Luckily it had no fence, but it also had no paths or lights. Worse still, it took up almost an entire block and had been neglected for many years by the council so it was full of trees and long grass, the natural Savannah Woodland reasserting itself. And he had to walk into that in the dark!

For a moment Graham stood remembering how it had been an initiation test forced on him (without the knowledge of the Scoutmasters!) by older Scouts when he had first joined. The challenge had been to walk diagonally through the old cemetery from the McLeod Street corner to Groves Street near the railway, alone and without a torch.

At the time, Graham had found he had been more afraid of snakes than ghosts and that had been before he was bitten. That now became the case again. Very gingerly he pushed his bike ahead of him into the long grass between the tombstones, his heart beating very fast and every nerve alert. He gave great, great grandfather a passing nod and again felt a flush of shame. Now he regretted hiding his bag of clothes so far into the cemetery. It hadn't seemed very far in daylight!

And despite trying to brush aside notions of ghosts, the knowledge that he was in a cemetery among hundreds of dead people, with the monuments and headstones showing white in the light from the distant streetlights and starlight, caused the hair on the back of his neck to stand on end. Several times he looked anxiously around and found he was breathing very rapidly.

Having found the clothes bag Graham leaned his bike against a tree and proceeded to change. And now, perversely, he was glad he was so far from the road as several cars went past, their headlights flickering through the trees and causing him to duck down in the long grass.

Bloody Spear Grass!

He swore as several sharp grass seeds stuck into him. It only took a few minutes to change but then he discovered that he had several grass seeds sticking through his underpants! Annoyed he groped for them and then adjusted his clothing.

Oh! I hope I look alright, he fretted.

Next was the challenge of walking back through the long grass to the road, and of avoiding being seen by the cars that drove past. There seemed to be a lot but in fact were only five. But two pulled in at the Scout Den and Graham gulped with anxiety as he saw people he knew get out. Seeing 'Silver Wolf' appear at the door of the Den caused him another flush of shame and he hesitated and almost changed his mind.

But lust had him in its grip and without conscious effort erotic images of Amelia were conjured up. She won. After taking a few deep gulps of air Graham walked out of the cemetery and he hurried away from the Scout Den. So afraid of discovery was he that he almost broke into a run, but the knowledge that such a move would make him sweat held him to a fast walk.

I don't want to stink of B.O., he reasoned.

Five minutes later he was standing on the grass footpath outside Christine's. The house was a typical old Queenslander, weatherboard and on high stumps. There were lights on upstairs but no sign of anyone. The sound of voices from the backyard led Graham to a grass driveway that went along the side of the house. Now almost gasping with anxiety, he made himself walk along it.

As he approached the backyard, which was lit by strings of coloured party lights, Graham saw groups of boys and girls standing talking and laughing. Several he recognised as being Year 11s which disconcerted him a little and he faltered in his step. Then he saw a very pretty Year 10 girl he thought was named Marlene and he made himself keep walking.

As more of the backyard came into view, he was assailed by a series of mixed emotions. The place was crowded. There looked to be several dozen people there, some sitting at picnic tables and others standing around in groups. A few were busy at a barbeque in the far corner. The numbers simultaneously daunted him and provided hope. At least he could hide in the crowd!

He noted a Year 11 named Nigel who had his arm around a shapely girl from Year 11. She wore a halter top that exposed half her breasts. To Graham's already aroused state the sight added more stimulation. At the back corner of the house he stopped and looked around. To his relief, he noted that most of the boys were even more casually dressed than he was, many just in shorts and T-shirts. The girls had, as usual, made more of an effort and looked very attractive.

And heavens! Isn't there a lot of bare flesh showing, he thought, noting girls just in shorts and bikini tops or in jeans and cut-off T-shorts that left their mid-riff bare. The sights were very stimulating. But where was Amelia?

Anxiously, Graham scanned the crowd, noting girls from Year12, Year 11 and Year 10. But the only girl from Year 9 he could see was Lucy from 9D. That sent Graham's anxiety shooting up. For a moment he stood there irresolute, thinking that he might have made a mistake and should leave before anyone noticed.

At that moment, Christine appeared from under the house. As luck would have it she looked his way and their eyes met. A puzzled look, half frown, half smile, crossed her face and she turned and walked over.

"Hi Graham! Are you looking for Millie?"

Graham could only nod. Christine smiled and gestured for him to join the party. "I don't think she is here yet. Never mind, come and join the party. Would you like a drink?"

Put like that, Graham did not feel he could now just slink away so he walked across into the crowd towards where tables laden with drinks and Eskis stood along the far side of the lawn. As he did, several of the people looked at him and a few gave quizzical looks, but they were all people he recognised as going to his school.

At the drinks table Graham was immediately set a challenge. A Year 11 boy named Barry grinned at him and asked what he wanted to drink.

"Beer or spirits?" he said.

Sharp memories if his previous dinking session flashed into Graham's mind and he hesitated. Partly he was shocked that there was so much alcohol visible, as he knew it was against the law to provide alcohol to minors. But there did not appear to be any adults present and almost everyone he could see was holding a beer or a glass of what looked like wine or spirits.

Then he was challenged a second time. Again he hesitated. *If I get drunk and mum finds out it will be boarding school for me!* he thought.

So he summoned up some courage and shook his head.

"No thanks. My mum might smell it and I will be in deep shit."

"Ah, ya bloody weakie!" Barry retorted.

At that another Year 11: Hoolihan, Graham thought his name was, joined in. "Have a drink, ya little wart. It'll do ya good."

Again Graham shook his head, hotly aware that others were now looking and listening. As embarrassment built, he began to nerve himself to try to withdraw.

Christine saved him. "Stop picking on him you guys. Here Graham, have a fruit punch." She gestured to a large punch bowl full of yellow liquid.

Graham nodded and gratefully accepted a glass. But as soon as he took a sip, he knew he had been tricked. The punch was heavily spiked with alcohol and the fiery liquid burned in his mouth and he gasped. His reaction sent up a howl of laughter and even more people turned to look.

Which led to the next incident. Through the crowd pushed several Year 11 boys. Among them was Larsen! Larsen came to a halt facing him, his thumbs hooked belligerently in his belt.

"What are you doin' here ya little Year 9 toad?" he snarled.

Graham swallowed and found his mouth dry with fear. But before he could moisten it and answer Christine spoke up. "He's in my class," she snapped. "So leave him alone. We don't want any trouble at the party."

"Oh yeah?" Larsen retorted.

But he then shrugged and moved to get a beer, sneering at Graham as he did. His cronies all curled their lips and did likewise.

"Thanks," Graham whispered to Christine. "Maybe I'd better go?"

Christine shook her head. "No, stay a while. Millie might make it yet. It's only seven now," she said. "Here, I'll get you a softdrink."

So Graham stayed, standing quietly to one side, sipping a lemonade from time to time. Christine stayed with him for a few minutes and then moved off to chat to two Year 10 girls who arrived, dressed in flowing caftans and laden with presents.

There was a lot of loud talk and laughter and some boisterous cheering when an obviously drunk Year 11 boy fell backwards into a garden bed. Graham felt lonely and wished he hadn't come. But he stood there in hope. If Amelia arrived, they would not be staying at the party. He began to plan where they could go for a bit of privacy.

Half an hour later she had still not arrived. But another group of people had, among them some tough looking older youths. And with them was another girl from his class: Janet. The sight of her brought sharp memories swirling back of how she and her friend Thelma had invited him to a party the previous year and pretended to be friendly and willing but were, in fact, using him to pass false information to the police.[1] The memory of that rankled, and Graham took several deep breaths and again wondered if he should just leave. But Thelma wasn't with the group, just an older girl who Graham thought was Janet's big sister.

By then the party was in full swing, with music, loud chatter and apparently copious amounts of dink being consumed. It all made Graham feel very young and out of place. Half an hour went by and still no sign of Amelia.

And then he was really put to the test. Just near him he saw a Year 11 boy, Groves was it?, hand something to a Year 11 girl named Felicity. The boy placed it in the palm of her hand, and she lifted it up between her finger and thumb to look at it. Graham saw that it was a tiny white tablet.

Is that drugs? Graham wondered.

Like everyone of his age, he had heard and read plenty about drugs at parties, but he had never been to one where they had been available, or at least not to his knowledge.

Anxiety swirled and he looked away, not wanting to be associated with anything like that. Out of the corner of his eye he watched Felicity slip the tablet into her mouth and then follow it with some drink. Graham had heard that mixing drugs and alcohol was not a good idea, and he became even more anxious. To calm himself he moved away along the garden to near the barbeque.

Only then did it occur to him that perhaps some of the shrieking and giggling and people looking unsteady on their feet might be because of drugs, not alcohol. He was appalled and determined to leave.

But as he began moving through the groups towards the driveway, he found a group blocking his path. They were all laughing and giggling and holding onto each other. Suddenly he found himself the centre of a circle of grinning faces. Barry stepped forward, swaying on his feet and put out his hand.

"Here's young Kirky, looking like he's lost his last penny. Here Kirky, have one of these. It'll do ya good."

---

[1] Read *The Boy and the Battleship* by C.R. Cummings

To Graham's surprise and horror he found one of the little white pills thrust into his hand. Such a mix of emotions filled him that for a few moments he was quite unable to speak or move. Topmost was fear, followed closely by the suspicion that he was being made the butt of some joke or set some test. He wasn't sure if it was to make sure he kept his mouth shut by simply implicating him, or whether Barry was just being friendly. But Graham also knew that such pills usually cost a fair amount of money, so he was confused.

Barry wouldn't just give them away, surely? he thought.

But now Barry was standing leaning on him but still sounding very friendly and affable. "Come on kid, have a go. You'll love it! You'll think you are the best in the whole world," he said.

Graham managed to force a smile, but his mind was racing. Different levels of fear were racing around inside his skull. Top of them was the anxiety that he might ruin his life. All those horror stories about kids who became addicted to drugs and then fell into crime or killed themselves with overdoses flitted across his consciousness. Coupled to that was the fear that he might actually really like the experience and that it might be an escape from his current misery.

The next level was concern about the effects of the drug. Not only was he afraid that he might like the drugs and succumb to them, but there was concern for his physical safety. In the few seconds while Barry grinned at him and urged him to take it, thoughts about the safety of what he was being offered flitted across Graham's mind. A class lecture came to mind in which a visiting police lecturer had pointed out that illegal drugs had no quality control.

"You have no idea who made it or what is in it," she had said. "And the drug pushers don't care about you. They just want your money."

Horror stories of kids dying disgusting deaths because of the toxic contents in the party drugs they had taken came to mind.

At the next level was fear of being thought a coward. Looking at all the watching faces he could only gulp. They were all older and would say things about him in school gossip. His pride and reputation were suddenly very much on the line again.

And there were also the possible legal consequences. If the police found out he would be really in trouble. Images of Constable O'Neill's grim face caused his bowels to squelch.

And there they all were, urging him to take it, daring him to take it. The eyes in the faces opposite seemed to glitter, partly from the party lights but also he sensed with morbid curiosity and malice, the desire to see someone take a foolish risk.

Barry nudged him hard. "Well, come on ya little bugger! Take it!"

Graham managed to shake his head, unsure what expression was on his face. "No," he managed to croak.

"Why not? Are ya scared," Barry jeered.

Others joined in, calling for him to take it. Graham gulped deep breaths and knew he was embarrassed and scared. His gaze flicked around, looking for a way out. Under that peer pressure he was sorely tempted to take the pill. To his dismay, he was also tempted by his own curiosity as he wondered what it might feel like.

Several others began to jeer and call that he had no guts. "Weakie!" "Piker!" "Little sook!" "Coward!" they called.

It was the jibe 'coward!' that did it. Graham stiffened and blushed, then took a deep breath. Shaking his head and forcing a smile he stepped aside. "Sorry, no." He thrust the tablet back into Barry's palm.

Barry shrugged and took it, releasing him. Others sneered and jeered but then a youth fell against a table, bringing glasses and bottles crashing to the concrete patio. In the resulting yelling and cheering, Graham smiled again and went to step around, only to have a person reach out and grab his arm.

It was Janet. "Well, if it isn't little Mister Dobber Kirk, the copper's informant. Don't you say anything to anyone Kirk, or you will wish you'd never been born."

Graham looked at her and was appalled at the malice in her expression. But now he was determined, so he just returned her stare and pulled himself free. A moment later he was striding along the driveway. To his relief, no-one followed or tried to stop him. Instead chanting began as someone was urged by the mob to 'Drink! Drink! Drink it up!'

Out on the footpath Graham almost jogged away. He felt scared and shaken and saddened. People he had admired and looked up to had been revealed as very unpleasant personalities. And the jibes about his lack of courage really stung.

Am I a coward? he fretted. And Amelia had not arrived. Clearly, she was not coming. Pausing to check the time Graham saw that it was still not quite 8 O'clock. *Still an hour or so of Scouts to go. Should I go there?* He wondered.

But that meant making up a story to tell the Scout Masters. As he jogged along the street, Graham concocted a simple tale. But inside he felt bad, and he sighed. This business of satisfying lust was turning out to be a lot more unpleasant and stressful than he had anticipated!

There was then the challenge of walking into that long grass and risking the snakes but by then he was so emotionally wrung out he made himself do it. Ten minutes later, now clad in his Scout uniform again, Graham wheeled his bike in the front entrance to the Scout Den yard. To his relief, the whole troop were out on the front lawn playing a game of Chariots and his arrival was barely noticed. Graham parked his bike and made his way over to where 'Silver Wolf' was umpiring the game. 'Silver Wolf' just raised an eyebrow, so Graham told his lie.

"Had a puncture, sir," he said.

Inside he felt bad as he really liked and admired 'Silver Wolf'. He also hoped he wasn't blushing, that 'Silver Wolf' would take his red face and perspiration as a sign of him having hurried.

With the guilt gnawing at him, Graham joined in, his friends luckily giving him only cursory greetings and not asking any questions as they concentrated on the game.

During the break between activities Peter again broached the idea of a hike but again Graham put him off.

I've got more important things to do on Saturday nights than camp in the bush, he thought, hopeful images of Amelia filling his mind.

When he got home, there had to be more lies. Graham simply described a couple of activities at Scouts to imply that he had been there all the time, and luckily his mother did not suspect or question. But it made him feel even more torn and ashamed.

But lust over-rode that. The mere thought of what he hoped would happen the following night made him horny again. This condition came and went, and it was an intensely frustrated boy who finally dropped off to sleep after hours of hopeful fantasising.

Chapter 17

THE MOMENT ARISES

Saturday morning dragged by with Graham in a state of continual excitement as he did his chores. Luckily, he was able to sneak his party clothes in with the normal washing, which he had to hang out. Also luckily, they were just ordinary casual clothes so attracted no attention and Graham could only hope his mother did not think about when he might have worn them during the week.

Saturday afternoon was even worse as he had nothing much to do; and while he was sitting on the front veranda reading, he saw Andrew Collins and his sister Carmen ride past on their bikes on their way to Navy Cadets. The sight of their happy faces and white uniforms made Graham's mouth twist into a bitter scowl. If only! Once again, he cursed his defective eye.

All afternoon Graham was aroused. He had to hide this from Alex and sister Kylie. Both badgered him from time to time to join in various games and activities, but he ignored their requests. In mid-afternoon, Margaret came over and wanted to sit and talk to him. Graham gave gruff, mono-syllabic answers and felt a real heel, particularly when he thought about being with Amelia in a few hours.

After a while, Margaret retired with a hurt look in her eyes and Graham withdrew to the Ship Room to be alone. The afternoon crawled on, and it was with relief he heard Margaret leave. By then he had implemented his next plan, but not without more shame at lying.

I will tell mum I am going out with Stephen, but not where, he decided.

And he had snuck his good clothes out. They were put in a bag which he smuggled out to hide in the front garden when nobody was looking.

After tea he launched his plan. He cleaned his teeth and dressed in old shorts, shirt, and gym boots.

As he walked through the house, his mother raised an eyebrow. "Where are you off to?" she asked.

"Just going over to Steve's mum," he answered, his heart thumping rapidly with concern that she might forbid this.

She gave him a hard look for a minute but made no answer, so he kept walking, knowing he was blushing with shame. Lying was not something he enjoyed. But he was out of the house. Before she could call him back to ask more questions, he ran downstairs, collected his bike and the good clothes, and set off as fast as he could pedal.

The next problem was changing into the good clothes. All he could think to do was ride to school and hide in the shadows down at the oval to change. That got his heart going again as the school was patrolled by security and police to stop vandalism and break-ins. He struggled quickly out of his old clothes then rapidly dressed. In spite of his care to try to keep his good clothes clean, he noted a couple of scuff marks.

By this time he was excited and almost tingling with anticipation. He was very aroused, and when he transferred the condom to his trousers pocket he felt a sharp thrill. Fear and lust began to war in him.

Hiding his bike and bag in a garden bed he walked to town and was thankful it was a cool night so that he didn't perspire too much. All the way he was beset by gnawing fears that Amelia would not turn up.

But she was there, with Rosemary and Lorna. With a sigh of relief, Graham walked up to greet them, hoping his arousal wasn't obvious.

Amelia greeted him with a big smile and moved to hold his hand, and to snuggle against his arm. It felt wonderful and sent his emotions into turmoil again. Soon afterwards Stephen arrived. The teenagers stood talking in the foyer of the theatre till the chimes rang. They then purchased their tickets and went in.

This time there was no hesitation. Amelia went to the far end of an empty row near the back, with Graham on her left, then Rosemary, Stephen, and Lorna. They settled down and Amelia at once snuggled against Graham. They began to kiss and caress.

Amelia eased her head back and looked at Graham. "Oooh! You are keen tonight!" she whispered, then giggled.

Graham felt his pulses race and slid his hand over her shoulder. She responded by snuggling up to him. As soon as the lights were dimmed, they began to pash in earnest. For days he had been yearning for this moment and he could hardly restrain himself. She murmured her appreciation and responded. From time to time, Graham glanced around to check whether the others were watching and noted that Stephen was engaged in a passionate embrace with Lorna.

Amelia was so passionate that Graham was amazed, delighted, and a bit scared. As they kissed and caressed each other, he thought he was in heaven.

Emboldened by his surging lust he stopped kissing. "Can we go somewhere where we can... can..." he croaked.

"Oh yes!" Amelia gasped.

But she kissed him again and then bit him on the side of the neck, stirring his passions even more. For several minutes more they stroked and petted, and he was both delighted and amazed at the pleasure in these actions.

Finally he could stand it no longer. "Come on!" he said as desire surged in his veins. "Let's go."

Amelia released him and nodded. Both then stood up. Graham was now so aroused he no longer cared what other people thought.

Stephen stopped kissing Lorna and turned to them. "What are you two doing?"

"Going outside," Amelia replied.

"Can we come too?"

Amelia giggled. "If you like," she said.

Graham didn't want that. He was now at the stage where he just wanted to get Amelia alone. But he could not find the words to tell the others to stay. To his annoyance they all stood up.

Led by Lorna they walked outside, Graham feeling incredibly hot and puzzled about how to get Amelia away on her own. He wasn't sure how to handle the situation.

Outside the theatre, Lorna turned to look at them. "Where are we going?" she asked.

"The park," Amelia replied.

"What are we going to do there?" Lorna asked.

Stephen snickered. "Whatever you like," he replied.

Lorna let out a little shriek. "Ooh! That'll be nice. I'll bet you aren't game though," she replied.

Graham was astounded but Stephen laughed and Amelia gave a giggle. "We wanted to be on our own for a bit," Amelia commented.

"Oh why? What are you planning to do?" Lorna cried.

To Graham's embarrassment and dismay Amelia now said, "We just want to get to know each other."

"Are you planning to be naughty?" Lorna replied, her voice squeaking with interest before she burst into giggles.

"A bit," Amelia replied.

"So why can't we come too?" Lorna queried, again bursting into giggles.

Amelia giggled too and said, "Because I'm shy."

"Aw, we might learn something," Lorna replied.

Graham looked from one to the other and now detected a feeling of tension between them. He was now so inflamed he knew he wasn't thinking clearly.

"You might!" he snapped, nettled at being thwarted. Stephen shot him a sharp look, but he didn't care.

Lorna now increased the tension. "Were you two going to take your clothes off?" she asked. When Amelia did not answer Lorna let out a giggling gasp. "Oh you are, aren't you!"

"You can if you want to!" Amelia snapped, clearly not happy with the way the situation was developing.

"We all will," Lorna replied in a cool and challenging tone.

This provoked another outbreak of embarrassed giggling before Rosemary said, "I'll bet you aren't game."

Graham did not know if he liked the trend of events at all, or if it was all just a joke. Anxiety and excitement both swirled in his already heated emotions.

But when they reached the park, he soon learned that Lorna was not joking. Lorna said to Stephen, "Well, come on big boy. Show us what you've got."

Stephen chuckled. "Only if you show us yours too."

"Show you what?" Lorna queried.

"Everything. Strip off for us," Stephen replied.

Graham was astounded at Stephen's casual tone. He was even more astounded when Lorna replied, "Okay, but only if you all take your clothes off too. I don't want to be the only one."

Rosemary looked shocked and worried. She looked around and said, "It's too light here. People will see us."

Lorna scoffed. "Oh, don't be a scaredy cat!" she challenged.

At that moment, they were walking along the concrete path near the monument in the middle of the park.

"Where will we go?" Stephen asked.

Lorna pointed to their right front. "Over there under those trees." She led the way across to the same tree Graham and Amelia had been under the week before.

By now Graham was very annoyed. He wished he and Amelia were alone, but equally excited with the hope of seeing the girls naked.

As they came to a stop in the shadows, Rosemary shook her head. "Oh, I'm shy," she admitted.

"We will make it a game then," Lorna said. "Each of us will take off one item in turn."

So saying she slipped off a shoe. Stephen grinned and unlaced one of his shoes. Rosemary looked worried. "What if someone comes along?"

"We tell them to clear off or we will bash them," Lorna replied. Graham was amazed at her boldness.

Amelia was next. She also took off a shoe. So did Graham. Rosemary did the same. Lorna then took off her second shoe and all the others followed suit. Graham thought the game would end there, but Lorna undid her skirt and stepped out of it. By then he was feeling very excited but also scared. Stephen pulled off his trousers. Then Amelia took off her blouse, her bra showing white in the night. Rosemary reluctantly did likewise. Graham slipped off his shirt and stood self-consciously, hotly aware of the cool breeze on his bare skin. By then they were all breathlessly excited by the dare.

To Graham's delight and surprise, the game continued until all were naked or nearly so. In a state of intense arousal, he feasted his eyes on the girl's wonderful curvy shapes and thought he had never seen such beautiful sights. He felt the blood pound in his veins as his eyes strained to see all the details in the shadows.

Rosemary reluctantly took off her dress and it was obvious she wasn't enjoying the situation. But Amelia clearly was, and she snuggled against Graham. The touch of her warm flesh set him ablaze, and he rubbed his hands up and down her back and buttocks. Rosemary was reluctant to undress further.

Graham did not care and was now only interested in Amelia. He turned and put his arms around her, then drew her against him. She sighed and hugged him hard. It felt very nice, and they kissed and stroked each other, almost oblivious to the comments of the others.

I wish they would all go away! he thought with annoyance.

"Cops!" Stephen cried.

That penetrated. Graham looked hastily around, and his flustered gaze followed Stephen's pointing finger. A wave of icy fear instantly swept over him. Stephen was right. A police car could be seen across on the Sheridan Street side of the park. It had pulled up and was shining a spotlight under the Mango Trees which lined the footpath. A policeman appeared on foot walking towards a person lying at the base of a tree. The police were a hundred metres away but that was way too close!

Rosemary gasped. "Get dressed, quick!" she squeaked.

There was a mad scramble to scoop up clothes.

"Not here. Over behind that shed," Stephen said.

He grabbed an armful of clothes and raced off through the garden beds. The others followed. Fifty frantic paces had them all around the corner of the brick shed. This put them right in the open beside Minnie Street and in the full glare of a streetlight, but they ignored this as they quickly pulled on clothes.

Graham was feeling torn up by fear and frustration. His arousal vanished. Rosemary kept looking around the corner of the shed as they struggled and fumbled with buttons and cloth which snagged in the most inconvenient places.

"They are driving this way!" she warned.

There was another scramble around the corner of the shed. By then most had at least tops and trousers or skirts on so it wasn't so bad. Graham stood on one leg to pull on a sock. Amelia leaned against him and held him. He slipped a shoe on and wrestled with the other sock.

Once again Rosemary warned them. "They are driving around the block!"

The teenagers scuttled to the next side of the shed, just in time to see a blinding beam of light slash across the garden where they had all been standing a few minutes before. As the police car came around the fourth side of the park, the group kept the building between it and the car. Thankfully, they watched it drive off towards town.

"Whew! That was close," Lorna cried. She burst out giggling.

Stephen joined in but Graham was too shaken to see anything funny. He just hugged Amelia.

Lorna turned to them. "We can keep going now," she said.

Graham was amazed, and scared. He now knew what a powerful emotion he was dealing with. He met Amelia's eyes and she nodded. Graham felt his desire surge afresh, but he shook his head.

"Not here. Someone in one of those houses over the road might have reported us and the cops could come back. Let's go somewhere safer."

"Where?" Stephen asked.

"The high school. Down at the oval," Graham replied.

"Good idea," Lorna agreed.

So they set off to walk the two blocks to the school oval, going along Grafton Street. Graham and Amelia walked with their arms around each other. That felt very nice to Graham, and he knew he was enjoying an experience he would remember for ever.

Suddenly a spotlight shone on them, and a car pulled up beside them. For a moment Graham went cold with fright and he took his arm from around Amelia. Then he went cold a second time. It was a police car. And the constable shining the spotlight on them was Constable O'Neil.

"What are you kids up to?" the policeman asked.

Graham felt sick with fear. What had he been up to! Only planning to break the law!

Stephen answered, "Just walking around."

Constable O'Neil shone the light full in Stephen's face. "Just walking around, eh Bell? Not up to any mischief tonight?"

"No," Stephen replied truculently.

Constable O'Neil grunted, looked hard at Graham, then said something to the other policeman in the car. The police car pulled out and drove on. Graham sighed with relief. Stephen swore.

Amelia looked curiously at Graham. "Do you know him?"

"Yes," Graham replied. He recounted the details of how they had met the police during their sailing races.

The group continued on but by then Graham was feeling intensely annoyed as well as frustrated.

I wish they would all just go away! he thought.

He urgently wanted to be alone with Amelia. In an attempt to achieve this he made a couple of hints but to his further annoyance he was ignored.

Once they arrived at the oval, they climbed over the fence and then went to the corner nearest the swimming pool under a large tree. It was still too open for comfort but there was almost no traffic on Grafton Street, and no pedestrians. An embarrassed silence settled, and they stood around self-consciously, Graham angrily wishing that he and Amelia were alone.

Stephen spoke first. "Well, come on you two. Get on with it," he urged.

Amelia responded sharply. "You can go for a walk or something," she snapped.

Lorna laughed but agreed. "Yeah, come on you guys, let's go back to the movies," she said.

To Graham's intense relief the others agreed, and after a few parting jibes they walked off. And now fear and lust surged in.

This is it! he thought.

But how to go about it? After a quick glance around to check that the others really had walked away, he moved closer to Amelia and they kissed.

Urgent desire was now causing the blood to pound in his brain. He was very aware that he was at one of those epochal life moments; that it could harm his whole life; that once it was done it could not be undone. Fear again warred with lust, and he wished he could back out with dignity, while his body surged with heated desire.

"Have you got a condom?" Amelia asked.

"Yes." Graham extracted it from his trouser pocket and held it up.

Embarrassment and distaste niggled at him, and he wished things were more private and romantic. The situation suddenly seemed very cold blooded and sordid. But he also sensed that if he did not take the opportunity, it might not come again.

Suddenly a bright light enveloped them. Graham looked around and felt a spasm of panic. Someone was shining a powerful torch on them!

Chapter 18

ANOTHER ATTEMPT

For an instant Graham froze in shock. On the edge of panic he sprang up and faced the light, fists raised. The torch shone directly into his eyes, blinding him.

A voice shouted at them, "You bloody kids, get out of here! Go somewhere else to do your pashing."

It was a night watchman. Graham stood facing him and slowly lowered his fists as waves of shock, shame and frustration surged within him.

They did not argue with the man. He took Amelia's hand and hurried to the side gate, annoyed that the man kept the torch beam on them all the way. A minute later they had fled out onto Grafton Street.

"Oh bugger him!" Amelia cried angrily as they walked quickly along the footpath back towards town.

Graham was acutely conscious of feeling intensely frustrated and annoyed but could not think of a new plan. He put his arm around Amelia.

"Sorry about that," he said.

She snuggled against him and shivered. "What will we do now?" she asked.

"Go back to the park?" Graham suggested. Desire was still surging in him and even after that shock he was still aroused.

But Amelia shook her head. "It is probably time we started back to the movies," she said.

Graham checked his watch in the light of a streetlight and was amazed to see it was already nine twenty. Where did the time go when you needed it most! Reluctantly, he agreed. And when they got to the park any hopes of continuing were dashed by meeting up with Stephen, Rosemary, and Lorna. They were walking along the pathway in the centre of the park and waved and called out. The group began walking back towards the movie theatre.

Desperate to win with Amelia, Graham clung to her hand and whispered, "Can I see you tomorrow?"

"I'd like to," Amelia answered. "But when?"

"In the morning maybe? I am supposed to go to church, but I could stay home and say I am sick," Graham suggested.

He blushed at the thought of lying but he was so intensely focused that he was prepared to do it.

"I will tell mum I am going to netball practice," Amelia said. "What time will we meet? And where?"

"About nine," Graham suggested. "At my place. Mum and Kylie will be at church and Alex usually goes out by then. We should have the place to ourselves for an hour."

"What about your father?" Amelia asked.

"He's away at sea. He won't be back for weeks," Graham replied.

So it was arranged. Graham put his arm around Amelia's waist and drew her close. She snuggled happily against him.

The group walked back to the theatre and were there by 9:45pm. Graham and Stephen both said their farewells, Graham pressing hard against Amelia.

"Tomorrow then," he whispered.

"You bet. We will manage it then," Amelia replied.

That put Graham over the moon. *I'm on a promise!* he marvelled. Thoughts of police and the law were swept aside by the urgency of his lust.

The boys left before the girl's parents arrived to pick them up. They walked back along Grafton Street to the high school. After scouting for the Security watchman Graham retrieved his clothes and bicycle. The boys talked for a while, mostly about sex and their chances with the girls.

"You are doing better than me," Stephen conceded. "If you don't win with Millie, then no bloke on earth has any chance."

Graham didn't want to discuss this as he had kept the planned meeting with Amelia a secret. Stephen then complicated this.

"What are you doing tomorrow?" he asked.

"In the morning? Going to church," Graham lied. He blushed with shame and was glad it was dark.

"What about after lunch then?" Stephen asked.

"Nothing. What do you want to do?"

"I was going to meet Lorna and Rosemary at the pool for a swim," Stephen replied.

"Yeah, that'll be okay," Graham replied.

By now he was urgently in need of relief, so he said goodnight and set off home. He was still dressed in his good clothes but did not know where to change so he rode home, hoping no-one would see him come in. In this he was lucky. He parked his bike under the house, quickly changed and hid his good clothes in the Ship Room and went upstairs.

His mother and Kylie were having supper in the kitchen, so he joined them. His mother smiled.

"Hello dear," she asked. "Did you have a good night?"

"Yes, Mum," Graham replied.

He did not want to answer questions so set about getting himself a cup of Milo. As soon as he had drunk this he went to the toilet. Feeling much relieved he took himself to his bed and lay on it to review the evening.

That got him all aroused again and he lay for hours fantasising and wondering what it would be like. At least now he was sure he would be able to do it.

"Oh I wish it was tomorrow!" he groaned.

* * *

His mother woke him the next morning.

"Come on lazy bones. It is eight O'clock. Get up or you will be late for church."

As usual when he woke Graham was aroused and he definitely did not want to get out from under the blankets as he realised, he was not wearing any pyjamas.

I must have kicked them off during the night, he thought.

Careful probing with his toes and feeling with his hands did not solve the problem. He could not seem to locate his pyjama pants. Anxiety about his mother learning this caused him to break into a cold sweat.

"I don't want to go, Mum. I don't feel very well," he replied.

"Are you sick?" his mother asked anxiously, bending to feel his forehead.

"A bit. More worn out though. I'd like to sleep in," Graham answered. As he said it, he felt a hot flush of shame and hated himself. To his relief, his mother did not make an issue of it.

"Alright. We will be home at the usual time. You can get your own breakfast."

"Thanks."

Graham snuggled thankfully down into the bed and closed his eyes. He began to fantasise about Amelia. For the next half hour he lay and listened anxiously. His mother and Kylie left at 8:30am in the car. Ten minutes later, Graham heard Alex wheel his bike to the front gate. Good! He got up to watch through the louvres to make sure Alex really was leaving. Then he lay back down again and waited in excited anticipation.

He woke with a start. *I must have fallen asleep,* he realised.

Amelia had woken him. As usual, the front door had been left open and she had walked in to stand beside his bed.

"Hi!" she greeted cheerfully. "I knocked and nobody answered, and I could see you sleeping there like a baby so I came in."

Graham rubbed his eyes and looked up at her. Amelia looked very fresh and attractive. She was wearing a short sports dress with a pattern of blue and white stripes on it, and it allowed a good view of almost all of her legs. These were close to his face and looked very inviting.

"You look lovely," he said, and meant it.

She smiled. "Thanks. Are we alone?"

Graham nodded. "Yes."

His heart began to thump at the implication of what she had asked sank in. *She wants it,* he thought. *Today is the big day!*

"Get up then."

But Graham felt unaccountably inhibited. Anxiety about legal consequences was added to shyness about exposing himself to her in broad daylight. Blushing he shook his head.

"You look the other way," he said.

Her face dimpled into a mischievous grin. "Have you been sleeping in the nuddy?"

Graham blushed again and nodded. Amelia laughed and grabbed at the sheet. "Show me."

Graham tried to stop her but wasn't fast enough. With a sharp tug, Amelia hauled the sheet and blankets aside. Graham clung to them and tried to cover himself. Amelia's eyes went wide, and she cried delightedly, "Oooh, you are too!"

A surge of excitement swept through Graham. He met her eyes, then accepted her dare. A storm of lust surged through him. He swung his legs off the bed.

"Come here!" he cried.

Amelia stepped back, giggling and wide eyed. She turned and started to run along the veranda. Graham instantly sprang after her. She didn't try very hard and he caught up with her in a couple of paces. As he grabbed her, she squealed and giggled even more.

By now Graham was fast losing control. He pulled her to him and started to kiss her. After a couple of heated minutes they fell onto the bed in a squirming, laughing heap, Graham on top. Millie giggled and gasped delightedly, encouraging him to continue.

For several minutes they enjoyed the kissing and caressing but at the front of Graham's consciousness was the desire to actually do it. Pausing with hammering heart and dry throat he met her eyes.

"Do you really want to?" he asked.

Amelia nodded. But still Graham hesitated. Fears and anxieties swirled amid the red mists of lust.

"You are sure?" he repeated.

"Yes. It's alright. I've done it before. I like it," she replied.

Still they hesitated, both panting and as anxious as they were aroused. Amelia met his eyes again.

"You can if you want. Just don't tell your mates please, and use a condom."

Condom! Graham thought. *Oh! What a fool I am!*

After another passionate kiss, he climbed off. For a minute they stared at each other, chests heaving with urgent desire and emotion.

"I'll get one," Graham replied.

He felt very self-conscious with her watching him as he walked to his bedside table. The condoms were hidden in the bottom drawer. He extracted one with shaking hands.

Half embarrassed, but still fuelled by burning desire, he opened the packet. Ripping it open he took out the condom. Then he froze.

Voices!

Alex!

Holy shit!

Graham moved to peer through the louvres. Yes, Alex and two of his mates. And they were dumping their bikes at the front gate!

"Quick! It's my brother!" Graham gasped.

Still holding the condom he turned and scuttled back to his bed. As he did, he spied his pyjamas lying on the floor. No time to even pull them on! He scooped them up and dived into bed, dragging the sheets up as he did. Amelia sprang up and sat on the side of the bed.

They were just in time. Alex and his mates, two Year 11 boys: Johnstone and Frazer, came through the front door. Alex stopped in surprise when he saw Amelia. He recognised her but did not know her name.

"Oh! G'day. Who are you? What are you up to little brother?"

Graham blushed fiercely. What had he been up to! The condom seemed to burn in the palm of his hand, and he surreptitiously pushed it up under his pillow.

Alex noted his discomfiture and grinned. "Have we disturbed you two in something?" he asked.

Graham noted the boys grinning and leering at Amelia who tried to pull her skirt over her legs. It was so short this was a failure.

Alex laughed. "You aren't sick, you little bugger! You sly dog! So that is why you didn't go to church eh?"

Graham wanted to deny it but knew he would be bright red with shame. Amelia sniffed and replied for him.

"Don't be crude. I just dropped in to say hello."

"Oh yeah!" Alex answered in a disbelieving tone. He laughed and met Graham's defiant gaze. "Give you something to confess about next time you do go to church though."

Oh my God yes! Guilt coursed through Graham, and he felt very torn. He was also acutely conscious he still had no pants on. *If Alex drags me out of bed like he sometimes does!* he thought anxiously.

But Alex made no move to do so. Instead, to Graham's intense annoyance he sat and began talking. Amelia was introduced and she did most of the talking. One of the boys, Johnstone, was in the army cadets.

"I know your dad: Warrant Officer Howley," he said.

The thought of Amelia's father made Graham feel very uneasy. If he found out! He felt his testicles contract involuntarily.

While they talked, Graham slowly worked one leg into the pyjama pants, then the other. After ten minutes, he had them on and did not think anyone had noticed. Annoyingly, Alex and the boys would not take a hint and leave. Instead, they sat there making crude innuendos and joking. Graham became more and more frustrated and irritated.

It was Johnno who tired of the game first. He turned to Alex, "Come on Alex, show us this new computer game."

The three moved into the house. As soon as they had gone through into Alex's room, Amelia leaned forward and hugged Graham and giggled.

"That was close!"

Graham tried to smile but was too tense and annoyed. He put his arms around her and kissed her. "Let's go downstairs," he said.

That raised the problem of whether to get dressed or not. His clothes were kept in Alex's room, and he had no desire to go in there. He decided to stay in his pyjamas, even though they were very loose and skimpy.

He got up and Amelia stepped forward to embrace him again. They clung together and kissed for a couple of minutes.

"Hey! It's Sunday you two," called Alex from along the corridor.

Graham stepped back and looked guiltily along to where Alex's grinning face showed in his doorway. Without replying he took Amelia's hand and led her down the front steps. They walked around to a side door which gave access to the Ship Room.

Amelia stopped in amazement when she saw the hundreds of model ships, and all the tiny balsa aircraft and tanks which made up the war game that Graham had been playing with Alex and Peter and Max for a year. He had to show her around and explain it and was quite embarrassed. He did not like people to know he was artistic and made models in case they considered him a sissy.

It took a while to show Amelia the models. All the while his frustration and desire was mounting. Finally, he just embraced her and held her tight. She made no attempt to escape but turned to kiss him. Graham gently but firmly began to kiss her. She responded passionately.

Damn! Alex and his mates were coming down the back steps. Graham stepped back just as Alex walked into the Ship Room.

"What ya's doin'?" he asked with a wink.

Graham badly wanted to tell him to bugger off but felt that would give away exactly what he and Amelia were trying to do, so he just made a face and went on explaining ship models to Amelia. She pretended that was what they were doing. To Graham's intense annoyance the two boys also joined them, and Alex proceeded to show them around and explain things.

It seemed they would never leave, but again it was Johnno who lost interest first. He said to Alex, “Come on. Let’s go. If we are going ter the football we’d better get a move on.”

Alex grunted agreement and gave Graham a knowing look. “Okay Johnno. You two behave yourselves, eh?”

Graham blushed fiercely again, and Amelia poked her tongue at him. Alex laughed and led his mates away. Five minutes later Graham watched them mount their bikes and ride off. At last! Now they could get on with it!

But they couldn’t. No sooner had they embraced and started kissing than his mother’s car drove into the yard and stopped in the car port, right next to the main door of the Ship Room. Graham was appalled. How would he explain Amelia to his mother? He heard voices. Worse and worse: Margaret was with Kylie. That was quite a normal Sunday proceeding but just at that moment was the last thing Graham wanted. He did not want Margaret to be hurt; and did not want Amelia to think he had a girlfriend, particularly one so young.

To his dismay he heard Margaret say, “I’ll just check to see if he’s in the Ship Room.”

Chapter 19

URGENT DESIRE

Oh no! Graham stepped hastily away from Amelia. She looked quizzically at him.

"Should I hide?" she whispered.

Graham just had time to shake his head. Margaret appeared in the door, and he saw her cheerful smile freeze into worried shock.

"Oh. Oh! Sorry... er... er... Hello," Margaret stammered.

Graham could tell she was hurt and that made him feel ashamed and even more guilty.

Kylie called out, "Is he in there?"

Margaret tried to answer, but had to swallow. "Ye... yes. Yes, he is."

She turned and walked quickly back out. Graham heard Kylie ask what the matter was. He could not make out all of Margaret's reply but did make out the word 'girl'.

"A girl?" Kylie cried.

Next moment she poked her head around the doorway and stared at Amelia, her face a mixture of curiosity and hostility. Graham blushed deep red. He just wished the concrete would swallow him up. His arousal quickly died away.

Amelia stood uncertainly and said, "Hi," but Kylie ignored her and went back out.

She's going to tell mum, Graham deduced.

And she did. He heard his mother's voice and then she walked in.

"I thought you were sick, Graham?" she said, raising her eyebrows. "Who is this?"

"This is Millie. Amelia Howley. She's in my class," Graham said, aware that he was blushing furiously.

"Hello," Mrs Kirk said in a very frosty tone.

"Hello," Amelia managed to say. "I was on my way home from netball practice, and I dropped in to see Graham's model ships. I've heard so much about them."

"I see," Mrs Kirk replied in a cold voice.

There was an awkward pause. Amelia then went on. "I'd better be getting home, or my mum will start to worry."

"Yes," Mrs Kirk agreed.

Graham led Amelia out to the side lawn past his mother. He knew Kylie and Margaret were watching from the back stairs and that made him even more embarrassed.

"I'd better go," Amelia whispered.

"Yes," Graham agreed. Strong emotions were now warring within him, desire predominating. He said, "I'm going to the pool this afternoon with Steve and Rosemary. Can you come?"

Amelia nodded. "I'll try. I should be allowed if one of the girls will drop by to come with me."

"Phone Lorna or Rosemary," Graham suggested.

Amelia agreed to do that, and they then said goodbye. She mounted her bike and pedalled off. Feeling very apprehensive and ashamed Graham walked upstairs to the kitchen wondering what he would say to his mother.

But Kylie attacked him first. "Who's she?"

"I told you. Just a girl in my class."

"Oh yeah! So why were you down in the Ship Room looking so guilty?" Kylie asked angrily. Margaret was with her but just sat and looked miserable.

Graham blushed, knew he was blushing and felt even worse. "Just showing her my model ships," he replied defensively.

"I hope it was only your model ships you were showing her!" Kylie snapped.

As she said this, their mother came in. "That will do Kylie. That is enough of that sort of talk. Now, do you children want some morning tea?"

Graham had been expecting a real roasting and was very conscious of only being in his pyjama shorts. However his mother changed the subject and sat them down to eat. Not having had breakfast, Graham was hungry and was thankful to eat, if only because it gave him an excuse not to talk.

Kylie and Margaret then left the kitchen and went through to Kylie's room. Urgently wanting to be out of the situation, Graham rose to go to his own room but to his dismay his mother stopped him.

"Did you know that girl was going to come over?" she asked.

Graham felt wretched. "Yes, Mum," he whispered. Shame scorched him. It got worse.

"And what is that mark on your neck?"

Graham was aghast. Mark? He blushed even more, remembering Amelia biting him the night before.

"Don't know mum," he mumbled.

"Well I do! It looks like a love bite!" Mrs Kirk snapped. She was angry and hurt. She went on, "Oh Graham, you be careful. Don't you do anything silly. She is too young and so are you."

"Yes, Mum," Graham replied.

"And please don't deceive me again please. If you want her to come over then tell me and we can arrange things properly."

"Yes, Mum."

Another wave of shame swept over Graham. He fled to the veranda and threw himself on his bed. By this time his body was in a state of considerable stress and his emotions were in turmoil.

For a while he just lay, thinking and reliving what had gone on. Amidst the guilt and shame was the triumphant knowledge that she had said yes! And he was intensely frustrated.

I'd better get rid of the condom, he thought anxiously.

Wrinkling his nose with disgust he slid his hand up under the pillow and gathered it into his hand. Carefully he slid out of bed and rose to his feet. After checking it wasn't visible, he listened to detect the location of his mother and the girls. Hearing nothing he quickly walked through the house to the toilet. Thankful to get there undetected he dropped the condom into the bowl and flushed it away. When he was satisfied it was gone, he felt happier, till another dreadful thought struck him.

The condom packet! I left it on my table on the veranda! I'd better get it before anyone finds it.

He had been going to have a shower before dressing but now rushed back to the veranda.

And it was gone. *I put it just here,* he remembered.

But it wasn't there. Where had it gone? He searched anxiously all around the spare bed. No sign of it. With a sinking heart he noted that the bedclothes had been straightened. Had his mother done that? Did she find it? Was that why she implored him to be careful? Graham felt stunned.

He went back to the bathroom, quite unable to look his mother in the eye as he passed her.

Later, after Margaret had gone home, Kylie had another go at him, "You are so cruel! You are always hurting Margaret," she cried.

"I am not! Anyway, that's her lookout. She doesn't own me," Graham retorted.

"But she loves you, and you know she does," Kylie replied.

"She's just a little kid," Graham answered hotly.

"Oh! And you are the big, grown-up man of the world I suppose!" Kylie snapped.

Yes I am, Graham thought.

He wanted to say that Margaret was too young and only just managed to keep the words unsaid. Awareness that Amelia was also legally way under-age made him feel very worried. But not so worried that he did not urgently desire to do it with her.

For the next few hours Graham kept out of Kylie's way and busied himself. But all the while his mind was on sex and how to get Amelia away on her own so they could get to do it. There was also worry that his mother might not allow him to go to the pool but, to his relief, she made no objection when he suggested it after lunch.

That put his spirits and hopes both back up. The thought of being with Amelia set his fantasies racing. He smuggled another condom into his pocket and set off on his bike.

But Amelia was not there. Nor was Lorna. Stephen and Rosemary lay on towels behind the same garden bed. Graham lay down beside them and tried to hide his disappointment. They discussed the previous night but not in any detail as Rosemary was obviously embarrassed by the topic.

And there was Amelia! She and Lorna came walking through the entrance half an hour later. Graham's heart leapt and his erection sprang to attention again. To his relief, Amelia gave him a big smile and did not appear to have any regrets about the morning's attempt. She spread her towel and lay beside him.

"Put some sun cream on my back please," she asked, handing Graham a tube of lotion.

Before he could start, he had to move to a crouching position and Amelia sat up, turned her back on the others and peeled her top down to her hips. Then she lay face down on the towel, but not before they all got a bit of an eyeful. The sight of her breasts bulging out helped keep Graham aroused.

So did rubbing the cream on her. The touch of her skin felt wonderful. When it came to putting the cream on her sides, he was unsure how close to her breasts he should venture but finally dared himself and rubbed it on all the exposed flesh. Amelia made no move to stop this and continued talking as though nothing was happening. Graham went very red and was hot and blushing the whole time. Awareness of the others watching added another level of thrill to the activity.

Fifteen minutes later, they all got up to walk to the pool for a swim. Amelia joined him and they both swam along the pool for 20 metres before coming to rest hanging on the side. Being winter the pool was almost deserted, so they were able to talk without being overheard. To Graham's delight, Amelia moved close so that her legs touched his under water.

"Did you get into trouble?" she asked.

"Not much. I think mum is suspicious though," Graham replied. He then described his search for the condom.

"Did you bring another one with you?" Amelia asked.

Graham's hopes soared. "Yes."

"Are you in the mood?" Amelia asked, and pressed against him. "Oooh yes!" she cried, sending his emotions boiling even more.

They clung together and kissed. Then Stephen and Louise swam over. Lorna grinned at them. "Come on you two, you will dissolve if you stay in the water any longer," she said. She and Stephen then climbed out and walked back to their towels.

Graham did not want to get out as he was enjoying the closeness so much. But Amelia snuggled against him and whispered in his ear. "Do you want to go somewhere to do it?"

Graham nodded. His mouth had gone too dry to be able to answer. He had to swallow and lick his lips. "Yes. Where do you want to go?"

"Anywhere where we can be alone," Amelia replied. She hugged him hard and sighed and he sensed she was just as frustrated as him.

"Centennial Park then?" Graham asked.

"Okay."

After a few more kisses they climbed out and walked over to where the others lay on their towels. This time Graham did not care if they saw his condition. He noted both Rosemary and Lorna look but he was too aflame to care.

When he and Amelia started rolling up their towels, Stephen asked, "Where are you two going?"

"Just for a walk," Amelia replied.

That caused laughter and ribald comments. "I've never seen people walking like that," Stephen jibed.

Graham blushed but was at the stage where he was so strongly in the grip of desire he did not care. Amelia must have felt the same way because she just laughed.

Rosemary frowned. "Be careful Amelia."

Lorna added, "That's right. Remember what my mum says. Be good children. But if you can't be good then be careful!"

They all laughed, and Graham forced himself to join in despite his embarrassment and urgent desire. He took Amelia's hand and led her towards the entrance. By this time his heart was pounding furiously, and he knew he was in the grip of both intense desire and strong fear. The great moment of testing as a man was upon him!

The pair walked out and across the street, then along the footpath and across the railway line. Five minutes' walk had them at Centennial Lakes. To Graham's annoyance, the place seemed to be swarming with families. Dozens of cars were parked there, and children ran in all directions playing hidey and chasey. Adults stood or sat in groups around barbeques and picnic tables.

"This is no good!" Graham muttered in annoyance.

He turned right at the walkway which led to the oil pipes. This led them to the footbridge over Saltwater Creek but that was hardly any better. Groups of people were strolling along the pathways or sitting on the grass. For a moment Graham considered trying the boardwalk through the pandanus swamp but even as he looked in that direction, he saw a family emerge from the thick undergrowth at its end.

"This is bloody hopeless!" he grumbled in frustration.

"Where else can we go?" Amelia asked.

"Up Mt Whitfield I suppose," Graham answered.

His mind was busy with options but that seemed the closest place. He led the way along to where the Red Track led up the mountain from a car park off Collins Avenue. The car park was no encouragement. Ten cars were parked there, and people sat around on the park benches.

The Bamboo Patch then, he thought.

The National Park walkway led into the jungle behind the old naval oil tanks and up onto the lower slopes of Edge Hill. Graham had often been there and usually enjoyed it as a walk. But this time he was so 'toey' with frustrated desire that he was just irritable. He slapped at mosquitoes and swore and glared at all the tourists and joggers who seemed to pass them every few minutes.

On arrival at the Bamboo Patch, Graham was wondering if he hadn't made another mistake and whether they shouldn't go somewhere else. But he could not think of anywhere close. Having come this far he stubbornly persisted, in spite of a few grumbles from Amelia. He led her up the right-hand track and along the walk through the Bamboo Patch.

This was a place he had explored dozens of times over the years and held a number of memories for him. He also knew it well enough to think he could find a secret corner where no-one would disturb them. The bamboo grew in a dense thicket several hundred metres across. Most was thin, yellow stuff about ten metres tall. There was virtually no undergrowth, just a mat of deadfall. The shoots grew so close together that in most places it was only possible to push through between them with great difficulty. It was also dark and gloomy and sound was muffled.

Several narrow foot tracks led off the walking track into the thicket. Graham knew that people were not supposed to leave the main track, but no-one was around, so he turned off and led Amelia along one of these. He moved slowly, eyes and ears alert, for snakes as much as people. Fifty paces in he came to what he sought, a small clearing a few metres across. From there they were not visible to people on the track. Now almost desperate to begin, he spread his towel on the leaf litter.

"Is this it?" Amelia asked.

She looked around, clearly not very impressed. Graham nodded and stepped forward to kiss her. She responded but both were inhibited. It seemed very cold-blooded and not very romantic. And he was now frightened. That close and that intimate he was very aware that Amelia was another person with emotions and hopes and he felt very conscious of the possible harm he might do her. But he also thought he could tell by her eyes, breathing and skin that she wanted to do it. It was all very scary!

Both began undressing, in between kissing and fondling.

Graham stripped right off and stood in front of Amelia. She did the same and they studied each other. Once again Graham felt his natural urges taking over and they kissed and caressed more passionately.

Voices!

They stopped and crouched together, hearts pounding and mouths dry. No. Just some walkers out on the main track. They resumed kissing and touching.

"The condom. Put it on now please," Amelia asked. "You might forget later."

Graham did as he was told. While he was rolling it on, and feeling embarrassed under her gaze, more walkers went past. He found his erection beginning to subside from fear. The people continued on, and Graham knelt and gestured to the towels. Amelia made a face and indicated she wasn't keen to lie on the towels spread on the ground.

"Ow! Bloody mosquitoes!" she said, slapping at the insects.

Several had settled on Graham's bare skin, and he slapped at them as well. Several bit him between his shoulder blades where he could not reach them, and he flexed and swore. Then a couple bit him on his bare bum. Angrily he slapped at them. Through a red haze of desire he was dimly aware that frustration and annoyance were building up to destroy their mood.

"Come on, lie down so we can get it over with!" he said.

A look of irritation crossed Amelia's face. "Oh that's not very romantic!" she replied, annoyance clear on her voice.

Graham swallowed and silently rebuked himself for being such an idiot. *Don't blow your chances now,* he told himself.

"Sorry. I didn't mean it like that," he replied.

To his relief, Amelia nodded and moved to lie down. Graham then knelt beside her. As he did, she half-lay, half-sat so that she could watch what he was doing. Fascination with her female body then held his interest. At length she let out a sigh of frustration.

"Oh come on!" she gasped.

By now Graham was very aroused and extremely scared. This was the big moment; and he knew it could have disastrous consequences. He nerved himself to do it.

More voices!

Bloody kids! And they were coming their way. The soft padding of footfalls sounded and figures flitted through the shadows. Two boys of about ten appeared on the narrow track. They took one look, then gasped and fled back the way they had come.

As soon as they reached the track the boys began calling to friends to 'come and look'.

"Oh damn!" Graham muttered. "Come on, we'd better get dressed and out of here before we have a bloody audience."

Feeling intensely frustrated and annoyed he stood up. For a moment strong desire caused him to tremble and he was tempted to get down and quickly do it. But Amelia rolled over and stood up, also muttering in annoyance.

She began to quickly dress. Graham tugged off the condom and tossed it into the scrub in annoyance, then quickly pulled on his clothes. After lacing his joggers up, he stood and scooped up the towels and dusted the leaves and dirt off them. By then they could hear whispering as the kids tried to pluck up the courage to sneak in to look.

"This way," Graham whispered.

He led the way off along a faint track going downhill in the opposite direction, only to freeze in fear.

A snake!

A big, brown snake more than a metre long. It was on the track only a metre or so from him and had curled into a striking 'S'. Graham stared at it in horror, his terror of the creatures rooting him to the spot. He swallowed and trembled, and his mind felt frozen.

It's going to strike! he thought. But he could not make his limbs move!

Amelia had not seen it and pushed at him from behind. "Come on! Let's get out of here," she muttered irritably.

"Snake!" Graham managed to croak in a sort of strangled gasp.

Amelia let out a squeal of fright and stepped back then leaned out to look past him. "Move back, quick!" she cried.

But Graham felt frozen by fear. Only slowly did his mind start to function and he noted the snake's forked tongue tasting the air. It looked to be staring straight at him with those wicked little dark eyes.

Amelia backed up a few paces and then called again. "Graham! Move back!" she said. "It might bite you."

To Graham, the reptile looked positively evil. He saw its head move slowly from side to side and some corner of his rational mind told him this was a very dangerous snake: an Eastern Brown or Taipan.

A Taipan bite can be fatal in minutes, he thought, remembering those First Aid lessons at Scouts. Then a wash of memories from the previous snake bite incident filled his mind, keeping him stock still.

"Graham!" Amelia muttered, anxiously plucking at the back of his shirt.

Graham still felt mesmerised but then his mind began to function again. *Can it strike that far? Am I in range? Will it strike if I move?* he wondered.

It took him a real effort of will power to ease his muscles and then tense them ready to spring. Gasping with anxiety he gingerly moved his left foot, the closest one, back half a pace. As he did, the snake flattened and looked to be about to attack. But it didn't and he carefully moved his right foot back. All the while his vision had narrowed down to just the snake and now seemed to blur.

Suddenly the snake lowered itself and turned away. It went slithering off to the right at a truly alarming speed. Graham gaped and then scuttled back, colliding with Amelia as he did.

"Sorry," he gasped, grabbing at her to keep his balance.

Looking back he was appalled to see that the snake had vanished into the leaf litter and was no longer visible.

"Where did it go?" he croaked.

Amelia pointed. "Over there. It's gone. Let's go," she said.

Graham nodded but found he had to cling to her and to a bamboo as a wave of dizziness swept over him. He realised he was hyperventilating.

"Are you alright?" Amelia queried, peering at him closely.

"Yeah," Graham croaked. "Sorry, I wasn't sure if I could spring back in time."

Now the incident was over he was ashamed of how he had frozen in fear. That shocked and embarrassed him. *Am I that much of a coward?* He wondered.

It was voices behind them and more mosquitoes that got him moving. Casting frequent nervous glances at where he had last seen the snake he quickly walked on along the narrow track. Amelia followed, muttering with annoyance and slapping at mosquitoes as she did. A few minutes later they emerged on the left fork of the Blue Track, under the curious gaze of several adults. Guilt made Graham burn with shame. He wanted to run but held himself to a fast walk.

From behind him Amelia called in an irritable tone. "Slow down! My legs aren't as long as yours."

Graham did as he was told, slapping at more mosquitoes as he went. Five minutes later they were back down at the car park.

Now thoroughly frustrated and annoyed, Graham waited for Amelia to join him "Let's find somewhere else," he suggested.

But Amelia shook her head. "I'm not in the mood now. Besides, I'd better be getting home. It is nearly five O'clock."

That put Graham into an even worse mood. Mustering some more courage he asked, "When can I see you again?"

"Do you really want to do it?" Amelia asked.

That question caused Graham to worry that his big opportunity might be slipping away. He nodded. "More than ever. I think I'm falling in love with you."

"Are you? Oh, that's nice," she replied, smiling brightly.

That made Graham feel a heel because he said it without meaning it. What he really wanted was sex.

To his mixed relief and astonishment, she said, "I need a fuck real bad. This is driving me crazy. If you are game, we can meet tonight."

The language shocked him, but also got his heart thumping again. "Where? When?" he asked.

"My place. After bedtime. I'll sneak out and meet you downstairs," Amelia replied.

That was a frightening concept, but Graham wasn't going to admit he was scared. Besides he badly wanted to do it.

"Okay," he agreed.

So, while they walked back to the pool, Amelia described exactly where to meet him. Graham's heart thumped with anticipatory excitement.

"Is your dad home? Or is he away on exercises?" he asked.

"Home. Why? Are you scared of him?"

"Bloody oath I am!" Graham answered truthfully. "But I'll be there."

Back at the pool they found the others sitting outside talking. They were all clearly curious as to what had happened but neither let on that nothing had. Amelia said, "See you later" and went off with Lorna.

Stephen and Rosemary rode off towards Edge Hill. Graham mounted his own bike and pedalled home in a state close to nervous exhaustion.

At home he avoided Kylie and Alex. Most of the time he lay on his bed and read a book, but he had difficulty concentrating. After tea he watched TV, then lay and read again, planning every move and getting more and more excited as time crept past.

That evening he was early to bed. For hours he lay fantasising, frequently checking his watch. Time seemed to drag slower than he could ever remember. He knew he was literally in the grip of a fever of impatience because, from time to time, he had bouts of nervous shivering.

At last midnight came around. With a soft sigh of relief Graham eased himself slowly out of bed. *Now, the challenge,* he thought: to sneak out of the house undetected; then to meet Amelia at her home in half an hour.

In preparation he slipped on a shirt and a pair of old shorts (*No underpants. They will just waste time,* he decided), placed a condom in his pocket and crept to the front door. By then his heart was hammering urgently with fear and excitement.

As he slunk down the stairs, urgent desire pounded in his veins.

Chapter 20

IN DEEP

As Graham rode along the road he shivered with emotion. The feel of the cool night air on his bare skin added a sensual touch. He pedalled as fast as he could, not wanting to be late for the tryst. From time to time he trembled as his rampant lust surged through him. He grinned with pleasurable anticipation.

Several cars went past but he ignored them. Thus it was a shock when a car drew up beside him. Graham glanced at it and went cold with fright. It was a police car, and Constable O'Neil was in it.

Damn! Graham thought.

Then worry replaced his annoyance. Constable O'Neil waved him over and he stopped and got off his bike. The policeman did not get out of the car, which was some relief to Graham, who was feeling very self-conscious. How could he explain riding along after midnight wearing only a shirt and pair of shorts (and with a condom in his pocket!).

Constable O'Neil shone a torch on him. "Kirk! What are you doing riding around in the dark kid?"

"Just... just..." *What on earth can I say? I can't say sneaking over to meet my girlfriend. She is underage...* "Just riding around," he mumbled.

"What? Couldn't sleep or something?" Constable O'Neil asked sarcastically. "You aren't up to mischief, are you? Like burglary?"

"N... no sir," Graham replied. He went cold at the idea of being thought a criminal. His arousal subsided from fear.

"Where's that mate of yours, Bell?"

Stephen? Graham was puzzled. "Don't know. At home I suppose," he answered.

"He'd better be. And that's where you should be. So turn around and go there. But get off that bike and walk. I should book you for riding a bike without a safety helmet," Constable O'Neil replied.

Graham was aghast. "Oh sir, please don't. I'm sorry! I won't do it again," he replied.

"I think I..." Constable O'Neil began.

Then he stopped as the car's radio crackled. The second policeman answered it. The message was about a domestic disturbance in Manoora.

"Okay, will deal," the driver replied.

Constable O'Neil put down the notebook he had opened. "Now you get home, Kirk. And make sure you walk. If we catch you riding you will wish you'd never been born."

The police car drove off. Graham stood and watched it turn at the next corner, then jumped on his bike and pedalled as fast as he could.

If I go fast, I will be away before they return, he thought. He was also worrying that he might be late.

The thought of Amelia got him aroused again. As he rode along his heart beat faster with the thrill. All the time he kept watching for any sign of the police car returning. It was very exciting. It took Graham only another ten minutes to reach Edge Hill. As he got closer to Amelia's caution took over. Now he put the next part of his plan into action. He had decided not to ride his bike right up to the house. The best place he could think of to hide it which wasn't far from Amelia's was the church on Collins Avenue.

When Graham reached the church, he dismounted and stood listening for a minute. There was plenty of light from streetlights, but the world seemed to be asleep. There was no traffic at all. Graham wheeled his bike into the church yard and hid it behind a garden bed. By then his heart was really thumping and his mouth was dry. He was scared but did not want to admit it. To further place his pride under stress he found that his desire was partly gone and that worried him.

What will she think if I can't perform? he thought.

It was a whole new level of anxiety. He licked dry lips and set off along the footpath. Pain from the soles of his bare feet on small stones on the concrete footpath added a new level of anxiety. Then a car came around the bend and he had to resist an urge to run and hide. It was not the police. He sighed with relief and padded on.

It was only two blocks up a side street to Amelia's. Graham had never been there before but knew the street. Slowly he walked along, checking the house numbers, his mouth dry and heart thumping so loudly it made it hard to hear. When he reached the right house, he stopped to study it. All appeared normal. No lights were on, so presumably they were all asleep. Except (hopefully) Amelia.

But Graham was afraid to go in. He knew he was getting in deep now. *I will be in deep shit if I get caught!* he thought.

A dog barked twice a couple of blocks away. Did Amelia have a dog? That would put the cap on things! His eyes searched the front and side of the house, then studied the garden at the side. That was where Amelia said she would meet him. The garden had deep pools of shadow among the shrubs and a stand of trees. And that was her window he was looking at. Was she watching? Could she see him?

"Go on coward. If you are a man, go in," he told himself.

He took a deep breath and slowly opened the garden gate. It squeaked slightly, making him pause, heart pounding, to listen. No sound from the house. Cautiously he went inside but left the gate open, lest it make a noise when he closed it.

Ten nervous steps took him to the tree opposite Amelia's window. He stood in the shadows and looked up at it. His eyes darted from window to window. According to her the next window was her little sister's room. Her parents slept on the other side of the house.

There was no movement and Graham began to tremble with anticipation and anxiety. *What if she is asleep? Should I climb up and try to wake her?* he wondered. He licked dry lips and wiped damp palms on his shorts.

There she was! An arm waved at the window. Graham felt relief and then excitement. He drew back into the shadows behind the tree. Now desire surged anew. His heart hammered urgently, and he felt himself harden up. That was a relief too. By the time Amelia came scampering across the lawn he was good and ready.

She wore only a slip-on cotton nightie, and he could tell instantly that there was nothing under it but bare skin. Without pausing she threw herself into his arms and kissed him passionately. He slid his hands up and down her body, lifting her nightie, revelling in the feel of her smooth skin. She groaned and pressed against him as he squeezed and pulled her against him.

"Oh I thought you would never come," she murmured. "I'm so randy I have been ready for hours."

That was interesting, shocking, and enlightening to Graham.

"Me too," he croaked. He had to lick his lips again he was so dry.

"Oh quick, give it to me," Amelia said, her voice sultry with passion.

Graham glanced anxiously at the house. "What about your mum and dad?"

"Mum might like it, but dad wouldn't," she replied mischievously.

"You know what I mean!" Graham replied in exasperation.

Amelia gave a soft giggle. "They are both asleep. Come on, quick. Here on this rug."

She pointed to a rug spread on the grass in the shadows. Graham had expected more foreplay. To check he wasn't making a mistake he asked, "You sure you don't want a bit of... of... of pashing first?"

"Stuff the pashing! I've been ready for hours. Give it to me. Then we can do a second one slowly," Amelia cried.

"Shhh! okay," Graham replied.

He was shocked and scared. But he was also fearfully horny. Amelia stoked the fires by whipping off the nightie and casting it on the grass. A few seconds later they were in a passionate embrace. She reached across and unbuttoned his shirt. With trembling fingers he helped her. The shirt was shrugged off and fell to the ground and she pulled herself against him, moaning softly.

She was ready alright. Her skin was warm and she was trembling with desire. Graham had never felt anything like the desire pounding in his veins- nor the gripping fear. The feel of her bare skin on his set his pulses racing even more.

They kissed again and he started to fondle her, but she impatiently stopped him.

"Later," she said.

She lay down, pulling him down with her. They kissed again and Graham thought he was already in heaven. As Graham pressed on her his whole being pulsed with urgent desire.

This is it! I'm going to really do it! he marvelled. And he knew he would be able to.

"Take off your shorts," she croaked. Graham agreed and moved back to a kneeling position, and later was glad he had!

For the fear was still strong. "Condom," he croaked.

He did not want to make her pregnant. Also lurking at the back of his mind was the dark fear that, if she had done it before, she might have some dreadful disease. He knelt between her legs and fumbled the packet out of his pocket. He was shaking so much he could hardly manage it.

But being inexperienced and never having done it Graham was not quite sure what to do next and as he knelt there, his heart hammering with lust and fear, he paused. Then the sound of someone running on the lawn made him glance over his shoulder.

It was her father!

For an instant fear froze Graham. Then, just in time, he reacted, springing up.

The boot, aimed between his legs from behind, took him so hard in the left buttock that he was knocked right over Amelia and onto the grass. Panic surged, overcoming the shocking pain. Desperate to escape, Graham rolled away across the lawn.

Her father, clad only in boots and pyjama shorts, was wild with anger. "You little bastard! I'll teach you!" Warrant Officer Howley shouted. He went to jump over Amelia, but she reached up and grabbed his leg and he tripped. Swearing loudly he fell in a heap on top of her.

Driven by near panic, Graham dived aside and scrambled to his feet. He didn't wait but fled. As he ran, he heard Amelia cry out and heard her father yell, "Let go of me! Let me go you little trollop!"

"Oh shit!" Graham cried as sheer terror took over.

He dashed through the open gate and fled along the footpath. From behind him Graham heard Amelia and her father yelling and what sounded like a fight. There was swearing and then a smack and then Amelia began sobbing. By then Graham was 25 metres down the footpath and running for dear life!

He felt several sharp stabs of pain as his tender soles landed on sharp stones, but he ignored the pain and ran on. There were more angry voices behind him, and a quick glance back showed Amelia and her father struggling in the shadows. Knowing how fit her father was added another spur of fear to Graham's efforts.

Twenty paces on another glance back showed Warrant Officer Howley at the gate, Amelia still clinging to him. He shouted, "Come back here you bastard! Come back so I can teach you a lesson you'll never forget."

Then he shook himself free and came running after Graham. Fear surged and so did the adrenalin.

In spite of a numbness which threatened to cripple him, Graham ran as he had never run before. He glanced back and saw that Warrant Officer

Howley was only about 50 paces behind. Amelia was standing naked on the footpath at the gate. But there was no way Graham was going to stop. Fear lent him strength and he ran desperately along the footpath. Terrible fears of being bashed, or worse, kept him running.

After a block it was clear he was drawing ahead. The Warrant Officer was fit, but much older. Also his boots were unlaced. As Graham reached the corner of the next street Warrant Officer Howley slowed down. He shouted and shook his fist.

"You wait, you little bugger! When I catch up with you, I will rip your balls off!"

Graham believed him. A spasm of fear gave him the strength to ignore the sharp agony of a stitch. Cursing at having to run under a streetlight he kept on down another block to Collins Avenue. Here he dashed around the corner and raced along the main road. Another backward glance showed that Warrant Officer Howley had stopped at the corner. Graham did not slow down. He ran along the concrete footpath, heart pounding and breath coming in hot gasps.

After another 20 paces he glanced back again. Warrant Officer Howley had definitely given up and was turning back.

He might be going to get his car, Graham thought. That kept him running.

A car went past, and Graham saw a man turn his head to stare at him. But, to Graham's relief, he didn't stop.

But he might call the police though, he worried. Or Warrant Officer Howley might. That made Graham feel sick. But he kept running, although he was now gasping for breath.

By the time he reached the church he was winded and in turmoil. Gasping and trembling Graham crouched behind the garden in the church yard while he recovered his breath. A quick check showed no one chasing him. All seemed to be quiet. But what to do next?

Then he became aware that he was still tightly gripping the condom in its packet. With a grunt of disgust he tossed it into the garden. Again he peeked around, fear and shame coursing through him.

I will have to ride home with no shirt! he realised. Fear and reaction made him sweat and tremble and he felt nauseous. Then he realised where he was and what he had done. *Never mind Warrant Officer Howley! This is God's house! And I am a terrible sinner,* he told himself.

Guilt coursed through Graham. He trembled and began to cry. *Oh what a fool I am! Now God will punish me too.*

He began to pray for forgiveness. Another car came along. He risked a glance. No, just some bloke on his way home.

Time I was going too, before the police arrive.

Almost hyperventilating with anxiety, and acutely aware of his bare torso, Graham picked up his bike and wheeled it to the gate. Now he was really scared. But then he paused, assailed by shame. He went back and found the condom. Feeling a wave of revulsion he picked it up and went back to his bike.

"I can imagine what Constable Bloody O'Neil will say this time!" he muttered.

With a sob he mounted his bike and began to pedal. Driven by fear Graham pedalled fast, feeling desperately anxious. The cold night air cooled his perspiration and he shivered. His heart still pounded and his mouth was dry. His hip and left buttock hurt at every stroke. He kept watching in all directions for any cars.

The roads seemed to be very well lit and that made him feel very conspicuous, but he saw no-one. As he crossed a large drain, he flung the condom into it.

During the fifteen-minute ride he saw only five cars. Three he detected early enough to be able to dismount and hide but two came around corners so fast he had no time to try. In each case he decided that running for cover would attract more attention, so he just crouched low, hid his face and pedalled on.

He half expected to find the police waiting for him at home but on turning into his street he saw that all looked normal. To his relief, his home was in darkness. With a mouth dry from fear he dismounted and wheeled his bike to the front gate, all the while aware that the streetlight across the road was illuminating him. Anxiety about being seen by a nosy neighbour had him glancing around as he wheeled the bike in the front gate. Now his heart was hammering harder than when he had been running as anxiety about being seen by Kylie or his mother gripped him.

As quietly as he could, he padded under the house and put his bike in its usual place. Then he crept up the front steps, his heart hammering and shame heating him. Before opening the front door, he listened for a minute. All was silent so he opened the door, slid in and closed it. A few seconds later he eased his perspiring, shaking body into bed.

Safe!

But am I really?

He began to ponder the consequences which would now flow. Depressing thoughts of the dreadful interviews to follow tortured him: with the police, with his mother and father; with her father! And then he fretted about the even more fearful legal consequences. Images of courts and prison added to his mental torment.

No. They won't send me to prison. It will be one of those juvenile detention centres, he decided glumly. That thought was even more depressing. *I will have to associate with all the scum and low life.*

From that it was a short step to realising that he might have destroyed any chance of ever having a good job.

Nobody will employ a crim, he brooded.

That led him to thoughts of running away. *I can be out of town by daybreak.*

But where could he go? He considered hiding in the jungle for a while but the more he thought about running away the less attractive it looked. He had heard a lot about homeless kids and how they were pressured into a life of crime and poverty.

The next dark step was to contemplate suicide. He brooded on this for a while. Time went by and he made himself more and more depressed. By the time dawn came he was exhausted and physically sick. He watched the glow of the rising sun and felt sure he now understood how it felt to face a firing squad.

Then the next problem arose. The police still hadn't arrived. *Should I just give myself up and hope co-operation will help?* he wondered.

In a fever of doubt he lay thinking and worrying. When he heard his mother get up, he realised he was still wearing his shorts, so he groped around for his pyjamas.

Breakfast time arrived and still no phone calls or police. Graham's mother came out to wake him.

"Come and eat. Time you got up or you will be late for school," she said.

School! How irrelevant! He'd forgotten that. "I don't think I'll go to school. I don't feel very well."

She felt his forehead. "Yes, you look a bit off. Do you want breakfast?"

Graham shook his head. He felt so upset he did not feel like food at all. His mother left him and went to rouse the others. Graham lay back and began to shake. Tears started to flow uncontrollably. He rolled over to face the wall and tormented himself with black thoughts. Uppermost now was guilt at what trouble his actions might be causing Amelia.

She must be in terrible trouble; and I have caused it. I have ruined her reputation and her parents will so be so upset!

At that he turned to prayer. He sobbed a confession to God and begged for help and forgiveness. After a while he cried himself out and calmed down. Time slid past slowly. Alex and Kylie left for school and his mother returned and took his temperature. He did not have to pretend. His worry had made himself genuinely sick by this, and he looked it.

Hours crept by. Still no police or phone calls. Graham continued to flail at his conscience. He could never remember feeling so wretched in all his life. The longer he waited for the axe to fall the worse it seemed to get until he almost wished something would happen.

Nothing did. He spent a miserable day lying in bed. In the afternoon he slipped into a fitful sleep. When Alex came home from school Graham asked how the day had gone to try to find out what was being said about the incident at school. When Alex just grunted and said, "Same as usual," and kept on walking Graham felt simultaneously deflated and relieved. Perhaps Amelia hadn't been at school either, so no-one knew about it yet? His next reaction was to despise himself as a coward.

I should face up to it like a man! he decided.

In the evening he rose to have a shower before tea. As soon as he tried to get out of bed, he was gripped by pain in his left hip. He let out an involuntary cry. Thankful that no-one had heard him he hobbled to the bathroom and examined himself. A massive bruise spread from his buttock down to his thigh. Gingerly he massaged it and eased himself into a warm shower. That helped but he felt very sore. After dressing he was called to come and have his dinner. Gritting his teeth to hide the pain, he walked to the kitchen as though nothing was wrong.

Even then his stomach felt queasy. He hardly ate anything. Afterwards he watched TV and then lay down again to read. It was apparent that no-one else in the family had any inkling of the event. That made Graham even more ashamed.

It will come as a terrible shock to mum, he thought. Once again, he contemplated running away. Another long, miserable night followed.

On Tuesday morning he woke from a bad dream feeling utterly exhausted. But now he was resolved to get it over. *I will go to school,* he decided.

Even though he felt worse than the day before he got up and went to get ready. His bruised buttock was very stiff, but he decided that would ease up with some exercise. His mother felt his temperature and looked thoughtful. She even suggested he stay home again and that they go to the doctor.

Graham shook his head. "I'll be alright. I want to go to school."

At 08:15am he set off. *I just have to know!* he thought. So he walked, his stomach all a-flutter and emotions in turmoil.

To get another shock. As he walked across the street towards the front entrance of the school, a grey sedan slid to a halt at the footpath. Warrant Officer Howley was driving, and Amelia was in the back.

Chapter 21

IN DEEPER STILL

Graham froze in fear. Warrant Officer Howley!

The warrant officer was speaking sternly to Amelia and had his head turned away. Graham felt a wave of cold terror sweep over him. With an effort he forced his paralysed limbs to move. Amelia had seen him but made no sign. She looked very upset, and her father's face was grim. Graham fled in through the main entrance, heart thudding.

Oh my God! I'm done for now! he thought.

He broke into a cold sweat and wondered what to do next. His first move was to place himself where he could see without too much risk of being seen. He had to know if Warrant Officer Howley was coming in to report the incident to the school authorities.

Someone touched Graham's elbow and he jumped nervously. It was Peter. "You look as though you've seen a ghost."

Graham nodded. Amelia had appeared in the entrance and she was on her own. He had to speak to her, to find out. Turning to Peter he said, "I was sick yesterday. I still feel a bit off."

Peter nodded and looked sympathetic. "I wondered where you were. When are we going on another hike? It's been weeks now."

Graham shrugged. Hikes seemed so irrelevant. "Don't know," he muttered.

"What about the weekend after next?" Peter asked.

Graham nodded but his attention was on the main entrance and on Amelia. He watched her walk past along the path towards B Block.

"Maybe," he mumbled. Then he started after Amelia without any explanation to Peter.

"Oh well, if that's how you feel!" Peter called after him in a hurt voice.

Graham knew he wasn't handling things well. He broke into a run. Amelia heard him and looked around but did not stop.

"Millie, what happened?" he gasped as he caught up with her, his sore buttock now making him limp.

She turned a pale and unhappy face to him. "What do you think!" she cried angrily.

"I'm sorry. I didn't want anything to go wrong. What did your parents say?"

Amelia stopped and faced him. Her eyes watered and her lips trembled. "I got the hiding of my life. You should see the bruises from where dad's belt hit me. He really whacked into me."

"He got me a beauty too," Graham replied ruefully.

For a second Amelia's eyes lit up and her mouth almost formed a smile. Then she went on, "He and Mum got stuck into me for the rest of the night. They both called me horrible names. I've never seen them so wild. Boy, when dad catches up with you, you will be in deep shit."

Graham swallowed and felt his stomach turn to water. "Do... do... do they know who I am?"

Amelia shook her head, then burst into tears. "I wouldn't tell them. Dad's been at me non-stop ever since, but I haven't said."

Graham was both amazed and relieved. "He didn't recognise me!"

"Why should he? He's only seen you a couple of times and it was dark," Amelia replied. She sounded very upset and bitter. She went on, "He and Mum are talking about sending me to a girl's boarding school. In fact, Dad has said that if I don't give him your name, he will send me to a convent school."

Graham was appalled. "I'm sorry, Millie."

For a minute he did not know what to say. His first reaction was enormous relief that her father did not know who he was. Perhaps he could scrape out of trouble!

"Did you come to school yesterday?" he asked.

"No. I wasn't allowed. I was too upset anyway."

"Neither did I," Graham added. Then he summoned his courage to ask the question which had been bothering him, "Are we still friends?"

Amelia nodded and a tear trickled down her cheek. Graham was moved to put his arms around her to comfort her, but she shook her head. "No. We had better pretend we aren't going together; in case dad asks the school who my boyfriend is," she explained.

That sent another wave of chill through Graham. He hadn't thought of that. It made him glance nervously towards the office. An urge to distance himself from her made him take a pace backwards.

"Alright," he said. "But I still love you."

Amelia smiled through her tears but looked very anxious. "Promise me you won't tell anyone what we were going to do; that you won't boast to your mates."

"I won't tell, I promise," Graham agreed.

He almost said 'Scout's Honour' but stopped himself. Not only would it sound corny, but he knew that what he had done wasn't what a good scout would have. Shame at his actions scorched him. Into his mind flitted one of those sayings his father was always trotting out:

A gentleman never tells.

Amelia turned away. "I'll go now. Don't talk to me again today please."

A deep sense of loss stabbed at Graham. "But when will I see you again?" he asked. The pain was very real.

She shrugged. "When it has all blown over, if it does."

Without another word she walked away leaving Graham feeling very guilty and hurt. He stood and watched her go, biting his lip in anxiety.

Stephen joined him. "Hi Graham! Things not going too well, eh? Did you try something she didn't like?"

Graham could only shrug but knew he was blushing furiously. Stephen noted this and grinned. "Never mind. If you don't win with her then nobody will."

"Yeah," Graham agreed. "How did you get on with Lorna?" he asked in an attempt to change the topic.

"Not too good. Think I might try my luck with Louise instead," Stephen replied.

"Helmut might punch your head in," Graham suggested.

To his relief, Stephen started talking about his own love life, or rather the temporary lack of it. It was an uncomfortable subject but carried them through till first period.

This was English. Graham returned to his old seat next to Stephen. He noted several curious glances from the girls at this and for a moment he met Amelia's eyes and thought he detected a wistful look. Regret? Possibly. But at having let him; or at things going wrong?

What also began to niggle at him was worry over his shirt. He knew his mother had printed his name in some of his shirts so he would get them back from washing on school camps. Was it one of those shirts?

The day settled into an exhausting grind. Graham hated the schoolwork and sat there brooding about what he had done and what the possible consequences might be. All his worst fears of the previous two nights swirled around in his head: detection, expulsion, police, disgrace, punishment. The more he thought about it, the blacker things looked. His mental state wasn't helped by the physical and emotional confusion caused by frequent hot memories of Amelia.

I could have done it! I'm normal! And I loved it! he thought. With deep certainty he knew he wanted to do it if he got the chance.

During Chemistry he was several times in trouble for not paying attention, but it all seemed so irrelevant. He sat and gazed wistfully out the window at the distant mountains.

How I wish I was up there, free, he thought. He imagined walking along a jungle track breathing the fresh mountain air, all his problems reduced to man sized ones of navigation and physical survival.

These thoughts led him on to considering running away again and he planned how he could get home, collect his hiking gear, and get out of town before the police could arrest him. This gave him a comforting daydream to push back his fears for a while.

During the break he sat with his friends. That prompted Stephen to say, "What's this, don't tell me you have given up your amorous pursuits? Has she turned you down mate?"

Graham blushed furiously as guilt coursed through him. He shrugged and did not reply. Stephen tactfully dropped the subject, but Graham noted him exchange a glance with Peter, who made a face.

Geography was next and Graham sat on his own and brooded. Mr Conkey noted this. "Come on Graham. It isn't the end of the world. Get on with your work."

Graham wanted to say that it was. By this time he had so depressed himself that he was again contemplating suicide. Worse still his conscience was tearing him apart. He knew he had intended to sin and the dreadful reality that it could never be undone, that he would have to carry it on his conscience for the rest of his days, was sickening him. Concern for Amelia added to his burden of guilt. He had done things to her, and his actions had resulted in harm to her.

It was my fault, he told himself. He glanced at her frequently but she looked calm, if a trifle pale.

Physics and lunch slipped by in a haze of gloom. Graham got into trouble for not working but could not care less. Then Maths B came around and he sat next to Stephen. Stephen kept cracking crude jokes which Graham was in no mood for. That attracted Mr Ritter's attention and he came and stood over them, then checked that they had done their homework. Neither had.

"Then you can both stay in till it is done. If you don't like that then get your parents in to see me," Mr Ritter said.

They were not the only ones. In all eight boys and three girls, including Amelia, had not done their homework. When the final bell went, Mr Ritter stood at the door talking to Mr Holden while the students settled to the chore.

After a few minutes, Stephen muttered, "Want to try another escape attempt? Ritter won't notice."

"No fear!" Graham replied. "I'm in enough trouble already."

In fact he urgently wanted to escape in case Amelia's father arrived to pick her up. In a dither of worry, he struggled to focus his thoughts to get the work done. It took twenty minutes and Graham and Stephen were among the last to be allowed to go.

Once outside, Stephen suggested going to town. Graham shook his head. "No thanks. I still don't feel well. I think I'll go home."

To his relief, Stephen accepted this. Graham said goodbye and headed for the entrance. Only then did it occur to him to go some other way in case Warrant Officer Howley was at the main office or outside the front entrance. Just in case he was, Graham detoured and went out a gate on the far side of the school and walked an extra three blocks to get home.

As soon as he reached home, he settled to afternoon tea, then lay on his bed. Reaction set in quickly. All his worries surfaced once again. If Amelia gave in and told he was done for! That led him back to thoughts of running away. Feeling thoroughly depressed he collected all his hiking and camping gear and carried it down to the Ship Room. His mother saw him doing this and asked why.

"Just checking it. Pete was suggesting a hike and some of this stuff hasn't been unpacked since our last expedition," he replied.

Last expedition might be right, he thought bitterly as he sorted and cleaned it all.

Regrets and guilt coursed through him like a physical force. As he worked, he brooded so that by tea time he had worked himself into a real 'fit of the dejections' and was physically ill.

His mother noticed this as he picked at his food and again asked what was wrong. Graham shrugged and said 'Nothing', then worried that she wasn't convinced. To his relief, she didn't press the issue and he was able to escape to the privacy of the veranda. He took himself to bed early and pretended to read.

It was another long, miserable night. He hardly slept at all and brooded on his possible fate. By daylight on Wednesday he was shaking and exhausted. Once again, he contemplated saying he was sick but worry about whether Amelia had told gnawed at him. He had to know. There was also the problem of Cadets.

Warrant Officer Howley will be there, he thought.

The only answer seemed to be to avoid Cadets, but his mother reminded him as he was about to leave so he reluctantly packed the uniform in another bag.

I will just not go to Cadets, he decided.

That thought made him even more miserable as it would mean lying to his mother again. With a heavy heart he dragged himself to school. All the way he considered his options: Juvenile Detention Centre; running away; hiding in the jungle and becoming a bandit; running away to a big city down south, or to sea. For a few minutes, romantic notions of joining the French Foreign Legion flitted across his mind, to be followed by thoughts of death or suicide.

By the time he reached school, Graham was in a state of morose surliness. And there was no sign of Amelia. She had still not arrived by the time classes began. Worry over what might be happening plunged Graham into a state of extreme anxiety. This was made worse by another confrontation with Larsen and his mates. They taunted him from a distance calling him a coward and a faggot.

Graham walked to class in a mood of savage hostility at the whole world. Everything seemed to be going wrong.

It all seems so pointless! I wish I was dead! he thought.

The lesson was Maths A with Mr Burgomeister. Like many previous lessons, Graham hated it. He had trouble concentrating and his homework was poorly done. Somehow, he forced himself to sit through the lesson when all he felt like doing was walking out. As soon as the period was over, Graham packed his books and stood up.

Stephen looked at him quizzically. "Where ya going?"

"Sick room. I don't feel well," Graham replied.

He actually did feel sick, and it took no play acting to get permission from the office to lie down for the next two lessons. All the while he lay there, he brooded. Life seemed so black and pointless that he again reviewed all his gloomy options.

To avoid speaking to his friends, Graham remained in the sick room during morning break. The next two periods went by in a haze of despair. Shame and guilt wracked him. By the end of Chemistry, Graham had made himself sick again. He spent the lunch break in the sick room.

He lay there for the whole lunch hour, slowly depressing himself even more. Suicide seemed an even more attractive option by the time the bell went.

It was Mr Conkey who noticed him as he walked past. The next lesson was Geography and Graham should have been in the class. Mr Conkey stopped. "You look a bit down. What's the matter?"

"Not feeling well, sir," Graham replied.

"Might be better if you get up and do something. It will take your mind off it," Mr Conkey suggested.

Reluctantly Graham agreed and walked with Mr Conkey to class. His real reason for going was to find out if Amelia had arrived. His first action on entering the room was to look to see if she was there. No. She had not arrived.

She can't have come to school, he decided. *I wonder if she has already been sent to that convent?*

During the lesson, Graham sat on his own and worked. It was map drawing and interpretation again. Mr Conkey did not bother him, and he was happy to be left alone.

Last period was Maths B with Mr Ritter, again in B7. Stephen rejoined the class after Art. As soon as he saw Graham his face lit up. He came and sat next to him in their usual seat.

"How are you feeling?" he asked.

"Not the best," Graham replied truthfully. In his mind he was preparing his alibi for not going to Cadets.

Mr Ritter arrived and surveyed the class. His gaze settled on Graham and Stephen. "Ah! The two desperadoes! We won't have any nonsense today, will we?"

"No sir," Stephen replied. Graham just shook his head.

Mr Ritter walked over to their desk. "Good. So show me your homework for today."

Graham bit his lip. *Bloody homework!* He had quite forgotten it. "Haven't done it, sir," he managed to croak.

"Oh well. You can stay in again and finish it," Mr Ritter replied grimly.

Graham gripped his chair and willed himself to nod and say nothing although fierce hatred flared in his heart.

Stephen spoke up, "It is cadet day, sir. Can we do the punishment tomorrow?"

Cadets! Suddenly Graham was glad he was kept in. To his relief, Mr Ritter shook his head and said no. Graham began wondering how he might get away unseen at the end of the detention.

Somehow, he got through the lesson without getting into further trouble. At the end of the forty minutes, Mr Ritter checked who had done their homework. Six others including Stephen, Angus McDougal, and Vincent were kept in. Mr Ritter took no chances and walked up and down inside the room. Graham was feeling really upset and sick by this but forced himself to work.

While Graham and Stephen worked in the classroom, the army cadet unit formed up outside on the grass quadrangle. The sound of their talking, then of the shouted orders carried clearly up into the room. CSM Grey called the markers and then ordered the company on parade. They were then ordered to 'Right Dress'.

At that moment, another voice came from outside: Warrant Officer Howley's. Graham felt his heart start to pound as anxiety gripped him. His first impulse was to run. That was replaced by a wave of shame at such a cowardly idea, then guilt at what he had done, and of the people he was hurting, or would hurt.

Poor Millie! It is my fault she is in trouble. I'm a gutless weakling, he told himself.

For the remainder of the detention he mentally flailed his conscience. After ten minutes he felt so physically ill he was shaking and nauseous. All he wanted to do was get away.

As the cadets came marching off parade to go to their training lessons, Mr Ritter finally said that he and Stephen could go.

Stephen stood up at once. “Come on, Graham. Come and get changed into your uniform,” he said.

“Don’t think I’ll go. I feel sick,” Graham replied.

“Well I’m going,” Stephen said. “My mum and dad have been checking up. If I’m not at Cadets today I will be in real trouble,” he explained. He dashed out of the room and down the steps.

Graham packed his school bag slowly, his mind and body in turmoil. With Mr Ritter standing there he could not remain in the room so reluctantly he walked out onto the veranda and cautiously went to the top of the stairs. Anxiously, he looked around.

Where is Warrant Officer Howley? I don’t want to blunder straight into him, he thought.

Chapter 22

MOMENT OF TRUTH

Graham stood at the top of the stairs and watched as a platoon of cadets came marching out from underneath the building. The platoon sergeant, Anastasia Mitrovitch, was calling the step and yelling at them to march properly. As they marched off towards the oval Graham knew he had to move. He was now the only person left upstairs and had become conspicuous by that fact.

I should have gone down with the others, he ruefully realised.

But where was Warrant Officer Howley? Was he under the building or had he gone somewhere else? Graham took a deep breath and started down the steps. As he went down, he tried to act calm while at the same time looking anxiously in all directions.

And there he was! Not ten paces away!

Warrant Officer Howley stood under the building talking to Mr Conkey (now dressed in his captain's uniform). Graham was almost paralysed by fear. Somehow, he kept on walking to the bottom of the steps and continued on away from the warrant officer. At every step he expected to hear a shout calling him back, but nothing happened. After 20 paces he glanced back and saw that Warrant Officer Howley was still standing side on to him and was deep in conversation with Captain Conkey.

At that moment, a file of cadets came between Graham and the two officers. Using the cadets as cover he turned and went off under C Block. Ten paces had him safely out of sight. By then he was panting as though he had run a race and had to wipe sweat from his palms.

Made it! he thought, sighing with relief. *Safe!*

At a fast walk he headed along the path past the library to the corner gate. Another anxious glance back over his shoulder showed no sign of Warrant Officer Howley. Graham turned right and started walking home.

And then it hit him. First shame at sneaking away: *like a bloody mongrel dog, a dingo!*

Then guilt at what he had done and the harm he was causing Amelia. The truth rose up and nearly choked him. He stopped and stood there on the footpath, panting and nauseous.

You gutless rat, Kirk! he berated himself. *Face up to it like a man.*

Graham sensed he was at one of those moments of truth. He knew he could walk away and probably never be caught. But he also saw, with a flash of agonizing insight, that the price of doing that would be one he would bitterly regret for the rest of his days. Pride, integrity, self-respect, all would suffer. The burden of guilt would weigh him down and corrode his spirit.

Graham shuddered and drew a deep breath. Biting his lip and sneering with contempt at his own cowardice, he turned and started walking back. As he went through the school gate, he could hardly see for the tears that blinded him, but he squared his shoulders and strode on. Better to get it over with, and quickly.

As he walked back under the school, Graham began to worry about how to get Warrant Officer Howley where he could speak to him privately as he did not want a public scene. The course to follow was resolved even as he saw the man. Captain Conkey had just finished speaking to him and turned away towards the small office and Q Store under B Block. Warrant Officer Howley came striding towards Graham. He was obviously on his way to the oval. No other cadets or adult staff were in sight.

Graham swerved to meet Warrant Officer Howley, whose face showed puzzlement and recognition.

Graham stopped. "Excuse me, sir."

"Yes, what do you want Graham?" Warrant Officer Howley asked.

Graham swallowed, "Sir, I am the boy you are looking for."

Warrant Officer Howley looked puzzled. "The boy I am looking for? What do you mean? I haven't been looking for any cadet."

Graham felt paralysed . His face seemed to be made of thick plastic and he had trouble holding the man's gaze. "It was me, sir. With Millie... I mean with Amelia, on Sunday night. So you don't have to send her to a convent. Please sir. It was my fault. Don't punish her."

As the import of what Graham was saying sank in, Warrant Officer Howley's face changed from a puzzled smile to shock and finally to anger. His colour became a deep red. Graham noted his large hands start to clench and unclench.

"You! Sunday night!" Warrant Officer Howley said, shaking his head in disbelief. "So why are you owning up now?"

"To save her from being punished, sir. It was my fault."

Warrant Officer Howley exploded. "Like bloody hell it was! It takes two to tango, boy! The little trollop! She planned and organised that. Why, she even had a blanket spread ready! Why... how...? I don't know..."

For a moment, Warrant Officer Howley was at a loss for words as he struggled with violent emotions. Graham braced himself for a beating and resolved not to flinch. The man glared at him, his chest heaving as he mastered his rage. For a long minute he held Graham's gaze. Then he shook his head again.

"You! God almighty boy, I hope you aren't in love with her."

"Sir?"

"I said I hope you aren't in love with her. Listen boy, you are not the first. In fact, you are just the last in a long line. Her mother and I are at our wits end over what to do about her. Christ almighty! Give me a minute to get over the shock of this."

Graham stood in shocked silence. It hurt to see the pain in the man's eyes. It also hurt to learn the truth about Amelia. He had expected abuse and even blows, and now was not sure what to do next.

So he asked, "What will you do to me now, sir?"

"Do to you? I should kick your silly little arse so hard your nose will bleed! Bloody hell! She's underage boy! Jailbait! Damn it all, what you've just done, owning up, was a really gutsy thing to do. But I'm sorry. She is going to be punished," Warrant Officer Howley said fiercely.

"Please don't send her away, sir," Graham cried. He was aware that Captain Conkey had walked up beside them and had stopped.

Warrant Officer Howley snapped angrily, "Why not? So you can go on secretly meeting her?"

"No sir. I won't. I promise," Graham answered. He was scared but also very worried.

Captain Conkey spoke up, "Is everything alright, Kevin? Has Cadet Kirk been causing you any trouble?"

Warrant Officer Howley's mouth formed a grim line. "Family business, sir," he said. "Nothing to do with Cadets."

"Oh. Why aren't you in uniform, Graham?" Captain Conkey said.

"I was kept in, sir. It is here in my bag," Graham replied.

"Then get changed and get to your platoon," Captain Conkey ordered. He turned to Warrant Officer Howley. "Sergeant Major, your squad is waiting for you over there when you are finished here."

Warrant Officer Howley nodded. "Thanks. I will just clear up this problem first if you will excuse me, sir."

Captain Conkey gave Graham a penetrating look but took the hint. "Yes, I'll leave you to it." He turned and walked away.

Graham swallowed and braced himself for the worst. For a long minute Warrant Officer Howley stared at him, his face a grim, angry mask. Then he shook his head.

"You get changed and get to training, Cadet Kirk. I will deal with you later."

Graham swallowed. He could see the flush of shame and anger mottling the Warrant Officer's face and neck and that made him ashamed too. The realisation of the pain he was causing really burnt.

"What will you do to me, sir?" he managed to ask. Pride made him try to speak normally but he knew there was a tremor in his voice.

Warrant Officer Howley shook his head angrily. "Damn it all! Now I will have to crucify you, son. Sorry, but her mother is pretty hostile. Bloody hell, what a mess!"

Graham gulped. Crucify! He braced himself for the worst.

Warrant Officer Howley glared at him. Graham forced himself to meet his eye, even though every instinct was to hang his head in shame. Finally, Warrant Officer Howley chewed his lip, then said, "Go on, get to your platoon. I will speak to you after Cadets."

"Yes sir."

With a heart feeling like it was made of lead, Graham turned and walked towards the change room. He watched Warrant Officer Howley marching towards where a squad made up of all the corporals stood waiting for him. As Warrant Officer Howley got closer, his voice began to bark sharp commands. The corporals snapped to attention.

In the change room Graham sat and battled with his self-pity and misery. Tears came but he managed to brush these away. Luckily, he had the place to himself. Once again, the temptation was to run, to get away from this place and these people. He sighed. What good would that do?

I have owned up. I will have to wear it now, he told himself. Part of him felt relieved and glad at this. *I deserve to be punished.*

Then another awful thought came to him: Would God also punish him? Or would God use Warrant Officer Howley as the instrument of justice? It was a sickening thought.

When he was changed into uniform, Graham took himself slowly to the oval. By the time he arrived, the first period was almost over. He reported to Sgt Masters, explaining that he had been with Warrant Officer Howley. Sgt Masters nodded and eyed him with a look of distaste.

"You aren't starting very well as a cadet, are you Kirk? Late all the time and giving NCOs cheeky back answers. If you want to do any good, you'd better change your attitude."

Graham swallowed, his pride hurt. Nodding he murmured, "Yes."

"Yes what?"

"Yes sergeant."

Sgt Masters took out his roll book to mark him present. "Join the lesson," he ordered.

With his emotions a seething swirl of resentment and anxiety, Graham did as he was told. The lesson was on the treatment of burns. Graham took no notice. He thought he knew it all from Scouts and his thoughts were focused on the ordeal to come. So serious and black did things look that it took all his will power not to burst into tears.

The next lesson was taught by the corporals; more Fieldcraft: Night Vision and Night Movement. Graham was in such a bitter mood he could not resist a sarcastic jibe at Cpl Grenfell.

"Bit light, isn't it? You forgot to ask God to turn out the sun!"

Cpl Grenfell bristled and turned to snap at him, "Shut up, Cadet Kirk! Speak when you are spoken to. I don't want any lip from you. You call me Corporal, got it?"

Graham seethed and wanted to lash out but somehow held his temper. The sight of Captain Conkey in the distance helped.

Cpl Grenfell went on to explain that they would be using the skills on the bivouac scheduled for that weekend. A bivouac! Graham had quite forgotten about it. At that moment, it was the last thing he was interested in.

The rebuke from Cpl Grenfell hardened Graham's feelings. He formed the resolve to find some way out of the weekend bivouac.

An opportunity to do this arose after the last parade was over. While on parade they had been handed a 'Joining Instruction' and Permission

Form for the bivouac. As soon as they were dismissed, Graham started reading the instruction out of curiosity, never having seen one before. He found Stephen beside him.

Stephen sneered and shoved his instruction in his pocket. "Lot of crap. Anyway, I'm not going."

"Don't you have to? Won't your parents make you?" Graham asked.

"Yeah, they'll try. But I won't," Stephen replied.

"How will you get out of it?" Graham asked.

"Easy. They will drop me off here with my gear, but we will just walk away and not turn up," Stephen replied.

Graham was amazed. "Where will you go? What will you do?"

"We will just go camping on our own and have good fun, then get back in time to be picked up by the oldies on Sunday afternoon," Stephen replied.

Graham was intrigued. "We? Who else?"

"Derek and Dru and me," Stephen replied. "You can come if you like."

It was a fascinating and frightening concept. Graham asked, "Where are you going to go?"

"Up to Stoney Creek and into the jungle," Stephen replied.

"But... but won't you get found out?" Graham asked.

Stephen sneered. "Not likely. We've done it before. You just get your oldies to sign the Permission Form and they think you are at Cadets. But you don't hand it in to the officers and don't turn up, so they think you aren't allowed or something. They only check when they are suspicious."

"You sure?" Graham asked. It sounded too easy to be true.

"'Course I am. It's too much paperwork for the officers to check all the time," Stephen replied.

On the other side of the quadrangle Graham spotted Warrant Officer Howley. *If I am quick, I can get away before he arrives,* he thought. Almost instantly he rejected the idea. *No. That would just make him even angrier.* That such an action would also damage his own self-respect even more, as well as lowering Warrant Officer Howley's opinion of him, was plain. *He will think I am a real gutless rat.*

So Graham excused himself and started marching towards Warrant Officer Howley. On the way he felt his stomach turn over and he knew he was scared. He took a deep breath and squared his shoulders. Warrant

Officer Howley saw him coming and stopped. Graham halted in front of him, remaining at 'Attention'.

Warrant Officer Howley pursed his lips and looked grim. He looked Graham up and down, keeping him in a cold sweat of suspense. Finally, he said, "You'd better go home, Cadet Kirk. I don't want to take action against you in a hot temper. Besides, I have to speak to my wife about what we should do."

"Will... will you be telling my mother?" Graham asked. He managed to speak without croaking but had to lick his lips.

"Probably. Holy mackerel kid, if Amelia's mother decides to make a real issue of this you will find yourself in court! Now get going!"

Almost sick with dread, Graham did as he was told. He battled with the tears until he was clear of the school, then sobbed with misery as he walked home. By the time he had arrived there, he had himself under control again. The next problem was whether to tell his mother or not. He decided not to.

Not until I have to anyway, he decided.

But that decision did nothing for his self-respect and he silently despised himself. To help hide his unhappiness he hid himself in the Ship Room all afternoon.

It was another miserable night. Homework was done. As soon as it was completed Graham took to his bed and pretended to read. For hours he brooded, his imagination conjuring up the worst that he could think of. He began to dread the next meeting with Warrant Officer Howley.

He will be on the bivouac I suppose, Graham pondered.

That made the event even less attractive. Into his mind crept Stephen's plan to avoid the bivouac. At first he rejected it as cowardly and impractical, but the idea kept returning to him repeatedly during the night. It sounded risky but also had an exciting thrill to it- to be able to beat the system.

On Thursday morning, Graham felt so wretched and exhausted that he considered telling his mother he was sick. He knew she was aware that something was wrong but could not bring himself to tell her. Feeling like what he imagined a condemned man on his way to the gallows might feel like, he dragged himself off to school.

All the way he prepared himself for the worst. On arrival he looked around for Amelia, but she was not there.

I wonder where she is? he thought.

Worry over what Warrant Officer Howley and his wife would decide to do gnawed at him till he wanted to throw up. He was not familiar with the law and legal processes (and doubly scared because of his ignorance!) so he conjured up dreadful images of his possible fate.

When First Bell went with no sign of Amelia or her father, Graham was even more concerned. *Is he just making me sweat as extra punishment? What is happening?*

Unsure and deeply distressed, Graham made his way to class. The sight of Amelia's empty seat added a twist to his misery. It was a dreadful day. The tension slowly built. At every moment Graham expected a summons to the office. His imagination constructed and replayed the awful scenes: the interview with Warrant Officer Howley and his wife; with the principal; with the police; with his own mother and father. That last thought really made him perspire.

Stephen could tell that something was wrong and several times sounded Graham to try to find out. One of his probes came very close to the truth when he asked if he had done something to Amelia. To Graham's relief, he changed the topic to what they were doing on the weekend.

"We are still going camping. Do you want to come with us?"

"I don't see how we could get away with it," Graham replied.

Stephen explained again how he and his friends had done the same thing earlier in the year and got away with it. "It's easy. Come with us Graham. It will be more fun than being bossed around by that pack of Little Hitlers."

Graham did not commit himself one way or the other, but the idea festered. It was one way to avoid Warrant Officer Howley. The idea of spending a whole weekend in close proximity to the man was enough to make Graham feel both scared and sick. When the day ended with no word from Warrant Officer Howley Graham took himself home to brood. The idea of going off with Stephen kept returning.

I could just go bush and stay there, he thought.

That led to fantasies of becoming a bandit or bushranger until the police finally tracked him down and put him out of his misery. One thing was for sure; he did not want to go on the cadet bivouac. But he did get his mother to sign the Permission Form, though not without some misgivings about possibly deceiving her.

On the Friday, the idea was given added fuel when CSM Grey stopped him in the school yard and told him he needed a haircut.

Resentment surged in Graham. "You can't tell me how to wear my hair!" he retorted. At that stage his hair was quite long and brushed well back.

"No, you are right, Cadet Kirk," CSM Grey replied. "But if you want to get promoted you will have to decide which group you want to belong to; the long-haired yobbos, or us."

"I'm not a long-haired yobbo! And don't call me Cadet Kirk when we aren't in uniform," Graham replied angrily.

"Suit yourself. See you tomorrow," CSM Grey replied.

"No you won't! I'm not going on the bivouac," Graham replied.

To his relief, CSM Grey did not ask why. Instead he walked away leaving Graham seething with emotion. His first move after that was to seek out Stephen.

"Can I come with you blokes on the weekend?" he asked.

Stephen nodded. "Sure. Be glad to have you," he replied.

"Where do we meet?" Graham asked.

"Outside the school at 0730. Derek's big brother Travis is going to give us a lift."

Graham was intrigued. "Where are we going?"

"Kamerunga and then up Smiths Track," Stephen replied.

That really interested Graham. During the hikes to Kuranda earlier in the year he had often studied the map and noted the old pioneer pack tracks which went from Cairns to the Tablelands over the coastal mountains.

"That'll be good," he said. "I've never been along Smiths Track."

He had been along Douglas Track which also went up from Kamerunga but on the other side of Stoney Creek, both tracks joining in the Speewah area. He knew that his Great, Great Grandfather, Robert Smythe Kirk, the one in the cemetery, had been a mule packer up those tracks during the Gold Rushes of the 19th Century.

Stephen went on. "We will find a good spot to camp and have a great time, then walk back down again on Sunday morning."

"Do we wear our uniforms?"

Stephen nodded. "Yes, but bring some civvies to change into."

Graham was both intrigued and excited. The idea of hiking over the mountains had great appeal. *And it gets me out of this cadet bivouac,* he told himself.

But it wasn't as easy as that. Once again, the day dragged by with Graham in a state of emotional turmoil. Amelia did not appear and there was no word from Warrant Officer Howley.

"The bastard! He is doing it deliberately to torment me!" Graham muttered. It made him even more determined not to go on the bivouac. "I will go with Steve and the others," he resolved.

That meant money for food, which presented another problem. Graham had very little. That afternoon at home he solved the problem by sneaking into his mother's room and taking a twenty dollar note from her purse.

I will pay it back as soon as I can, he told himself, to ease an already sore conscience. He had never done anything like it before and it left him feeling troubled and upset.

Lying to Peter bothered him as well. This happened at Scouts when Peter asked him if he was looking forward to the bivouac.

Graham swallowed and shook his head. "No. I won't be going."

"Why not?" Peter asked in astonishment.

"Mum has grounded me. I have lots of chores at home I have neglected," he concluded lamely. The bit about the chores was true enough but the lie still hurt.

To his relief, Peter did not question him further. He just said, "Pity. I reckon you would have really enjoyed it."

Graham thought about that later and decided that Peter was probably right. He did think that the exercise sounded interesting; each platoon hiding in an allotted area and trying to locate and raid the others. He began to waver over his decision and wondered if he shouldn't change his mind and go to the cadet bivouac.

Worry over this kept him awake much of the night. By 0600 Saturday morning when his alarm went, he was feeling sick inside and very nervous.

"I'm being stupid," he told himself. "I should go to Cadets and not take the risk of getting into even more trouble."

This was what he said to Stephen as soon as he met him at 0725 outside the school. He had walked, carrying his gear, and wearing uniform. Stephen curled his lip.

"Not scared, are you?"

Graham licked his lips. He was but did not want to admit it. Stephen twisted the knife. "If you ain't game then don't come. We don't want any weakies with us."

At that moment, Dru and Derek arrived. Graham did not wish to argue in front of them as he knew they would tease him unmercifully and accuse him of being a coward. Feeling sick inside and berating himself for lacking the guts to stand up to them, he started walking with them along the footpath to where a 4WD utility was parked.

At that time there were dozens of vehicles coming and going as parents dropped off cadets, so nobody paid them any attention. But at any moment Graham expected someone to ask them what they were doing as he and his friends slung their packs and webbing into the back of the ute

But as he climbed into the back seat and the ute drove away from the school, Graham felt very anxious. In his heart he knew he was doing the wrong thing. He also despised himself for being weak and for being scared. He bit his lip and hoped it would all come out right.

They passed several other vehicles with cadets in them making their way to school and that caused more worry. What if they mentioned they had seen them? It was a very unhappy Graham who arrived at Kamerunga at 0815 with the other three deserters.

Derek's brother did not stop at the Kamerunga picnic area but drove on along the bitumen road towards Rainforest Estate, the small suburb nestled in the jungle at the bottom end of the Stoney Creek valley. Two hundred metres further along, he was directed to park in a small parking area on the right of the road. This was in rain forest with the bottom of the mountain on the left and a steep drop down into the Barron River on the right.

"This is it," Stephen said.

The friends climbed out of the ute and collected their gear. As they did, a car drove past towards Cairns. The driver looked at them curiously as they went past. The fact that they were all in uniform and therefore very noticeable added to Graham's discomfiture.

"Do we change now?" he asked.

Stephen shook his head. "No. We can do that later. Let's get off the road so we aren't as conspicuous.

As he said this, both Derek and Dru picked up long bundles from out of the back. These were so obviously rifles wrapped in cloth that Graham felt another spasm of anxiety. He knew there were very strict laws about who could have a firearm and under what conditions. He did not know the details but did know that minors under 18 years of age could not have them unless supervised by a qualified and licensed adult. And the only adult was the driver of the ute, and he was obviously not staying.

"See you after lunch tomorrow," he called.

Then he backed the ute out, gunned the engine and raced away back towards Cairns. As the vehicle vanished from view Graham's spirits sank further. He was gripped by doubt and anxiety and now really regretted he had joined the group.

Stephen pointed across the road. "That way. Let's get into the jungle before more cars come along," he said and swung on his webbing.

Hoisting on his pack he led the way across to where a tiny sign said, SMITHS TRACK. It was a rough foot trail and not at all what Graham had been expecting. Back in April they had come down a track from the railway and it had been bench cut and easy to follow. That track ended at the old Scout Hut he could just see half hidden in the jungle a hundred metres away across the small creek to his left front. The memory of that adventure held him for a few moments, and he wished he was on a hike with his usual friends, not with this group.

For a few seconds Graham contemplated leaving the group and walking back to town on his own. *I could phone mum from Redlynch,* he thought. But the thought of having to explain to his mother what had happened daunted him. So did the other option- of walking all the way home. *That would be halfway across the city, and in cadet uniform.*

So, despising himself as a weakling and regretting his foolishness, he swung on his webbing and pack and followed the others off the road and up the winding foot trail into the jungle.

It was at least a relief to get out of sight of passing cars. In fact they had only just climbed about 50 paces before one did. *Just in time,* he thought. To cheer himself up he began to imagine that they were group of bandits fleeing into the mountains to escape the police.

It was 0830 by then. *The cadets will be on parade having the roll called now,* Graham thought unhappily. *If only I hadn't allowed myself to get talked into this!* He knew his mother would be very hurt if she found out. *I'll never do it again!* he vowed.

Chapter 23

CAMPING

Hiking over the mountains was one of Graham's favourite activities, usually filled with happy memories of other expeditions and adventures. But this hike he found to be nothing but misery. All the way he fretted and worried, although he tried to hide this and joined in the laughter and jokes with the others. Even the scenery held no interest for him. The only good thing was noting that he was very much fitter than any of the others, even Stephen. Derek and Dru were so unfit they had to stop to get their breath back nearly every hundred paces.

The narrow track zig-zagged up the spine of a steep ridge, coming out of jungle into more open country. Lantana and other bushes grew thickly in places and the track wound up through these thickets. The narrowness and overhanging long grass added to his anxiety. Fear of snakes rose up to grip him and often to cause his steps to falter. For that reason he went last, working on the theory that the snake would bite the first or second person. But that was small comfort.

Much of the time Graham just plodded slowly up, sweating and puffing and lost in his thoughts.

These included stark memories of the hike earlier in the year when they had encountered the jungle madman nicknamed 'Tarzan'. These memories were at the top of his mind when the trail they were on led up over the top of the Kuranda railway. The railway and some of its tunnels were visible a hundred metres below them and also on a bench cut on the slope across the far side of the valley. From that direction the scene was dominated by the massive craggy bulk of Glacier Rock.

Stephen pointed to it. "Remember when we climbed that with the Scouts last year?" he commented.

Graham nodded, and Stephen proceeded to relate the adventure of Tarzan to the others. He described the camp site above Stoney Creek Falls railway station and the drama when Roger had nearly slipped over the falls to his death. Graham had climbed down to save him, and it had been the riskiest and most terrifying thing he had ever done.

"We aren't planning to camp there are we?" he asked.

Stephen shook his head. "Nah! We will camp on top of the ridge where there is a better view," he said.

That was some relief to Graham, and he lapsed back into his brooding thoughts as they slogged on up.

It took the friends three hours to reach the top of the climb and another hour to walk down a gently sloping crestline towards Tobys Lookout. On the way they met three middle-aged hikers going the other way, two women and a man. They looked at them curiously and one of the women looked hard at the rolled-up bundles containing the rifles. That made Graham glad they were in cadet uniform.

He might think cadets are allowed to have guns, he thought. But Graham felt very guilty. He had to make an effort to nod a greeting.

At Tobys Lookout they dropped their packs and rested. As they did, four more bushwalkers arrived, having hurried up behind them. After a few greetings these people moved on down a track into the jungle, leaving the four boys alone.

"That's better," Derek said. "Now we can enjoy ourselves"

Dru looked around the small clearing among the she-oaks on the narrow ridge top. "Where will we camp?' he asked.

Stephen pointed northwards along another narrow foot trail. "Somewhere along there, where there aren't liable to be as many people. I reckon we should go along that way a bit until we are above Stoney Creek Falls."

Graham agreed. "This looks like the main track," he said, pointing down the well-worn trail the four hikers had taken.

So they walked for another 200 paces before finding a small open area just where the almost overgrown track doubled back and plunged down a steep slope towards where Stoney Creek could be heard down in thick jungle.

Derek dropped his pack. "This will do," he said.

Dru dropped his pack as well and then began to unroll the bundle containing his rifle. "Good spot. Now we can get out the weaponry."

Stephen agreed and dropped his back and undid his sleeping bag. Graham watched in horrified surprise as Stephen unrolled his sleeping bag to reveal a dismantled rifle. It had been sawn short, both the stock and barrel, to make it small enough to hide in the pack. The rifle was a .22". Both Dru and Derek also unrolled .22s of one sort or another. Graham was aghast. None of them was old enough to own or carry a firearm. He knew that the state gun laws were very strict and that they had to be 18 to do have them. And there was no adult to supervise them.

"You blokes could get into real trouble with those," he said.

"Crap!" Dru sneered. "Who's gunna see us here?"

"It's a National Park. You shouldn't have guns in one, not even with a permit," Graham went on.

The others laughed. Derek jeered and waved his arm around. "So! Where are the Rangers? Do you think Smokey the Bear is going to drop out of the trees and arrest us?"

Graham shook his head and looked around uneasily. Dru sneered again and said, "You don't have to stay with us. If you are scared, then piss off! Run off home like a good little boy."

That burnt Graham's self-esteem. So did the fear he felt when Derek added, "And don't you dob on us. You say anything to anyone, and we will deal with you, see!"

Graham swallowed. "I won't say anything. I'm just surprised that you have the guns, that's all," he said.

He almost said that sawn-off weapons were illegal, but he knew they would sneer at that as well, so he held his tongue. Much as he now regretted being there, he did not want to endure more scorn by leaving.

Stephen ended the argument by saying, "It'll be okay. We aren't likely to meet anyone here."

But Graham was still worried. "Do you think we should camp here?" he asked. "Isn't that the track that comes up past the falls?' he added, pointing to an even fainter foot track that led on down the spine of the ridge northwards. The last time they had climbed it had been on the hike when Tarzan had chased them. He looked anxiously around.

Stephen curled his lip and laughed. "It'll be fine. Anyway, your mate Tarzan isn't around anymore. And even if he is we can blow him away."

To demonstrate this, Stephen pointed his rifle down into the jungle and pulled the trigger. Graham was appalled. The crack of the shot echoed around the mountains.

"Christ, Steve! Stop that! We will get into real strife if we get caught. Come on, let's get out of here before anyone comes."

The others laughed. Stephen shook his head. "No. This is a good spot to camp. Don't be such a bloody scaredy-cat. If anyone comes, we will just hide the guns."

Reluctantly, Graham took off his pack and webbing. Then he stood and had a big drink, thinking hard all the while. Dru also had a drink then held his water bottle upside down.

"I'm out of water," he commented.

"Have you only got one water bottle?" Graham asked in astonishment.

Dru just scowled in reply. "No, two, but they are both empty. Let's go down to the creek and refill," he said.

This was agreed to. Packs were left hidden in the grass and the four made their way down the steep track with webbing and rifles. A hundred paces down the slope the track crossed Stoney Creek. The creek flowed down through a beautiful setting of jungle and moss-covered boulders. There were several pools of waist deep, crystal clear water.

Graham was enthralled. He thought it one of the most beautiful places he had ever seen. The trees met overhead to form a shady tunnel through which the crystal-clear water rippled over small stones. Ferns and vines made it the perfect jungle setting. Beams of sunlight shone through to give it a delightful pattern of light and shade. Butterflies and other small insects flitted through the glade.

"Bloody nice spot," Derek voted. "What about a swim?"

"Be bloody cold," Dru said.

But they were all hot and sweaty, so a swim was agreed on. The boys dumped their webbing and rifles and stripped off. Graham had been half expecting this and it was what he and his friends of the 'Hiking Team' normally did, but in this case he felt a bit inhibited. It made him glad he was 'normal' as a male. But he became uneasy and embarrassed as he had heard rumours that Dru and his brother were both 'gay'.

I hope he doesn't try to do anything to me, he worried.

To hide himself he hurried into the icy cold water. The others followed. For the next ten minutes the boys splashed and swam happily. But there was more embarrassment as both Dru and Derek stood up and made crude gestures and jokes.

Graham was embarrassed and even more worried. *I hope he isn't going to suggest things,* he thought anxiously.

He was able to relax a little when Derek grinned, and said, "What we need are a coupl'a sheilas."

That comment was a relief to Graham, but he was still embarrassed. To add to his own problems, he was ashamed to realise that memories of swimming nude with girls was also causing him to stiffen up. To forestall this, he quickly walked out of the water and began to dry himself.

Stephen joined him. Glancing at Graham he said, "Are you wishing Millie was here?"

Graham blushed bright red and a flood of hot memories swirled in his mind. They were replaced by images of Amelia and then her father. *Warrant Officer Howley, is he wondering where I am? What story will I tell him when he asks?* he worried. For he was sure Warrant Officer Howley would ask. The fear of that probable confrontation was enough to kill his desire.

Quickly he dressed while Dru and Derek played rude games in the water. To Graham's relief, Stephen also got dressed and looked a bit askance at their goings-on.

After the swim there was a debate as to whether they should camp there or not. Graham shook his head. "There isn't enough level space and it will be damp," he said. Having camped in such spots before he had no desire to do so again.

Stephen supported him in this, so they refilled their water bottles, pulled on their webbing and set off to climb back up to the ridge top.

On reaching the crest, Graham stopped and looked around. The view across the valley was spectacular. Directly opposite was the rugged grey mass of Glacier Rock. He breathed deeply and revelled in the freedom and in the feeling of physical well-being. To him the jungle-covered mountains looked marvellous, and he felt very much at home, knew himself to be so.

That's because Great, Great Granddad was a mule packer over these tracks way back in 1876 during the Hodgekinson Goldrush when Cairns was founded, he mused. *My country,* he thought happily. And he knew he was doing what he loved best, walking around the bush exploring it.

"We will camp here," he agreed.

Packs were dragged from their hiding places and dumped in a rough circle. The four then sat on them to cook and eat lunch. Graham was a bit annoyed when Derek and Dru just tossed their empty tins and litter into the grass, but he said nothing. For an hour the boys sat and ate, talking and telling jokes as they did.

But in spite of the surroundings Graham was tense and unhappy. He could not stop thinking about the cadet bivouac. It was at Davies Creek, another 20 or so kilometres further west.

Warrant Officer Howley will be there. He must think I am a gutless rat, Graham thought bitterly. In his heart he knew he had made a series of mistakes. *I wish I hadn't come with these blokes. This was a mistake too.*

Misery twisted his lips, but he said nothing, just made the decision to try to get it over with as quickly as possible.

After lunch the boys set out to explore and hunt. They walked down to the creek again and crossed it then followed a foot trail which led up into the rainforest. The boys walked slowly along 'hunting' but the only living thing they saw was a scrub turkey. Dru snapped off a shot at it but missed. The scrub turkey scuttled out of sight.

Derek and Stephen both jeered. Dru was annoyed and fired twice more, missing both times. Then he tried to shoot butterflies. The bullets went whacking off rocks into the jungle. This caused shouts of laughter and more gunshots. Graham felt very uneasy about this. He was not only worried about the noise attracting other people but about safety. He was not impressed with the way both Derek and Dru carried their rifles. They slung them casually over their shoulders or wandered along gripping the stock, with fingers on triggers.

"Yaah! Shit!" Derek cried as he slipped on a wet rock.

Bang!

There was a moment of shocked silence.

Dru swore. "Bloody hell! That nearly got me!" he cried.

For a minute the boys stood in silence. Graham felt sick inside. What if the bullet had hit Dru? He contemplated the awful task of getting him to medical help, or worse still, of having a corpse to explain to the police.

"For God's sake, be more careful with those guns!" he snapped. "Keep your fingers off those triggers, and watch where you are pointing them!"

The others made no reply to this but both Derek and Dru scowled. Stephen changed the subject and suggested they try hunting further along. The group moved on, following the track up out of the creek and up a slope to the end of an old, overgrown timber snig track.

As they walked, Graham came last. He watched uneasily as the boys swung the rifles from one side of the track to the other as their eyes searched for game. Derek and Dru still walked with their fingers on the trigger. Stephen at least did not. His French manufactured semi-automatic looked very businesslike.

Apart from a few screeching cockatoos which fled at the first shot, and some crashing noises in the undergrowth, they saw nothing to shoot. That pleased Graham as he wasn't in the mood for killing anything. For lack of anything better to shoot at they stopped in an overgrown clearing and fired at pieces of paper set up as targets.

Graham was allowed to fire Stephen's rifle but only ten rounds. The others each had several packets of 50 rounds and they blazed away for well over an hour, trying all sorts of tricks such as firing one handed, or snap shooting. Derek was the better shot, to Dru's obvious annoyance. It was fun in a way, but Graham knew he wasn't really enjoying it. He kept thinking about the cadet bivouac, wondering what it was like. Every few minutes he would worry about what Warrant Officer Howley and his wife were going to do. The result was a physical pain in his chest and a sick feeling in the stomach.

I should have gone to the bivouac and gotten it over with it, he told himself miserably.

Back at their camp he found the contrast between it and his memories of the previous weekend expedition quite marked. Here there was camaraderie of a sort, but not the relaxed mateship of the cadet staff. Nor were the stories as interesting. Dru and Derek spent most of the time trying to outdo each other with tales of bravado, or of how good they were at hunting. The conversation moved to sex and Derek implied he was an expert on women's breasts. That was a subject which fascinated Graham, so he listened with avid attention. His own experiences then swamped his consciousness and reminded him of Amelia and of the trouble he was in. It was all he could do not to burst into tears.

As darkness set in, they lit a fire and sat around it cooking and eating. Graham sat and watched the last glow of the sunset on Glacier Rock and tried to tell himself he was happy, but he knew he was not. He just wanted the weekend to finish so he could escape from a situation he now recognised he should never have gotten into at all.

Then things got worse. To his dismay, all three of the others produced bottles of alcohol. Stephen had Vodka, Dru had Bundaberg Rum, and Derek had Bacardi Rum. Graham was invited to join in as they sipped and swigged. Rather than admit he did not want to, he smiled and pretended to enjoy it. The fierce raw liqueur bit at his throat and made him gasp and his eyes water but he pretended it was great and laughed and joked with the others.

Soon they were all drunk. Graham had only been really drunk that once before, but he found this both enjoyable and disconcerting. After an hour or so, his eyes were becoming unfocused and his head was spinning, but he felt very happy and quite uninhibited. Crude jokes became the thing and Graham offered some of the best. They laughed and sang filthy songs and it seemed that they were really having a great time.

Then things changed very quickly. First Dru nearly slid over the edge of the cliff as he staggered over to have a pee. Just in time, Stephen grabbed him He was dragged back up with much giggling and joking, to be teased by Derek about his penis which still dangled out of his trousers. Dru waggled this and they all told penis stories and jokes. That made Graham uneasy because there was more than a hint of homosexuality about some of the comments.

Then Dru surprised Graham by sitting beside him and putting his arm around him. Next he suggested they 'do things'. It took a moment for Graham to realise what Dru was hinting at. Then the shock hit him like a drenching of cold water.

He is gay, and he fancies me! he thought. Shame and anxiety caused him to burn, and he moved away.

As he sat to one side, Graham found his heart hammering with disgust and anxiety. *This must be how girls feel when they are the victim of an unwanted advance,* he thought. Memories of how he and Stephen had said things to Rosemary and other girls caused him to burn with remorse.

But it was Derek who really spoiled it all. He became surly and bad-tempered, then wanted to fight. It took quite an effort to calm him down. To Graham's dismay, but the drunken amusement of the others, Derek grabbed his rifle and blazed angrily into the night until the magazine was empty. One of the shots hit Stephen's billy, which was simmering over the fire. The bullet ricocheted between Graham and Stephen with a vicious whine. Steam and smoke billowed. It was with difficulty that Stephen persuaded Derek to let the rifle go. For a few minutes Graham was worried that the two would fight over it, as Stephen had hold of the rifle as well.

It was very sobering, and equally unpleasant. Derek subsided, cursing and swearing onto his sleeping bag and picked up the rum bottle to swig from it. In one gulp he drained it dry, then swore and threw it over the cliff. To everyone's relief, he then lay back and began to snore.

Then a drunken Dru made several more hints about 'enjoying themselves'. This really bothered and embarrassed Graham, but Stephen helped to end the situation and finally a grumpy, but very drunk, Dru collapsed on his sleeping bag.

It was a dreadful night for Graham. He found himself vomiting, clinging to a sapling on top of the cliff. Then he experienced the world revolving and making him nauseous again. He tried to sleep but kept having bad dreams and waking up. All the time he seemed to be conscious of the trouble he was in, and of the wrong he had done. Sheer misery finally dominated his thoughts.

He woke in the grey of dawn with a splitting headache, tasting the horrible furriness of a hangover in his mouth. His vision seemed blurry and he felt awful. It was definitely a new experience; and not a pleasant one. He rolled over and groaned, holding his head and wishing he could slip back into oblivion.

Derek woke them all with a start. "Bloody pig!" he cried.

Graham squinted in the morning light and saw a small black bush pig sniffing at the empty cans that had been tossed down the slope. Derek reached across for his rifle, grabbed it by the muzzle and hauled it towards him.

Bang!

Graham gasped in shock. Derek cried out and dropped the rifle, his hands flying to his face.

Oh my God! he's shot himself! Graham thought. He and Stephen sprang up and ran to him.

It was only a graze. The bullet had nicked the corner of Derek's temple. There was plenty of blood, but it was only a flesh wound. Derek was badly shaken and broke into a fit of shivering when he realised just how close he had come to death. His recovery wasn't helped by Stephen suddenly throwing up beside him.

Graham found a Band Aid in his webbing and, after washing the wound and stopping the flow of blood, put it on.

"It isn't too bad," he reassured Derek.

"Do you think my mum will see it is a bullet wound?" Derek asked.

Graham shook his head. "No. It just looks like you caught yourself on something. Tell her it was a barbed wire fence you were crawling under."

Derek nodded and mumbled to himself. "Gawd, I've got a headache! That was a bloody good night. Hey! Wake up Dru, ya slug!"

Dru lay sprawled on his sleeping bag. He had taken off his trousers in the night and his penis was hanging out of his underpants. It was obvious he had pissed himself and Graham found the sight disgusting. He rose and walked over to his own gear and sat with his back to them, watching the sunrise shining on Glacier Rock.

Out of perverseness he made a special effort to wash and shave, then brushed his boots before cooking breakfast. *I wish I'd gone on the bivouac!* he told himself for the hundredth time.

The others took a long time to get up. Dru was surly and ill-mannered. Stephen lay down after vomiting again. Derek kept nursing his head and muttering. Graham looked at them with disfavour, then around the campsite with disgust. The place was a litter of cans, bottles, and paper. Someone had done a turd during the night and left it lying unburied nearby. Flies buzzed around it.

"What a mob of pigs we are!" Graham muttered, then got up and picked up all the rubbish and buried the crap, not caring what the others thought of him. Then he sat and stared moodily across at Glacier Rock. The others lay down and appeared to have dropped off to sleep.

Once again, Graham catalogued his failings and sins and then contemplated his options. Everything looked desperate and pointless. Leaning against the tree beside him was Stephen's rifle.

That's an option. I'll shoot myself now and end it all, he thought bitterly. He reached across and picked the rifle up. An examination showed it had a full magazine.

For a time Graham sat with the rifle across his knees, feeling the harsh, cold reality of the metal. Into his mind crowded images of death. What would it really be like? Would he go to heaven, or to hell? Or was there no such thing? Was it all just like sleeping, a black nothing? In his misery he berated himself once more for being a coward, for not having the courage to end it all.

With a determined move he placed the butt of the rifle on the ground and moved the muzzle to the centre of his forehead. The steel was cold and the thought of the bullet smashing through bone and flesh made his head feel as though a cold hand was gripping it firmly. Goosebumps stood out. He trembled and realised he was sweating, despite the chill.

With his right hand he pushed the cocking handle back. The sear clicked audibly as it engaged. *Now, all I have to do is pull the trigger,* he thought.

He rested his head against the muzzle and moved his hand to the trigger. It was cold as well. He shivered.

Go on! Do it, you coward! his mind cried.

In the depths of his misery he thought of all the bad things he had done. *Perhaps God will forgive me,* he hoped.

He dwelt on trying to have sex with Amelia, and was annoyed that he remembered it with pleasure and began to get aroused. To help psych himself up he switched to topics which might feed his misery.

School. I hate school. And I hate the teachers; well, not all the teachers. Mr. Captain Conkey is okay.

That made him remember the cadet bivouac and the unhappiness welled up. "Go on, pull the trigger. Nobody will care," he told himself.

But he knew they would. *Mum will be dreadfully upset. And so will Kylie,* he thought. For a time he contemplated gaining savage revenge by hurting other people through his death, but he knew it wasn't his way. There were people who would be terribly hurt. *Amelia might need me; and her old man will think I just took the coward's way out. And there are people who do love me and care about me. I've got good friends,* he told himself.

He catalogued his friends, starting with Peter and Roger and only later thinking about Stephen. Derek and Dru he now saw clearly as false friends.

And I am loved. Poor little Margaret will be heartbroken, he mused.

With a sigh he moved the rifle muzzle aside, unloaded the weapon and eased the working parts forward before applying the safety catch. He stood up and stretched, while the ideas in his mind crystallised.

I will take my medicine like a man, then make another start, he resolved. With that decided he began his preparations.

It was nine O'clock before the others stirred again and another hour before they were sitting around eating breakfast. During this time Graham sat staring out across the valley, moodily brooding on how he would explain the weekend when he got home.

It will mean more lies, he realised. The thought made him feel even sicker.

Stephen joined him. "What do we do today?" he asked.

Graham grunted and turned to him his mind made up. "I'm going home."

Stephen nodded. "I'll come with you."

Dru had been listening. "Aren't you staying with us?"

Graham shook his head. "No. I'm going now."

"Well stuff you then!" Dru yelled angrily.

Graham just shrugged but stood up and began gathering his gear. Both Derek and Dru watched for a while then Derek said, "You will have to walk. You ain't comin' back in my brother's ute."

Again Graham shrugged. It just meant more walking, but he almost looked forward to the pain as a sort of penance.

Stephen pointed down the slope. "We can go home on a train," he said.

Graham shook his head. "The tourist trains only come back from Kuranda after lunch. That will too late for us," he said. Having walked and travelled the railway half a dozen times only a few months before he knew the timetable.

Stephen bit his lip and looked at Derek and Dru. They scowled and bent to their cooking. Then Stephen shook his head.

"If we walk or go by train, we will be very late home."

Graham's mind had been busy. "There are busses between Mareeba and Cairns. We could catch one at Speewah," he suggested.

"How far is that?" Stephen asked.

"Five or six kilometres from memory," Graham replied. He hauled out his map and studied it. "At least six, two hours if we step it out," he said.

"Train then," Stephen said.

Graham shook his head, suddenly sick of the whole situation. "No. I am walking to Speewah. I'm sick of sitting around here," he said. Driven by a desire to get away from Dru and Derek, he stood up and bent to pick up his webbing and pack.

"Are you going now?" Stephen asked in surprise.

"Yes," Graham replied as he pulled on his webbing.

Stephen looked worried and glanced from him to the others. Graham picked up his pack and swung it on.

Derek made a face. "Piss off then, Kirk. We don't want ya with us."

"I'm going," Graham replied. Determined to act he started walking down the track towards the creek.

"An' don't you dob on us, ya gutless turd!" Dru shouted after him.

Graham did not reply. He just kept walking. He was scared, both because he was walking off into the jungle alone, and because of what the others might do.

From behind him, Stephen called, "Hang on, Graham! I will come with you."

Graham looked back and saw an anxious looking Stephen picking up his rifle and gear. He slowed down to allow him to catch up. When he did, he said, "Get that gun out of sight then."

Stephen made no complaint. They stopped and Stephen dismantled the rifle and wrapped it in his sleeping bag. This was strapped into his pack. Graham was greatly relieved that his friend was coming with him. While Stephen did up his pack Graham studied his map.

As Stephen swung his pack on, he said, "They are bad news those two."

Graham grunted agreement and started walking. As he did, a rifle shot rang out behind them. The bullet cracked through the trees above them. Dru's jeering laughter carried to them. Both Derek and Dru began to shout obscenities and insults. More shots snapped through the trees. Graham flinched anxiously but could hear the bullets striking tree trunks well above him.

Just trying to frighten us, he decided. He kept walking but did not increase his pace.

The two friends headed down into the rainforest and soon came to the creek. There was a pause to refill water bottles before they continued. Graham breathed the cool, fresh air and felt immeasurably happier.

Now we are free, he thought. Then gloom clouded his brow again. *No we aren't. I still have to explain the weekend when we get home! And there was still Warrant Officer Howley to face!*

Chapter 24

SOONER THAN HE EXPECTED

The walk to Speewah took less time than Graham had expected. He walked fast, ignoring Stephen's muttered grumbles, and was out of the rainforest of the National Park in just over an hour.

The only event of any note was a red-bellied black snake that Graham had nearly stepped on in the jungle. The reptile was sunning itself in the weeds on the overgrown timber track. Just in time Graham saw it and he momentarily froze. But the creature remained coiled up and did not move. Stephen, who was following, bumped into his pack.

"What the…?" he cried. Then he looked and quickly scuttled back.

Graham stared at the coiled snake, fascinated by the glistening sheen of its black scales and the rich red of its underbelly. But once again he felt frozen, unable to make his muscles move.

Move you idiot! he told himself as he noted the snake finally lift its head. To his shame, he found he was trembling and breathing rapidly. His focus began to come and go.

Only after making a conscious effort, and after a few seconds, was Graham was able to make himself act. After taking a deep breath he sprang backwards, and when he was sure he was out of striking range did he bend forward and peer at the reptile.

"Trying to warm itself in the sun," Stephen suggested.

Graham agreed. He knew that snakes were cold blooded but had never seen one that was so cold it could not move. *Not even to save its own life!* He marvelled. Then he blushed ashamed of how he had frozen up.

"Will I get out my rifle and shoot it?" Stephen suggested.

Graham shook his head. It didn't seem fair somehow. "No, snakes are protected remember," he replied, then added, "Besides we must be close to some houses by now and we don't want any trouble."

So the pair stood and watched until the snake slowly uncoiled itself and slid out of sight into the long grass. Then they were on their way again.

While still in the jungle, Graham halted and said, "I think we should change into our cadet uniforms now."

"Why? We can do it when we get back to Cairns," Stephen replied.

"Where will we do that if we go back on the bus? It will drop us off right at the school, won't it?" Graham replied.

Stephen thought for a moment then nodded. "Suppose so. Okay."

So the two boys changed into their camouflage cadet uniforms, then continued to walk. The change made Graham feel much more comfortable, but he wasn't sure why. He supposed because it had solved one of the numerous small problems he could see looming.

Then it was just a 90-minute slog in hot sun along a bitumen road past small farms and 5 Acre lots. At the Speewah Service Station and shop, the boys purchased drinks and pies. They then sat in gloomy silence outside while they ate.

When he finished his food, Stephen licked his fingers and said, "You are in a bloody bad mood today. Just because you can't win with Millie there's no need to take it out on the rest of us!"

Graham bristled at the insinuation but clamped his jaw shut till he had mastered his temper. "You don't have to be with me. You can walk back and join your mates."

Stephen muttered they weren't his mates and relapsed into grumpy silence. Graham picked up his webbing. "Come on, we had better get up to the bus stop or we will look bloody silly. I don't relish trying to hitch-hike home."

They trudged the kilometre through the bush to the junction with the Kennedy Highway and seated themselves in the bus shelter. Neither spoke much. Graham was in no mood to talk. He was too miserable and worried.

Cars and trucks rushed by in both directions, hundreds of them in the hour they sat there. Graham barely noticed, except to feel conspicuous in the army uniform. Suddenly, Stephen grabbed his arm.

"Bloody hell! That was an army Land Cruiser with cadets in it. Lt Hamilton was driving it. The bivouac must be over."

Army cadets! Graham felt his heart flutter with anxiety. "Did they see us?"

"Not sure. Hope not. Hey! Here is the bus," Stephen cried.

He stood up and signalled to the bus to pick them up. It was a

Tablelands 'Whitecars' bus and he guessed it had left Mareeba at about 1:30pm. The bus pulled up and the driver muttered about their dirty clothes and their camping gear but let them on. Their webbing had to be stowed under the seats and their packs on their laps. The bus was almost full, so Stephen settled himself in the empty front seat directly behind the driver. Graham would have preferred to be in one of the less conspicuous seats in the middle but said nothing and joined him.

After they had paid the driver, the bus started up again and drove on towards Kuranda. Graham sat in gloomy silence, rehearsing the ordeal of explaining what he had done on the weekend. In his bones he felt sure that the deception would be seen through, and he knew there was more trouble looming. He also tried to imagine what would happen when he next saw Warrant Officer Howley.

This happened sooner than he expected. The bus detoured into Kuranda, dropped off a couple of people and picked up four more, then drove back out to the highway. As it waited at the road junction for the traffic lights to change, another army Land Rover went past in the direction of Cairns. It was towing a trailer and was carrying cadets in the back. The driver was Warrant Officer Howley.

Warrant Officer Howley! Graham felt his heart skip in fear. To his dismay, the bus pulled out directly after the Land Rover and began to follow it towards Cairns.

"We should move back to another seat in case one of those cadets recognises us," Graham suggested.

He peered at the faces of the cadets in the back of the Land Rover. A couple he recognised as being from their school. The cadets were all laughing and joking. That hurt too. Obviously, they had enjoyed the bivouac.

Stephen turned and looked behind. "I think all the seats are full now," he said. "It'll be alright. Stop fretting. They aren't looking at us."

Graham wasn't so sure and sat worrying, his heart beating faster than normal and a cold sweat breaking out from time to time. To his relief, on the long straight on the run up to the crest of the range on the other side of the Barron River, a white van and a yellow car passed the bus and placed themselves between it and the Land Rover. Graham relaxed slightly.

The position remained unchanged up over the crest of the mountain and much of the way down the other side. Graham hardly noted the drive.

He had done it too many times and was too pre-occupied. On the lower half of the winding range road the line of vehicles was slowed right down when they caught up with a large Shell petrol tanker which was grinding down the mountain in low gear. Graham didn't care. It was just another irritation on a bad day.

"Bloody hell!" Stephen cried.

Graham jerked his head up and looked. The petrol tanker was grinding around a sharp curve to the right. The white van had suddenly pulled out in an impatient attempt to get past it, the driver apparently ignoring the double white lines. As the white van attempted to accelerate past the petrol tanker, a red Porsche flashed into view from the other direction. The Porsche was travelling very fast.

It all happened in the twinkling of an eye. The Porsche attempted to brake, failed, and slammed into the white van, which swerved to the right in an attempt to avoid it. A second later, Porsche slammed in under the huge petrol tank on the trailer of the tanker. The white van struck a tree and crashed onto its side next to the Porshe. The yellow car, Land Rover and bus braked to a halt at once.

"Oh my God!" Graham cried in horror.

He had watched the driver of the Porsche fling up his arm in a futile attempt to shield himself before he was crunched in under the steel chassis of the huge trailer. The petrol tanker shuddered to a stop and the driver's head appeared, staring back, his face a mask of horror.

Stephen gasped. "He's on fire!" he yelled.

The Porsche had burst into flames, wedged in under the huge fuel tank and against the rear wheels of the trailer. Graham had half stood as the tragedy unfolded. His mind received impressions at bewildering speed: another car coming around the bend up the range stopping just in time and was trying to reverse away from the fire but was struck from behind by a blue station wagon, which was following it too closely; people climbing out of the yellow car; the driver of the petrol tanker jumping from his cab and running back to stand appalled at the carnage; Warrant Officer Howley and cadets piling out of the Land Rover.

Cadet CSM Grey came running back up the road, holding up his arms.

"Back up! Back up!" he shouted to the bus driver. "Back up in case the petrol tanker explodes!"

Graham watched open mouthed as Warrant Officer Howley ran down the road to the white van. An arm was waving through the side window. Warrant Officer Howley scrambled up onto the side of the overturned van and leaned in. A moment later, he hauled a hippie-looking woman out and lowered her to the bitumen, where she collapsed. Graham saw Warrant Officer Howley waving his arm and shouting. Although he could not hear him through all the other sounds, Graham knew what he was saying: He wanted help, and urgently.

Before he realised what he was doing, Graham had dumped his pack on his seat and was standing at the door yelling for the driver to open it. The driver was in the process of trying to reverse and swearing.

"Sit down kid!"

"Open the door! He needs help!" Graham shouted, pointing to the wrecks. He felt someone grab his arm.

It was Stephen. "Graham, don't be crazy! You'll get us into trouble!"

Into trouble! Graham thought they were anyway. Besides, what did that matter? There were people there in desperate need and no-one was going to help Warrant Officer Howley. Even as Graham watched, he saw Warrant Officer Howley drop down inside the crashed van. A spray of burning petrol began to spurt from the stalled petrol tanker. The tanker driver ran to get an extinguisher. The woman still lay on the road. Two cadets, corporals from HQ, stood gaping at the scene from beside the Land Rover. CSM Grey had vanished back up the road.

Once again, Graham shouted to the driver, "Let me out, quick!"

To emphasise this he hammered on the door. The driver swore and glanced at him, then went on trying to reverse. But the road behind was now blocked by more cars arriving and he had to stop. Passengers began to stand and scream as more flames billowed at the petrol tanker.

Graham turned to the driver. "Open the bloody door and let these people out. If that tanker explodes, we will be caught in the fireball. Quickly!"

The driver stared at the burning vehicles and licked his lip. He was very pale and on the edge of panic. With a convulsive jerk he pulled the lever that operated the door. It hissed open. Graham was out and running even before it was fully open.

As he raced down past the Land Rover, he yelled to the two corporals, "Come with me, run!"

Warrant Officer Howley's head appeared from the window of the van. He held up a baby. The woman still lay on the road. By this time more blazing petrol was squirting from the ruptured tanker. Flames were spraying across the road just beyond the van in a way that made Graham think of movies he had seen of flame throwers in action. The heat hit him like a solid thing as he pounded down past the yellow car.

The people from that were backing up the road and the driver was trying to turn it around.

"Come and help!" Graham called to a teenage youth from the yellow car.

He did not wait to see if the youth responded but raced on to the van. As he arrived there, his eyes met those of Warrant Officer Howley. A look of surprise crossed Warrant Officer Howley's face, followed by a mixture of emotions: puzzlement, anger, relief?

Warrant Officer Howley held out the baby. "Grab the baby, quick! There are more kids in here, and the driver," he ordered.

Graham did as he was told. He grabbed the baby and started running back up the road. He then had to stop and jump aside as the yellow car revved across the road and swung to face uphill. Graham swore, dodged around the car, and kept running. Ahead of him were the people from the yellow car, all running away.

CSM Grey came dashing back down the road. He yelled at the two corporals to help him and kept on going. Then he saw Graham and his face registered relief and puzzlement.

"Kirk! What the…?"

"Grab that woman CSM. I'll come back and help you," Graham cried as he ran past.

CSM Grey nodded and ran on down the road. Graham dashed up to the two corporals, who still stood transfixed beside the Rover. He thrust the baby into the arms of one.

"Take the baby and get back up the road to safety, quick!"

The corporal licked his lips and nodded, then fled, the baby gripped tightly across his chest. Graham grabbed the shirt of the other corporal.

"Come on! Come and help CSM Grey with that woman!"

The corporal tried to pull away, but Graham was in no mood for argument and dragged him with him. He set off back down the road again. It was only 50 paces, but his mind seemed to register every impression:

blazing petrol dripping and squirting from the tanker; the sports car a flaring mass of wreckage; tyres on the back of the trailer beginning to smoulder and flare.

CSM Grey had taken another young child, a girl of two or three, from Warrant Officer Howley, who was still inside the van. Graham met CSM Grey's eye and nodded as they passed. The CSM looked very grim and determined and was sweating heavily. Graham was too but barely noticed it. He was aware of the scorching heat though. It was now so hot that he shielded his face with one arm while he grabbed at the unconscious woman.

To his enormous relief, the corporal was still with him, although he looked very scared. Graham grabbed one of the woman's arms and yelled for the corporal to do likewise. As he did, he saw Warrant Officer Howley again put his head and arms up through the side window of the van. This time he was holding a struggling boy of three or four who was screaming in terror. Once again, their eyes met. Graham hesitated. Should he leave the woman to the corporal and take the boy?

At that moment, Stephen came racing down. "I'll take the kid. Get going!" he called.

Graham felt a surge of relief and affection. Good old Steve! He yelled to the corporal and they began running, dragging the woman with them. By now the heat was so great that it seemed his shirt would burst into flames on his back.

They had covered about 20 paces when there was a sharp 'whumpf" from behind them. Graham glanced back, just in time to see a ball of flame billow up and out from the Porsche.

Petrol tank has exploded, his mind registered.

The next concept was to dive for cover, but the shock wave and debris struck them before his body could act on the thought. They were blown flat, skidding painfully on the bitumen.

Get up! Run! Graham thought; or perhaps he shouted.

He wasn't sure. The fall had banged his knee and skinned his knuckles but that only spurred him on. He scrambled to his feet and grabbed at the woman. The corporal hauled himself to his feet as well but seemed disoriented. To Graham's intense relief two strange men, one a big, burly man in singlet and shorts, came running down to them.

"We'll take her. You kids get clear," the burly man shouted.

They grabbed the woman and ran on up the road, followed by the corporal.

Steve! Is he alright? Graham thought.

He turned, just as Stephen came pounding past with the little boy, still struggling and screaming, tucked under his left arm.

Someone else was screaming too; a dreadful, piercing shriek of terror. It made Graham's hair stand on end just to hear it. The scream was coming from the van. Graham stood and stared in horror. Where was Warrant Officer Howley? There was no sign of him.

He must be inside the van, Graham decided.

He ran back down the road. Ahead of him it looked like a scene from hell. The whole rear of the petrol tanker was now aflame, with blazing streams of petrol squirting, dripping, and running from the tank. The tyres were now on fire, adding choking clouds of black smoke to the conflagration. There was no sign of the driver. Streams of burning petrol were now washing across the road close to the van.

As Graham got closer, he saw that the van was also beginning to smoulder. The paint was blistering and bubbling. There was still no sign of Warrant Officer Howley. Graham's heart leapt in anxiety.

He might have been overcome by the fumes or heat, he thought.

He was dimly conscious that he needed to be aware of the same dangers himself. By now the heat was fierce, drying and scorching. Graham ran to place the van between himself and the worst of the fire and bent to peer inside through the windshield.

The windshield had cracked in the heat and it was hard to see in because of the reflections of the flames on the glass, but Graham was able to shield his face enough to see that Warrant Officer Howley was in there. He was struggling to pull the driver from his seat. The spine-chilling screams were coming from the driver; a thin, weedy looking individual with a long, wispy beard.

An instant's appraisal made it clear to Graham that Warrant Officer Howley would never be able to drag the driver back over his seat, then lift him out of the side window. If nothing else the metal of the vehicle was now so hot it could not be touched. A single accidental touch with his left hand determined that for Graham.

Graham snatched his hand back and sucked it. At that moment, a flaring swirl of blazing petrol flowed past, almost engulfing the front of the van. Glass cracked with sharp snapping sounds. The blazing liquid flowed off the bitumen and down into the jungle. The leaves on the tree next to Graham shrivelled and blackened. A gust of wind engulfed him in acrid, hot air and smoke. The sickening stench of roasting flesh made him gag. The driver of the Porsche being barbequed, his mind told him.

Only one thing to do, Graham thought.

So he did it. Trusting to the strength of his army boot he kicked at the shattered windshield as hard as he could. It finally broke and fell into pieces but was much tougher than Graham had expected. He kept kicking as more of the sickening stench enveloped him. Flames flowed by only a metre from him. His clothes felt as though they would burst into flames.

Coughing and spluttering and with his eyes streaming, Graham knelt and looked in. The driver and Warrant Officer Howley were still there.

"I'll take him, sir. Push him this way," Graham shouted.

The roaring noise of the fire was so great he wasn't sure if Warrant Officer Howley heard him or not. But he had, or at least it was clear what was needed. Warrant Officer Howley pushed hard and the driver half fell out through the hole. Graham grabbed him and hauled with all his strength, ignoring the nearby fire and the fact that the driver was being cut by the jagged edges.

The man was still screaming and was struggling so much Graham nearly lost him. He pulled as hard as he could, but the man would not come more than half out.

"Push him! Push him!" Graham shouted at Warrant Officer Howley.

Warrant Officer Howley met his eyes. He looked quite calm. "You call Warrant Officers 'sir', Cadet Kirk; now stop shouting. His foot is caught. I will just release it, then you drag him out."

"Yes sir." What else could he say?

Warrant Officer Howley crawled half over the back of the seats and reached down among the man's flailing legs and hauled. The man's bare foot struck Warrant Officer Howley in the face. Warrant Officer Howley didn't hesitate. He picked up a spanner and whacked the man on the skull with it. The man went limp and Warrant Officer Howley was able to reach down.

"Okay, pull!" he ordered.

Graham pulled. The skinny man slid out like a long sack of potatoes. He was still breathing. Graham took three paces backwards with him to get the van between them and the petrol tanker. Then he dumped the man on the edge of the jungle and ran back to the front of the van.

Coming from the relative shelter of the van into the full blast of the flames was like opening the door of a furnace. The heat was so intense that breathing was painful. Graham knew he was weakening and in great danger.

Warrant Officer Howley had crawled over the seat and had his head and shoulders out through the hole where the windshield had been. Graham grabbed at him to help. Warrant Officer Howley shook his head and yelled, "Get going, Cadet Kirk. That tanker is going to blow any moment."

Graham grabbed him and pulled. Warrant Officer Howley again shook his head. "Stop pulling. I'm caught somewhere. Get going, Cadet Kirk, before the tanker explodes!"

"No sir."

Graham shook his head and kept a grip on Warrant Officer Howley's clothing. He could see his shirt and hair smouldering.

Radiant heat, he thought. *Run!* his mind screamed.

There was a loud *crump!* and a ball of flame billowed up from the tanker, almost engulfing them.

I think I've left it too late! he thought. *I am going to die!*

Chapter 25

RECKONING

Warrant Officer Howley's face twisted in pain as he struggled. He met Graham's eyes and ordered him to get going.

"No sir."

"A good soldier obeys orders. Now run!"

Into Graham's mind slipped a quote from his Grandfather, who had battled through World War 2. "A good soldier also uses his initiative when circumstances demand it sir," he replied.

He knelt and looked in. Warrant Officer Howley swore at him and called him an insubordinate young bugger. Graham ignored him.

Warrant Officer Howley's army boot was tangled in the seat belt. Graham passed this information to him. Warrant Officer Howley curled up and groped for it. His hands reached but it seemed for ever before he untangled the offending belt. By then he was gasping in short, rapid breaths and was very red in the face. The heat was intense.

"Okay, pull!" he gasped.

Graham heaved. Warrant Officer Howley was a solid man and heavy. It took all of Graham's strength to drag him out. Then, just as most of him was clear, he snagged again. Graham glanced and saw his other boot was caught under the steering wheel.

"Lie still sir. I'll clear it," he ordered.

Without waiting Graham crouched and half crawled in through the broken windshield. His hands and knees were both cut by jagged metal and glass, but he ignored the stinging pains. By stretching right in he managed to grasp the boot at the ankle and hauled it back and up. It came free. Graham wriggled backwards, bumping Warrant Officer Howley in the process. As soon as he was out, he grabbed and pulled. Warrant Officer Howley slid clear.

Graham just wanted to collapse. He was gasping and felt like he was on fire. A wave of dizziness swept over him, and he reeled. Warrant Officer Howley rolled over and sprang to his feet. He reached out and grabbed Graham and dragged him behind the van.

The respite was immediate, but illusory. It was still very hot, and the petrol tanker was now a raging inferno. Roaring flames were billowing across the road and licking at the van. The paint of the van was now on fire as well.

Graham pointed down the slope into the jungle, but Warrant Officer Howley shook his head. "If she blows all the burning petrol will flow down there. Come on, run for it!"

He took a grip on Graham's sleeve and started to run. Graham ran for all he was worth. They bolted up the bitumen as fast as they could go.

Behind them there was a sharp metallic *crack!* Warrant Officer Howley suddenly swerved and dragged Graham with him over the bank and behind a large tree. Even as they fell behind it, the petrol tanker exploded. The blast shook the ground and lit up the jungle so brightly that all the greens went bright white. The shock wave picked up dust, leaves and loose objects. A wave of searing heat engulfed them.

"Don't breathe!" Warrant Officer Howley cried as he muffled his face into his sleeve.

Graham did likewise, shutting his eyes as he did. Something slammed into the tree. That caused Graham to open his eyes in alarm. He saw a jagged piece of steel strike the next tree with a vicious *thud!* It stuck there. Several windows on the bus vanished simultaneously. Objects clattered and thudded around them, but the white glare faded to an angry red.

Alive! Graham's brain registered. What he had feared had not happened; they had not been engulfed in blazing petrol.

They stayed sprawled in the dust and dead leaves for a few more moments. Warrant Officer Howley glanced back, then stood up.

"Safe now," he said.

Feeling battered and half stunned, Graham stood up as well and glanced back. They were still only about 30 or 40 paces from the burning tanker but the fire was now flaring upwards, not spewing outwards. The huge steel tank was shattered. The van and prime mover were now also in flames.

"Where is the van driver," Warrant Officer Howley asked.

Graham suddenly felt sick. He had forgotten the driver! "I left him beside the van," he said.

"Come on, let's get him then."

They ran back down the road to the burning van, ignoring calls from up the road. Luckily there was almost no wind, so the flames and smoke were rising straight up. To Graham's intense relief, the unconscious driver appeared to be still alright, although his clothes were smouldering and his hair gone. They grabbed him and started dragging him back up the road.

The same two men, plus CSM Grey and Stephen, came running down to help. Stephen had two water bottles, one in each hand, with the caps undone. As soon as he arrived, he tipped them over Graham and Warrant Officer Howley. The splash of the cool water was an instant and enormous relief.

"On him," Warrant Officer Howley said, pointing to the van driver.

"Bugger him! He caused the crash," Stephen replied.

He finished emptying the water bottles over them. Graham let go of the van driver as one of the men took over. With his hands he wiped the water over his face. What luxury! The two men and CSM Grey took over and whisked the injured man off. Once clear of the worst of the heat, Graham slowed down. He felt absolutely exhausted. Warrant Officer Howley stayed with him. Stephen walked back up the road with them.

Warrant Officer Howley stopped beside the Land Rover. Its windshield had cracked in the heat but otherwise it looked untouched. He grunted, then turned to face Graham. For a moment he rubbed water over his face and cleared his red-rimmed eyes. He looked very grim.

The time of reckoning! Graham thought. With apprehension turning his stomach to water he stood to attention and faced Warrant Officer Howley.

"Well, Cadet Kirk, what's the story?"

No point in lying, Graham thought. He began to explain the camping trip. As he spoke, Warrant Officer Howley looked stony faced. Then his facial expression changed to annoyance as people began swarming down the road.

"Tell me later. Keep it to yourself till Captain Conkey is here. Let's get this mess cleaned up," Warrant Officer Howley ordered. He turned to the men who had arrived, who included the bus driver. "Has anyone used a mobile phone to call the emergency services?"

A middle-aged man in business clothes nodded his head. "Already done. They are on their way," he replied. He reached out and took Warrant Officer Howley's hand. "Bravest thing I ever saw. Well done!"

The man then shook Graham's hand. Graham felt a warm flush and winced as it was the hand which had been burnt.

"Well done kid! Hey! Are you okay? Here, sit down."

Graham and Warrant Officer Howley were both seated on the edge of the road in front of the Land Rover. Water was found in the back by CSM Grey and poured over them. A water bottle was thrust into Graham's hand by Stephen and he gulped it greedily. Almost instantly he began to sweat.

CSM Grey stood in front of Graham. "Where have you and Bell been, Cadet Kirk? You weren't at the bivouac."

Warrant Officer Howley looked up, wiping water from his face and hair. "I'll deal with this if you don't mind CSM. We will wait for the OC. Now, Cadet Kirk, do you have any injuries? Do you need medical treatment?"

Graham shook his head. "No sir. Just a few small burns and a couple of scratches." As he said this, he held up his hands and noted blood trickling from half a dozen small cuts.

Warrant Officer Howley nodded. "Okay, good. CSM, get my mobile phone from the vehicle please."

CSM Grey brought the phone and Warrant Officer Howley called up Captain Conkey who was in another Land Rover somewhere back up the road. He quickly outlined the situation. The problem was getting the cadets home in their coaches.

"This road will be blocked for hours. I reckon it'd be quicker to turn around and go back along another road," Warrant Officer Howley said.

Captain Conkey agreed. A short discussion decided them to go back via Kuranda to Mareeba, then north through Mt Molloy and down the Rex Highway to come south along the Cook Highway. Warrant Officer Howley then phoned some army officer at Porton Barracks and passed on the details.

By then Graham had begun to shiver. Reaction set in hard as he contemplated his own bleak future. This was made worse by constant memories of the driver of the red car flinging up his arm, and of the smell of him being incinerated. Suddenly, Graham felt sick. He leaned forward and vomited between his legs. It came out as mostly bile. He found himself gripped by Warrant Officer Howley's arm around his shoulders.

When he finished puking, a water bottle was thrust into Graham's hands and he rinsed his mouth and washed his face. Warrant Officer Howley stood up and lifted him to his feet.

"Spread a sleeping bag CSM," he ordered.

Graham found himself half carried across the road to a grassy spot on the edge of the jungle. Warrant Officer Howley lowered him onto the sleeping bag and made him drink some more.

As Graham handed back the water bottle, Warrant Officer Howley gripped his right hand. "You are a gutsy bastard, Graham Kirk. You are a good man to have around in a tight spot. Thanks. I reckon I owe you my life."

Graham met Warrant Officer Howley's eyes. A feeling of intense pleasure flooded through him, as well as embarrassment.

Gutsy! Good man to have around! Good man! The words of praise pounded in Graham's mind. All he could do was shrug and mumble.

A buzzing roar indicated the arrival of a helicopter. Graham looked up and saw it was an Emergency Services chopper. It hovered just out of sight around the bend downhill. People were still milling around, hundreds of them. They came from the vehicles stopped further up the range and had walked down to see the show. By this time the tanker was just a smouldering mess of twisted metal, but the van was still blazing fiercely.

More uniformed figures appeared: Captain Conkey and a cadet corporal carrying a First Aid Kit. The medic was set to work but there was little for him to do. Graham had his hand treated and the few scratches cleaned and coated with antiseptic. As soon as Captain Conkey saw Graham and Stephen, his eyebrows shot up.

"What's going on then?" he asked.

Warrant Officer Howley answered, "CSM, you keep those others away." He waited till CSM Grey had moved the other cadets out of earshot, then explained the crash and the cadet's subsequent part in it.

Captain Conkey stared at the burning wreckage and was suitably impressed. "Holy Moses! What a mess! And these cadets helped get the people out? Good! But how did Kirk and Bell get involved. Neither of you was on the bivouac." He turned an accusatory eye on the pair.

Graham flushed and bit his lip. Warrant Officer Howley said, "Okay, Cadet Kirk, give us the story."

Graham nodded. Nothing to be gained by keeping silent now. For the next 20 minutes, while the place suddenly swarmed with police, paramedics and firefighters, he quietly told how and why he and Stephen had gone camping. Captain Conkey looked grimmer by the minute.

When Graham was finished, there was an interruption as paramedics wanted to check their condition. There was a pause while this was done. One of the paramedics suggested they both be transported back to hospital by ambulance at once.

Warrant Officer Howley shook his head. "I'm okay. Besides, I've got a Land Rover to drive. What about you, young Kirk? You can go in the ambulance if you want."

It was an attractive idea, but Graham immediately shook his head. It would only delay the reckoning. He preferred to get it over with.

"I'll go back in the vehicle with you sir."

"Good lad. Where's your gear?"

"In the bus sir," Graham replied.

Stephen stood up. "I'll get it. You stay there, Graham."

Then a TV crew arrived and started filming. Graham was embarrassed but also pleased. Warrant Officer Howley explained the rescue, leaving out that he had done most of it and giving credit to the cadets. The TV men wanted to interview Graham, but Warrant Officer Howley firmly refused and sent them off. Policemen arrived and their questions had to be answered.

As the police walked towards them, Warrant Officer Howley leaned over and said quietly, "You two say nothing about where you've been. That is cadet business, and we will deal with it later, got it?"

"Yes sir."

Capt Conkey nodded agreement. He looked very serious. Graham felt even sicker.

One of the policemen was Constable O'Neil. He saw Graham and made a face. Graham returned a wry grin.

Constable O'Neil walked over. "What's he done this time?" he asked.

"Been a hero," Warrant Officer Howley replied.

Graham could only blush and stammer a denial, but he felt extraordinarily pleased. Then there was half an hour of questions and note taking before the police were satisfied.

During the questioning, Warrant Officer Howley and Capt Conkey walked off to one side and stood talking. Graham could tell it was about them by the glances and gestures. The two men looked very serious and grim and worry over what they might decide made his stomach churn.

When the police were satisfied they had all the information they needed at that moment, they went off to interview other witnesses. By then the flames had all been extinguished, the scene photographed, and a tow truck brought up. It winched the burnt-out shell of the van aside and the traffic began moving, under close police direction.

Capt Conkey said, "Wait here, Kevin. I'll go and get my Land Rover."

He walked away. Warrant Officer Howley told the boys to get into his Land Rover. Graham stood up but felt very shaky. He leaned on the vehicle for a moment as a wave of dizziness swept over him. Stephen steadied him and helped him climb into the passenger seat. Stephen climbed in the back with CSM Grey and the two corporals.

"You got our gear?" Graham asked.

Stephen patted a pack. "It's here. Relax," he replied.

Graham tried to, but fearful images and gloomy forebodings kept swamping his consciousness. He knew he was shaking and gratefully wrapped the sleeping bag about him and snuggled into it. Another water bottle was passed to him. Warrant Officer Howley stood at the door and drank a whole water bottle while he waited. In the back the two corporals began quizzing Stephen where they had been.

Stephen shook his head. "Not allowed to tell you. It's a secret."

Hundreds of cars, trucks and busses had been delayed. Graham overheard one of the corporals mention that it was nearly five O'clock. Five O'clock! The crash had happened at about 2:30!

The traffic movement was very slow because only one lane of the highway was clear, and the police would only let a hundred or so vehicles through from one direction before stopping them to give the other lane a chance. It took nearly half an hour before Capt Conkey's Land Rover appeared. He stopped to allow Warrant Officer Howley to pull his vehicle out into the slowly moving line of traffic.

As they started moving, Graham heaved a sigh of relief. He stared unhappily at the twisted remains of the tanker and red Porsche.

So quick! he thought.

One moment alive and vibrant, enjoying the drive, then dead! Just like that! It was sickening to contemplate. He looked away and stared out at the jungle instead.

On the drive back to Cairns, Graham was acutely conscious of Warrant Officer Howley in the driver's seat beside him. From time to time he glanced at the man to see what his mood was. It looked black. He also noted the strong, sun-tanned arms working the gear lever and steering the vehicle. Admiration could not be withheld. Warrant Officer Howley was a great man.

That made Graham feel even worse. By his actions he had hurt him; by trying to seduce his daughter.

He has every right to punish me, he decided gloomily.

It was 6:45pm and dark by the time they arrived back at the school. The main body of the unit had already arrived and been dismissed. Several parents were waiting, including Stephen's and Graham's mother. Lt MacLaren, the 2ic, and Lt Hamilton, the QM, were both there as well. When Graham saw his mother, he felt both intense relief and concern. Now it would all come out and she would be so hurt!

The two Land Rovers were parked and Capt Conkey climbed out. "You cadets please help unload the vehicles and put all the stores back in the Q Store. I will speak to your parents."

As Capt Conkey went to meet the anxious parents, Graham and the other cadets climbed out. As Graham walked to the rear of the Land Rover, Warrant Officer Howley came around and called to him.

"Cadet Kirk! Come here. I want to talk to you."

Graham swallowed and felt his stomach turn over. The moment of reckoning had arrived!

With his heart in his boots, Graham walked over to where Warrant Officer Howley had stopped. Warrant Officer Howley stood four-square, feet firmly planted and apart, clenched fists on his hips. In the light from the Q Store his face looked implacable and deadly serious. The sight of it made Graham shiver and fear the worst. He braced himself.

There was a long pause. Graham stood to attention and waited. Warrant Officer Howley looked him up and down then said, "I've made my mind up about you, Cadet Kirk. By rights I should throw the book at you and kick your silly little arse so hard your nose will bleed. But I've got another plan for you. Whether you like it or not, you are going to be my offsider. I am going to turn you into the best soldier I have ever trained. And there will be no arguments about it. Or else! Got that?"

"Yes sir." His offsider? What was he talking about?

Warrant Officer Howley went on. “As I see it, this is the situation: you are a silly young bugger going nowhere fast. Or rather, you are going downhill fast. And that is a real shame. You’ve got real ability; and you’ve got guts. You’ve demonstrated that twice to me, no, three times. It must have taken some guts to sneak over to my place to meet Amelia.”

He paused and Graham felt queasy in the stomach, despite the compliments. Amelia! God yes! That had taken an effort.

Warrant Officer Howley went on, “The other thing you’ve got that is worth its weight in gold is leadership. I watched you take control back up there. You saw what needed to be done and took over. You just ordered the CSM and that pair of useless corporals around; and they obeyed. That means you’ve got it, son. That is real leadership. We won’t waste that. This country needs all the good leaders it can get. Your problem, apart from feeling sorry for yourself over your bloody eyesight, is that you don’t have any goals; no aim to channel your energy and ability constructively.”

“Yes sir,” Graham muttered.

Warrant Officer Howley looked around to check they were still alone. Graham could see his mother talking to Capt Conkey over near the Q Store. She looked worried but pleased.

Warrant Officer Howley turned back to him, and continued, “I’ve talked this over with Capt Conkey. And I’m going to discuss it with your parents. As of tomorrow, you are going to work with me. And when I say work, I mean bloody well sweat-till-you-drop-work; and no complaints or back answering. Now get this straight. I am making you an offer you can’t refuse, because if you want to try to buck, then we will take that other matter up with the police. Got it?”

Graham swallowed. He ‘got it’ alright. “Yes sir.”

Does that mean he isn’t going to tell the police about Amelia? he wondered.

Warrant Officer Howley went on, “Capt Conkey will want to talk to you; and I don’t doubt he will tear a strip off you for your deceit (That made Graham wince). He has agreed to keep you in the unit and to back my plan. He is going to talk to the principal about it to get approval. So you stay a cadet; although he would be fully justified in chucking you out.”

“What about Stephen, sir, Cadet Bell?” Graham asked.

Warrant Officer Howley took a deep breath. "That's another good thing about you. You are loyal to your mates. All the best Australian soldiers are. Well, if we keep one, we must keep both of you. But I am singling you out, not him."

"Thank you, sir," Graham replied.

"Don't thank me. That was Capt Conkey's decision. Now, any questions?"

Graham licked his lips. It had to be asked. He had to face up to it. "What about me and Amelia sir? What punishment do I get?"

Warrant Officer Howley grunted, then answered, "Yes, you've got guts. A lot of blokes would have tried to duck that one. I reckon you are a kid with pretty high morals really. In this case, your dick just took control. Okay, your punishment is to promise me you will become a good soldier, with no complaints. Now be clear this has no legal basis. This is between you and me, man to man."

Man to man! The words glowed in Graham's mind. "Yes sir," he replied. *A good soldier, eh? I'll show him!*

"So that is the end of it then, got it?"

"Yes sir, but... but is that what Mrs Howley has agreed to?"

"She doesn't know about you. I didn't tell her," Warrant Officer Howley replied. "I didn't see the point. Handing you over to the police would just be a waste. Putting you through the legal mill wouldn't make you a better person. You can repay me by becoming a good leader. And it wouldn't stop Millie from playing up either."

Graham was astonished. "Am I allowed to see her, if I promise to behave?" he asked.

Warrant Officer Howley shook his head. "I'd let you, but she is gone. Her mother has packed her off to a convent school. So you won't see her at this school again. Sorry son. I hope you weren't in love with her. Were you?"

"Ye... er... I... I thought I was, but I'm not sure now," Graham replied truthfully. "Isn't that a bit hard on her sir?"

"Maybe, but it was her mother's decision. Her mother is really angry with her." To Graham's surprise, Warrant Officer Howley suddenly chuckled. "The real reason is that she was just the same at that age. That was when I met her, when I was a young soldier and she was still in high school. She was a hot little number. Still is. That's why I love her. And I have to live with her. So, if she says Millie goes to boarding school, she goes. Got it?"

"Yes," Graham replied.

Into his mind came images of girls: Margaret who loved him; Kylie who cared for him; Amelia who had shown him the gates of paradise! He sighed.

"Right, that's enough of this. Your orders are to keep your mouth shut, and obey orders. Now come and help unload," Warrant Officer Howley said.

"Yes sir."

With his mind reeling from the implications of what he had just been told Graham followed him over to the trailer of the second Land Rover and, ignoring the pain in his hands, picked up two empty water jerrycans.

As soon as the work was completed, Capt Conkey thanked them all for their efforts. He then called Graham and Stephen aside.

"I will speak to you two later, but I am not happy as you can guess. Cadet Kirk, I know Warrant Officer Howley has spoken to you. By now he will have also spoken to your mother. We will discuss it all tomorrow at school. A final decision will be made then. Good night."

"Yes sir. Good night, sir," the boys echoed.

As they walked over to where their parents waited, Stephen asked, "What was all that about?"

"Sorry, I can't say," Graham replied.

Stephen had no chance to continue the questioning as they reached the parents. Mrs Kirk hugged Graham and looked him over for signs of injuries.

"Capt Conkey tells me you have been a real hero and saved people's lives."

"Aw Mum! Fair go. There was a whole group of us," Graham replied.

"Well, that is not how Warrant Officer Howley described it," his mother said. "He thinks you are a very brave young man."

"He spoke to you then?"

"Yes, he did," his mother replied.

By the subtle change in her tone Graham could tell that she knew something. He sighed. *There will be more questions when they were alone at home,* he thought.

But there weren't. His mother filled him with Milo and supper and stopped Kylie and Alex asking too many questions before hurrying him through his bath and into bed. Only when she came to tuck him in did she allude to the trouble he was in. She kissed him and stroked his hair.

"It will be alright Graham. Warrant Officer Howley will do the right thing. He and Captain Conkey are very good to you."

"Yes, Mum."

Graham badly wanted to confess to his mother and wondered just how much she knew. After swallowing and licking dry lips, he summoned the courage to ask.

"Mum, I've been in trouble again," he began.

She put her fingers to his lips. "Hush! Yes, I know. Don't talk about it now. Tomorrow will do. Now say your prayers and just thank God for your safety."

"Yes, Mum."

And Graham did. After she was gone, he even slid out of bed to kneel while he confessed his sins and to beg forgiveness. To his annoyance, confessing about Amelia made him get randy and he had trouble picturing it as evil or sinful. With a sigh he climbed back into bed and lay back.

A few minutes later, he was sound asleep.

Chapter 26

JUST DESERTS

Monday morning Graham woke to find the sun streaming through the louvres onto his face. It took him a few minutes to remember the events of the previous few days. The throbbing of his burnt hand helped. As full realisation came to him, he felt his stomach turn over. What exactly had Warrant Officer Howley told his mother?

Then the agreement with Warrant Officer Howley came to mind. What exactly had he promised? And had it been a promise anyway?

Or did I just say yes under duress?

Pondering these issues Graham took himself to the bathroom for his morning shower and shave. At breakfast, he discovered that his name and photo were in the newspaper and he was being hailed a hero. It was simultaneously thrilling and embarrassing. Kylie was very pleased and Alex pretended to be, although Graham thought he was really jealous.

It was his mother's reaction he worried most about. She smiled but it didn't seem to reach her eyes. When breakfast was over, she called him back to the kitchen after the other two had left.

"I have been asked to come to school after classes finish this afternoon," she said. "Have you been in trouble again?"

Graham bit his lip and hung his head. "Yes, Mum."

"Do you want to tell me about it?"

"No, Mum." Graham shook his head and felt the shame suffuse his face and neck.

"Well it can't have been too bad because both Captain Conkey and that regular army fellow think you are a good lad. I hope it isn't something serious," she said.

"Yes, Mum," Graham replied.

I hope so too! he thought.

"I think you'd better tell me. I don't want to go to a meeting about you and be made to look silly because I don't know what happened."

Graham felt a rush of shame and desperately tried to find an honourable way to escape. There was none. For an instant his anguished gaze locked with his mother's worried eyes. Then he lowered his head in shame.

"I did something to a girl," he said.

"Oh my God!" his mother gasped. She shook her head in dismay.

"It wasn't rape, or assault or anything like that," Graham hastened to assure her. "She wanted me to."

"Oh dear! You haven't made her pregnant, have you?"

"No Mum," Graham said.

But that made him blush even more because he was sure he might have if Warrant Officer Howley hadn't caught them.

His mother shook her head and looked upset. "Oh well. I suppose we can cope with that. I just knew you were heading for trouble. Oh dear! Oh dear!" She was silent for a moment. Then she asked, "Who is she?"

Graham had been hoping she wouldn't ask that. He bit his lip. "Amelia Howley, the girl that was here that Sunday morning."

His mother nodded sadly. Then she asked, "So how do Captain Conkey and that regular army man come into this? Did it happen at cadets? Is she a cadet?"

"No Mum, she isn't a cadet. She is Warrant Officer Howley's daughter."

His mother's jaw dropped open in surprise. "But he spoke so highly of you last night. He must like you and think you are good, or he wouldn't have. Does he know?" She was clearly puzzled.

Graham could see that it all had to be explained. He took a deep breath and said, "Yes, Mum. He... he caught us."

A look of pain crossed his mother's face, and she again shook her head. "Well, I hope for your sake we can sort things out," she said.

Graham blushed again and bit his lip. *Get it over with, you coward!* he told himself.

Straightening up and battling to prevent his lips from quivering he said. "There's more to it, Mum. I didn't go to the cadet bivouac. I went camping with some friends."

The look of distress that crossed his mother's face hurt more than anything. Graham knew it would remain burned into his conscience for years to come. Having got that far he now unburdened himself of the whole sordid tale but made no mention of who he was with. When he was finished speaking, his mother sat shaking her head in unhappy disbelief.

"Oh Graham! Why? You are such a good boy? What's happening? Why are you acting this way? It's not like you. Oh, I wish your father was here. Oh, you poor boy! You must be very unhappy. You should have told me." Another look of deep distress crossed her face. Tears formed. As she mopped at these, she said, "It is my fault. I haven't been paying enough attention. I have been too busy working and going to meetings, to see that you weren't happy."

"No Mum! It's not your fault. You are a great mum!" Graham cried. He was appalled that she should blame herself. His own tears were now forming. He stepped over and put his arm around her. "It will be alright. I promise I will be good from now on."

She looked up and met his eyes. Hers sparkled with tears but she smiled. For several minutes she hugged him closely. It was Kylie coming back to the kitchen for her lunchbox that ended the conversation. Graham took the opportunity to rush off to get ready.

Only when he was halfway to school did he remember Amelia. Already gone! Sent to a convent school! It was a real shock. So sudden! Somehow it seemed unfair, but he knew it was really none of his business what parents did in a case like that. He could only be thankful he wasn't going to face the police and the disgrace of a court.

That led to ruminating over the comments Warrant Officer Howley had expressed about his own daughter. It was all amazing to Graham. Obviously Warrant Officer Howley loved her; but equally he and his wife were at their wits end over how to control her. It was all very adult and saddening.

That led Graham to thinking about what he and Amelia had done. To his confusion he found the memories very arousing and enjoyable but that led to the painful question: Did he love her?

It was a question he could not honestly answer. He thought he did. Certainly he missed her and regretted she was gone. *But that is probably because it means I won't get any more sex,* he decided sadly.

Then even more worrying questions arose: What did Amelia think of him? Did she love him? Or was she just using him? It was all very upsetting to think about.

Once at school, the new status of public hero pushed all thoughts of Amelia out of his mind. Graham found himself the object of an amazing mixture of praise, admiration, envy and malicious spite. Larsen and his cronies orchestrated the latter with insults and jibes; calling him a coward and challenging him to a fight to prove he wasn't.

The intervention of Captain Conkey ended that. He called Graham to his staffroom as soon as he saw him. "Don't forget that you have a meeting at the office after school," he said.

"I won't sir."

"And don't react to any of that taunting from Larsen and his scaly mates. Show your strength of character by ignoring them. No more trouble, thank you."

"Yes sir."

Graham made his way to where his friends sat. Peter was the first to speak. He stood up and shook Graham's hand, being careful not to grab the bandage covering his burn.

"Bloody well done! You and Stephen both. Really well done!"

"Thanks," Graham replied, his heart surging and expanding at the warmth and sincerity in Peter's voice.

Roger added his congratulations. Stephen had already been praised and he made a wry face at Graham.

Peter then tested Graham's defences by asking, "Where were you blokes on the weekend? I didn't see you at the bivouac, yet you were with Warrant Officer Howley at the crash?"

Graham met his eyes and was sorely tempted to confess. He was aware that Stephen had an anxious look in his eyes. Then Warrant Officer Howley's words ran through his mind: 'say nothing.'

He shook his head, "Sorry. We've been ordered not to say."

To his relief, Peter nodded. "Like that other weekend when you went off with the officers, eh? They must be planning another one of those really good seven-day exercises. I hope so. I've heard they are great."

Graham grunted and shrugged. He was relieved that Peter had seized on that explanation and was content to leave it at that. Curiosity about the week-long exercises Peter had mentioned made him want to ask about them, but decided that, in the circumstance, he should not display any ignorance of them.

Period One was Geography with Captain Conkey (He was no longer 'Mister' in Graham's mind). The only jarring note was seeing Amelia's empty desk. Several times Graham glanced at it wistfully. He felt the loss sharply.

His emotions must have shown on his face because at the end of the period Rosemary said to him, "Amelia has been sent to boarding school by her parents."

Graham nodded. "Yes, I know thanks. Her dad told me."

"It was very sudden. She said she would be if she was naughty," Rosemary said, "I wonder what they caught her doing?"

Guilt made Graham flush and he hoped it didn't show. *She's fishing,* he thought.

Partly to divert the conversation; and also because he wanted to know he asked, "Do you know which one she has been sent to?"

"No, I don't. Sorry. Did you like her?" Rosemary asked, her eyes soft with sympathy.

"Yes, I did."

It was not a topic he really wanted to discuss, so he was relieved when Christine turned and said, "That's what my mum is threatening if I don't do better at school."

To Graham's relief, the girls began to discuss boarding schools and Amelia was dropped as a topic of conversation. However she kept cropping up in his thoughts throughout the day. To his surprise many of the memories did not arouse him but made him feel sad. He decided he did not really love her.

But I did like her.

His conscience remained sensitive to what they had done together, but mostly he just felt satisfaction that he was an apparently normal man who could perform. The knowledge gave him a feeling of deep contentment.

In English Mrs Ramsey insisted he and Stephen amplify the news reports of what happened at the accident. Graham did not really want to. Not only was he embarrassed at the praise, but it brought back with painful force the memory of the driver of the red Porsche being killed and then incinerated.

Only twenty-one! What a dreadful way to die, he thought. *And gone even faster than Amelia, and for good!*

Now that was very sobering to contemplate.

* * *

Maths A was different. Mr Burgomeister was sneeringly sarcastic.

"You can't make a career of it son, so get on with learning some mathematics."

Graham took a deep breath and thought of Capt Conkey's words: *Don't react.*

"Yes sir," he replied; nodded agreement, and lowered his head to work. To his relief, the tactic worked and the teacher left him alone to spend the period picking on Vincent.

The day dragged by. In every lesson there were painful reminders: either of Amelia, or of the tragedy on the Kuranda Range Road. Graham felt very stressed and tired. He was also becoming more and more anxious about the meeting after school.

I hope Capt Conkey can agree to whatever it is Warrant Officer Howley has in mind, he thought.

Morning break, German, Physics, History (Capt Conkey again, but still no clue of what was to come), lunch, Music, Maths B (and miracle of miracles, Mr Ritter not only did not keep them in for not doing their homework but congratulated them both most handsomely). Finally it was 3:10pm.

"What are you doing now?" Stephen asked.

"I have to go to see Capt Conkey, then go to the office. They are going to decide what to do with me. What are you doing?" Graham replied.

"Captain Conkey wants to see me too," Stephen answered, making a wry face as he did. "Going to tear a few strips off us, I suppose."

Graham felt a surge of anger. "Well? And why not? We deserve it! Be thankful he isn't going to chuck us out in disgrace."

"Yeah, I suppose so," Stephen replied.

The two walked to the office and were met by Capt Conkey. "Both of you come with me into this classroom," he ordered.

They did as they were told. In the room were Lt Maclaren, Lt Hamilton, Lt McEwen and Mrs Standish. They looked very serious.

Capt Conkey sat beside the other OOCs. The boys were not invited to sit. Graham stood himself at attention and waited.

After a pause, Capt Conkey began. "Both of you came into the Cadets in unusual circumstances. In both cases it had to do with bad behaviour and the hope by others that service in Cadets might help you. I accepted you both because that was also my belief. It is still my belief.

I think both of you are mixed up kids who need some guidance and help to set you on the right paths, so you can use the very real talents you both possess. In short, I think you are both good kids with a lot of ability and potential. If I didn't think that I wouldn't waste my time on you."

He paused and met the eyes of each in turn. Graham nodded and broke into a cold sweat. Shame was already coursing through him, but Captain Conkey's next words made him burn.

"When you joined, you each promised me personally that, while you were at cadets, you would behave. Now, I suppose a bush lawyer might argue that you weren't at Cadets on the weekend, at least until you got off that bus, but it doesn't look that way to me. In both cases your parents thought you were with us. In other words you used us, and you deceived your parents. You used us and we don't like being used; and we don't like liars and cheats. Got that?"

Graham nodded and managed to meet Captain Conkey's flinty gaze. Shame scorched his cheeks and he felt sick inside. Captain Conkey then went on, "Both of you are going to decide right now if you are going to stay in Cadets under those conditions. If you choose to do so, you will promise again not to cause trouble at Cadets. If you aren't willing to do that then you are out; and I mean as soon as we can discharge you. In that case the full story goes to your parents. Now wake up to yourselves and stop behaving like idiots. Both of you are heading down the juvenile delinquent track fast. Why? To what end? What is your aim?"

Captain Conkey paused again to let his words sink in, then continued, "You can't be proud of the way you are behaving. It is almost mindless rebellion, with a lot of pointless self-pity involved. Wake up! Both of you have enormous potential. You are both very intelligent, fit and healthy, able to do all sorts of skills. You have leadership and ability, and it is a real waste not to use it. So I am again giving you a chance. You might not think Cadets is worth anything; or that it won't help you. That is your prerogative. But here and now you choose. So what is it to be?"

His eyes moved to Graham first. Graham swallowed, then (to his secret relief) spoke in a clear, loud voice, "I want to stay in Cadets, sir. I promise not to misbehave again."

"Good. And you, Bell?"

"Yes sir. I promise not to misbehave at Cadets," Stephen said.

"Fine! Okay, you can go, Stephen. Graham, you have another interview now, in the principal's office. Let's go."

Graham was led to the principal's office. The door was closed so Captain Conkey knocked and was told to come in. He beckoned Graham to follow and then indicated a seat. As he walked in, Graham noted that the room seemed to be full of people: The Principal, both Deputy Principals, his mother and Warrant Officer Howley. It was all he could do to sit calmly and focus his eyes. To him it appeared that they all looked very grim and knowing.

It was immediately apparent that the principal did not know about Amelia, as he only mentioned the camping trip when he went over the problem. His summary was simple. "Graham, we seem to be almost back where we were a few weeks ago. You were given a chance then and you have thrown it back in the faces of Captain Conkey and your parents. At the very least that is unwise. It is also ungrateful. As fate would have it, you have been found out in rather dramatic circumstances, which showed us perhaps your true worth."

He paused and looked directly into Graham's eyes with a steely glare. "I know, and so do soldiers like Warrant Officer Howley and Captain Conkey, that it is in a real crisis that we see what a person is truly capable of; and what they are worth. When the chips are down people forget to play act roles which mask their real personality and they stand exposed. Well, you have been tested and not found wanting. I have it from a dozen sources that your actions yesterday showed both courage of the highest order and also a cool head in an emergency. You also have real leadership.

"If it were not for how you acquitted yourself, I would be recommending you try another school. I will admit you have been something of a problem over the last month or so and we had several staff meetings to try to formulate a strategy to help you. Now, Captain Conkey and Warrant Officer Howley are offering one which is somewhat unusual." At that he smiled. "Or actually, it is a very ancient and traditional one which has fallen into disuse, because it is no longer fashionable. That is placing you in the army."

Graham nodded. He was amazed how hard his heart was beating and he sensed that it was now very important to him to be given that chance.

The principal went on, "Now, you cannot be placed in the army of course. You are too young. And the Cadets are only part-time, much as Captain Conkey would argue they would do more good if they were full-time!" He and Captain Conkey exchanged glances, and both smiled. It was obviously an old argument.

The principal resumed, "So, what we can do is make it possible for you to do some extra cadet training on top of your schoolwork. We can only do this with your permission of course. You cannot be forced. You must volunteer."

Graham glanced at Warrant Officer Howley. Must volunteer! He remembered Warrant Officer Howley's words and demeanour the night before: 'An offer you can't refuse!' Would he really carry through with legal action if Graham now said no? To his own surprise he decided he did want what Warrant Officer Howley was offering. He managed a grin and Warrant Officer Howley's lips came together in what might have been a sardonic smile.

"I want to do it, sir. I volunteer," Graham said.

There was a noticeable easing of tension in the room. The Principal and Captain Conkey both smiled and Warrant Officer Howley nodded with satisfaction.

The principal nodded. "Good! Good! Then I will leave all the details to be worked out by you Mrs Kirk, with Captain Conkey and Warrant Officer Howley," he said.

The meeting broke up and there was the usual flurry of handshakes and farewells. As they did, Graham overheard the principal say to Warrant Officer Howley, "It is very good of you to concern yourself in the boy's welfare, sergeant major."

Warrant Officer Howley grunted and replied, "He has the makings of a really good soldier. It would be a shame to waste such talent. Besides, he needs a firm hand to help him from going bad. I have a personal interest in that."

Graham was very interested in that, and also worried in case the principal inquired further what the 'personal interest' might be. *I am going to pay for those minutes of pleasure with Amelia!* he mused.

He was not wrong. After a few words to Graham's mother, Warrant Officer Howley called him over. "Right, Cadet Kirk, you and I both know the score. From here on you obey my orders and work for me. Start by going home and doing all your homework. Be in bed by 2130hrs. Be at my house at 0600 tomorrow morning. You know where I live, and I know you won't have any trouble finding it in the dark."

Graham almost gaped at that. *Is the old bugger making a joke about it?* he wondered. Sensibly he just nodded.

Warrant Officer Howley went on. "Wear shorts, T-shirt and joggers. Bring a pullover. Now off you go."

0600! That means I will have to get up at about 0530 at least to get over there! Bloody hell!

Graham met his mother's worried gaze. Yes, he was going to pay alright!

Chapter 27

HOW TOUGH ?

At 0600hrs the next morning, Graham stood in the cold darkness outside Warrant Officer Howley's house. Warrant Officer Howley was dressed in T-shirt, shorts and running shoes. He stood hands on hips and looked Graham up and down.

"Okay, let's see how tough you are. And I don't mean how physically fit. I am going to test your character. Do what I do. Leave that pullover here. Let's go."

Then he was off, running. Not jogging, but running. After a hundred paces, Graham was feeling the strain. He began to lag. Warrant Officer Howley glanced back at him.

"Come on, run. You can do better than that! I've seen you run faster than me, so get cracking!"

Graham could not resist either retorting, "I had more incentive then."

"Sir! You call warrant officers and officers 'sir'. Now run or I might decide that I should cut off your offending appendages!"

Graham wasn't sure if he had overstepped the mark or not. He ran. Somehow, he kept on running, even when he felt ready to drop. He ran till his heart was pounding fit to bust and every lungful of air was a hot agony. Pride helped.

Grumpy old bastard! I'll show him, even if it kills me! he told himself through clenched teeth.

In the end he thought it would kill him, but by then he didn't care. He just kept pushing himself. Warrant Officer Howley did not slow down till they were at the Esplanade. Abruptly, he stopped running and began flexing and stretching his muscles.

"Not bad. I'll try you out on a fifteen kilometre when I reckon you are ready."

Graham could only pant. Fifteen kilometres! Could any human run that far? Warrant Officer Howley then led him through a series of muscle strengthening exercise: push-ups, sit-ups, heaves and so on till the sweat poured from him in rivers, even though it was a cool winter morning.

After fifteen minutes they ran back to Warrant Officer Howley's. It was 0645. Warrant Officer Howley eyed him with what might have been satisfaction.

"Not bad. But you aren't fit. Remember, if you build your body right while you are young it will carry you through life well. Now, don't forget the program for today."

"No sir," Graham gasped.

"Put on your pullover so you don't get a chill and get home."

"Yes sir."

A fast pedal had Graham home by 0700. Straight into the bathroom for a shower and shave ('Do both at once,' Warrant Officer Howley had advised. 'Saves time, and you don't need a mirror. You know where your face is.'). Breakfast was under the grinning jibes of Alex. His mother looked concerned and so did Kylie, who did not know the whole story and was plainly mystified and worried.

School by 0845. No problems in class. Graham concentrated and kept his mouth shut. He did not sit next to Stephen, and that helped. He avoided trouble, even when Larsen and Co. taunted him. Graham just clenched his jaw and walked off, seething with rage and humiliation.

The hardest experience was a brief confrontation with Derek White and Wally Dru. Both glared and sneered but, as neither Graham nor Stephen had mentioned their names, they made no real issue of things. They just taunted him for being a 'hero' and curled their lips.

By mid-afternoon, Graham was feeling exhausted. Worse still, his muscles were protesting vigorously at the unaccustomed exertions. Graham walked home and immediately did his homework, much to the astonishment of Alex. Then he brushed his army boots and checked his uniform and webbing.

Straight after tea, and now dressed in uniform, he was picked up by Warrant Officer Howley and taken to Porton Barracks. Being Tuesday night, the active reservists of the General Army Reserve (part-time volunteers) were holding their weekly 3 hour 'Home Training' parade. Under certain circumstances Army Cadets could participate in their training. Warrant Officer Howley had arranged for Graham to do this. Warrant Officer Howley inspected him, explained what was going to happen, then marched him in to be introduced to an officer, then taken to meet a sergeant named Thompson.

For the next three hours, Graham was placed in a platoon of soldiers and did the army training. At first he felt very self-conscious, but he soon lost most of that. He was dressed the same (except for the blue 'cadet' patches on his upper sleeve) and, he realised, he was as big as most of them. He also knew just enough of the basics to avoid making serious gaffes. Sweating with anxiety, he watched and learned so as not to be singled out and made look foolish.

There was a theory lesson on 'Radio Antennas' which he found very interesting, although some of the jargon and technicalities of the radio sets they were talking about were unknown to him. Next was a lesson on using an 84mm Karl Gustav Anti-Armour weapon. This was revision to the others, so a corporal took Graham and two others aside and ran through the basics. The weight of the weapon came as a real surprise, but Graham found the lesson fascinating and he thoroughly enjoyed it. The last period was on 'Preparation for a Recon patrol' and he found that even more interesting.

It was a tired and sore boy who was dropped off at home at 2230hrs to find his anxious mother waiting up with a cup of hot Milo for him.

"How did it go?" she asked.

"Good. Really interesting! I can do all that stuff," he enthused.

"That's nice, dear. Now into bed. I've set your alarm."

A dreamless sleep. Then another similar day. This time Warrant Officer Howley ran slower and led him up the Red Track up Mt Whitfield to a lookout. Passing the Bamboo Patch gave Graham some mixed emotions and he was thankful Warrant Officer Howley did not know of that incident. The walk up the hill Graham found really testing. The only other worry was over possibly encountering a snake. But he saw none. Then home and ready for school.

The school day slid past without any trouble. Graham hated it but he gritted his teeth and made himself behave and work. As he worked, another piece of Warrant Officer Howley's advice kept coming to mind. 'Remember this, Cadet Kirk. You might not have much control over what is happening to you. But you can control how you feel about it. Now think about this. You may be going through hell, but you can still focus your thoughts to be cheerful. That's what separates the really good soldiers from the second raters. When everything is going wrong: the enemy is winning, your best mate has just been killed, it is cold and raining, and the world all looks black, you can either be a miserable weakling and feel gloomy, grumble, and give up. Or you can grin and bear it, help your mates and lift their spirits, and show you can take it.

"That makes you a winner. Remember, you control your emotions. Don't let them control you. And even in the blackest situation there is still some good. So train yourself to look for it, to be positive. You'll be amazed how it changes your life. You can be certain that grumbling and moaning won't make things any better. Being positive will."

Graham did try it, and he was amazed. Several times he forced himself to find nice things in every lesson and they seemed to go much faster.

As it was Wednesday, there was the cadet 'Home Training' after school. Graham quickly changed from school uniform to cadet uniform and went to join his platoon. He was very self-conscious doing this as he was the object of much curiosity and speculation, and he knew all sorts of stories were circulating. To all questions he simply answered that he was ordered not to say anything. To his surprise, people accepted this and appeared to be even more impressed.

The admin parade he now found easy. Graham had time to look around and notice small details. He noted that Sgt Masters screwed his hands together nervously behind his back when he was standing 'at ease' in front of the platoon. He also noted that CUO Grant was watching him!

The lessons were: First Aid (Sprains and minor fractures), Map Reading, and Night sentry duties in the field. Once again, Graham concentrated and kept his mouth shut. He learned a lot and even decided he was enjoying himself. The only thing he found hard to take was that he felt a bit lonely as the others had decided he had some special status. As a consequence, he was somewhat excluded socially but he shrugged his shoulders.

Part of the price I have to pay, he told himself.

After cadets he went home, had a shower and changed, then had tea. In the evening he did his homework. By then he felt thoroughly exhausted. He was in bed by 9:15pm and asleep within minutes.

The Thursday morning run was along the Esplanade all the way to the Pier. During this they encountered a group of drunken Aborigines who threatened and shouted abuse. As they approached them, Warrant Officer Howley slowed down and asked, "Can you fight?"

"Yes sir. My dad taught Alex and me," Graham replied.

But there was no fight. The gang just called insults and jeered. They were soon far behind. This time, when the pair stopped, instead of physical exercises, Warrant Officer Howley sparred with Graham. He grunted qualified approval.

"Not bad. But we can improve on that. I'll teach you how to defend yourself with a bit of unarmed combat."

Then Graham learned that Warrant Officer Howley had served in a commando regiment and his admiration grew even more. After school that day, and on Friday, Graham had to go to the army depot straight from school. Warrant Officer Howley made him bring his cadet uniform and change into it. Then he was put to work. One day it was simply moving boxes of stores and helping with a stocktake in the Q Store. The next day it was helping take out hundreds of weapons and read their serial numbers for a routine check. It was hard work, but he still found it interesting.

On Friday night his mother took him to Scouts and picked him up afterwards. That caused him more secret guilt as memories of sneaking off to the party from the old cemetery came to him.

By the time he slipped off to sleep he felt very tired and sore but paradoxically quite content.

* * *

There was no morning run on Saturday. Graham made himself get up and go for one anyway. It took a real effort as his muscles were stiff and sore. The morning was spent in household chores, including washing his two uniforms and socks (Warrant Officer Howley insisted he do his own army laundry). The afternoon and evening were devoted to schoolwork. The following week was the last week of term and there were exams scheduled for most days. Part of the deal was that all schoolwork would be done before there was any play.

Two written assignments for Capt Conkey; one for History and one for Geography, took up most of this time. By 9:30pm they were finished, and Graham was allowed to telephone Peter to finalise arrangements for the next day. That done, Graham climbed wearily into bed and slept soundly.

On Sunday morning Graham again rose at 0530 and forced himself to go out and run. It was a cold morning and that made it even harder to get up. At 0830 he went to church with his mother and Kylie. That led to a slightly difficult series of experiences.

Firstly, he found himself seated next to Margaret. He had not seen her for two weeks and she looked very anxious. From the way she spoke he could tell she knew he had been in trouble. She fairly oozed sympathy, which annoyed him. Her concern also made him feel guilty.

I hope she doesn't know what I've done! he thought.

That revived sharp and erotic memories of Amelia. Being in church and with confession due this was not what Graham wanted. He battled against the images and feelings but still found himself aroused. Embarrassment and guilt both combined to make him burn. There could be no escaping the fact that God knew!

Feeling genuinely contrite, Graham silently confessed his sins. He also took the opportunity to give thanks for his survival, and for being able to help in the rescue on the previous Sunday. All in all he found church a cleansing and healing experience and came out feeling much calmer.

Peter was at church and he and Roger both talked to him later. A short hike to get fit for annual camp was planned. Stephen was grounded so could not come. Nor could Roger as he had to go with his parents to visit an aunt in Atherton. So it was just Peter and Graham. That suited Graham.

I've had enough of Stephen for the moment, he decided.

On arriving home after church, Graham changed into his hiking clothes, collected his basic webbing, pack and a cut lunch, and climbed into the car. He could tell that Margaret was dejected by this as she obviously wanted to be with him. That made him happy to go.

I've had enough of girls for the time being, he thought.

His mother drove him to Peter's. Peter was also in hiking clothes and had his gear. Both boys climbed into Peter's mum's car. The two mothers talked for ten minutes and then Mrs Bronsky drove them up to Kuranda. On the way they passed the site of the road smash. The place was only obvious from a few scorched leaves and scars on the bark of the trees.

Seeing the place gave Graham some bad memories, but it was also a sobering reminder that life went on. The traffic whizzed up and down the road oblivious to the tragedy. Peter kept a tactful silence, but his mother wanted to know the details. Graham gave them in outline, then sat and stared out at the view and reviewed the whole series of experiences. They were painful to remember.

Did I really do all that! Graham thought in agonised embarrassment. It seemed too much and as though someone else had done them.

Mrs Bronsky dropped the boys at the Black Mountain turnoff. They set out to route march along it. Both had full packs and despite the coolness of the day they soon worked up a sweat. Graham found it a real relief to get out of the area where there were houses tucked away in the rainforest. After that it was just pure rainforest till McKenzies Pocket and he enjoyed walking through that.

It was mostly an uphill slog for ten kilometres, but the very air seemed to be cleaner and fresher. Graham took pleasure in pushing himself along. Peter had trouble keeping up although he made no complaint. The sheer hard physical work was balm to Graham. It seemed as though he sweated his problems away.

At McKenzies Pocket they turned right and followed a dirt track along the edge of a vast pine plantation to Forgan Smith Lookout. They stopped there for lunch and hotly debated the story about a man digging a fence post finding an ancient Egyptian coin in that area.

Peter did not buy the theory that Ancient Egyptians had visited North Queensland. "Most of the blokes who came to the Gold Rushes came from Britain and they came on British ships through the Suez Canal. I'll bet the bloke who dropped this famous coin got it in Egypt on his way here, and then dropped it accidentally when he slogged his way up the mountain on his way to the diggings," he said.

Graham wanted to believe in the more romantic notion of ancient Egyptians navigating to North Queensland but had to concede Peter's theory made more sense.

They followed the track down the mountain to Greenslopes Street and walked out to the Cook Highway. Both felt self-conscious trudging along with pack and webbing in the middle of a suburb. They stopped at a shop and drank and talked till Peter's mum arrived to drive them home.

That night Graham slept as though drugged, and his mother had to rouse him for his morning run. As it was, he was ten minutes late. Warrant Officer Howley was not amused.

"We will just go ten minutes longer to make up," was his comment.

Once again, they ran. At the end of it he said, "That's not too bad. So, tomorrow, we will run in boots and basic webbing. Wear your uniform. Wash it as soon as you get home."

School was exams, all day long. Graham sat for each with a determination he had never displayed before. The day seemed to race by.

After school Graham again went to the army depot. This time Warrant Officer Howley taught him more unarmed combat. He tossed Graham a bayonet in its scabbard.

"Okay, Cadet Kirk, attack me with the knife and I will show you how to protect yourself from people who do," he instructed.

Graham gripped the knife in the way his father had instructed him: thumb on the blade, blade flat and in line with his forearm. Warrant Officer Howley grunted approval.

"Who taught you to hold a knife like that?"

"My dad, sir. He is a ship's captain. He taught all of us how to fight with a knife, and with a broken bottle. He reckoned that we might run into trouble when we were down at the docks."

"He wouldn't be wrong. Not nice places usually," Warrant Officer Howley agreed. "What did he say to do with that?"

"Strike upwards," Graham said. He demonstrated.

Warrant Officer Howley blocked the thrust and spun Graham around and into an arm lock. He grabbed his little finger and pulled it. Graham let go.

Warrant Officer Howley let go and bent to pick up the bayonet. "Easy when you know how. Come on, I will show you."

For the next hour he trained Graham until both were bruised and sore. At the end of the session, Warrant Officer Howley said, "Now, don't you ever use this knowledge except in self-defence. And don't talk about it to your friends. And don't try to teach them. Got it?"

"Yes sir."

It was a very pleased and confident Graham who rode home.

The Tuesday morning effort was a trudge up Mt Whitfield with pack and webbing. Graham was very glad he had done the walk with Peter as he managed to keep up. As they stood at one of the lookouts gazing out at the airport, Graham summoned the courage to ask a question that had been nagging at him for a week.

"Sir, would I be allowed to write to Amelia?"

Warrant Officer Howley turned to face him and scowled. "No! Her mother is adamant about that. You are not even to know what school she has been sent to. My advice is to forget her. If you still want to write when she is sixteen, then ask me again. Until then drop the subject and be thankful I don't throw you down that bloody mountainside!"

Graham could only swallow with embarrassment. He wouldn't have minded if Warrant Officer Howley had bashed him and tossed him over the edge. *I deserve it!* he told himself.

On the next section of track up the mountain he forced himself to keep up, pushing himself until his breathing came in rasping gasps and black dots danced in his vision. Only later did it dawn on him that Warrant Officer Howley loved his daughter and missed her. That made Graham feel even more guilty.

School that day included three more exams: Maths A, Maths B and Chemistry. To his own amazement Graham managed to do most of the Maths B paper.

I might even pass that! he thought.

The other two were dismal failures, he knew, but he also appreciated he had done better than he otherwise would have (In fact his Maths A went up from 4% in the previous exam to 23%).

After school he went home and studied for the last two exams: Physics and German. He held out no great hopes for either, but did try. However the study time was only two hours as he had to wash his uniform and prepare for the evening. Tea was early: 5:30pm. By 6pm he was dressed in uniform.

Soon after that Warrant Officer Howley arrived in an army Land Rover. Graham climbed in, feeling quite excited. They were going to Mareeba and he was looking forward to that. First, they went to Porton Barracks and loaded six Light Machine Guns and other stores into the vehicle. A second vehicle, driven by a corporal, came with them. It carried the weapon's bolts and was for security in case one vehicle broke down or had an accident.

"Road accidents do happen, you know," Warrant Officer Howley commented as he steered the vehicle up the Kuranda Range in the dusk.

Going past the accident site in the dark was another emotional experience. Graham was moved to ask if he knew what had happened to the people from the van.

"Released from hospital yesterday, so I heard," Warrant Officer Howley replied.

"They didn't come to thank you?" Graham asked.

Warrant Officer Howley shook his head. "No. People rarely do that. In this case I expect the bloke feels pretty guilty, so he wouldn't want to be reminded of it."

It was very sad to Graham. As he pondered human nature, he remembered a sermon at church a few months before about how only one of ten lepers who had been cured by Jesus had come back to thank him.

They drove on in silence up the winding mountain road. It grew colder and Graham was glad to pull on his field jacket as they went down towards Kuranda. After that it was half an hour's fast drive with little traffic to Mareeba. On that stretch, Warrant Officer Howley talked about the army and his experiences in various parts of the world.

Mareeba by night was another experience. Graham had been there half a dozen times by day but now it seemed to be almost a ghost town. Apart from a few drunks in the main street, the place appeared to be deserted. Not a single car moving in the main street and that at 7:15!

They drove to the Army Reserve Depot. This was also the Air Force Cadets Depot. The army had a small room in the downstairs at the back. The local platoon, numbering only 15 men, was on parade when they arrived. There was no officer, only a sergeant. Graham looked around with interest and happily took part in the training.

Two of the lessons were on the Minimi light machine gun. Warrant Officer Howley was the instructor for both. He placed Graham in the squad and just treated him as another soldier. That suited Graham. The local Reservists were mildly curious about him. On asking Graham was informed there were no army cadets in Mareeba.

"Some in Atherton," his informant replied.

The two lessons were on 'Holding, aiming and firing' and 'Stoppages'. 'Degrees of weapon readiness' was the revision. With a bit of help from the others Graham was able to manage these. Despite being the odd one out he thoroughly enjoyed the lessons. He was also impressed by Warrant Officer Howley's instructional style.

He really knows his stuff. And he puts it across really well, Graham thought.

Best of all was when Graham had to carry out the gas stoppage practice. As he finished, Warrant Officer Howley nodded and said, "Good! Very well done, Cadet Kirk."

The glow of that praise warmed him all the way back to Cairns after the parade. They drove back with hardly a word. Graham looked out at the dark bush and felt happy. After they had returned the weapons to the armoury at the barracks and Warrant Officer Howley had dropped him off at home, Graham stood at his front gate for a few minutes.

What was occupying his mind was the thought, which had grown over the evening until it seemed to be a marvellous thing: This man, who had every reason to hate him and to punish him harshly, was going out of his way to help him.

He is treating me more like a son than like a delinquent juvenile!

Chapter 28

ADVANCE PARTY

There was no let up on Wednesday. Graham was up at 0530 and at Warrant Officer Howley's by 0600. Five minutes later they were stepping it out in a forced march wearing packs and webbing. This time Graham actually enjoyed it. He was feeling much fitter. More importantly he was feeling valued. Another factor helping him was mounting excitement. The cadet unit's Annual Camp was due to start on Saturday. For Graham, this really meant that afternoon as he and Stephen had been selected (ordered?) to go on the Advance Party.

School went by in an impatient blur. The two exams were coped with. Graham was sure he had done well at Physics and even thought he might have come close to passing the German. Another boost came from Capt Conkey who told him he had marked both his History and Geography exam papers and that he had done well in both.

"Good work Graham. I knew you could do it!" he said.

The praise was like a drink of cold water in the desert. Graham drank it in and flushed with satisfaction. He also felt a stirring of affection for the tubby captain.

He is giving me a chance when I don't really deserve it, he told himself. *The least I can do is not let him down.*

After school was Cadets. This was mostly taken up with administration for the camp. About twenty new recruits had just joined and they were placed in sections to bring the 'First Year' platoons up to strength. Captain Conkey then checked the Enrolment Forms and Next-of-Kin Forms and Permission Forms. During this, Graham sat quietly in his section near the back. Only one person was added to their section; a girl from another high school named Harriet Harris. She was a very tall, slender girl and appeared very nervous. Graham gave her a friendly smile and tried to make her feel at ease.

Of more interest and concern were two girls added to 5 Section: Angela and Rita. Both were Year 9s and already had a reputation around the school for being 'hot numbers'.

What on earth are they joining the Cadets for? Graham wondered. *It must be because of all the boys.*

This suspicion was confirmed a moment later when Angela, an attractive brunette with lively brown eyes gave him a bright smile. Stephen added to his suspicions later when he commented on the two girls.

"You'll be right on camp with Rita the Rooter and her mate Angela in your platoon."

Graham eyed the two girls with a speculative eye, and with mixed emotions. They were certainly horny looking chicks. And, if rumour was correct, they were both 'easy'. What a temptation!

At the end of the parade, those people going on the Advance Party were called aside for final instructions. The group included the QM, Lt Hamilton; the CQMS, Sgt Strutton; Cpl Storeman Vince Brooke; two of the 'Control Group' (older cadets who had not been promoted but had stayed on): Sgt Green and Cpl Holbrook; plus Stephen and Graham. All were boys (because of the problem of supervising girls in the circumstances). Lt Hamilton briefed them on the program, then dismissed them.

As they walked away, Graham felt his spirits soar. School was over for two weeks! He found he was really looking forward to the cadet camp. Stephen was not so keen but accepted the situation.

Peter was mystified. "How did you two get on the Advance Party?"

Stephen and Graham looked at each other. Graham answered, "Just better looking I suppose."

"Oh poop! I wish I was going," Peter said. "That means you lucky buggers miss out on two more days of school."

Stephen nodded. "That's right. Some have it... and some don't," he replied.

Peter made rude raspberry noises but then laughed. "Oh well. Have fun. I'll see you on Saturday."

Graham made his way home feeling extremely happy. It was as though a huge burden had lifted from him. No school for more than a fortnight! At home he washed his uniform and hung it to dry. For the next hour, he laid out every item of clothing and equipment he would need for the camp and checked. It was all then carefully packed. As each item was put away, he ticked it off on the list of 'What to Bring' on the back of the Camp Joining Instruction.

With every passing minute he became more and more excited. Several times he walked around whistling and smiling. As he worked, he hummed cheerfully. His mother noticed this and smiled happily. Once she stopped him and gave him a spontaneous hug. That embarrassed Graham as he thought he was too big for hugging.

His mother laughed. "You are never too big for your mother to hug! And don't you forget it!"

"Yes, Mum."

"Are you looking forward to the camp?"

"Yes, Mum."

She sighed, then hugged him again, "Oh I'm so glad that Warrant Officer Howley had taken you under his wing. The school says you are a different boy these last two weeks. Is he going on the camp with you?"

"Yes, but I think he has to help look after more than one cadet unit," Graham replied.

"Good. Now you have a good time, and be good."

"I will be, Mum."

That night Graham could hardly sleep. So many images flitted through his mind that he lay awake for hours. Among them were images of Amelia. These made him very aroused, as well as ashamed and guilty. He was also dismayed to find that he seemed to be having trouble remembering exactly what she looked like.

There was no time for a run the next morning. Graham had to be at the school by 06:45. He insisted on walking. His mother offered to drive him, but he declined. In line with the family tradition of no sentiment on partings, he briefly hugged Kylie, shook Alex's hand, and gave his mother a hug and kiss, then picked up his gear and strode off.

Two Land Cruisers with trailers were parked at the Q Store. Lt Hamilton was the driver of one and Warrant Officer Howley of the other. They said a cheery good morning and told him to start loading the water jerry cans. Graham greeted the other cadets and happily set to work. It felt like the start of a great adventure.

Stephen arrived just before they departed. He was in a bad mood, but Graham ignored this. He was not going to let anything spoil the day.

"Cheer up you grumpy bugger!" he chided. "We could both be in jail instead."

At 0730hrs they were loaded into the two vehicles. Graham wanted to go in the front of Warrant Officer Howley's Cruiser but Sgt Green took that seat, so he had to sit in the back. Stephen sat next to him and Cpl Holbrook on the other side.

The annual camp was being held at Speed Creek, about 50 kilometres west of Townsville in the dry country. That meant a five-hour drive to Townsville along the Bruce Highway to begin with. Graham had only done the drive once before, so he found it interesting enough. There was a stop to eat and refuel at Tully and then on.

They arrived in Townsville at 1230hrs. Graham was not impressed with the city. It appeared a drab, brown, dry, industrial city. The things which interested him were seeing all the army helicopters at the Garbutt RAAF base and Lavarack Barracks.

To his amazement, Lavarack Barracks went on for kilometres, sprawled along the base of Mt Stuart. It housed a brigade of regular troops and Graham was fascinated to see platoons of real soldiers marching along with weapons and in full kit. A glimpse of lines of armoured fighting vehicles and the sight of a gun crew practising with a field gun all added to the interest.

Their first destination was a HQ, where the cadets sat and waited while the adults went in to get training area clearances. From there they went to a huge store depot. Graham was amazed at the scale of it all. He gaped at the huge sheds full of every conceivable type of military stores. It was another world and an eye-opener.

A camouflaged truck driven by a soldier appeared and was loaded with an assortment of camp stores. Graham even enjoyed the sweaty task of helping load the truck. Everything was new and novel, and it was also good physical exercise. Warrant Officer Howley helped with the loading. All the time he worked he cracked jokes. Even Stephen laughed and cheered up.

Once the stores were loaded and signed for the group drove out of the barracks. It was 1500hrs by this. The next part of the trip took them along the Ring Road past the hospital and across Ross River, then out of the city along the Herveys Range Road. Graham enjoyed this drive. The suburbs gave way to dry savannah woodland and grassland. Rugged looking mountains grew closer by the minute and the little convoy then ground its way up the side of a steep, rocky escarpment.

As it did, Warrant Officer Howley pointed ahead. "That pass where the road goes through is called Thorntons Gap. In the pioneering days it was the main road west to the goldfields around Charters Towers."

Graham leaned forward and looked with interest. He had never been to Charters Towers but had seen pictures of it. "It must have taken an effort to cut a road up this mountain," he commented.

Warrant Officer Howley shook his head. "They didn't. This bit of road was made in the 1970s. The old road went up that ridge over there on the right. It was much steeper."

Graham followed his pointing finger and picked out a faint scar, which wound its way back and forth up a steep spur covered in savannah woodland. "Do they still use that?" he asked.

"No. It was closed years ago. But there is an interesting story about it. Back in World War Two, the sappers prepared the road for demolition in case they had to delay the Japanese."

"Sappers?"

"Army Engineers," Warrant Officer Howley explained.

Graham blushed and felt very ignorant. He said, "Where were the Japanese coming from, sir?"

"I'm not sure if it was to cover a Japanese advance from the north overland from the Tablelands or whether it was to cover our withdrawal from Townsville if the Japanese landed and captured it," he explained.

"What did the engineers do?" Graham asked.

"They dug a tunnel under the road up near the top of the range and filled it with explosives, what's called a prepared demolition," Warrant Officer Howley explained.

Graham was fascinated. He found it both exciting to imagine being part of but also puzzling. "But they didn't blow it up, did they?" he asked.

Warrant Officer Howley shook his head. "No. After the Americans won the Battle of the Coral Sea there was no danger of invasion. But they left the charge in place, just in case. Then they forgot about it."

"Forgot about it!" Graham cried, wondering how anyone could forget about a large quantity of explosives.

Warrant Officer Howley chuckled. "Forgot it. This the army, son. The sappers detailed to guard it were obviously ordered to another task and not replaced but the demolition was left, just in case. I suppose the HQ staff officers also changed and nobody remembered. It was only a few years ago it was discovered that it was still there," he said.

Graham could picture that, but it bothered him as he had always had the image of the army being super organised.

"So what happened?" he asked, amazed at the idea of civilian vehicles driving unknowingly over such a dangerous thing for many years."

"Some old veteran mentioned it at a reunion, I gather. So the sappers sent a team to look and there it was. So they removed it."

A discussion on the laying of prepared demolitions and their command and control kept them occupied all the way to the top of the range past Piper's Lookout.

As soon as they were on top, they turned into Camp Gedling. This was a school camp belonging to Ignatius Park College and consisted of a dozen widely spaced buildings set on lawns on a hill slope. The camp was surrounded by bush. The kitchen of the camp was to be used to cook for the cadets. As the vehicles drove slowly in, Graham saw other army vehicles and uniformed figures.

Stephen pointed to them. "Who are these blokes, sir?"

"There are three other cadet units using this as their base camp as well: 15 Army Cadet Unit from Townsville and some from 130 Heatley. There's also a group from St Michael's College."

Cpl Holbrook sniffed, "Oh that Heatley mob! They think they are so good. They are right up themselves."

Warrant Officer Howley laughed. "Oh well, you will have a chance to find out which unit is better. The OC has organised a couple of exercises against them this camp."

That sounded very interesting to Graham, and he felt his pulse quicken. "Do we get to take part, sir? First Years I mean."

"Yes, I think so."

Graham peered out of the vehicle as Warrant Officer Howley parked it. "How do you tell which unit they come from?"

"You can't with most units unless they are in their ceremonial uniform. But all of these with the blue and white patch on their right shoulder are from 15ACU."

"What about the others, sir?"

"130ACU, that's Heatley and Charters Towers, don't wear any unit patch, nor do most units. But 130 aren't here. They spend all their camp in the bush, the same way we are going to this year; and St Michael's haven't marched in yet."

They climbed out and Graham looked around with interest. He met the curious stares of several strange cadets but was too shy to speak to them. Sgt Strutton and Sgt Green knew several and called out to them, a mixture of teasing and greetings.

They were told to unload their gear and to place it in an open-ended shed with a concrete floor. The other end was a Q Store, and they were growled at by a grouchy old, grey haired lieutenant who ordered them to keep their thieving fingers off his stores. A shower and toilet block further down the slope were pointed out to them.

"Have your bath later. It is time for mess parade," Warrant Officer Howley said.

This puzzled Graham as there did not seem to be any sort of parade occurring. All he saw were half a dozen cadets drifting over to the mess hall with their mess tins and cups. Unsure what to do, he just followed the example of the others and collected his own 'eating irons', then walked over and joined the end of the short queue.

When his dixies were filled with food, Graham followed Stephen to a table and sat down. A couple of cadets from 15ACU were seated opposite. One, a corporal, looked up and nodded a not particularly friendly g'day. Graham felt quite self-conscious, and the corporal's next words reinforced this.

"You blokes Second Years?"

Graham shook his head and blushed. "No. Only First Years."

The corporal made a face to indicate he wasn't impressed and from then on ignored them. The feeling of being a 'green reo' made Graham flush. He disliked it intensely. To hide this he just sat and ate. Stephen was not so easily put off and made several attempts to enter the conversation. By listening, Graham discovered that the 15ACU cadets had only arrived that morning, and that they were their own unit's Advance Party. He was surprised to learn that 130ACU had been in camp for three days.

"They get a whole week off school, the mob of posers," the corporal from 15 explained.

The whole concept of rivalry between cadet units was new to Graham and he became quite anxious that their unit would do well and not be sneered at.

After the meal, Graham went and had a shower, finding them communal with no dividers between each shower rose. That was a little bit embarrassing. Stephen made crude jokes about dropping the soap and other innuendos. Graham also took the opportunity to wash the uniform he had been wearing. He hung this on a clothesline strung between two trees behind the shed. The cadets then sat around and talked before joining the 15ACU cadets in a hall to watch a movie.

When he bedded down for the night, Graham was tired but happy. It had been an interesting day. The cadets slept in a line side by side on the concrete floor. Despite the discomfort, Graham slept soundly.

He was roused by Sgt Strutton's call to get out on 'Check Parade'. To his surprise, Graham found it was freezing cold. He had slept in uniform so only needed to pull on his boots. He hurried out, pulling on his pullover as an icy wind was blowing up through the pass. It was an experience he did not enjoy. They were lined up and Sgt Strutton called them to attention, then called gruffly, "Where's your hat, Cadet Kirk?"

"In the shed," Graham replied.

"In the shed, sergeant," he was rebuked. "Go and get it. You always wear your hat on check parade."

"Yes sergeant."

Graham blushed and ran to get his hat, annoyed by a snicker from Cpl Holbrook. When he came back, Sgt Strutton began calling the roll.

As he did, Cpl Holbrook whispered out of the side of his mouth, "You might be Howley's pet, but you can still lump it with the rest of us."

Graham flushed with embarrassment and anger. Angry words of rebuttal sprang to his tongue. With an effort he bit them back. What would be the point? It wouldn't stop comments like that.

Once the roll was marked, the small group was fallen out. Graham made his way to the shower to wash and shave. Breakfast followed. He was then detailed to help wash up in the kitchen. This was a messy and greasy job, but he made no comments and got stuck into it. He suspected he might wear more such tasks, but the knowledge just made him shrug.

As he worked, he watched the officers and Warrant Officer Howley talking at one of the tables. They looked as though they all knew each other well and were enjoying themselves.

A Land Rover drove in and parked. Cadets climbed out and unloaded metal containers. The cook turned to Graham.

"Go and help bring those Hot Boxes in and then wash them up."

Graham hurried out to help. A captain with a moustache wandered over from the Rover, to ribald jests from the seated group. Graham learned that he was also named Hamilton and was the brother of Lt Hamilton. The captain was the QM of 130ACU. Graham now found that the 130 cadets had collected their food while he had still been asleep and were returning the empty hot boxes. They also began filling empty water jerries.

The chores done, Lt Hamilton instructed them to load themselves into the vehicles. Graham remembered just in time to retrieve his washing. He hastily packed this, then tossed his gear into the Land Cruiser. They climbed in and set off, following the 130ACU Rover.

Now Graham was even more alive and interested. They were heading out into the bush to the training area, and he was curious to see what it looked like. The road was a good bitumen highway with almost no traffic. For the first few kilometres it ran through bush with a scattering of houses on large allotments. Then the bush became drier, the houses ended, and it was just rolling, open country. To the left, hills lined the road. To begin with they were a few kilometres off, but after a few more kilometres the road and the hills converged. Then the hills ended and only a few stony hills covered in scattered iron barks stood up from the gently rolling ridges. The grass was so short it was mostly only ankle high. The ground cover was so sparse that bare earth showed through as often as not.

"Certainly dry country," Stephen commented.

At that moment, they turned right off the highway onto a gravel road. This was corrugated and very dusty. The dust billowed into the back of the Land Cruiser. Graham sat with his eyes half closed and tried to keep track of where they were going. The road ran over a wide, low ridge and then down a long gentle slope for a kilometre. At the bottom they turned right again, this time onto a dirt track.

The dust thinned and through the windshield Graham saw an area of gently sloping ground. This was sparsely grassed and eroded. A scattering of iron barks covered the area. It did not look very attractive or inspiring to Graham.

The vehicles stopped. Captain Hamilton from Heatley pointed to the low rise. "This is your area. We are just over the road about a half a kilometre away."

He pointed through the trees towards the other side of the gravel road, which was still visible a couple of hundred metres back.

After a few more words to the officers, Capt Hamilton climbed back into his vehicle and drove off. As they departed, the Heatley cadets in the back of the Rover grinned and called, "You'll be sorry!"

That sent a little stab of concern through Graham. *What did they mean by that?* he worried.

Lt Hamilton turned to the Cairns cadets. "Okay, this is home for the next few days. Unload and we will start setting up."

As they worked, Stephen looked around. "What a dump! I'm not impressed with this place."

Graham looked around. It was certainly ordinary Australian bush. Off to the west a hundred metres or so was a white painted water tank with a windmill near it. Beyond that a line of darker trees marked a creek line, which he learned was called Speed Creek. Distant mountains showed through gaps in the straggly tree canopies. He shrugged. It would do.

For the next three hours they worked solidly. All the vehicles were unloaded. Stores were stacked in groups: jerry cans for water, camp stores, sleeping bags and warm clothing, tentage, boxes of Ration Packs and all sorts of miscellaneous stores. On an open area near where the vehicles were parked, three 14' X 14' tents were erected.

"Do we have to put up enough tents for everyone?" Graham asked Lt Hamilton as he hammered in a tent peg.

"No, just these three," Lt Hamilton replied.

Stephen made a face. "Who gets to sleep in these? The officers I suppose," he said.

Lt Hamilton gave him a sour look. "One is for stores. The next is the Command Post and Orderly Room, and the third is for the female officers," he replied. "And seeing you are so interested, you can dig the storm drains."

Stephen looked up at the clear blue sky. "Storm drains! You've got to be kidding!"

"Got to be kidding sir," Lt Hamilton reminded. "No. If we get a thunderstorm, it will really pour. Now, remember that the real function of the drain is to give you the dirt to build a dam around the inside of the tent. So all the dirt must go inside the tent in a neat mound."

"Yes sir," Stephen replied sulkily.

Lunch was collected by Lt Hamilton and his 'Q' staff from the kitchen at Camp Gedling. It was a tasty stew and Graham quite enjoyed it, although Stephen grumbled a lot. After lunch the pair were set to digging the storm drains. When that was finished, they were taken to a spot a hundred metres off and tasked to dig a latrine.

Stephen swore. "Bloody digging! That's all we've done all day," he grumbled. "Bloody ground's as hard as a rock too! Bugger it!"

Graham was nettled. He was enjoying the physical exercise. "Stop moaning and give me the pick Steve. It could be worse; we could be in school!"

Once the hole was dug, they were given the job of erecting a Hessian screen around the latrine. While they were engaged in this, a line of six cadets suddenly appeared out of a nearby gully and walked towards them. Graham stopped and looked at them, first with shock because they seemed to have popped up out of nowhere, then with interest.

All six were camouflaged and wore a sort of shapeless covering made of netting festooned with a straggle of Hessian strips. Their faces were all splotched with camouflage cream and they looked tired and dirty. They also looked tough and confident.

As they got closer, Graham noted they were carrying binoculars, a spotting telescope and a camera. One had a radio. Graham nodded and grinned.

"G'day. Who are you blokes?"

"Heatley. Recon patrol. Who are you mob?" answered the hard-faced looking sergeant leading the patrol.

"Cairns," Graham replied.

The Heatley sergeant grunted. "Heard you were arriving. Come and dig a dunny for us when you finish this one."

His patrol all grinned and offered helpful advice on dunny digging as they walked past. Graham experienced a series of emotions: irritation, annoyance, shame at being a mere 'First Year' digger of dunnies; and a sharp sense of jealousy.

That's what I want to be like, he thought with sudden determination. It was as though a hazy picture had cleared. *I want to be as good as them, or better,* he decided.

Later that afternoon, they had a chance to go over to visit the Heatley unit in their camp. The first impression was that there wasn't much of a camp; just a couple of vehicles parked under camouflage nets and a scatter of the small camouflage plastic two-man shelters nicknamed 'Hutchies'.

Then other impressions were overlayed as platoons of cadets filed in out of the bush. First was a sense of order, of an organization that knew what it was about. Then he experienced an indefinable but very tangible sense of mood, of atmosphere. Graham realised it was that thing he had read about described by the French term *Esprit d' Corps*.

This mob think they are good, he thought, but not in the sense of sneering at them. He could tell by their speech, faces and bearing that they were proud of themselves. *That is what we must aim at.* He had experienced inter-group rivalries in the Scouts, but this somehow felt more important.

The Cairns cadets returned to their camp for the evening meal, minus Warrant Officer Howley, who stayed to take part in the night exercise Heatley was planning. Back at their camp, the Cairns cadets sat around on logs and boxes to eat. Graham looked around and sniffed the air. It was noticeably cooler and the air was very crisp. A magnificent sunset of red and gold bathed the bush in a russet glow. The evening hush had settled and it was very peaceful.

This is great! Graham thought. He felt very much at peace.

He was also very tired. After tea he went on the vehicle which returned the hot boxes and had a shower at Camp Gedling. On returning to the bivouac, he found that the only light was from a small campfire and a single lantern. There was a sliver of a moon, but it was already low down among the trees to the west.

The group sat around the fire and told stories and jokes. Graham lay to one side on his sleeping bag and listened avidly. It was all interesting to him. The older cadets and officers talked about experiences, mostly funny, from previous exercises. Graham wished he had some experiences to add of his own but wisely held his tongue.

Twice patrols from Cairns dropped in for a few minutes. They were doing a night Recon Patrol exercise. Graham was seized by a wish that he was taking part as well. Heatley's OC, Major Wickham, also dropped in to chat for a while and once again Graham was struck by the cheerful camaraderie of the adult staff. To his delight, Warrant Officer Howley also arrived. After speaking to the officers for a minute, he caught Graham's eye.

"How's it going?" he asked.

"Great, sir. Really interesting," Graham replied.

"Fine. Keep up the good work."

The comment caused a glow of satisfaction in Graham. This was still with him when they were ordered to bed at 2100hrs. Stephen and Graham quickly strung their hutchie between two ironbarks and unrolled their bedding. Having done dozens of hikes there was no novelty in this for either. Graham carefully scooped out a small 'hip hole' to make himself more comfortable. By the time he slid into his sleeping bag, it was quite cold. As he lay back and relaxed, a feeling of deep content suffused him.

Despite the cold, Graham slept well. He was roused by a vehicle starting up. He opened eyes gummed by sleep and peered out. It was still dark, the first streaks of dawn just showing in the sky. A Land Rover drove off.

Going to collect the food for breakfast, he realised.

Being awake he checked his watch: 0530hrs. He pulled on his boots and took the opportunity to go to the latrine, then stood alone in the stillness and breathed deeply.

"I think I'm going to enjoy this camp. I'm glad I had to join the Cadets!" he told himself.

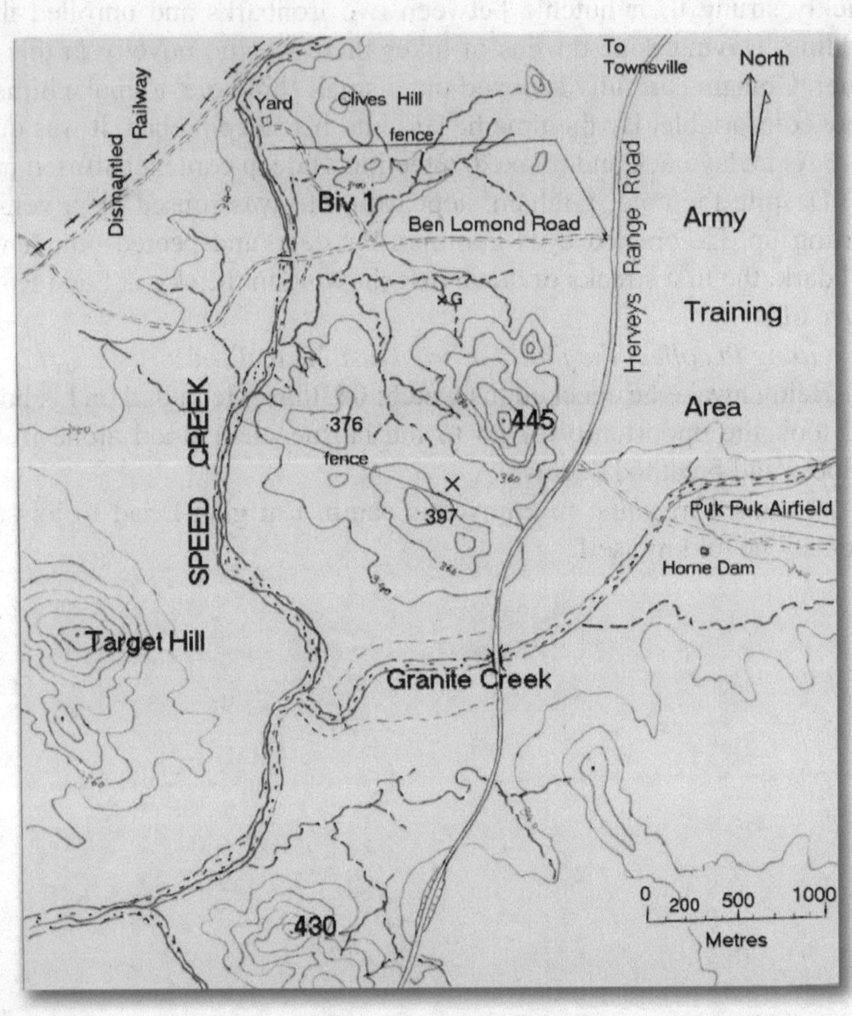

Map 1: Speed Creek

Chapter 29

CADET CAMP

Saturday morning was spent digging two more latrines, one for boys and one for girls. Stephen and Graham were also briefed as guides to show the platoon commanders which area was allocated to their platoons. During all this time Warrant Officer Howley was over with 130ACU. Graham was aware that he was vaguely uneasy about this. He would have liked to visit 130 again to watch but there was neither the time nor opportunity for this. Once he saw a section of Heatley cadets walking through the bush in the distance, but that was all.

At 1100hrs Lt Hamilton loaded the two Q cadets, plus Stephen and Graham into the Land Cruiser. Sgt Green and Cpl Holbrook were left to guard the camp. The army driver followed in his truck when they drove out to the bitumen road. Here Stephen and Graham were told to get out and the truck was parked. Lt Hamilton gave them instructions on what to do when the unit arrived. He then drove on back to Camp Gedling to pick up lunch.

The unit was due at 1130hrs. It was a hot, still day with no clouds. Stephen moved into the shade of a tree and sat down. Graham joined him and sat chewing a piece of grass. He was aware that he was tired, sun burnt and dirty.

"It feels like we've already been here a week," he commented.

"Yeah. I miss the bright lights already," Stephen said. "I... Hey! Here they come."

A convoy of army trucks had come into view from the direction of Townsville. The vehicles looked very businesslike and had camouflage nets and all sorts of bags and boxes festooned on them.

The army driver shook his head. "Not them. That's an army convoy," he said.

As the vehicles drove past, he added, "4 Regiment, Artillery."

"How can you tell?" Stephen asked.

"The 'Tac' signs on the vehicles," the driver explained.

He pointed out the small, coloured plates with numbers on the front and rear of each vehicle. Graham was fascinated. Each vehicle had soldiers in it. They looked very dirty and worn but also had that air of unit pride about them. Ten trucks and four Rovers went past. Six of the trucks were towing big guns. Graham had never seen real guns being moved and stared at them with great interest.

"Regulars," the driver added. "Long range snipers."

"What?"

"Long Range Snipers. Drop shorts. It's a nickname," he replied.

Graham felt very green and ignorant. The soldier then entertained them by teaching them the soldier's nicknames for as many branches of the army as he could remember.

A cattle truck went past the other way. Then there were no vehicles for ten minutes before a Land Rover came from Townsville and roared past. Stephen stretched out on the grass and put his hat over his eyes. Graham stood up and walked up and down.

Three motor coaches came into view. The army driver ran out to flag them down. The coaches slowed and turned around at the junction. Graham walked down to the edge of the road to watch. As soon as the coaches were parked, Capt Conkey jumped off, followed by CSM Grey. Capt Conkey saw the waiting cadets and grinned a welcome.

"Camp all ready?"

"Yes sir," Graham replied.

Capt Conkey nodded. He briefly met Graham's eyes, then turned to supervise the de-bussing. Cadets hurried off and were formed into groups to unload their gear from the cargo bays underneath each vehicle. There were some shouted orders and a bit of milling around. To Graham, the new arrivals all looked very clean and fresh. He was also conscious of cadets glancing at them. It was suddenly born upon him that they thought he was some sort of 'veteran' because he was there already and looked grubby.

Peter waved and called out as he struggled through the throng with his gear. "G'day! How's it going?"

"Good," Graham replied. He moved to help Peter.

Peter shook his head. "Better find your own platoon and help them," he suggested.

Graham saw the sense of this and made his way to where CUO Grant and Sgt Masters were grouping 2 Platoon on the side of the road. For a moment Graham hesitated over whether to salute or not. In the end he did.

CUO Grant returned it. "Hello, Cadet Kirk. How are you?"

"Good sir. I'm your guide to show you where the platoon is to camp," Graham explained. "All the kitbags and packs are to be loaded onto the truck. We have to walk."

"Good. Yes, I know that, thanks," CUO Grant replied. Then he lowered his voice and said, "By the way, the Australian Army doesn't normally salute when it is in the field, but thanks anyway for doing the right thing."

Graham burned with shame at the gaffe. He also felt a wave of warm appreciation at the way CUO Grant had tactfully explained it to him. He stood to one side while the platoon sorted its gear.

As Graham stood there, Rita came past, struggling with a huge kitbag. She gave a cheeky smile.

"Hi Graham! How's it going?"

"Good," Graham replied.

He was a bit taken aback at her forwardness but responded. She winked and gave an impish grin. That set his mind and body going. *She is a 'sure thing', or so all the boys say. I wonder...?* he speculated. He watched her locate her gear and then move to sit with her section.

When everyone had their gear, the coaches drove off back towards Townsville. A platoon at a time, under the direction of the CSM, the cadets filed up to pass their kitbags and packs onto the truck. While they were doing this, another Land Rover arrived. This was driven by Lt Maclaren. Lt McEwen was in the passenger seat.

As each platoon completed loading their kitbags they pulled on their webbing and started walking along the gravel road. 1 Pl went first. CUO Grant called to Graham.

"Okay, Cadet Kirk, lead on!"

Graham stepped off. CUO Grant followed him, then each section led by its corporal. Sgt Masters brought up the rear. As they walked Graham kept looking back and then at the platoon ahead. The cadets walked in long lines in single file on the right-hand side of the road. They seemed to stretch over a huge distance. It looked quite impressive.

As they topped the first rise, CUO Grant said, "Slow down, Cadet

Kirk. Don't catch up to the platoon in front. Remember, some of these kids aren't as fit as you."

"Yes sir." Graham looked back and saw that several cadets were already sweating and looking red in the face. "I can help carry some of the webbing sir," he offered.

"Thanks for that. Let them lug it for a bit longer first," CUO Grant replied.

From then on Graham kept a careful watch on the platoon. After about a kilometre, he was handed the webbing of a young Year 8 boy in Cpl Telford's section. After another 300 metres, he offered to take a second set off another Year 8 boy, a fat little slug in Cpl Gayney's section. However, CUO Grant vetoed this and instructed Cpl Gayney to organise her section to carry the webbing by its straps between two people.

Graham enjoyed the march back to camp. He was fit and knew he was. It felt good. So did being the leader of the line. As soon as they arrived, he led the platoon past the row of tents to a clump of ironbarks 50 metres on.

"This is our area sir," he said. "From that big tree there over to that log. 1 Pl is on that side and 3 Pl on the other side."

"Good. Thanks Cadet Kirk. Right troops, sit! Section commanders to me!" CUO Grant called.

Within a few minutes CUO Grant had shown each corporal which area their section could have, and he and Sgt Masters had dropped their webbing between the two trees they had selected for Pl HQ. Sgt Masters then sent them a section at a time to collect their packs and kit bags from the truck. The corporals then called the sections to join them in the allocated areas. Cpl Grenfell pointed out the trees they were to use. That now presented a small problem for Graham. Who would he team up with to share a hutchie?

There were seven in the section. The two girls, Gwen and Harriet, had to be in one hutchie. Cpl Grenfell and LCpl Bannister teamed up and so did Crane and Morris. That left Graham on his own.

Perhaps I can stay with Stephen? he thought. He put this idea to Cpl Grenfell.

Cpl Grenfell shook his head. "Bell is in 3 Pl. You have to be with your own section. You will have to rig a hutchie on your own. Do you know how?"

"Yes corporal," Graham replied.

He was not really disappointed at the decision. He went off to collect his gear from the HQ area.

As he put up a single hutchie, Graham discovered that the closest hutchie of 5 Section belonged to Angela and Rita. They did a lot of giggling and asked him to help.

He was feeling very fit and that made him horny. Just looking at the two girls started his pulses speeding up.

Setting up camp was interrupted by the arrival of the lunch vehicle. CSM Grey took charge. This time there actually was a mess parade. Platoons were called one at a time and marched over to the serving point. This was just a line of hot boxes laid out beside the vehicle track. Once they were served a meal, the cadets went to eat, sitting in the shade of trees on logs or on the ground in platoon areas.

Graham seated himself, then found that Rita and Angela had joined him. "Tell us about the camp. What is going on?" Rita asked.

Are they making a pass at me? Or are they just a pair of flirts? Graham wondered.

He began to describe the camp. While he talked, Crane seated himself and struck up a conversation. That suited Graham as he did not really want to get involved.

After lunch, work resumed on setting up camp. As he tidied his gear in his hutchie, Graham noted two Land Cruisers drive in. One was driven by Warrant Officer Howley. The other contained Major Wickham and officers from 130ACU. The adults stood and then sat on folding chairs and did a lot of talking and laughing.

CUO Grant and Sgt Masters came around and checked every hutchie. Later, Capt Conkey and CSM Grey also came around and looked over each platoon area.

Soon after that, Sgt Masters called the section commanders to move their sections. Graham walked behind Cpl Grenfell as they made their way over to where CSM Grey was seating the company in section groups in the shade of a large ironbark. Each section was seated in numerical order so 3 Section of 1 Pl was Graham's right and 5 Section of his own platoon on his left. They sat in a line behind their section commanders. Right next to Graham, and so close that her knee actually touched his from time to time, was Rita.

CSM Grey explained they would normally sit like this for briefings. Not only did it seat them all into a small area so that they could easily hear what was said, but it allowed the section commanders and Pl Sgts to quickly and easily do a head count to see if anyone was missing.

As they waited for the other platoons to arrive, Graham noted that the officers, including the four CUOs, were seated in a group over beyond the HQ tents. Capt Conkey was speaking to them. Graham was curious to know what they were being told.

When the whole company was seated, CSM Grey checked they were all present, then went over to report to Capt Conkey. Capt Conkey and the officers walked over to them. Capt Conkey stood at the front and began speaking to them. First, he welcomed them to Speed Creek and to the Annual Camp, particularly welcoming the new recruits. In his own mind, Graham no longer considered himself to be one of them.

Capt Conkey then explained the Camp 'Standing Orders' and safety rules. He had everyone issued with a photocopied map of the area and pointed out the main features and the boundaries of the area: Speed Creek to the west; Granite Creek to the south, the Herveys Range Road (Main Road he nicknamed it) to the east; and a fence line to the north.

All of this took nearly an hour. Capt Conkey then said, "Now, to conclude, I am going to ask those who haven't yet made a promise to me to abide with the Code of Conduct to do so. What I am talking about is this. The staff are all giving up a week of their holidays to be here; to give you the chance for this experience. They also give up all those weekends during the year for bivouacs; and they don't get paid for most of them. We do get pay for this camp but, as I said, they are giving up nine days of their holidays. So, in return for the sacrifice that the staff are making, we ask you to promise to behave for the duration of the camp. That is your side of the bargain."

He paused to let this sink in, then went on, "Now, you don't have to promise. Nor do people who have previously promised have to do so. To me a promise, once given, stands. Nor do we want any 'bush lawyer' quibbling over what constitutes misbehaviour. What we are asking for is that you don't give us any problems or grief. That includes obeying the school rules, the army regulations, and state law. I will also point out that this promise is not an army requirement. It is a personal one: you to me. And you don't have to promise. If you do, we will trust you. If not, we will keep a close eye on you. So, if you haven't previously promised then move out and form one line here."

Graham blushed as he listened to this. He also wondered if he should go out to promise. As he puzzled over this, he found Capt Conkey looking at him. Their eyes met. Capt Conkey distinctly shook his head. Graham relaxed and remained where he was.

I have promised, he thought. *And from now on I will keep it.*

But he quickly discovered that it might be easier said than done. When Rita came back from making her promise she met his eye and smiled. Then she put her hand on his shoulder as she sat down, ending with her knee touching his, causing him a surge with desire.

Oh bloody hell! he thought as he became aroused.

After the briefing, the platoons were moved back to their areas. CUO Grant then gave them a lesson on Field Hygiene. The section commanders then took over and gave them a lesson on 'Field Cooking'.

Graham thought he knew all about this and was inclined to the school of thought that said weight should be kept to a minimum, so mess tins were a waste. Cooking out of the tin he thought was good enough. Cpl Grenfell pointed out that this was very inefficient as the top usually stayed cold and the food at the bottom burned because it was difficult to stir. He taught them how to use a hexamine stove and demonstrated that using the aluminium mess tins was twice as fast as using the steel canteen cup to heat water. The most useful part of the lesson to Graham's mind was when Cpl Grenfell showed them how to wash up and wipe the mess tins clean using a piece of toilet paper. Within a minute he had removed the grease and the dirty paper was stuffed into the used tin. It was very easy and economical.

Dinner was next. Graham found he was hungry and happy. He seemed to be accepted in the section, although he was also aware none of them were likely to become close friends. With that in mind, he made a point of doing little things to help others and to be cheerful. Once again, he found himself drawn into talking to Angela and Rita, to Crane's obvious annoyance.

After dinner there was half an hour of free time. Graham wandered over to 1 Pl and chatted to Peter. Peter was in a happy mood and seemed to be in a good section who all got on well with each other. While he was talking, Graham noted all the officers and CUOs over at HQ being briefed by Capt Conkey again. At 1850hrs, the Pl Sgts began calling on the cadets to get ready. Ten minutes later, the company was seated in sections over beside the vehicle track near HQ.

It was dark by then and the only light came from a couple of lanterns and from torches. Capt Conkey briefed them for a night navigation exercise. Mostly this was on safety rules, and he reminded the corporals that the aim was not for them to do the navigation but for them to ensure each cadet knew how to use the magnetic compass at night. One of the things that concerned Graham was hearing that there was no moon that night. He had never really thought about it before, but now understood that there were times when the moon was not up at all during the night.

The officers, CUOs and Sgts tested the small radios they had all been issued and headed off into the night to act as check points while Capt Conkey gave each corporal their first leg. Graham watched and noted that the corporal was required to plot the two grid references, then use a protractor to work out the grid bearing, then convert it to a magnetic bearing. It was something Graham had learned in the Scouts, but he was not entirely confident he understood what to do. Cpl Grenfell clearly knew how to do it and quickly worked out the bearing and paces. He showed these to Capt Conkey and was told he could move.

Because he was next in line, Cpl Grenfell selected Graham to be the first to use the compass. "Here, Cadet Kirk. Do you know how to use this?"

"Yes corporal," Graham replied confidently.

That was something he had learned in the Scouts. He took the compass and asked for someone to hold a torch so he could see. When that was done, he turned the milled vane until the required number was lined up on the lubber line. That done, he showed it to Cpl Grenfell who nodded, and said, "Good. Now, shine the torch on it for a minute."

"Why?"

"To brighten up the luminous inside. It will be easier to see it in the dark then," Cpl Grenfell explained.

This was done and the torch was then turned off. Graham was amazed at how brightly the luminous markings on the compass glowed. He then positioned the compass level in front of his stomach and turned himself until the luminous north pointer was positioned between the two luminous dots.

He pointed along the compass. “That way corporal.”

Cpl Grenfell had been watching. “Good. Off you go. LCpl Bannister and Cadet Morris, you count the paces; six hundred.”

Off they went into the darkness, Graham leading. He hated that. His deep fear of snakes welled up to cloud his mind. It took an effort to keep putting one foot in front of the other, to just walk through the dark bush.

“Why don’t we use our torches?” he asked.

Cpl Grenfell snorted. “Huh! Soldiers can’t walk around the battlefield with torches on! The enemy would spot them immediately and blast them.”

“But we aren’t soldiers. We are cadets,” Graham retorted, stung by his fear into being snappish.

“Don’t speak in that tone of voice, Cadet Kirk! Too bad if you are scared. Just get on with it,” Cpl Grenfell retorted.

That hurt too! Having his courage publicly questioned really stung Graham’s pride, so he clamped his mouth shut and silently seethed. And after a while he forgot to worry about snakes as he concentrated on keeping the compass needle between the two luminous dots and on not falling into washouts or over logs or anthills.

The others trampled along behind in single file. Another section was moving off to the right but on a course which diverged. From time to time someone in that group stumbled over something and the sound of their curses carried plainly.

Cadet Morris asked, “Corporal, what do we do if we run into enemy?”

“This isn’t a tactical exercise. There won’t be any,” Cpl Grenfell replied. “And cadets don’t use the word enemy. We only have an opposing force on exercises.”

Graham had been wondering the same thing and was glad someone else had asked the question.

They blundered down across a small dry creek and then across a flat which seemed to be covered in logs and bushes. The checkpoint was a gate. CUO Madden and Sgt Mitrovitch were the staff. Cpl Grenfell moved up beside Graham and held out his hand.

“Yeah, that was good Cadet Kirk. Give me the compass.”

Graham did as he was told and then moved to the back of the line. He stood there in the dark feeling both relieved and satisfied that he had managed to navigate straight to the check point.

I can do that, he thought happily.

CUO Madden gave Cpl Grenfell the grid reference of the next check point and he sat to work it out, Gwen Copeland holding a torch for him. After ten minutes they moved off again. This time Cadet Morris led with the compass and Graham had to count paces. They went up a small, rocky hill for four hundred paces to where CUO Hansen and Sgt Cleland waited in the darkness. By then it was quite cold, and a million stars twinkled overhead. In the distance they could see occasional torch flashes and hear voices as other sections stumbled around.

The next leg took them down the hill and across a flat to a creek junction seven hundred paces away. Gwen did the navigating and they arrived spot on. This was just as well because Capt Conkey and Warrant Officer Howley were there. This was Checkpoint D and was the very centre of the exercise. Graham was mildly surprised to find Capt Conkey seated there in the dark. He had obviously had to walk there through the dark bush, the same as the patrols had to. It gave Graham further respect for the man.

Cadet Harris led them up a long slope to the gravel road. Lt Hamilton waited there with a safety vehicle. When 4 Section arrived, 8 Section was already there and Lt Hamilton was calling on the radio to ask if Section 2 had left Checkpoint E.

"Someone lost," LCpl Bannister suggested to the section.

"Better not be us," Cpl Grenfell replied.

He was given the next grid reference and sat to work out the bearing and paces. Graham stood with the other cadets and listened. He was now thoroughly enjoying himself.

I can do this, he thought happily.

Cadet Morris was given the compass next and the leg took them 400 paces down a gentle slope to a small dry creek to Checkpoint G where Sgt Brown and Cpl Holbrook from the Control Group were the 'DS'. 9 Section was already there, standing or sitting in a group while one held the torch for their section commander.

Cpl Grenfell was given the next grid reference and moved the section a few paces away while he sat to work out the bearing. LCpl Bannister held his torch to light up the map.

While he stood watching this, Graham was surprised to find Angus MacDougal, a cadet from his own class, beside him. Angus leaned forward to watch what Cpl Grenfell was doing, and then whispered to Graham, "Your section commander seems to know what he is doing."

Surprised, Graham turned to him. "Doesn't yours?" he whispered back, casting a glance across to where Cpl Hungerton was sitting with map and protractor. Cpl Hungerton was sucking his pencil and frowning.

Angus shook his head and muttered, "No. This is only our second checkpoint and we've gone the wrong way twice."

Graham looked again and then frowned in puzzlement. *Is that protractor the right way up?*

He wondered. He dug into his memory and wished had paid more attention in lessons in Scouts. To check he moved closer and leaned over to look. Then he was sure. The semi-circular protractor was placed horizontally along a northing.

Pointing to it he said, "You should have your protractor vertical Corporal Hungerton. The Zero should face north."

Hungerton looked up, annoyance and anxiety both showing on his face. He opened his mouth to reply but Derek White, who was a cadet in that section, snapped back first.

"Shut up, Kirk! Mind your own business. You might be the officer's pet but that doesn't mean you can tell people what to do."

"Yeah," added Cadet 'Pigsy' Pike, a Year 9 bully who had clashed with Graham at school. "Piss off and mind yer own business, Mister 'Goody Goody Know-all'!"

Taken aback and a bit shocked at the reaction, Graham stepped back and re-joined his own section. But he was still sure he was right and was a little bit concerned when Cpl Hungerton stood up and told Sgt Brown he was ready. Cpl Grenfell was showing Sgt Brown his calculations at that moment, but Brown just nodded and told Cpl Hungerton to get going.

He should have checked the calculation, Graham thought.

But after the last altercation he was wary of getting snapped at again, so said nothing. Instead, he just shrugged as 9 Section headed off into the night behind Cadet 'Dimbo' Doyle.

The next leg for 4 Section was only 300 paces and Crane did the navigating. The leg took them to a prominent pile of rocks out on a wide, bare flat where Lt Maclaren was the DS. The last leg was back to the Start Point and by 2100hrs they were there. Two other sections were already there, and others came tramping in. CSM Grey had them all seated in section lines behind their corporals. At 2115hrs, the 'ETR', there were still two sections missing: the unfortunate Section 2 led by Cpl Hunter and 9 Section.

On hearing that, Graham shook his head and muttered, "I told them so!"

By then the DS from the Check Points were walking in or being collected by vehicles. Lt Standish, who had been at the CP all the time, called both sections on the radio. 2 Section replied at once and because every corporal had their radio on the whole company could hear the reply. They reported they were at a fence beside the road.

"Which road? Over," Lt Standish queried.

"The main road, the bitumen one," came the reply.

There was a groan from the seated cadets. Graham shook his head. He was sure none of the Check Points was within a kilometre of the main road! Capt Conkey came on the radio and called Lt Hamilton to take his vehicle to look for them.

Lt Standish then resumed calling 9 Section. Graham detected a sense of tension among the senior cadets and the OOCs. He realised a lost section with a medical problem could be a serious problem for the adult staff.

Then Cpl Hungerton answered. The reply was very faint and distorted but the gist of it was that 9 Section had run into a barbed wire fence. They knew they were not to go through a fence, so they had looked both ways along it but not found any check point.

Capt Conkey again came on and told them to walk back to their last known check point with DS.

There was a crackled reply and then a distorted query. "How… do... crackle… we do... that? Over."

There was another sigh from the whole company. Capt Conkey spoke again, exasperation clear in his tone. "On the Back Bearing, over."

"Roger, over." Cpl Hungerton replied.

The company were told to relax and wait. Corporals were told to turn off their radios. Capt Conkey and Warrant Officer Howley came walking in out of the night along with some CUOs and sergeants. Graham talked quietly to Gwen and decided he liked her very much.

Not my type though, he mused.

He also found himself talking to Rita, who sat beside him. Her knee frequently bumped his and he could not decide if it was accidental or not as she did so much wriggling around, continually turning to talk to others and to joke.

Twenty minutes later, Lt Hamilton's Land Rover drove in. In it were the missing 2 Section. As the section climbed out and made their way over to join the seated company, there were sarcastic and cutting comments from dozens of people.

Ouch! I hope I never get a section lost, Graham thought. Only later did he realise exactly what that meant. *I want to be a section commander,* he told himself. In his heart he knew he had accepted being an army cadet.

Capt Conkey spoke briefly to the section and sent them to sit down with the company. He then consulted with the OOCs and told CSM Grey to get the sergeants to mark their rolls. They did this while the CSM did a head count. When it was certain that only 9 Section was missing, Capt Conkey spoke briefly about the lessons learned and the company were then dismissed. They dispersed happily into the night with much chatter and many jokes.

For most of them it had been a long day and they were glad to brew a cup of hot chocolate and relax. 1 Pl was providing the security piquet, so the others had no duties. Graham sat next to Gwen and Harriet, now nicknamed 'Harry', and lit his hexamine stove. The glow of the tiny flames was very cheering, and he realised he was really enjoying himself. He heated water for the girls to make Milo with, then made himself a cup of hot chocolate.

Ten minutes later they were ordered to bed by Sgt Masters. "Lights out you mob! Get to bed and go to sleep. Reveille is 0600. Don't disturb me before then, or else!"

As Graham walked with the others towards his hutchie, he noticed that there was still a cluster of OOCs and CUOs at the CP.

9 Section must be still missing, he decided.

Hearing Capt Conkey calling on the radio and obviously not getting satisfactory answers niggled at Graham. He knelt to unroll his bedding but kept thinking about the unpleasant scene at Checkpoint G.

Should I tell Capt Conkey? he wondered.

Chapter 30

FRICTION IN THE NIGHT

Looking out of his hutchie Graham saw Capt Conkey talking to Warrant Officer Howley. That decided him. Standing up he began walking towards the CP.

"Where are you going, Cadet Kirk?" Cpl Grenfell called.

"To see the OC corporal."

"Why?"

"To help find the missing section corporal."

"You! What's it got to do with you?" Cpl Grenfell replied.

"Because I think I know what they did wrong," Graham replied. Now he feared being told to go back to his hutchie more than he fretted over the possible ridicule.

His voice laden with scepticism, Cpl Grenfell called back. "So how would you know that?"

"Because I saw Cpl Hungerton put his protractor wrong on the map."

The answer plainly astonished Cpl Grenfell who shook his head. "How would you know? You are only a cadet. You haven't been taught that yet."

"I learned it in the Scouts," Graham replied. "Please corporal."

Cpl Grenfell hesitated. As he did, another figure loomed up out of the darkness: Sgt Masters. "What's all the talk! Get to bed!"

"Sorry sarge, but Cadet Kirk is claiming he knows where the missing section is," Cpl Grenfell replied.

Sgt Masters was also incredulous and then sarcastic. "How would you know what another section was doing, Cadet Kirk?"

Graham blushed but made himself describe the scene at Checkpoint G. Sgt Masters looked thoughtful and glanced towards the group at the CP.

Graham saw that he was wavering and acted. "Please sergeant. I will just tell Warrant Officer Howley."

"Oh alright. Come with me," Sgt Masters said. "Cpl Grenfell, get your section to bed."

Sgt Masters led Graham over to near the CP and then told him to wait. He walked across and beckoned CUO Grant who raised his eyebrows but left the group and joined him.

"Yes sergeant?"

"Sir, Cadet Kirk has a theory about the missing section," Sgt Masters replied.

CUO Grant's eyebrows shot up even higher. "Has he! Well, I hope so because nobody here can work out where they are, and they don't know either."

Graham blushed at that, but he was aware of the sense of worry in the group and again told his story. CUO Grant listened and then nodded.

"Okay, let's see what the officers think of this one. Thanks Sgt Masters. You go and put the platoon to bed."

"Sir!"

Sgt Masters vanished back into the darkness and Graham was led forward into the light of the CP lanterns. It was even more obvious to him close-up that the adult staff were really worried. As he was ushered forward, he braced himself for sarcasm and ridicule.

Capt Conkey also raised his eyebrows on seeing Graham move into the light. "Yes CUO Grant? What is the problem?"

"Sir, Cadet Kirk has a theory about where the missing section is."

Lt Maclaren grunted. "Let's hope so! Nobody else has one!"

Capt Conkey faced Graham, "Well, Cadet Kirk, what do you know?"

Graham was suddenly very nervous with all those adult faces and CUOs watching. In particular he was extremely conscious of Warrant Officer Howley looking at him. He licked his lips.

"Sir, it is just something I saw at Checkpoint G." He then described the scene in outline.

Capt Conkey frowned. "And what did Cpl Hungerton say to that?"

"Nothing sir," Graham replied, blushing as he remembered the retorts from Derek and Pigsy.

"Did he act on your advice?"

Graham shook his head. "I didn't see, sir. Some of the others told me to go away."

CUO Madden curled his lip. "I'm not surprised! I would have too," he commented.

Warrant Officer Howley had been listening. He now gestured Graham forward. "Okay, young fella, show us what you reckon," he instructed. He pointed down at the map board on the small table under the CP shelter.

Graham edged in next to Lt Standish who moved aside. Now Graham felt very nervous and his heart was hammering fast. He was regretting having spoken as all eyes were on him, and not all looked friendly. Blinking to clear his suddenly blurred vision, he bent to study the map. To his relief, the map had an overlay on clear plastic of the Navex Plan, each route shown in a different colour. Beside it was a legend which indicated which colour 9 Section was. Quickly he followed their route around until he found Checkpoint G.

Placing his finger on Checkpoint G, he looked for a paper map and pencil. There was a pencil next to his hand and beside it another loose map and a protractor. Quickly he picked up the pencil and made a dot on the loose map at the location of Checkpoint G.

Capt Conkey was watching intently and frowned. "Who were the DS at Checkpoint G?"

"Sgt Brown and Cpl Hollbrook sir," Graham replied.

Capt Conkey looked around. "Where are they? Why aren't they here? Go and get them Sgt Strutton," he snapped angrily. Then he turned to Graham. "So show me what you saw Cpl Hungerton doing, Cadet Kirk."

Aware that the OC was very angry, Graham bent to the map board and checked on the legend which Checkpoint 9 Section had been heading for.

According to the plan, 9 Section was meant to go to Checkpoint J, he noted.

Using the pencil, he marked that on his paper map and took the protractor and used the edge of it as a ruler to draw a line joining the two places.

Warrant Officer Howley leant across, and said, "Make the line across the map longer. It needs to be longer than the width of the protractor. It doesn't matter how long it is."

Graham did as he was told, nervously aware that he was perspiring and that he was starting to fluster. Then he paused, trying hard to remember what he had seen.

Where do you put the centre of the protractor? he fretted, *on the check point or on the grid lines?*

Suddenly, Mr Ritter's words during a Maths B class came to him. "Remember Pythagoras! Equal angles. It doesn't matter where you measure an angle of a line on a square grid, all angles are equal."

Guided by that Graham placed the protractor upright on the map and rotated it so that the second half of the circle was being used. He then positioned the centre on the pencil line. He then slid the protractor down along the pencil line to an easting.

"That's how he should have done it, sir," he explained.

Capt Conkey nodded with approval. "How do you know that?"

"Mr Ritter taught us that in Maths B sir, and 'Silver Wolf' taught me in the Scouts," Graham replied, blushing with embarrassment at the use of the name 'Silver Wolf'.

For the first time that evening Graham, saw Capt Conkey smile. "So you have paid some attention in school! I will tell Mr Ritter. He will be pleased," he commented.

"And don't forget good old 'Silver Wolf'," Lt Hamilton added.

"What bearing is that?" Lt Standish asked, leaning over to peer at his map.

Graham squinted at the tiny gradations on the plastic protractor and did some adding in his head. "Five thousand three hundred and sixty mils ma'am," he replied.

"So what did Cpl Hungerton do?" Capt Conkey asked.

That got Graham really worried, but he made himself picture the scene at Checkpoint G. *The protractor was sideways on the map, I'm sure,* he thought, moving the protractor to match his memory.

Quickly, and as calmly as he could, he read the bearing and noted it. "That way, sir," he said.

Lt Maclaren shook his head. "Bloody hell! That means he has gone off at a right angle to his proper course."

"Yes, gone southwest when he was supposed to be going northwest," Capt Conkey agreed. He turned to Graham. "What bearing is that, Cadet Kirk?"

Graham bent closer to check then said, "They should have been moving on 5360 mils sir, but I think they calculated 3760 instead," he replied.

Capt Conkey nodded. "That is a grid bearing. Do you know how to convert it to a magnetic bearing?"

Graham blushed and had to admit he wasn't sure. Capt Conkey went on, "In this part of the world the magnetic variation is east, 140 mils east. To get a magnetic bearing subtract the variation, that's 140 mils, from the grid bearing."

Graham did this. As he wrote the calculation on the edge of the map, he was aware that a very hostile looking Sgt Brown had joined the group. He was followed by an equally annoyed Cpl Hollbrook. For a brief moment, Graham met his eye.

Then he looked away and said, "Three thousand six hundred and twenty mils, sir," he said.

Capt Conkey looked up at Sgt Brown. "What bearing did you write down when 9 Section left, Sgt Brown?"

Sgt Brown looked surprised and then shrugged. "Er… er... er. I don't know, sir," he mumbled.

"Then look in your notebook!" Capt Conkey snapped testily.

Even as Sgt Brown dug in his trouser pocket for his notebook, Graham guessed by the way he was fumbling that he hadn't written the bearing down. Knowing that all the staff at the Checkpoints were supposed to check bearings and record them before any section left their location, he tensed ready for an explosion.

Sgt Brown made a play at leafing through his notebook before an increasingly sceptical audience, and an obviously irritated Capt Conkey, before shrugging and saying, "I can't seem to find it, sir."

Graham saw Capt Conkey's lips purse and he expected harsh words and anger. Instead, Capt Conkey just said mildly, "Did you write the bearing down, Sgt Brown?"

Sgt Brown flushed and looked down. "No sir. I forgot."

"Cpl Hollbrook?"

"No sir. I thought Brown was doing that."

"Sergeant Brown you mean, Cpl Hollbrook," Capt Conkey said. Then he sighed. "Oh well, we will just have to try with what we have."

At that, Lt Hamilton spoke up. "What about the back bearing, Boss?"

"Yes, good idea Hamish. You can check it with the CUOs. Warrant Officer Howley, will you please take the CSM and CUO Hansen and walk back around the route 9 Section was supposed to walk. Okay, Jill, I mean Lt Standish, you and the HQ keep manning the CP. I will take Lt Maclaren and Sgt Strutton with me. Sgt Brown, you and Cpl Hollbrook can come for the walk, seeing as you are partly to blame for this. And you can carry a stretcher and First Aid Kit. So go and get them and your webbing and be back here in five minutes. And make sure you have full water bottles."

He then turned to Graham. "And you, Cadet Kirk. This is your theory so you can navigate. So get your webbing."

"Yes sir," Graham replied, half pleased and half dismayed at the way things were developing.

He moved to stand up and again noted another venomous glare from Sgt Brown. *I've made an enemy here,* he thought.

That was confirmed a few minutes later when he re-joined the groups forming up outside the CP tent. Both Sgt Brown and Cpl Hollbrook gave him resentful looks and did not speak to him.

Capt Conkey told Graham to take the map and then swung on his webbing and spoke to Lt Standish. "Call 9 Section, Jill, and see if we have coms."

Lt Standish did but there was no answer. She tried again and then shook her head. "Nothing sir."

Capt Conkey looked grim and nodded, then spoke to Lt Hamilton briefly before doing a radio check. "Okay, Sgt Brown, lead us to Checkpoint Golf," he said.

So it was back into the darkness again. Graham joined the end of the line and was glad he was well away from Sgt Brown, who had to lead. Their route took them back along the entrance track to the Ben Lomond Road. That was easy walking, even after a long day.

At the junction, Capt Conkey halted. "This was Checkpoint Juliet," he said. "We will now walk the back bearing to Checkpoint Golf. Cadet Kirk, you worked it out, so you lead."

That put a whole new aspect on the situation. Up until then Graham had been happy to just trudge along, but suddenly he found himself thrust into the metaphorical limelight. Worse still, he now had to lead through the dark bush and all his fears of snakes again surged to the top of his consciousness.

But there was no way he could think of to escape, so he quickly took out the map from the CP and his pocket torch while Capt Conkey radioed the CP to tell them where they were. Graham checked the bearing he had written and then found he needed to calculate the back bearing. Rather than make a mistake he dug out a pencil and did the maths on the edge of the map.

To get a back bearing you add half a circle if the bearing is less than half and take it away if it is more, he told himself. As he did, the calculation he was very aware that everyone was watching. So he pencilled: 5360 – 3200 = 2160

Hotly conscious that both Capt Conkey and Lt Maclaren were leaning close to watch, Graham took the offered compass and turned the Graduated Dial until 2150 mils plus a tiny bit was set against the Lubber Line. Then he turned off his torch and held the compass horizontal against his lower chest. Once his eyes had adjusted to the dark and he could see the luminous marks he turned his whole body until the luminous mark on the north pointer was quivering between the two luminous dots on the base.

Pointing with his right hand, he said, "That way, sir."

Capt Conkey nodded. "Good. Lead on. Sgt Brown, Cpl Hollbrook, count the paces."

After taking a deep breath, Grahams started walking, glancing up every second step to watch where he was going. The bearing took them off the gravel road after a few paces and into the bush. To his satisfaction, Graham found he could see well enough in the starlight to see the tress, which were mostly black-trunked ironbarks. He was even able to detect a few logs and was able to warn those behind as he stepped over them. Ahead, he saw a dark line of trees and knew they were the creek they had crossed on the Navex.

It was harder to cross because they had to weave a course through the trees and thick clumps of lantana bushes, but the bed was dry sand and once they climbed up the other bank they were out in gently rising open country with very few trees.

After a while, Graham realised he had forgotten about snakes and hope that the vibrations and noise of the group were scaring them away.

Even though it was nearly 2300hrs and quite cool, Graham found he was perspiring. It was a considerable relief when Sgt Brown called 650 paces.

Capt Conkey called back, "Is this Checkpoint Golf?"

"I think so, sir. It was just up on the rise from that little gully in front of us," Sgt Brown replied.

Capt Conkey turned on his torch and swung the beam around. Flickers of white showed up on the ground and the torch beam settled on them. Graham saw that they were lolly wrappers. He also noted trampled grass and boot prints on the sandy areas.

Capt Conkey grunted and said, "Yes, Checkpoint Golf. Okay, Cadet Kirk, reset your compass and start moving. Sgt Brown, you and Cpl Hollbrook pick up all this rubbish and catch us up. You should have made sure your checkpoint was clean before leaving it."

Graham glanced at Sgt Brown and saw him and Cpl Hollbrook both look sheepish and annoyed in the glow of the torch beam. *Serve the lazy buggers right!* he thought. It also told him how anxious and annoyed Capt Conkey was, as he rarely reprimanded an NCO in front of junior ranks.

Graham did as instructed and then used his torch to check the map for the 'going'. *We will have Hill 445 on our left and we will cross its lower slopes, then cross a wide valley with some gullies before passing between these two small hills: Hill 376 and Hill 397.*

Satisfied he knew what he was doing, he switched off his torch, held the compass for night marching, and began walking. As he did, he glanced to his left front and sure enough he could see the dark loom of Hill 445 and that gave him comfort.

The first few hundred metres were easy; short grass, few logs or termite mounds, and only a few bushes. As the group walked, Capt Conkey again began calling on his radio trying to contact 9 Section. There was no response.

As the group began ascending an ever-steepening slope on the west side of Hill 445, Graham heard Sgt Brown and Cpl Hollbrook catch them up.

As the ground got steeper and studded with rocks, Lt Maclaren queried their course. Graham blushed but was sure he was right.

"The pencil line runs over a spur running west from Hill 445, sir," he answered, pointing up to the hill which now loomed above them on the left.

Capt Conkey made no comment but again tried the radio. Graham resumed walking. Fifty paces on he saw a faint pale line crossing his front at a diagonal angle. It puzzled him until he reached it and saw it was a cattle or animal pad, the grass worn away by the hooves of the animals.

Glancing along it to his left he noted something, and on an impulse stopped. Capt Conkey almost ran into him. "What's the problem, Cadet Kirk?"

"Just checking something, sir," Graham replied.

Risking a rebuke he slid his torch out of his pocket and held it low to the ground before clicking it on. *Ah yes! They went this way,* he told himself.

"What is it?" Capt Conkey queried.

"Boot prints sir. Someone has walked across here recently," Graham explained. He was sure that the tracks were recent, or the cattle would have obliterated them.

Capt Conkey and Lt Maclaren bent to look, and Graham shone his torch along the pad to illuminate the prints.

"My word yes! We are right in their tracks," he said.

Once again, he tried the radio but there was still no answer. Capt Conkey then stood and shouted into the night, "Corporal Hungerton! Cpl Hungerton!"

The shout echoed around the low hills and caused some night bird to squark but there was no reply. Graham looked and listened but could only hear his own heart and the rustle of the gentle breeze in the leaves. He looked out and noted they were at the height of the treetops in the small valley. He wondered when the moon might come up but did not ask.

"Will I keep going, sir?"

Capt Conkey turned. "Sgt Brown, how many paces have we come?"

Sgt Brown gasped and then muttered before calling back, "Sir, I lost count."

"What about you, Cpl Hollbrook?"

"I… er…er... I was looking where I was going, sir."

"Damn!" muttered Capt Conkey.

But Graham had been counting and despite knowing it would increase Sgt Brown's animosity, he said, "Seven hundred and twenty sir."

"Oh well, keep going on this bearing," Capt Conkey muttered.

So Graham did. The course began to trend downhill across the side of the slope, and within five minutes they were down in the bottom of the low valley with Hill 445 now looming up to their left rear and a low saddle between two hills staring to show against the stars ahead of them. Capt Conkey called out twice more, shattering the silence and causing more echoes. But there was no response and Graham could tell that the officers were really worried.

They came to a steep-sided gully and, after finding a safe way down into it, Graham noted it had a sandy bottom, so he again turned on his torch. He was rewarded by seeing churned up sand only five paces to his left. He moved there and studied the marks in the sand and was pleased to see the clear imprint of an army boot in the damp sand.

Capt Conkey studied it and nodded. "Fresh. That is definitely them. Keep going. You are doing very well Cadet Kirk."

"Sir." Graham found where 9 Section had climbed out of the gully and followed them. Up on the flat ground he turned off his torch and resumed doing a compass course.

As they trudged across the floor of the small valley, Capt Conkey again called out and tried the radio but with no response. Then they crossed another small dry gully and once again Graham found the boot prints of the missing section.

They began to climb a gentle slope towards the low saddle between Hills 397 and 376. The going was easy with almost no grass or small obstacles. Capt Conkey radioed the CP with the information and then called Lt Hamilton and told him to return to camp.

At 1135hrs the group reached the crest of the saddle and Graham saw a vast panorama of dark bush opening out ahead of them in the starlight, a couple of large hills standing up in the distance. Graham stared at that vast area of darkness and felt his stomach turn over with dread.

Bloody hell! If they are lost out there, we are in trouble, he thought. Then he modified it, remembering that Speed Creek was to the right and curved across his front.

"How far have we walked now?" Capt Conkey queried.

Luckily, Graham had kept counting and was able to answer. "Twelve hundred paces sir."

Again Capt Conkey shouted, his voice seeming to be swallowed up by the vastness of the bush. Now there were no surrounding hills his calls did not echo.

"Bloody hell! Where are they?" he muttered.

Chapter 31

ENEMIES

Graham stared at the vast expanse of dark bush and felt slightly ill. *Poor old Captain Conkey!* he thought.

Capt Conkey called again and then ordered them to keep walking so Graham again led, now moving down a long gentle slope. A hundred paces down the slope they came to a barbed wire fence.

"Now where are they?" Lt Maclaren queried.

"They said they had reached a fence," Capt Conkey replied.

"Yes, but the fence is the boundary for the exercise. They were told not to go through a fence," Lt Maclaren retorted.

"Let's look both ways along it," Capt Conkey suggested.

He then turned on his torch and began studying the ground. Very quickly he found more boot prints in the sandy soil. It took them a few minutes to determine that the boot prints going right only went a short distance but the ones going left kept on going.

Capt Conkey groaned audibly. "Oh bloody hell! They have gone south towards the highway."

"I'll call Hamish and get him to drive around to look along it for them," Lt Maclaren suggested.

"Good idea," Capt Conkey agreed. "As we go further around behind these hills, we might lose radio coms with the CP."

Lt Maclaren started talking on his radio. As he did, Sgt Brown and Cpl Hollbrook came and stood nearby. "Bugger! I'm getting cold," Cpl Hollbrook muttered.

Graham was now also cold and was feeling weary. His feet had begun to hurt and his muscles ached. "Bloody idiots! Why didn't they turn right? Speed Creek is just over that way and they could have followed it back to the road."

To his surprise, Sgt Brown snapped back, "Shut up Kirk! You've got us in enough trouble already."

Cpl Hollbrook stepped closer and shoved at him. "Yes, you bloody smart-arse know-all, shut your mouth."

Graham was shocked and felt hurt. What particularly niggled was the accusation that it was somehow his fault that Brown and Hollbrook were in trouble. He opened his mouth to defend himself but then shut it. *Nothing to be gained,* he told himself.

Sgt Brown then thrust the stretcher at him. "Here, you take a turn at carrying this!" he snarled.

At that Capt Conkey turned. "No Sgt Brown! We are here because you and Cpl Hollbrook did not follow orders. You keep carrying it."

Even in the starlight Graham could sense Sgt Brown's hostility and he suspected it would lead to more accusations of being the officer's pet.

Capt Conkey and Lt Maclaren began walking again, following the fence south. This led them back over the low saddle and then across the north slope of Hill 397. Graham stared to his left front at the bulk of Hill 445 and was hotly aware that every step was staking them further from their camp. He wasn't looking forward to the walk back.

The fence slowly descended the side of the hill and went across another low saddle, this time the one between Hill 397 and Hill 445. As they did, Capt Conkey called the CP to inform them of where they were and to caution them that they might lose coms.

A sudden flicker of light a kilometre or so ahead caught Graham's eye. His mind quickly worked out that it was the headlights of a vehicle heading north along the main road. Then he jumped with fright as Capt Conkey suddenly shouted again, "Cpl Hungerton! Cpl Hungerton!"

From some distance ahead came an answering yell. "Help! Help!" the voice cried.

Two minutes later the search group had reached a small gully where the missing patrol were. They were huddled in a group and Graham could not work out what was going on until Capt Conkey reached them and began questioning them.

"What's the problem, Cpl Hungerton?"

"Sir, Cadet Moloney has hurt his ankle and we were trying to get him back to camp."

"So why are you going this way?"

There was an embarrassed silence. Then Cpl Hungerton replied, "Because we thought it was the right way, sir."

"Which direction are you heading?"

"Sir? Er... err... I'm not sure, sir."

There was another short silence, then Capt Conkey snapped, "What does your compass say?"

"Compass!" Cpl Hungerton replied.

For a moment Graham thought the corporal was going to say he had lost his compass but then saw him fumble it out of his shirt pocket and take hold of it.

He stared down and then said very softly, "Southeast sir."

Graham saw Capt Conkey shake his head. Then he asked, "Why didn't you call on the radio?"

"Because we didn't need help then, sir."

"What do you mean by then?" Capt Conkey queried, obviously annoyed.

"Er... er... before the batteries went flat, sir," Cpl Hungerton replied.

"Haven't you got spare batteries?"

"I did have sir, but I gave some to Cpl Moore, sir."

This time Capt Conkey muttered something under his breath and Lt Maclaren spoke. "Don't you have batteries in your torch?"

"They went flat, sir," Cpl Hungerton replied and Graham realised the boy was about to cry.

"What about you other cadets? Don't any of you have batteries in your torch?" Lt Maclaren asked.

The group all fidgeted and hung their heads and it transpired that of the seven of them three had not brought torches, even though it was on the 'What to Bring' List for camp; and three more had them but the corporal had not asked.

Capt Conkey then asked, "When you reached the fence and realised it wasn't a checkpoint, why didn't you do what the exercise orders said and just turn and go back to the previous checkpoint on a back bearing?"

There was another strained silence before an obviously upset and miserable Cpl Hungerton muttered, "I don't know how to do that, sir."

Graham was now feeling a mixture of contempt and sympathy for Cpl Hungerton. *He's a corporal. He should know,* he thought. But he was glad when Capt Conkey changed the subject.

"Well, never mind navigation. Let's get ourselves home. Can you walk at all, Cadet Moloney?"

Cadet Moloney was helped to his feet and tried to walk but quickly cried out in pain and made a big show of limping.

That looked serious to Graham, but Capt Conkey just said, "Okay, open the stretcher, Sgt Brown."

There were a few minutes of instructions and movement before Moloney was lying on the stretcher with eight people around it. Graham took a hold in the middle of the right-hand side and at Capt Conkey's orders they lifted and started walking.

"Go on east," Capt Conkey instructed. "We will get down to the highway and see if we can get Lt Hamilton to pick him up."

He tried calling on the radio but there was no reply. "Screening, from this high ground," he said. "Lt Maclaren, would you walk back up to the saddle there and pass that message, then come back and catch us up please. Sgt Brown and Cpl Hollbrook, go with him."

The group split and began slow movement down into the wide flat bottom of the valley. Luckily there was very little grass and the ground was clear of small obstacles.

As they moved slowly along, Graham saw the headlights and then rows of red side lights that could only mean a road train or semi-trailer go past southwards.

"What's that?" called Cadet 'Pigsy' Pike in front of him.

"A truck you dumbo!" replied Cadet Derek White from behind.

"I told you I seen a car!" Pigsy retorted.

Graham had not realised White was there and wished he could move away, not wanting any part of the section's troubles or any more friction. But he had to stay carrying until it was lowered after hundred paces and other people were instructed to take over.

Lt Maclaren and the other two cadets re-joined them and reported that the message has been passed. "Hamish says he will be here in a few minutes," he reported. Then he watched the struggling group and commented, "If we had copied that 130 mob and given every section two broom handles to make improvised stretchers with, then this bunch could have carried him down to the highway before we arrived."

In reply Capt Conkey grunted and Graham gathered it was an old argument. But he secretly agreed. Looking around he could not see any small trees or saplings that might have been cut down to make a stretcher.

And even if there was, we haven't got anything to cut them down with, he thought.

More headlights appeared from behind Hill 445. These slowed and came to a stop at the bottom of the valley. That made Graham wonder if it was Lt Hamilton with his Land Rover and his spirits lifted. A radio call from Lt Hamilton confirmed that it was and his morale went up even more.

I hope I get a lift and don't have to walk back, he thought.

It took another ten minutes to get Cadet Moloney down to the fence beside the highway and another five for them all to crawl under. By then it was plain to Graham that Moloney was not badly hurt and he clambered into the back of the Land Rover quickly enough.

Probably just a twisted ankle, Graham thought.

"Okay, Sgt Strutton, you and 9 Section get in," Capt Conkey ordered.

They moved to do so but Lt Hamilton snapped at them, "Webbing off first! You don't get into vehicles wearing webbing."

The cadets did as they were told and squashed into the back.

"Nearly midnight," Capt Conkey said. "Take this lot back and then come back for us, Hamish," he said.

The Land Rover accelerated away and Graham stood with Capt Conkey, Lt Macalaren and Sgt Brown and Cpl Hollbrook.

"Thanks Cadet Kirk," Capt Conkey said. "That was good reasoning and good navigating."

"Thanks sir," Graham replied, hotly aware that Brown and Hollbrook were listening and were probably sneering.

But he was still enjoying himself. He looked around the dark bush and decided it had been a good little adventure. The group stood there waiting. Several vehicles went past in both directions, the main road being a major road connecting Townsville to the mines and cattle stations further west.

Suddenly there was a distant thudding rumble to the south, and when Graham looked that way he was amazed to see brilliant lights bursting out in the sky. The other cadets gaped, and Cpl Hollbrook cried, "What's that?"

Capt Conkey answered. "Mortar flares. Some army unit is calling for illumination."

"Does that mean they are being attacked, sir?" Sgt Brown asked.

"Most likely," Capt Conkey agreed. "There is a major army exercise going on over there in the High range Training Area involving the whole Regular Army Third Brigade and some Singaporean and Tongan troops."

More flares lit up the sky in the distance, and even though they were a long way away Graham noted that they still lit up the faces of those with him.

Cpl Hollbrook said, "I didn't hear any mortars then."

"Probably hand-held parachute flares," Capt Conkey replied.

Graham found he was intensely interested. These were real soldiers and they were training for the real thing. Then the air seemed to shudder and vibrate and a series of heavy but distant thuds carried to his ears and body and even seemed to come through the ground.

"What's that?" Sgt Brown cried.

"Artillery," Capt Conkey replied. "The infantry have called in a defensive fire mission."

Even as he said this, there was an even more distant rumble of explosions. "That is the shells landing and exploding," he explained.

Cpl Hollbrook frowned. "Is... are they real shells sir?"

"Yes."

"But… but won't that kill any soldiers acting as enemy?"

Capt Conkey shook his head. "The guns are firing live ammo, but they are not aimed at any soldiers. They will be firing at targets in what is called the Impact Sector. That's an area where no-body does exercises and is used for practice firing and bombing."

This was all a revelation to Graham, both of how the real world might function and of how much Capt Conkey might know. It reminded him that the teacher had been a soldier and seen active service when he was younger. A memory of seeing him on the School Anzac Ceremony in his uniform with medals on his shirt flitted across his mind. He experienced a sudden yearning to be part of that world.

The guns fired several more 'Fire Missions' and then the flares died out and the action ended. Graham hoped for more but then Lt Hamilton returned in his Land Rover and parked for them to get in. Capt Conkey moved to sit beside the driver and Graham went to climb in.

"Webbing off, Cadet Kirk," Lt Hamilton reminded.

Graham blushed and then burned at the sniggers from Sgt Brown and Cpl Hollbrook. He climbed in the back of the Land Rover and moved to the front. Suddenly he was struck hard in the right thigh by the steel foot of the stretcher.

"Grab this, Kirk," Sgt Brown called.

Graham looked and saw he was shoving the end of the stretcher in. "Ow! Watch it," he cried.

"Aw, sorry!" Sgt Brown replied, his insincerity obvious to Graham. But there was nothing to be done so he just gritted his teeth and rubbed at where he had been whacked.

Once everyone was in, they were driven north along the highway to the junction of the Ben Lomond Road where the unit had debussed. Here they turned left and drove in the 2 kilometres to the bivouac site.

When he went to climb out Graham was surprised and somewhat dismayed to discover that his right thigh had gone stiff, and he had to rub it and stretch before it would function.

Bloody Brown! He thought.

After climbing out, Graham limped with the others over to where 9 Section and some others stood near the CP. Among them were Warrant Officer Howley and CUO Grant. Capt Conkey looked at his watch and said, "Well after midnight. We will do a post-mortem on what went wrong in the morning. Cpl Hungerton, you will get a Patrol Report from the CP and fill it out. Give it to me by 0900 tomorrow."

"Yes sir," Cpl Hungerton replied, plainly embarrassed and upset.

"And you can thank Cadet Kirk we found you so soon," Capt Conkey added. "He came up with the idea of what had gone wrong and led us there."

"Yes sir," Cpl Hungerton replied, flashing Graham a resentful glance.

Warrant Officer Howley stepped forward. "Yes, well done young fella."

The praise washed over Graham, and he felt warm with pleasure but also hot with embarrassment. The muttering and jealous looks of some of the other cadets made him sure he would be teased.

Capt Conkey nodded. "Thanks Warrant Officer Howley. Now get to bed all of you. Reveille in five and a half hours."

They dispersed into the darkness. Graham found he was still very 'hyped-up' from the experience and the exhilaration and praise sent his spirits soaring. But he did need a pee before he got into his sleeping bag, so he silently padded through the bivouac area to the latrine, limping slightly because of his sore right leg.

As he relieved himself, he stared up at the millions of stars and felt he was glowing with them. *That was great!* he thought. The notion of maybe becoming a soldier lodged deeper in his mind. *I can do this stuff,* he told himself, despite a niggling worry that he might actually be a coward if there was a real enemy firing live ammunition.

But he also worried that his personal enemies might punish him. And he didn't have to wait long!

Graham made his way back to his hutchie, sure that he would not be able to sleep. But he did. Within minutes of taking his boots off and snuggling into his sleeping bag he was asleep. He slept soundly till footsteps woke him at 0540.

The mutter of soft voices woke him and he pulled the sleeping bag away from his face and blinked, wondering what it was he was looking at. Then he realised it was cold plastic that was touching his face.

My hutchie has come down, he thought.

He pulled the plastic aside and looked out. It was light but the sun was not yet up. Moonlight, he realised, noting a half moon low to the east. As he did, he saw CSM Grey and Sgt Masters standing nearby and looking at him.

They both walked over as Graham pushed the shelter aside. As he did, he noted that the nylon cord which had tied his hutchie to the tree at that end was still tied around the trunk. One end hung down. CSM Grey bent down and took hold of the end and looked at it.

"Cut," he commented.

Sgt Masters joined him and looked at it. "Cut alright, and cut at the other end too."

Graham twisted around to look and only then did it occur to him that the hutchie had been deliberately cut down.

Sgt Masters looked down at Graham. "Looks like you've got an enemy, Cadet Kirk."

CSM Grey nodded and added, "After last night, probably more than one."

That hit Graham hard, and he experienced a surge of anxiety, anger and upset that for a moment rendered him speechless.

Enemies! he thought. *And more than one.*

Chapter 32

JEALOUSY

For a second or so Graham felt his emotions surge, a mix of anger and hurt.

"Bloody Brown and Hollbrook!" he snapped. "They will regret that," he added, blustering to cover his upset.

"No they won't, Cadet Kirk," CSM Grey said firmly. "You have no proof, and they aren't the only ones who don't like you. So don't go off half-cocked and cause more problems. Just put this hutchie back up and keep yourself under control."

"Yes CSM," Graham replied, shuddering with the effort of restraining his temper.

He moved to stand up, then cried out in pain as the muscles of his right thigh protested. Pushing the pain aside he straightened up, stepping off his bedding in his bare feet.

Sgt Masters pointed down at them. "Put something on your feet first. You know the rules, no bare feet."

"Yes sergeant!" Graham replied between gritted teeth.

He was close to tears, both from his boiling emotions and the pain in his thigh and was worried they might see that. Thankfully the CSM and Sgt Masters turned and walked away.

But by now the talking had woken others nearby and Graham could see heads spoking out. Not wanting to shame himself, he managed to hide his feelings. Quickly he found his socks and boots and pulled them on. As soon as he had his boots laced up, he limped as fast as he could to the nearest male latrine, the need to pee becoming urgent.

As he walked to the latrine, Graham rubbed at his thigh and luckily the pain eased as the muscle warmed up. As he relieved himself, his mind churned with upset and suspicion. Mostly that was because he thought of himself as a good person who tried to help and found it really wounding to think others did not like him. As he came back out of the gully on the way back to his platoon, he looked around to see if anyone was looking at him.

A glance in the direction of the Control Group's bivouac showed him Sgt Brown standing watching him. As their eyes met, Sgt Brown's face changed to what looked like a smirk.

Bloody Brown! He did cut my hutchie down! Graham thought.

Once again, the anger surged and he was strongly tempted to detour across and accuse him. But another glance around showed Sgt Masters calling 2 Platoon out for Check Parade so he kept walking. But it was hard to restrain the anger and the tears of self-pity that welled up!

This time it actually was a parade. Sgt Masters called them out, 'boots and hat', and moved them as a platoon to the dirt vehicle track near HQ. This was the 'parade ground'. 2 Platoon was the first there and Graham stood in the rear rank feeling resentful and upset. That got worse as 3 Platoon moved past behind them, and he saw Cpl Hungerton and Cadets Pike and White scowling at him.

It's not fair! Graham thought. *Just because Hungerton can't navigate. They should be thankful, or they'd still be out there.* He also realised that every cadet in his section was just acting normal and he received only a few grunted 'good mornings'. *They don't know I was out looking for the lost patrol,* he thought. The temptation to tell them welled up and he shook his head. *No, they will just think I am boasting,* he told himself.

Once all the platoons were there the CSM called the company to attention, right dressed them and told the sergeants to mark the roll. By then it was full daylight. After the roll call the CSM called out for all those who had been issued a radio or compass had the correct one, and that no-one was sick.

From the ranks of 4 Platoon a voice called out, "What about 9 Section? They have a compass haven't they!"

A wave of snickering swept the company and Graham felt genuinely sorry for Cpl Hungerton.

"Silence in the ranks!" CSM Grey snarled. "Sgt Cleland, keep 4 Platoon quiet. That section can dig the next latrines."

"Sir!"

The platoons were told to return to their platoon areas, so Sgt Masters marched 2 Platoon back and fell them out.

"Pack your bedding and get ready for breakfast," he ordered.

They did as they were told. Graham walked to his hutchie and hoped that no-one would notice. But Rita did.

"What happened to your hutchie Graham?" she asked.

Graham just shrugged and knelt to roll up his mosquito net. He did not want to explain but Cpl Grenfell came over.

"What happened, Cadet Kirk? This has been cut."

"Somebody doesn't like me, corporal," Graham replied.

The others now crowded around. Rita looked shocked. "Oh! Why ever not?" she queried.

But Graham did not want to explain and just forced a grin and continued rolling. Cpl Grenfell ordered the others back to do the same and Graham was able to place the mosquito net in his pack. Then he simply retied the cut cords and restored the hutchie. To his own surprise he did not feel tired.

Having packed the mosquito net Graham had a few moments to look around, surprised that the others were taking so long to do such simple tasks. Already he noted that the different personalities were starting to emerge. He observed that Morris was a real whinger and that LCpl Bannister was good at avoiding work. Harriet looked like she was having second thoughts about having joined. Gwen looked cheerful and competent. Cpl Grenfell had his own gear prepared very quickly. He walked around supervising.

"Roll up those sleeping bags and groundsheets," he instructed. "That is the rule in this unit, as soon as you get up. Bedding is never left unrolled or unpacked during the day. That is to stop snakes crawling in."

The image of sliding his feet down into his sleeping bag, only to have them bitten by a poisonous snake formed a fearful picture in Graham's mind. He needed no second bidding to roll up his bedding, and never after forgot the lesson.

Breakfast was next: a typical army breakfast with bacon and eggs. Graham enjoyed it. He then went back to his hutchie and lit his stove to heat water for a shave.

As he shaved, Harriet came and squatted to watch. "I've never seen a man shave before," she explained. "Not even my own dad. I hope you don't mind."

Graham puffed with male pride. "No, of course not," he replied.

Later, Morris teased him. "Next thing you'll be showing 'Harry' your other male things I'll bet."

Graham snorted and did not reply, pretending such an idea had not crossed his mind. It had of course, but with it went images of Amelia, of being in trouble, and of his promise to Capt Conkey. He sighed.

Oh well. After camp maybe?

But his leg still ached, and when he went to the latrine and pulled his trousers down he saw a large bruise had developed. Again he muttered dislike of Sgt Brown and gently massaged it until the arrival of another cadet hurried him on with his morning business. To his relief, the pain subsided and after a while he barely noticed it.

Graham found Day 2 of camp hard work, but very interesting. The day was divided into periods of instruction, each 40 minutes long with 10-minute breaks between. The weather was hot and clear with hardly a cloud in the sky. Period 1 was by Cpl Grenfell on Field Hygiene. Graham found that fairly boring but understood the need for them to know. Period 2 was by Sgt Masters on Field Routine. That was also potentially boring, but Sgt Masters managed to make plenty of humorous comments which kept them laughing and interested. Then it was back to Cpl Grenfell to learn how to tie various knots. Graham knew all of these from Scouts so had no difficulty and was even able to help some of the others.

CUO Grant took the whole platoon for Period 4 on map reading. Most of this was revision for Graham. He had learned it in the Scouts or in Geography at school. During the lesson he kept getting flashbacks to the previous night and several times he saw CUO Grant glance at him, obviously thinking the same thing. But he made no comment and Graham was surprised that nobody in his section seemed to have heard about it. In spite of that he still found the lesson interesting.

After that there was a 20-minute break. Jokes were the order of the day, some of them quite crude. This embarrassed Graham as he could see that Harriet and Gwen were not happy about it. Gwen solved the problem herself.

She glared at Crane and snapped, “You can stop those sort of crude jokes, thank you Crane. We don’t like them.”

“Well too bad! You can go somewhere else then,” Crane retorted.

“No. We have every right to be here. Capt Conkey made it quite clear that people’s rights are to be respected. Just because we are on a cadet camp doesn’t take away our normal civil rights. I don’t like what you are doing. Stop doing it or I will complain about sexual harassment.”

Crane sneered and muttered under his breath but there were no more jokes in Gwen's hearing. Later, he grumbled about 'bossy, stuck-up bitches who were frigid.'

Graham was present and replied, "Well, she was in the right."

"Oh was she! Who are you to tell me I'm wrong! You, you bastard! What a little crawler you've become. You hypocrite! After the way you've been carrying on at school," Crane retorted.

Graham blushed and made no reply. He hadn't set out to cause a split in the section. Crane went off mumbling to join a couple of his mates in 5 Section.

Period 5 was by Cpl Grenfell on how set up and use an army radio. That pleased Graham and as it was new knowledge and he thought it might be important. Period 6 was by CUO Grant on measuring distance on a map. Lunch followed. Graham found himself ignored by Crane and Morris. To his mixed pleasure and annoyance, Angela and Rita came and sat with him. That caused Crane to sneer again.

It was during lunch that the whispers of what had happened during the previous night reached the section, brought by Crane and whispered with some behind-the-hand sneering.

Graham noted this and was relieved when nobody asked him about what he had done. *Crane is just jealous,* he told himself. But it was still upsetting.

After lunch were four more lessons. All were on fieldcraft: Why things are seen; Personal Camouflage and Concealment; Day Movement (creeping and various crawls); and Night Movement (the same crawls adapted to the dark). During the Day Movement lesson Crane made another comment, deliberately Graham thought. Cpl Grenfell had just mentioned that the lesson was on crawling and stalking.

Crane said, "Kirk can do all the crawling. I'll do the storking!"

With that he leered at Harriet, to ensure she got the double meaning. She did, as witnessed by a blush which mottled her neck and cheeks, but she pretended not to understand.

Graham also blushed but as much with anger. *Don't react,* he told himself. With an effort he controlled his temper.

Cpl Grenfell was annoyed. "Don't interrupt, Cadet Crane! And don't tease people," he snapped.

Crane scowled but did not reply. The lesson went on, with much sweating and dirt as they practiced crawling and rolling on the sandy ground. After a break, Cpl Grenfell announced they would be learning night movement.

Graham couldn't help himself. He indicated the sun blazing down. "It's still daylight, corporal!"

"Don't be a smart-arse Cadet Kirk. We will learn it now, when we can all see the demonstrations. Then we will practice them tonight," Cpl Grenfell snapped.

Graham blushed. "Yes corporal. What do we do tonight?"

"Look at the camp program you were given. We have a lantern stalk," Cpl Grenfell replied.

The lesson proceeded. Graham actually found it very interesting, and he did not mind getting extremely dirty. They crawled through long grass and along washouts and gullies, then tried to sneak up on 5 Section. This led to some good-natured rivalry and more sweaty crawling.

As they were called in, Harriet dusted herself and wiped grime off her face. "Urk! I didn't like that. I wish we could have a bath."

"Tomorrow night," Cpl Grenfell said.

Harriet looked unhappy. "But I'm filthy. I need one today."

"Use a bucket then," Cpl Grenfell replied.

"Bucket?" Harriet replied looking puzzled.

Gwen spoke up. "We will get a washbasin and have a bird bath," she said.

Graham's mind filled with images of naked girls washing themselves from a bucket of water and he felt a surge of lust so powerful it surprised him.

That would be nice to see, he thought.

The section filed back to their hutchies. On the way they passed 3 Pl. Graham waved to Stephen, who looked as grubby as he was sure he was himself. Stephen grinned back.

"What a grub you are, Graham!"

"Talk about the pot calling the kettle black!" Graham replied. Both grinned and laughed and Graham felt very happy.

And then it was spoiled when Graham saw Cpl Hungerton scowling at him. Cadet Pike joined in. "Piss off, Kirk! We don't want crawlers like you around here."

That brought a puzzled frown to Stephen's face, but Graham got no opportunity to explain. Embarrassed he kept walking.

After the evening meal, Graham decided it might be a good time to have a chat to his friends, so he walked around looking for Peter. He was in 1 Platoon, and luckily they were nowhere near 3 Platoon so he encountered no jibes of hurtful comments before he found Peter.

Peter grinned and greeted him warmly. Graham gave a wry grin. "I seem to have made a few enemies," he replied.

Peter nodded. "Yeah, I heard about last night. Cpl Hungerton and his section are not very happy."

"I was just trying to help!" Graham cried, the self-pity welling up again to make his eyes prickle.

"I know you were. Ignore the mongrels. You did a good job from what I hear," Peter answered.

"They'd still be out there, the noddies," Graham muttered.

"The OC appreciated your efforts," Peter added.

"That's what's causing the problems," Graham replied. "They all think I'm just crawling to get a stripe."

Peter shrugged. "They are just jealous because you can do it and they can't. Just keep trying. Remember that everything in life has a price."

Graham could only nod and give another grin in response and he was so upset he felt like bursting into tears. He turned and limped away, his leg again bothering him. As he made his way back towards his section, he briefly entertained the idea of asking to go home. The notion of just sneaking out and hitch hiking he instantly rejected as too dishonourable-too much like cowardice and desertion.

Half an hour later, he and the other cadets were again seated in their sections and Lt Hamilton gave them a lesson on night vision. As part of this he explained the modern night vision devices which armies used and four night sights were passed around for them all to look through. When Graham focused the sight and saw the clear green picture it presented, he was astounded.

Holy Moses! How could anyone creep up if the enemy have gadgets like this? he wondered.

Others wondered this as well and one asked. Lt Hamilton explained that, because of expense, not every soldier would have one. "Also, they tend to draw the eyes. Soldiers don't keep watching every second. They get bored, they stop to rest. As well fog, smoke, rain and so on all degrade the performance of this type of equipment." Then he smiled and added,

"Besides, what other option do you have? If you are going to fight an enemy at some stage, you are going to have to try to close with them and the old-fashioned creeping and crawling is still the best way to stay alive."

He then briefed them on the safety for a fieldcraft exercise called a Lantern Stalk. He pointed out that the guards had been instructed to use torches and to keep moving.

"The exercise is planned so that, if you do the right thing, you will be able to creep past the guards to reach the lantern. The lantern is your objective. It is also a navigational aid."

The guards were the CUOs, CSM and Sgts. The OOCs were on the flanks to prevent cheating. Capt Conkey and Warrant Officer Howley led the company to their start point. The lantern was pointed out and they were told to start. They had been told to group into pairs. Graham thought about Peter and Stephen but found Angela and Rita were beside him.

"Can we come with you?" Rita asked.

"Suppose so," Graham replied, half pleased and half worried.

I can imagine what Crane and his cronies will say if they see me heading off into the night with the girls, he thought. But he could not think of any reason to say no.

What bothered him more was snakes. As he crawled along in the short grass, Graham kept thinking of them and trying to re-assure himself with what Capt Conkey had said.

"Don't worry about snakes when you are crawling. You are going so slow they have plenty of time to hear you coming and to get out of your way. The danger is when you run and they think you are coming to attack them. They strike in self-defence. So don't run and don't dive behind logs for cover!"

After a while, the fear wore off and was replaced by the thrill of the game. Pride helped. Graham wanted to do it well, to creep the 200 metres and not get caught. To his great satisfaction he managed this, reaching the lantern tired and dirty just before the end of the exercise. The girls were with him and sat beside him at the lantern. Capt Conkey was there and Graham saw his eyes note the fact. That made him feel uneasy, but he could not think of any way to explain that he had no designs on the pair.

To his annoyance, Crane had also noticed. He sneered and called, "What sort of storking have you been doing, Kirk?"

Graham burned with angry embarrassment and ignored him but was worried about what others thought of him. He was more bothered by the fact that several times Rita had bumped against him and was now sitting close enough for their legs to touch so that he had become aroused. Luckily, the darkness and the camouflage uniform hid this.

At the end of the exercise the guards were called in. CSM Grey and the sergeants checked that no-one was missing. Capt Conkey then congratulated them on a good exercise and led them back through the darkness to the camp.

As they went to bed, Angela and Rita made it plain they were interested in some sort of meeting. Both seemed to be making a few hints as they chatted to each other and to him.

Graham's mind raced. His body also reacted. He became very aroused. As he arranged his bedding and took off his boots, the two girls crawled into their hutchie, which was only five paces away. With much giggling and talking they prepared their bedding.

Graham then heard Gwen call to Sgt Masters. "Can we have a wash now please sergeant?"

"Yes, but be quick."

Rita stuck her head out of her hutchie. "My clothes and hair are all full of sand. Can we have a wash too?" she asked.

"Yes," Sgt Masters growled.

Cadet Lewis, a boy in 5 Section, called from the darkness. "What about me? I'm full of sand too."

Another male voice called out in reply. "Full of shit, you mean!"

Crane called softly to Rita, "Can I come too? I could scrub your back."

Angela snorted. "Oh dream on!" she replied.

Gwen was walking past at that moment. She snapped, "That's enough of that sort of talk!" She walked over to Rita and Angela's hutchie with Harriet following. "You girls coming with us?" she asked.

"Where?" Rita asked.

"Down in the gully. Harriet and I are going now," Gwen explained.

Graham listened to the conversation with growing interest, mental images of girls bathing feeding his fantasies. Then Sgt Master's voice sounded, "You girls hurry up! And keep quiet. Everyone else is trying to sleep."

"Yes sergeant," Gwen replied. She bent to the end of her hutchie. "We will just get a jerry can and some wash basins from the Q. You two get your soap and towels and thongs," she explained.

"Thongs?" Angela asked.

"So you don't stand on the sand in bare feet," Gwen explained. She and Harriet hurried off and Rita and Angela dug in the kit bags for their towels.

A few minutes later, Gwen and Harriet returned and the four girls made their way by torchlight down into the gully out of sight. Graham watched them go, his mind filled with images of soaping naked girls.

I could sneak down and watch, he thought. Then he blushed with shame for having such an idea.

But the sound of the girl's voices, mostly murmuring but occasionally little squeals and giggles, kept his mind in a riot of fantasy and he became very aroused.

There was a loud sigh of pleasure from down in the gully and Rita cried, "Oooh, that was nice! Do it again."

Crane called loudly from his hutchie, "I'll do it!"

"Be quiet and go to bed!" Sgt Masters snapped from the centre of the platoon area. "Hurry up you girls and stop making so much noise."

A few minutes later, the girls came walking back up from the gully. In the starlight they were just dark shapes as they weren't using their torches. Suddenly a torch came on from Crane's hutchie and its beam lit up the girls. Gwen and Harriet were leading and were carrying the jerry can and washbasins. They were fully dressed and had towels slung over their shoulders. Behind them were Rita and Angela and Graham got a tantalizing glimpse of bare flesh: long legs white in the torchlight and of bosoms half covered by towels and bundles of clothes.

"Turn that torch off!" Gwen snapped.

"Sorry," Crane said, not sounding sorry at all. "I thought it might have been kids from some other unit."

"Rot! You knew perfectly well who we were," Gwen replied, clearly unimpressed.

Graham was impressed. *Gwen certainly isn't scared to say what she thinks,* he thought.

But his focus was on Rita and Angela who had obviously not dressed after their wash. As they went to their hutchie, he was granted several tantalising glimpses of bare skin in the starlight as they draped wet towels over a clothesline and then crawled into their hutchie.

Rita and Angela continued preparing for bed. Their talk and actions fuelled the fires of Graham's lust.

"Get your bum out of my face, Rita!" Angela laughed.

Graham looked at the girl's hutchie. It was side on to his so he could not see into it. A torch came on and Rita cried, "Turn off your torch, Angie! I haven't got any clothes on."

"Strewth, you look nice, Rita!" Angela replied.

"That's what all the boys say," Rita replied.

"I'll bet they'd all like to see," Angela added.

I would! thought Graham, his mind swamped with images of Amelia. His imagination went into overdrive, and he listened with mounting interest.

Angela went on, "Are you going to sleep in the nuddy?"

Rita giggled. "I always sleep with nothing on. It saves me having to undress if some spunky hunk comes crawling in later."

Holy Moses! Graham thought. *Is that a hint?*

At that moment, Sgt Masters called out, ordering the girls to stop talking and to go to bed. With some muttering and whispering they did. Silence and darkness settled. Graham lay alone in the dark, his mind developing fantasies about the two girls.

Were they hinting they want a boy to join them? he wondered. Heated images of what would it be like in a tent with two naked girls caused him to stay very aroused.

But he did not dare put the situation to the test. *If I am wrong and they call out I will be done for,* he thought.

But it was a wonderful temptation, and a delightful fantasy. Frustration gripped him and tried to go to sleep. But sleep would not come.

Hours went by but he was so randy he was wide awake. Desire tormented him like an all-compelling itch. From time to time he considered going to the girl's hutchie and trying his luck, but fear and his promise held him back.

Finally, he drifted into a restless sleep.

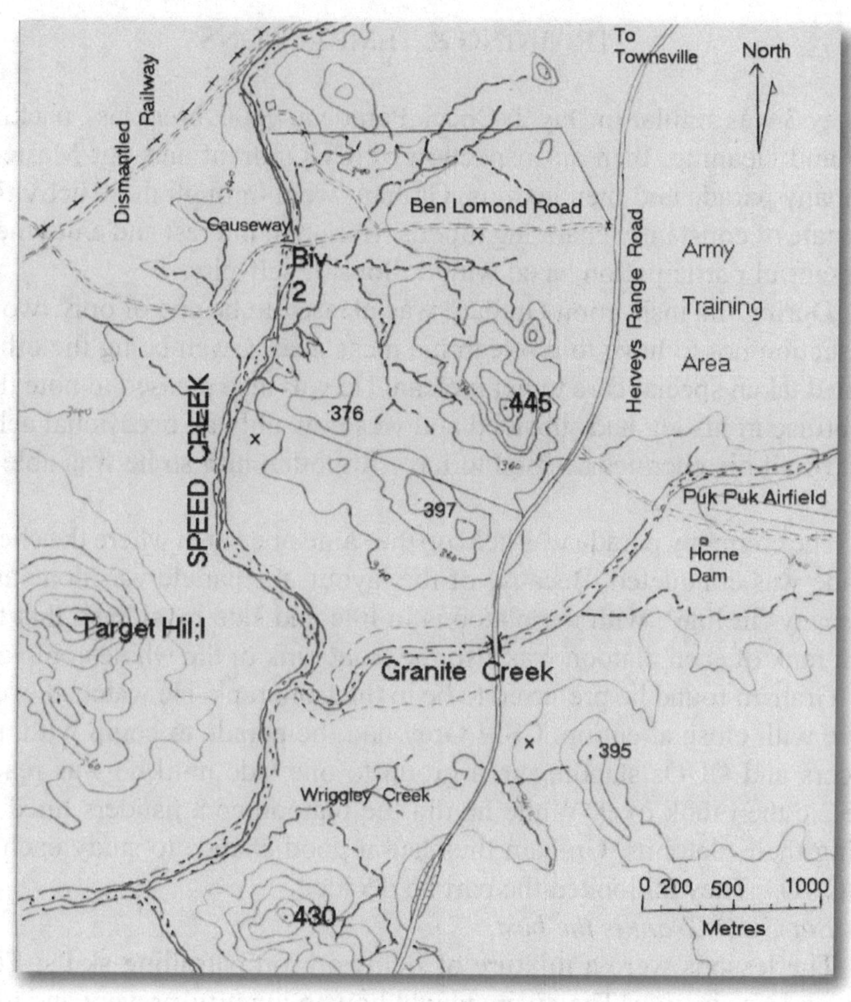

Map 2: Speed Creek

Chapter 33

TRAINING & TEMPTATIONS

Day 3 was similar to Day 2: Check Parade at 0600, breakfast, packing and cleaning, then an inspection by CUO Grant and Sgt Masters; company parade and then lessons. Graham went through these activities in a state of constantly changing moods: from real interest and enjoyment to resentful participation laced with dollops of self-pity.

During the inspection Graham was pleased to be one of only two in the section not to have to re-clean his mess gear, Gwen being the other. He had taken special care to get it clean. He was also pleased to note that the bruise in his leg had subsided and was now only an occasional ache. Best of all his enemies seemed to have forgotten him so he was able to relax.

The company parade was held on the same open area where the check parade was conducted. Because of the layout, the parade was done as a company 'in line': with the platoons in line and side by side so that the front rank of each platoon was also the front rank of the whole company.

Graham found he preferred to be in the front rank. He watched every move with close attention. CSM Grey had the parade to begin with, the officers and CUOs standing in a group to one side until he was ready. The 2ic then took over. While he did the platoon commanders lined up facing their platoons. Graham thus had a good chance to study each of the CUOs. They all looked the part he decided.

But CUO Grant is the best.

The lessons were a mixture of fieldwork on patrolling skills; First Aid; and Navigation. They were taught how to identify, prevent and treat Heat Exhaustion. Period 2 was Section patrol formations. Period 3 was how to find direction by the sun and the stars. During this, Graham was tempted to point out that it was daylight so they could not see the stars but managed to contain himself. Period 4 was on how to move a casualty. This included armchair lifts, crawls to drag unconscious or disabled casualties, how to make improvised stretchers and stretcher drill.

This brought back clear memories of having carried Cadet Moloney on the stretcher two nights before and he understood it was an important skill. He found it all good knowledge to have but did not enjoy it much as he had to work with either LCpl Bannister or Morris during the practices.

Period 5 was 'Field Signals', the silent hand signals used to communicate on the battlefield. That was interesting and Graham tried hard to memorise them all. Period 6 was Navigation: compass revision and how to orientate a map by the ground and with a compass. Graham loved maps and found this fascinating. He knew he had an excellent sense of direction and was keen to polish the skill. Once again, it brought memories of navigating across past Hill 445 while looking for the lost section.

After lunch he was given an opportunity to show his skill. The afternoon was devoted to a Day Compass March. The three junior platoons spent three hours zig-zagging around the area in section groups from check point to check point. At the same time the 'Senior' cadets from 4 Pl and HQ carried out an 'Escape and Evasion' exercise to try to sneak through the area without being seen or caught. The 'Seniors' were given two yellow cloth flashes to wear on their hats. These were 'lives'. If caught once, they forfeited one flash to their captors and continued. If caught twic,e they were 'dead' and had to go with the section.

The compass work was the same as the night Navex. The corporal worked out the bearings and paces and the cadets did the compass work. Graham found it ridiculously easy. He was also childishly pleased when they spotted three 'enemy'. Gwen saw them first. They were about a hundred metres off, trying to hide behind some ant hills. Graham let out a yell and started running.

The three senior cadets sprang up and bolted. The section set off in pursuit, stringing out as they ran. At length one of the seniors gave up: Cpl Travis from 4 PL. The other two kept running. Graham kept on after them. He was dimly aware that his name was being called but he kept on running till he had caught both of them.

When he looked around, Graham was astonished to see that the nearest person from his own section was Cpl Grenfell, and he was still a hundred metres back. The others were scattered for half a kilometre. Some were not even in sight. Graham's delight at capturing the two seniors evaporated as he saw Cpl Grenfell's face. The corporal was red with anger.

"When I tell you to stop, Cadet Kirk, you bloody well stop!" he shouted angrily.

"But... but corporal, they would have got away," Graham replied. He was puzzled because he was pleased at his own fitness and at the exploit.

"I don't bloody well care!" Cpl Grenfell yelled, waving his arms and pointing back the way they had come. "Don't you listen to orders? Safety first! The section must stay together. We cannot scatter ourselves all over the bush in case someone gets lost or injured. One prisoner would have been fine. Now I don't even know where Harriet and Morris are!"

Graham flushed at the rebuff. "Yes corporal. Sorry."

Cpl Grenfell grunted, then turned to the two prisoners. "Okay Jonesy, give us a flash. You too, Smith."

The prisoners handed over a yellow cloth strip each and were let go. Graham and Cpl Grenfell then walked back to re-join the section. To Graham's astonishment, Morris was almost back at where they had started. Both he and Harriet complained of blisters. It was all Graham could do to hide his contempt. Blisters! After walking only a couple of kilometres!

They trudged on around the remainder of the two-kilometre course, meeting Capt Conkey and the CSM in the middle. By the time the section were on the last leg, Morris and Harriet were trailing far behind and limping. The others looked tired and hot. Graham felt hot but happy.

That was good, he thought.

On arrival back at camp they were told to get organised for a shower. But as Graham walked towards his hutchie, he was puzzled. Where was it? Then he saw it. It was lying on the ground amid a scatter of clothing and belongings.

Oh no! Bloody hell! Who has done that? Graham wondered.

Names like Brown, Hollbrook and Hungerton flitted across his mind, but he conceded it might also have been Derek White or Pigsy Pike. He walked over to the mess and stared down at it with his temper rising, mingled with embarrassment. The others crowded around to stare.

Sgt Masters joined them. "Looks like your fan club has left their calling card, Cadet Kirk," he said.

"Bastards!" Graham cried, clenching his fists and looking around to see who might be smirking or laughing.

But there were no obvious suspects in the area and he looked back down at the tangle of clothes, toiletries and other gear lying scattered in the dust.

Sgt Masters shook his head. "Well, we will sort this out later. You lot stop gawping and go and get ready for a shower: towel, toiletries, change of underwear and change of clothes. Cadet Kirk, just get what you need and shove the rest back in your kitbag."

Stephen had joined Graham, but he now called out, "You just reminded me of the World War Two Prisoner of War Camp joke sarge."

"Oh yeah? What's that?" Sgt Masters queried. The others lingered to listen.

Stephen went on, "The prisoners were all on morning parade and the commandant got up to speak to them. 'Gut morning prisoners,' he said. 'Today ve haf der gut news und der bad news. First the good news. Zere vill be a change of undervear. Now der bad news; Hut A, you will change vith Hut B."

Despite his upset Graham found he had to grin. Most laughed but a couple took some time to get the joke. Sgt Masters laughed and then repeated the order to go and get ready. The cadets turned and moved away.

Stephen nudged Graham. "Come on, cheer up. It isn't the end of the world."

Graham grunted and was tempted to reply that it was and that he wished he could just end it all, but he knew it was not true and seeing Stephen's friendly face reminded him that he had some good friends. With that knowledge a warm feeling flowed in to lift his spirits. Still feeling hurt and annoyed, he knelt and began quickly sorting his belongings and stuffing things back in his pack and duffle bag. Only then did the thought come to him to check whether anything had been stolen. But without carefully laying it all out he could not tell.

Cpl Grenfell came over, his laundry bag over his shoulders. "Leave that, Cadet Kirk. Grab your clean clothes and get moving."

Graham did, not wanting to be the cause of holding the platoon up. He could see an army truck and the Land Rover returning from shuttling 1 Platoon to the showers.

2 Platoon were loaded into the truck and a Land Rover with their webbing and washing. Graham went in the truck, squashed in between Stephen and Gwen on the near side bench seat. Lt Stanton sat in the

back with them to supervise for safety and Lt Hamilton drove. Twenty minutes later, they were back at Camp Gedling. This time it was teeming with cadets from 15 ACU and St Michael's College. Graham looked out at them with interest as the truck drove slowly past the buildings. His impression was not favourable. They looked very clean and many of them looked very young and unfit.

The Cairns platoons were debussed at the rear of the showers. Under the direction of the CSM and sergeants, they laid their gear out in section lines, posted a piquet and then took off their boots. Thongs were placed on feet (except for a few cadets who had not brought them and had to pull their unlaced boots back on). They were then lined up to wash clothes and shower.

The hot water was a definite luxury and sent morale soaring. After washing his dirty clothes and showering, Graham dressed in a clean uniform and then went for a walk around. He found that just being clean felt really good. It was sunset by then and he was struck by how cool it was. As before, a cold wind was being funnelled up through the pass, the camp being on the very crest of the ridge.

As Graham strolled around, he was joined by Peter.

"How's it going, Graham? Do you like the camp?"

There was a strong temptation to play the martyr; to claim he had been press-ganged into attending, and that he hated it. But this was his best friend, Peter.

"I love it," he replied.

I can do all of this, he thought. *And I'm good at it.*

He was careful to make no mention of his hutchie being cut down again or of his gear being tipped out in the dirt.

Peter was pleased. "I said you would. That's great. How's your section?"

They fell to discussing their respective sections and platoons. Peter was adamant that 1 PL was the best in the unit; and that his section was the best in the platoon.

Graham was reluctant to claim that his section was better. Instead he said, "My section commander, Cpl Grenfell is the best section leader in the company."

Peter laughed. "Yeah, you might be right. But I'll bet mine is the prettiest."

His section commander was the gorgeous black-haired Sheila Sherry. There were five other female corporals, but Graham had to concede that. They changed to discussing girls, a fairly delicate subject for Graham. He soon changed it to discuss the other cadet units.

"Our unit is better," he commented, gesturing to where a large group of cadets was engaging in rowdy behaviour nearby. "This St Michael's mob don't seem as well organised, or as well disciplined," this last prompted by a shouting match between a large female warrant officer and a thin male corporal.

Dinner was eaten in the mess hall at Camp Gedling. This gave more opportunities for the three units to eye each other jealously, and for frequent interchange of comments and challenges. Luckily, the Cairns cadets were put on their truck to return to camp as soon as they had finished their meal, and this prevented any unpleasant incidents.

On return to their camp the platoons were allowed to light campfires. No training was scheduled for the evening. Graham dug some nylon cord out of his webbing and strung a clothesline between two nearby trees. He was busy hanging his wet washing on it when Rita strolled over.

"Can I put my washing on your line please, Graham?' she queried.

There was clearly room for more clothing, so Graham smiled and nodded. "Yes, sure," he agreed.

But he was suspicious. *Is she going to make a play for tonight,* he wondered anxiously.

While Rita did that, he returned to the tangle that was his hutchie and gear and resumed sorting it out. As he did, he tried to check whether anything had been taken but could not think of anything that was missing. It only took him a few minutes to repack and a few more to get more cord and retie the hutchie. While he worked, he found he was more philosophical about it and kept thinking of what Stephen had said.

I will just ignore the mongrels, he told himself.

Feeling much better, he then strolled over to where Sgt Masters was organising the fire. This resulted in him being roped in to collect firewood. Graham didn't mind. It was a task he often did on hikes and Scout camps. He took his torch from his pocket and went off to look. But even so he was very careful to use the beam of his torch to check that any twisted looking stick was actually that and not a snake!

The campfires were a great success. Despite some trepidation at how he might be received, he went with Stephen and Gwen and visited every platoon in turn. He soon found that 4 Pl were anti-social and jealous of their status and discouraged First Years. HQ and the 'Control Group' were even more so. Sgt Brown in particular scowled at him and told him to, 'Bugger off!'

So it was a choice between the three First Year campfires. Suspecting he would not get a friendly reception at 3 Platoon, he avoided them. After a while, Peter joined the group and between Peter's smart comments and Stephen's jokes Graham's spirits quickly rose.

A 'canteen', comprising Lt Hamilton and his Q Staff seated on Eskis, was operating. Graham purchased a chocolate and a soft drink and sat with his friends to yarn. He found it incredibly relaxing and enjoyable.

The officers were walking around visiting each campfire. They also had their own. At one stage Graham and his friends called there. Capt Conkey was there, with the CSM and HQ. To Graham's disappointment Warrant Officer Howley wasn't there. Out of curiosity he asked Capt Conkey where he was.

Capt Conkey pointed westwards into the night. "He's helping run a night patrol exercise for Heatley Cadet Kirk. How are you anyway?"

"Good sir."

"Enjoying the camp?"

"Yes sir."

"Good."

Peter asked where the Heatley unit was. "They were just over the road when we arrived sir but they have gone now."

Capt Conkey nodded. "Yes, they walked off cross-country just after lunch. They are currently defending a hill a couple of kilometres away."

"Do we do that sir?" Graham asked.

"Yes, we do. In four days' time."

That sounded good. Graham was surprised at himself. *I actually want to do these military exercises!*

Soon after this Graham found himself put to the test. When they were told to go back to their platoon areas and to go to bed, he found Rita beside him. Angela was nearby, talking to Crane.

Rita was very direct, which Graham found disconcerting. "Hi Graham. Having a good night?" she asked.

"Yes thanks."

"Would you like to have an even better night?"

That stunned him. *What does she mean?* he thought, his hopes and anxiety both shooting up. Surely, she didn't mean that? But she did.

When he mumbled an answer, she said, "You know what I mean. I've heard you are a real spunky guy; and I'm feeling really horny. How about it?"

Graham's body began to respond. So did his mind. He sensed instantly that this was one of those critical moments. The idea was immensely attractive, even with a tart like Rita.

To his own surprise, the decision was very easy to take and only took a few seconds to arrive at.

"I'd love to," he said. "But not at camp thanks."

"Oh, why not spoilsport?" Rita asked, clearly peeved.

"Because I promised Capt Conkey I would behave," Graham replied simply.

He knew his manhood would now be ridiculed and called into question but somehow it didn't matter. *My integrity is more important,* he told himself.

Rita gave a scornful laugh. "Promise! What a load of crap! He won't know."

"Maybe not, but I will," Graham replied.

When she realised he meant what he said, Rita was really stung. "Well stuff you then! I'll go and find a real man!"

With that, she stormed off into the darkness. Graham took several deep breaths and went to his hutchie. This time as he lay there in the dark, he was assailed by regret and lust; but also felt a strong sense of pride at having faced the temptation and won.

He slept very well that night and woke feeling rested and refreshed. The only niggling worry was whether Rita had actually gone off and found some other boy who was willing. It worried him to think people might be misbehaving. At check parade and breakfast he found that both Angela and Rita ignored him and spent their time flirting with Crane and his cronies. That suited Graham. He shrugged philosophically and sat next to Cpl Grenfell and Gwen during breakfast.

Day 4 was a day of patrol training and preparation. The training was harder, with more running and sweating as they grappled with the problems of working as teams. Capt Conkey ran the training. First, he had a demo squad made up of the Control Group, CSM and HQ show how something was done. Then the sections went to practice the skill. Before they did, Capt Conkey reminded them that the aim of cadet training was not to train soldiers and that anyone who did not wish to take part in 'warlike' training had the option of doing medical and signals training.

He also gave them a lecture on the morality of military service and told them to examine their own consciences and decide for themselves whether they would, or should, ever fight in defence of their country. Then the training began.

First was revision of the patrol formations followed by one on how scouts operate. Two-man fire and movement was next. That was an eye-opener to Graham. He took to the practice with relish, teaming up with Cpl Grenfell. As he ran forward, he dived to cover and pretended to give covering fire (They had no rifles and no blanks but like most of the others Graham picked up a stick as a pretend weapon). As he did, he discovered that it roused a savage lust in him. A fierce determination to do it, and to do it well, made him exert himself to his utmost. At the end of the practice he stood, chest heaving and eyes alight with the sheer joy of it and knew he had arrived.

He wiped sweat and dirt from his face and grinned. *That was real excitement!* he thought.

He sat and watched with critical but hungry eyes while the others in the section had a go. Because there were only seven in the section, he volunteered to have a second go with LCpl Bannister. Once more he relished the physical exertion, the drama and the adrenalin rush.

Graham knew that the real thing would be a terrifying and bloody business. Capt Conkey reminded them of this; and he knew. As a young soldier he had fought in a real war at that very level. Even so Graham wondered: *Am I good enough? If I have to fight in a war, will I have the guts to do this; to get up and run when someone is shooting at me?*

It was serious food for thought. He was left with a nagging doubt but felt sure he would rise to meet the challenge. There was also a lurking suspicion that there might be dark depths to his own character that he had not suspected.

There were lessons on section patrolling, tactical obstacle crossing, and just a hint of the drills that soldiers carried out when they encountered the opposing force. Graham thought that these were even more fun; with some shouting and running and lots of excited sweating. For the last two periods they learned how to do a section attack, and how to deal with prisoners and to search bodies. It was all interesting to Graham. A lot of what they were taught was in stark contrast to what he saw in movies on TV.

After lunch, they pulled down their hutchies and packed them. The area was then cleaned up. Sgt Masters organised an 'Emu Bob' to pick up the litter. A work party led by LCpl Bannister was sent off to fill in one of the latrines. While they worked, Graham noted that the HQ tents had been dropped and packed and that all the stores were loaded on the truck. The CUOs and officers stood talking in the shade of the 'HQ tree'.

CUO Grant walked over and checked that the platoon area was clean. As soon as he was satisfied, the platoon was ordered to pick up their gear and form up in single file behind their corporals. Graham hauled on his webbing and pack and helped Morris and Harriet with theirs. He then hoisted his kitbag onto his shoulder.

When all were loaded up, CUO Grant set off. The others followed: Corporal, cadets, Lance Corporal, then the next section; with Sgt Masters bringing up the rear. CUO Grant had wanted to beat the other platoons. In this he was successful. They moved just before 1 Pl. Their route led straight through the trees past the windmill and across to the gravel road. They crossed this and followed a dirt vehicle track. Close on their right was the tree line marking Speed Creek. Off to the left was the same small dry creek which they had been training along for three days.

The platoon tramped in through a stand of large trees and past a clump of twisted mulga scrub for a hundred metres to where Capt Conkey now waited.

How did he get here? Graham wondered. He hadn't seen him leave the other camp and no vehicle had driven over. *He must have walked,* he concluded.

Capt Conkey indicated 2 Platoon's new bivouac area as CUO Grant reached him. CUO Grant led the platoon off to the left side of a flat area studded with trees. It was the area the Heatley unit had been camped in but was clean. Apart from a few marks in the bare earth there were few signs of previous use.

For the next two hours they set up a new camp. Hutchies were erected in a few minutes. Then grease traps and latrines were dug. Once again, Graham found himself wielding a pick. He stripped off his shirt, till ordered to put it back on ('Sun safe'). It felt good to use his muscles, to swing the pick. He wanted to sing but was too self-conscious about showing his feelings.

A lesson on Night Patrolling was then given by Lt Hamilton to the whole company. While they were learning this, Graham observed Capt Conkey and the CUOs seated on a log over at HQ. They had done this every afternoon so far and he had heard it referred to as an 'O' Group. Lt Hamilton now made the term clear. It was an Orders Group, where detailed instructions were given according to a set sequence.

An hour later, he watched from a distance as CUO Grant held a platoon 'O' Group with Sgt Masters and the three corporals. Then Graham took part in one when Cpl Grenfell returned and gave a Section 'O' Group. As the planned night patrol was explained, Graham was again impressed. It was all so logical and well thought out. It was also real 'army stuff' and that made it more important.

Later, Graham voiced this opinion to Cpl Grenfell. He laughed.

"Should be. I think they worked the method out in the First World War. Heaven knows they have had enough opportunities to get it right since then!"

The last hour was devoted to patrol preparation. Webbing was packed, water bottles filled, faces camouflaged, torches and compasses checked. Graham found it interesting and exciting.

A night patrol! Even if they were only going to look, and not to fight, it would still be an adventure.

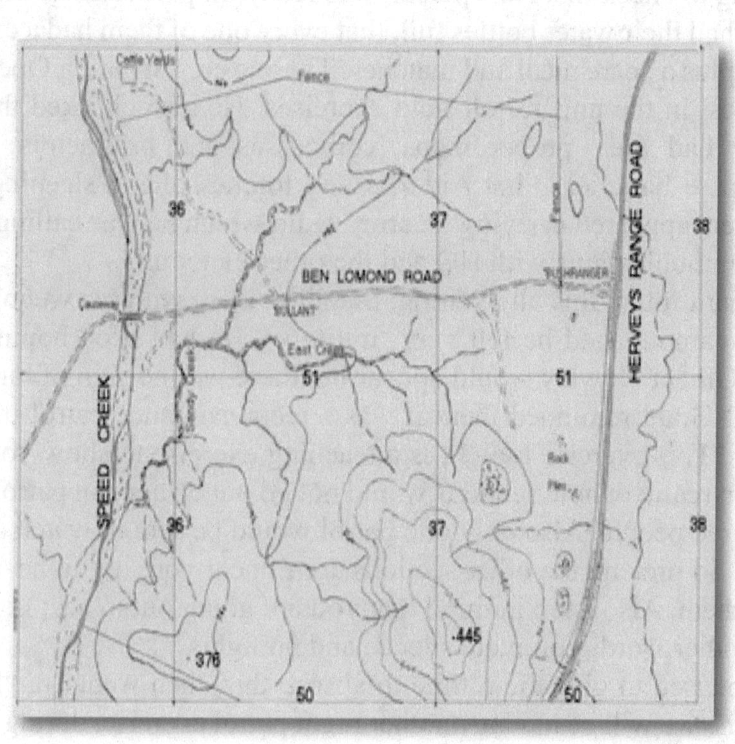

Map 3: Speed Creek

Chapter 34

NIGHT PATROL

As it began to get dark, the platoon was lined up. CUO Grant went along to check that each person was ready. In particular he checked that they had their water bottles full, that every one of them had a copy of the map, plus a spare meal and matches. These were 'Standing Operating Procedures' in the unit for all field exercises. He also checked that the corporals had their proper maps, compasses and protractors, small radios, spare batteries, First Aid kits and torches plus a sleeping bag. Sgt Masters appeared carrying an army radio which he was calling on to check communications with HQ and the other platoons.

Graham found this all exciting. Standing there with his webbing on and face camouflaged he felt very 'military'. He had been hoping that Warrant Officer Howley would appear but there was no sign of him.

CUO Grant reminded them it was a reconnaissance patrol training exercise. "This exercise tonight is a teaching exercise to show you how to do it. In reality whole sections would not go out on a recon patrol; only two or three people. Also only one patrol would be sent to watch a road, not nine. So pretend the other sections aren't near you, if you hear them or meet them. Also keep in mind that you are going out to see; not to be seen. In other words complete silence and no lights."

He paused to give them time to absorb this, then went on, "In two nights time we will be having another night patrol exercise, during which we will practice what you learn tonight, but it will have a more active opposing force and harder navigation. Now, follow me and move as quietly as you can. Let's go."

CUO Grant turned and led them off in single file. They filed out of camp down towards the small dry creek just to the east. As they did, Graham noted 3 PL also starting to move. It all looked very military, and he enjoyed the sensation of being part of a team. In his imagination he pretended they were commandos setting out to carry out a dangerous mission.

Their route took them due east across the dry creek and then across fairly open ground beyond it. Darkness set in. There was no moon. Millions of stars shimmered in the clear sky above. The temperature dropped steadily. Graham had his pullover strapped to his webbing and he wondered if he shouldn't have put it on before they started.

Progress slowed to a crawl as they encountered another dry creek with steep, eroded sides. They slid down into this one at a time and clambered up out the other side. Beyond it was another gently undulating area several hundred metres across. This was dotted with small ant hills and stones and there were frequent stumbles and muttered curses. Using Orion as a guide Graham estimated they were still heading almost due east.

This is where Checkpoint Golf was for the night Navex, Graham thought.

Remembering that experience gave him very mixed feelings, the main one being satisfaction. He looked to his right in the starlight, noting the bulk of Hill 445. The memory of finding the lost patrol's tracks gave him another spurt of fierce satisfaction.

After about half an hour of slow walking, they stopped at another creek. CUO Grant walked back along the line to check they were all there. Graham was re-assured by this. The CUO gave the impression he knew exactly what he was doing, and that made Graham feel better.

Once CUO Grant had returned to the front of the line, they moved off again. This time they filed down into the creek bed, turned left and trudged along its sandy bed to a creek junction a hundred metres on. Here they paused for another check and for the tail to catch up. Then they turned right and went along the sandy bed of the other creek.

By then Graham was perspiring, despite the cold, and was glad he didn't have his jumper on as others were muttering about being hot. It was slow going and there were frequent stumbles on rocks and logs. The cadets walked one behind the other, mostly within touching distance. Graham could now see what had been meant in the lecture when Lt Hamilton had explained that, on really dark nights, troops actually held onto the webbing of the person in front.

The darkness wasn't such a problem this time as the starlight gave enough light to see the other people close up. The platoon kept heading east. The creek line became deeper, with steeper banks. Twice CUO Grant stopped to check his map by a shaded torch as they came to small creek junctions. After about 300 metres, which took 20 minutes to cover, they came to another creek junction and stopped. A huge boulder on the left marked the spot.

CUO Grant stopped and told them to close in and sit down in section groups. This took a few minutes, with muttering and cursing as people bumped into each other or trod on others. The section commanders were then called out. Sgt Masters reported all present and was told to send the nickname 'Grasshopper' on the radio. He did this and got good clear reception.

"Bloody miracle!" CUO Grant exclaimed. "A radio that works! Okay, this is the platoon rendezvous. For those of you whose French isn't all that good we will call it the 'RV'. This is where you come back to. Corporals, set your compasses and show me which way you reckon you are supposed to go."

Each of the sections was to move out at a different angle, spreading out in a fan pattern, but all would end up watching the gravel road. The plan was for them to be about two hundred metres apart. While CUO Grant checked the bearings, Graham took out a water bottle and had drink. Then he quickly unstrapped his pullover and draped it over his back, crossing the sleeves on his front. Now that they had stopped moving the sweat was rapidly chilling.

I might not get a chance later, he decided.

Cpl Grenfell came back to where the section waited in line. "Righto Four Section, up you get. Let's go! No noise."

They stood up and Graham and several others hastily took off pullovers and bundled them up. The section headed up out of the creek line to the left of the large boulder and onto gently rising flat ground. As before, this was studded with rocks and ant hills. There were also a few small washouts leading down into the creek. The section made its way slowly over these in single file, Cpl Grenfell leading.

Graham had the job of counting paces. Five hundred was the distance they had to travel. He could just see the crestline of the ridge ahead through the trees. The sky and stars showed up lighter than the trees and grass. He knew, from studying his map, that the gravel road ran along the crestline at an angle to the bearing they were following.

After a hundred paces, Cpl Grenfell stopped to check that the tail of the section was still with them. He looked at his luminous watch and muttered, then set off at a faster rate. They were supposed to be in position by 2000hrs and it was already 1945.

There was a thud and a cry, and Cpl Grenfell suddenly went down. Graham was so close behind he almost fell with him. He stopped and looked. Cpl Grenfell had tripped or fallen into a small washout which was almost impossible to see in the grass.

Cpl Grenfell let out a groan and did not get up. "Ah! Oh! I think I've broken my arm."

The section crowded round. Graham and Gwen helped Cpl Grenfell to move. They eased him over so he was not lying on the arm. As they did, Cpl Grenfell let out a wail of such pure agony they stopped moving him, fearful lest they were doing more damage.

"Where does it hurt?" Gwen asked, assuming the role of First Aider.

"Upper arm. Shoulder and elbow. I... ah! I can't move it without it hurting real bad," Cpl Grenfell replied.

Gwen knelt and began to gently feel along his arm. LCpl Bannister joined them from the back. The others stood in worried silence.

"Give me some light please," Gwen asked.

"But we were told not to use lights or the enemy will see us," LCpl Bannister replied.

Gwen snorted. "Oh piffle! The orders said that if there was a real accident then we were to stop the exercise and carry out First Aid," she snapped back.

At that Graham pulled out his pencil torch and turned it on. Gwen went on with her examination.

"I don't think it's broken," she said. "Or, if it is, it is split along the bone. It isn't snapped in two, or anything like that."

"Might have damaged the joints," Graham suggested.

Gwen nodded. "Yes, that's what I'm worrying about," she replied. "Anyway, it needs proper medical attention. We will immobilise it and get help."

She stood and took off her webbing and rummaged around for bandages. Graham stood holding the torch. Cpl Grenfell lay back, groaning and holding his arm.

"What'll we do?" LCpl Bannister asked anxiously.

Cpl Grenfell spoke, his voice quavering from the pain. "Use the radio to call for help," he said.

Gwen knelt and took hold of the small CB radio Cpl Grenfell had tied to his shirt. "Headquarters, this is Two One Alpha, over," she called.

There was no answer. She tried again. Then she put the radio to her ear and pressed the press-to-talk button. Looking at Cpl Grenfell she shook her head.

"I can't hear any carrier wave when I press the transmit button," she explained. "I don't think it is transmitting."

Cpl Grenfell reached up, just beating Graham's twitching fingers. He also tried calling. But there was no response. Graham turned the beam of his torch on it. The small radio was covered with dust and the antenna was bent over sideways.

"I think it got broken when you fell," he said.

They tried again but the radio made no sound. LCpl Bannister, who had been squatting beside them, looked very anxious in the torchlight.

"What will we do?" he cried, his voice rising with alarm.

Gwen answered. "Take him out to the road and send two runners to the safety vehicle. That's what the exercise orders said to do," she answered.

"Where is the safety vehicle?" LCpl Bannister asked. He sounded very nervous and unsure.

Cpl Grenfell groaned, then snapped angrily, "You were told in the bloody orders! If you didn't write it down then dig out my notebook and look up the grid reference."

"I've got it corporal," Graham replied. He dug into his pocket and extracted his notebook. A moment's searching showed him. "Grid Reference 374 513."

He then took out his map photocopy. With his torch held in his mouth he scanned the map. "That is here, at this track junction. Where are we?"

"Somewhere near our objective. About two hundred metres from it I'd say," Cpl Grenfell replied.

He then lay back with his eyes closed. Graham saw that he was shaking and had beads of sweat on his forehead. While Gwen and Harriet set to work to immobilise the arm with triangular bandages Graham and LCpl Bannister plotted their position. Graham put a pencil mark on the map.

"About here, I reckon."

"How do we get there? What compass bearing?" LCpl Bannister

asked. There was an edge of panic in his voice that worried Graham. It also aroused his contempt.

"We just walk north to that crestline and we should come to the road," he said. "Then turn right and run along it till we find the safety vehicle."

"Are you sure? Don't we need to work out the magnetic variation and all that?" LCpl Bannister queried.

"Yes, I'm sure. And no, we don't have to worry about magnetic variation," Graham replied sharply. "The distance is so short the variation is meaningless. Anyway, the gravel road runs east-west. If we go north, we must come to it somewhere."

LCpl Bannister managed to look both nettled and anxious at the same moment. Then he suddenly looked to his left. "Ye... yes. Hey! There's a light over there! Maybe they can help?" LCpl Bannister pointed off along the slope.

Graham looked. A torch flickered in the darkness on the slope a few hundred metres off. He snorted, "Just another section. Be 2 Section or 3 Section. The mob of noddies! They shouldn't be showing lights."

"I'll get them to help," LCpl Bannister replied. Before anyone could say anything, he began running towards the torch. As he ran, he shouted, "Help! Hey! Over there, help! Hel... aargh!"

There was a thud. LCpl Bannister went down in a dark heap. There was a moment of silence; then he cried out loudly in pain. "Aargh! Argh! Oh! Oh helf! Helf!"

Graham swore. He flicked off his torch and stood up. "Keep on with Cpl Grenfell, Gwen. Harriet, Morris, come with me."

He strode over to where LCpl Bannister was writhing on the ground in agony. A quick examination by torchlight showed him to be lying on his side holding his face.

Graham was annoyed. "What's wrong?" he snapped.

Through the groans came the muffled answer, "I finkf I haff bfroken fmy noth."

"Broken your nose?"

"Yethf. Oh! Oh! Helpf."

Graham held him still and eased his hands away from his face. Blood was flowing freely from the nose, which certainly looked to be at an odd angle and was starting to puff up.

"Looks like it. What happened?" he asked.

"I trippff... oh! Tripped on thuff... argh... on an ant... ant thill. Oh!"

Graham looked and saw a small ant hill of about knee height. It was just visible in the starlight.

Bloody drongo! he thought.

Cpl Grenfell snapped at him. "You shouldn't have been running, you nong. You were told never to run in the dark. Ouch!"

It was obvious that Bannister was in great pain as well. The blood kept flowing and soon clotted to block his swollen nostrils. Tears and groans escaped in a continual flow. Graham stood up and bit his lip. What to do?

Gwen joined him. "What about going back to the Platoon RV and getting CUO Grant. He's got a radio."

For a moment Graham weighed this course; then shook his head. "No. Just waste more time. I will go and get the safety vehicle. Crane can come with me. You get this lot out to the road. It should be just up there."

"But there is only one compass. How will you navigate?"

"By the stars. We had the lesson," Graham replied.

"Are you sure?" She sounded genuinely concerned.

Graham smiled. "Yes I am. Look, there's Orion almost overhead and there's the Southern Cross." He swung round and pointed to where the constellation just showed through the treetops behind them. Then he pointed up the slope. "Anyway, I can see the crestline from here. The road is just over there. Come on, you get this lot moving."

Gwen shook her head. "But we will need two people to carry each of these."

That raised the problem of whether the casualties could walk or not. Cpl Grenfell assured them he could, if he could lean on someone. It was obvious that LCpl Bannister needed two people to help him as he was very distressed and nearly hysterical.

"Let's not argue about it," Graham said. "Morris, you and Harriet help Lance Corporal Bannister. Jeff, you help Cpl Grenfell up, then Gwen can help him to walk. Gwen, you navigate with his compass. Go due north. Don't bother to reset the compass, just walk along the north pointer."

Graham helped to get Cpl Grenfell to his feet. Gwen had removed his webbing, so Graham picked this up.

"Don't... ah! don't... argh!... forget my pack," Cpl Grenfell groaned.

Graham searched for this and picked it up as well. As soon as he was sure Harriet had the compass, he said, "Come on, Jeff. See you soon Gwen, out on the road."

Without waiting to see if he was obeyed Graham set off. He didn't care if Jeff Crane came with him or not. He only took him because it was unit policy in this situation for two people to go for help.

For speed and safety he used his torch, directing it at the ground about three metres in front. Crane followed in his footsteps. "Where's your torch?" Graham asked.

"Lost it," Crane muttered.

Graham shrugged. Typical!

Only after he had gone about 50 paces did Graham remember snakes. For a few steps his stride faltered but then he shook his head and kept walking. *Not much ground cover and any snake will hear us coming and get out of our way,* he reasoned.

Within three minutes he had reached the gravel road. His own webbing and the pack he placed in the grass beside the road. Cpl Grenfell's webbing he dumped in the centre of the road as a marker. As soon as Jeff Crane dropped his webbing, Graham turned off his torch and began to run. The road was plain to him in the starlight.

Crane followed. "You sure we are going the right way?" he asked.

"Yes," Graham replied shortly.

He pushed himself to run even faster. Crane was obviously unfit as he soon fell behind. Graham didn't care. He pushed himself on.

Three black figures loomed ahead. "Who's that?" challenged CUO Hansen, 4 Pl commander.

"Cadet Kirk, sir. We've had an accident. How far to the safety vehicle?"

"Just along there a few hundred metres," CUO Hansen replied.

Graham did not stop to explain. He ran on. *Thank God for those early morning runs!* he thought. He was surprised how well he could see the road in the starlight once his eyes adjusted.

The road went over a low crest and curved gently to the left. By then Graham was puffing but still felt quite capable of running a lot further. Square black shapes loomed up in the darkness: parked vehicles, two of them; a Land Rover and the truck.

Warrant Officer Howley's voice called out. "Who's that? Why are you running in the dark?"

Graham heaved a sigh of relief. Warrant Officer Howley! Now everything would be alright!

"Cadet Kirk, sir. We've had an accident; two in fact."

He skidded to a stop. Warrant Officer Howley and Lt Hamilton were both there, along with a dozen cadets from HQ and 4 Pl. As quickly as he could, Graham explained the situation. By the time he finished Crane came panting up to join them.

Warrant Officer Howley listened, then said, "In the Rover. Let's go!"

Lt Hamilton jumped into the driver's seat. Warrant Officer Howley sprang in beside him and began calling Capt Conkey on the radio. Graham and Crane clambered in the back, along with Cpl Kelly, the medical corporal. She was an extremely attractive Year 11 girl. He had never spoken to her, only admired from afar.

Within a few seconds, the Rover's engine was going. With headlights blazing, the vehicle accelerated back down the road. As they drove, Graham sighed with relief. He was sweating now. It took only a minute or so to reach the place, marked by Cpl Grenfell's webbing. By then Graham was recovering his breath. There was no-one there, but torches were flickering among the trees off to the left. He scrambled out and located his webbing then headed through the bush towards the torches. The others followed.

Within another minute they had reached the torches. The section was only 50 metres from the road. Harriet and Morris were supporting a sobbing LCpl Bannister between them, and Gwen was helping Cpl Grenfell. There was a pause while the two injured cadets were examined again. While they did this, the lights of another vehicle came up the road from the west. It stopped near theirs and Capt Conkey appeared through the bush with CSM Grey and a signaller.

The adults had a quick discussion, and it was decided to send both casualties to the hospital in Townsville at once. The group continued walking slowly out to the gravel road. Once there, Lt Hamilton's Rover was quickly turned around. Cpl Grenfell was eased up into the passenger seat and LCpl Bannister placed on a stretcher in the back. Cpl Kelly climbed in to tend him on the journey. Their webbing was collected by CSM Grey and placed in Capt Conkey's Cruiser.

While they were doing this, torches appeared from down towards the creek. CUO Grant and Sgt Masters joined them. They had heard over the radio and had come to check if they could help.

Lt Hamilton checked that he had the cadets' medical documents and then climbed in. The Rover was started up and roared off into the night. As the dust settled, Capt Conkey gathered the section together and asked what had happened. Gwen did most of the talking and the story was soon told.

Capt Conkey nodded his approval. "You have done well," he said. "Okay, CUO Grant, you had better take this lot back with you to your RV."

Chapter 35

RIVALRY

Graham felt a sharp stab of disappointment.

"Oh sir! Can't we go on with the exercise?"

"Do you want to?" Capt Conkey asked in surprise.

"Yes please," both Graham and Gwen chorused.

"Do you think you can do it without an NCO?" Capt Conkey asked. "Who will navigate to get you home?"

"I can sir," Graham replied.

"Oh, yes? So how will you find the platoon RV?" Capt Conkey asked.

"By walking back the way we came, sir," Graham replied.

"How will you know that?"

Graham thought for a moment. "Using the back bearing, half a circle," he replied.

"Good! That's correct. Except you probably aren't in the right place here," Capt Conkey replied.

"No sir. We should be about a hundred paces down the road that way," Graham explained, pointing to the west.

Capt Conkey rubbed his chin. "Hmm. Yes. What do you think, CUO Grant? You are the one who is going to have to find them if they get lost."

Graham was indignant. Before CUO Grant could reply he said, "Oh sir! We won't get lost. The RV is just down the slope in that creek line. Even if we miss it, we will just go up and down the creek till we find it. We can't miss the creek. I can see it from here."

Capt Conkey laughed. "I've known it to happen! But yes, in your case I think you can do it. You happy with that CUO Grant?"

CUO Grant nodded. "Yes sir. At the worst they will still be somewhere between the road and the creek. As long as you don't cross any creeks and keep going Cadet Kirk."

"This is 4 Section sir, not 9 Section," Graham replied.

Capt Conkey snorted. "Don't get cheeky, Cadet Kirk! Now, do you know what you have to do when you are in position?"

"Yes," both Gwen and Graham replied. Gwen continued, "We have to note down all enemy movement along the road. I've got a notebook and pencil."

"How are you going to write in the dark?" Capt Conkey asked.

Graham thought about the orders. But before he could answer Gwen did. "Cpl Grenfell was going to hide his head and shoulders inside a sleeping bag so he could use his torch without the enemy seeing it. The sleeping bag is in his pack."

"Very good, Cadet Copeland. Well done," Capt Conkey replied.

That nettled Graham. He had known that and was jealous and annoyed. Gwen had suddenly emerged as a distinct rival. In spite of that, he still liked her. *She is certainly very capable.*

The pack was found and handed to Gwen. Graham and Crane picked up their webbing. CUO Grant then led the section along the road to where Graham thought it should be. He was a bit anxious about that but was confident he could still find the RV in the dark. Capt Conkey turned his Rover and drove off back towards Speed Creek with CSM Grey. Warrant Officer Howley walked with them but said nothing beyond praising the whole section for how it handled the crisis.

"This is the spot sir," Graham said to CUO Grant.

"Okay. Get the section hidden just back from the road. Make sure you can see anyone walking along it," CUO Grant said.

Graham was reluctant to antagonise the others by giving an order, but when he walked into the bush they all followed him. The place had almost no cover other than a couple of trees and a few ant hills. The grass was very short. He got them to lie down in a line, side by side. Gwen lay close beside Graham with Harriet beside her.

When they were in position CUO Grant turned on his torch and gave the compass to Graham.

"Okay, Cadet Kirk, set it on the back bearing."

"We could just turn the compass around and hold the front towards us, then walk with it that way sir," he said.

"I know that! But I want to be sure you really do know what you are doing," CUO Grant replied testily.

Graham did a quick mental calculation. *We came out on 6200 mills. Half a circle is 3200 mills. So take off 3200... er... that is 3000 mills.*

He told CUO grant this and then turned the graduated dial to set the compass.

CUO Grant checked it and nodded. "Good. Now, remember, when you come to the creek don't cross it. We are in it."

"Yes sir."

While they were doing this, two cadets from HQ came along the road pretending to be two enemy soldiers returning drunk from leave. Warrant Officer Howley told them to keep going. Gwen then set up the sleeping bag, torch and notebook. When they were ready, CUO Grant and Sgt Masters did a radio check with Capt Conkey, then set off back through the bush to the RV. This time they did not use torches.

Warrant Officer Howley said, "That was well done 4 Section. Keep up the good work. Okay, you are on your own now." He walked off back along the road towards the truck.

Graham settled down; unclipping the belt on his webbing and wriggling to get comfortable. He moved a few sticks aside and then relaxed. Silence settled. The only sound was the occasional gentle sighing of the breeze in the trees. Time began to crawl past. Graham checked his watch. Only 2030hrs! All that in less than an hour!

After ten minutes there were sounds, the crunch of footfalls on gravel. From the direction of the truck came four cadets. They were moaning about always being the ones selected to dig latrines. One carried a shovel. A second had a pick. The other two had large boxes on their shoulders.

"Are they the enemy?" Morris whispered after the group had passed.

"Yes, of course," Graham replied.

"Pretending to be a work party," Gwen said.

She stuck her head into the sleeping bag, clicked on the torch, noted the time and wrote the information down.

For the next hour they lay there watching. Morris kept fidgeting and grumbling about ants. Crane let out several loud farts. Harriet dropped off to sleep and started to snore till Gwen shook her. During that time, groups of 'enemy' passed every five or ten minutes. They went past in both directions, and all were play acting some role. Capt Conkey and CSM Grey went past soon after two runners. Capt Conkey was pretending to be a prisoner of war and kept making comments to his guard. Some of these were so funny Graham had to bite his thumb to stop from laughing out loud.

Morris nudged him. "There are a lot of them. Where are they all coming from?" he asked.

"It is only HQ and 4 PL," Graham replied.

Four enemy with a radio came from the left. Then three came from the right. One was groaning loudly in pain.

"There's been another accident!" Morris hissed.

"There has not!" Graham replied. "They are just pretending. They have come from the truck."

Gwen noted this. Another ten minutes dragged by. Capt Conkey and CSM Grey came back pretending to be two 'Lost Navigators'. This time the comments were so funny some of the section actually did chuckle.

"Sssh!" hissed Gwen angrily.

More groups went by. Just before the time when they were due to withdraw a long line of armed troops came tramping past from the left. Graham counted them as they went past. He was astounded. His total was 32. He found it very impressive; the long line of troops marching determinedly and silently to the front.

Morris gaped. "There's a lot of them! Where'd they all come from?"

Graham couldn't answer but he suspected that Capt Conkey had somehow collected all the 'Control Group', HQ and 4 Pl at one end without them being seen by the patrols.

"Time to go," he said.

They stood up and thankfully dusted and stretched themselves. Gwen rolled up the sleeping bag and shoved it into the pack. Graham checked the compass and set off down the slope. The others followed.

It was easy. Ten minutes later they arrived at the RV, coming down beside the same large boulder. CUO Grant spoke as they reached the creek bed. "Which section is that?"

"4 Section sir," Graham replied. He felt relieved but also satisfied.

"Good. Well done. Did you get the job done?"

"Yes sir," Gwen replied.

"Excellent. Right, just sit there and wait for the other sections."

They did this. Graham was bursting for a pee by this and took himself off into the darkness. Then it was just a 15-minute wait. When all three sections had returned and CUO Grant was sure there was no-one missing, he led them back to camp. This took about half an hour. By then it was very cold, and Graham was glad of his pullover.

On arrival back at camp the three 'First Year' platoons were directed to sit in section lines by the CSM. Before Graham could act, Gwen took control and told them to sit in line behind her. That got him annoyed, but mostly at himself for not taking the initiative. There was another wait until all patrols had returned. The CSM and sergeants then did a headcount and Capt Conkey did a short debrief.

Capt Conkey then pointed to the lantern at the CP hutchie. "Okay CUOs, send your section commanders over to fill out patrol reports. You are also needed for an O Group. CSM, the platoon sergeants can put the others to bed. They can have half an hour to have a brew if they wish."

"Yes sir."

The question of whether 4 Section were supposed to fill out a patrol report flitted across Graham's mind. He opened his mouth to ask but Gwen beat him to it. She put her hand up.

"Sir, do you want us to make out one of these patrol reports?" she asked CUO Grant.

"Yes, you and Cadet Kirk go and have a go," CUO Grant replied.

None of the others said anything to this. Graham felt it was a real mark of confidence and hoped it meant he had done well. He and Gwen went with CUO Grant and the section commanders to the CP. When Capt Conkey looked at them Gwen spoke for them.

"CUO Grant said we were to fill out the patrol report sir."

"Oh good. You don't have to. I use it to assess which corporals might make good sergeants, but you can if you like."

Gwen nodded. "Yes please, sir," she replied.

Capt Conkey handed them the form. The pair sat side by side. Graham held his torch and Gwen did the writing. The form was self-explanatory and they had no trouble with most of it. Graham provided the navigational data and Gwen took the rest from her notebook. While they worked other corporals came and went. Among them was Cpl Hungerton, and when he saw Graham sitting there he gave him a sneering glare. Graham was tempted to ask him if he had managed to get to the right place but held his tongue just in time.

A few minutes later the truck drove in and dumped 4 Pl. It went off again and returned with HQ. CUOs and the HQ team came to the fire nearby. Warrant Officer Howley walked in out of the darkness and stood talking to the officers.

When the patrol report was completed, Gwen handed it to Capt Conkey. He thanked them and told them to go back to their platoon.

"You have done a very good job you two," he added.

That was good to hear. Graham felt his spirits lift. Then as he walked away, Warrant Officer Howley called out to him.

"Just a minute, Cadet Kirk," he said, and walked over to where Graham had stopped and took hold of his sleeve.

Graham was mystified and worried. *Am I in trouble for something?*

He examined his conscience. Warrant Officer Howley told Gwen to keep going, then, when she was out of earshot, said, "That was very well done tonight, Cadet Kirk. I knew you were a good man to have around in a crisis. From what I hear and see, you are doing very well on this camp. Good! Keep it up."

To Graham it was as though a warm fluid was flowing out from a heart that was suddenly too small, but expanding by the second.

"Thank you, sir," he replied, almost too choked up to reply.

"Off you go."

Graham walked off into the dark in a state close to euphoria. *Good man to have around in a crisis!* he told himself. He glowed at the praise.

Only to discover that his hutchie was down again and that his gear was scattered around the area. But so buoyed up was he by the praise that he just shrugged and quickly tidied up and quickly re-erected the shelter.

Then tiredness took effect, and he was asleep within minutes.

* * *

At check parade the next morning, Graham was surprised and pleased to see that Cpl Grenfell was back. He had his arm strapped and in a sling, but he was smiling.

"Not broken," he explained. "The hospital X-rayed it. It is only badly bruised; and they think I might have wrenched some muscles and things."

Graham opened his mouth to say how glad he was to see Cpl Grenfell back, but before he could say anything Gwen spoke, "That's good. We are so pleased you are back. Now we won't be split up among other sections; or have someone else made section commander."

Irritation at being cut out niggled at Graham but was diverted by the concept Gwen had mentioned: the section split up! It hadn't even occurred to him, but he now saw it as a distinct possibility.

Gwen then went on, "What about LCpl Bannister? How is he?"

"Definitely broke his nose. He will probably be in hospital for a day or so. They might even send him home," Cpl Grenfell replied.

"So we will need an acting 2ic today?" Gwen suggested.

Graham hadn't thought of that either but now saw the need. Cpl Grenfell laughed and was about to answer when a bellow from Sgt Masters urged them to hurry on parade. Later, while having breakfast Graham mulled over the events of the night. It had been exciting, and the glow from Warrant Officer Howley's praise returned. He breathed deeply and looked happily around. The air suddenly seemed fresher and the colours of the sky and trees brighter.

The morning was taken up by two activities: an individual static observation exercise and an individual moving observation course. For the first one the platoon was marched back over to the creek crossing near the turn-off to their first bivouac area. They were then seated in the shade of a tree and taken one at a time to a 'Stand'. Here either Lt McEwen or CUO Grant took a cadet and made them look at the opposite creek bank.

When Graham's turn came, he went to Lt McEwen. He liked her but had so far barely spoken to her. She asked his name. He told her, and she then said, "Now, Cadet Kirk, within twenty-five paces of you are twenty-five items of military equipment. You have three minutes to detect as many as you can. When you see something tell me at once. Your time starts... now!"

Twenty-five items! Graham looked out in a flutter of anxiety. Quickly, he scanned the area. His eyes focused and he relaxed.

"There is a boot Miss. And there is a water bottle. And over there is a set of webbing."

As quickly as he could, Graham searched with his eyes. Twenty-five! He found a matchbox, a mess tin, a hat, a sock, a shovel, a helmet, a hutchie, a hexamine stove and a packet of hexamine, a spoon, a green nylon rope, a can of food, a green container he couldn't identify (it had once contained a trip flare he was informed), a green hand towel, some camouflage cloth, a notebook and a compass.

When he ran out of time with only twenty items located, Lt McEwen pointed out a pencil, a protractor, a shiny brass cartridge case right near his feet, some green nylon cord tied between two trees, and an entrenching tool.

Having missed five items was annoying to Graham. He berated himself for being so hopeless. His feelings weren't helped by learning later that Morris had also got twenty, Crane twenty-two and Gwen twenty-four. That put him in a bad mood, and he sat alone and sulked.

The second exercise he enjoyed more. For this they moved a hundred paces back across the road to the small dry creek. Lt Maclaren briefed them for the activity. The story was that their platoon was fighting the enemy and was running short of ammo. They were a runner being sent back with an important message to company HQ, which was at the junction of the small dry creek and Speed Creek. They had to move individually along the creek bed (for navigation they were told, but actually to make sure they encountered the various incidents). On the way they would see things and must avoid trip wires, land mines, and booby traps.

Having been briefed, they sat in the shade and waited their turn. CUO Grant was sent first, and Sgt Masters remained to control the platoon and to send them off at 3 minute intervals. This exercise really appealed to Graham, and he became quite excited. When it was his turn to go, he determined to do as well as he could.

With beating heart he set off along the dry sandy creek bed, eyes questing for any sign of trouble. It came thick and fast. At almost every bend there was something, either an item to detect, or a booby trap. There were also some senior cadets playacting. Some were dressed as Opposing Force with yellow flashes. The problem was that not all the people he met were OPFOR. Some were supposed to be 'Friendly' troops. To complicate things, there were dummy 'land mines' (food tins) and 'booby trap trip wires' (green cord) to avoid. Looking for these meant constantly looking down, when all his attention was needed to search for the lurking enemy.

After being caught once, Graham quickly improved and detected all the mines and trip wires. He even detected an enemy hiding up a tree. All in all, Graham thoroughly enjoyed the exercise. At one stage he passed Capt Conkey and the CSM who were standing on the creek bank watching. That put extra stress on him as he was convinced there would be a problem to cope with. Sure enough, he met a trip wire and an enemy close together. He saw the trip wire just in time and then went into a crouch and the enemy, who sprang out from behind a big tree, missed him.

"Bang! Gotcha!" Graham called. He stood up and moved on, feeling pleased with his effort.

At the Speed Creek junction was Lt Standish. She was grouping them into pairs and sending them upstream to move along as a scout team. The creek bed was a hundred metres wide and had three distinct sandy channels separated by low sand ridges covered with bushes, weeds, and trees. A shallow trickle of water flowed along the channel nearest to the bank where they were bivouacked. Graham was teamed up with Gwen and the result was nearly a disaster as neither wanted to take orders from the other. Both wanted to be the boss.

After 500 metres and five incidents, which Graham thoroughly enjoyed, they arrived at the concrete floodway where the gravel road crossed Speed Creek. CUO Grant was waiting there. As the scout teams arrived, they sat in the shade on the sand. All were full of their exploits and there was much laughter and boasting.

While they sat there, Gwen got CUO Grant talking about the other camps and exercises he had been on. Graham learned for the first time about the Adventure Training Award. This was earned on a 9-day course run by the army. It sounded very interesting and challenging.

I'd like to have a go at that, he thought.

Gwen asked how a person got on the ATA course. CUO Grant's answer was real food for thought.

"Each unit is only allowed to send three or four candidates each year," he explained. "They must be Third Year cadets who are sixteen or older and have one more year to go and they have to be selected by the officers and pass a 'Barrier Test'."

As soon as he said that Graham was oppressed by the spectre of his past.

With my record of misbehaviour, I probably don't have much chance, he thought gloomily.

Chapter 36

STRESS

This theme was reinforced after lunch. The platoons were sent to march back across to the area where they had first camped, then on along the vehicle track past the low hill where they had done the lantern stalk and through the gate to the cattle yards. It was a very hot and sticky afternoon. The marching cadets stirred up the dust and the place swarmed with flies, which rose in buzzing clouds from the cattle dung which littered the area.

The march ended down in the bed of Speed Creek below the cattle yards. Here they were met by Capt Conkey and CSM Grey. Capt Conkey called all the CUOs and sergeants to join him while CSM Grey seated the sections. Capt Conkey and the CUOs and sergeants walked off downstream along the sandy bed of the creek. Cloud came over and a light drizzle began to fall.

The rain was very welcome to start with as it cooled them nicely. Graham had been feeling very sweaty and sore and found it a relief to sit and relax. They had nearly half an hour to wait. While they sat there several cadets asked Lt Hamilton if they could go to the toilet. As there was none nearby, he merely told the boys to go one way across the creek and the girls to go another.

I had better go, Graham thought.

To his own shame he realised he needed a nervous pee. So he stood up and hurried up the creek bank and then along it, looking for a place out of sight of everyone else. This took him about 50 metres and also straight into another stressful incident.

The ground was almost bare of grass but was covered by a thick layer of dead leaves and sticks. Deciding to go back down into the creek bed behind some bushes he could see, he changed direction and angled quickly down the slope. As he did, he glanced back out of his shoulder to check he was not visible to anyone.

As he did, he heard a sound that stirred some instinct and he slid to a halt on the slope and looked to his front, and froze. To his horror, he saw that there was a large brown snake only a couple of paces ahead. Graham was aghast. The snake was so big and so close that it was within striking distance, and it had coiled itself back ready to do so.

Graham stared at it in horror, noting that it was a very big brown snake, well over a metre long and with a sightly flattened dark head. Its beady eyes seemed to be staring straight back at him and that horrible little forked tongue, blue he noted, was flickering in and out.

Taipan! he thought, the deadliest of all North Queensland snakes.

To his dismay he found that he could not seem to make his muscles move. Then his racing mind decided that it might be best if he did not.

If I make a move, it might think I am attacking it and then it will strike, he reasoned.

For what seemed like an eternity, but was probably less than a minute, Graham stared at the reptile, appalled at the way it kept swaying its head from side to side and tensing and flexing its body, preparatory to striking. The little black eyes seemed to mesmerise him, and he saw the tip of its tail give several tiny twitches.

I must move or it will strike, Graham told himself.

But that required him to muster up more courage than he seemed to possess at that moment, and for several more seconds he stood there, rooted to the spot by fear.

Taking a deep breath, almost sobbing with anxiety, Graham summoned the courage to force himself to move. Very slowly he slid his right foot back half a pace. The movement instantly attracted the snake's attention and it flattened itself even more.

Again Graham froze. He tensed, wondering if he could spring back faster than the snake could strike. He doubted that so stayed still. He was sure that this was one of the venomous snakes whose bite would probably be deadly.

When the snake did not lunge forward, Graham again took another anxious breath and this time eased his body weight back onto his back foot, causing the snake to draw its head back a fraction. Then he slowly slid his left foot back past his right, the boot rustling the damp leaves as he did. Again the snake watched with an intensity that made Graham break into a cold sweat.

But it did not move, so Graham eased himself back and then slid his right foot back, reasoning he was now probably out of range. As he did, the snake suddenly swung away and lowered itself. It then slid off away along the slope. Graham stood and watched it go with a mixture of relief and dismay at the speed. The dismay increased when the snake slithered into a small bush and became instantly invisible.

Bloody hell! How can it hide in that? he wondered, at the same time thinking of how many similar bushes he had walked past during the week.

For several more seconds he stood there, staring at the bush and then scanning the surrounding leaves. But there was no sign of the snake and he slowly relaxed. To his shame, he realised he was sweating and panting as though he had run a race. Through his mind flitted images of what he would have down if the snake had bitten him.

Then the urgent need to pee got him moving. *At least I didn't wet myself!* he thought ruefully.

Stepping back a few more paces he glanced around and saw no one. Even though he was out in the open he quickly relieved himself. He did not want to go and stand behind a bush at that moment.

Still trembling with shock he turned and walked back, watching very carefully where he put his feet as he did. But then pride got involved and when he got back closer to the others he pretended to be sauntering casually along, despite an occasional shudder as the image of the snake slid across his mind.

Graham sat himself down with his section and listened to their conversation, his mind still full of images of calling for help while he tried to stay calm. Bit by bit the incident receded from his consciousness and his thoughts turned back to the exercise they were about to do. He knew the activity was called a 'Leadership Evaluation Exercise' but the full import of it did not strike him till Capt Conkey returned.

Capt Conkey had obviously just walked fast along the sand as he was red in the face and puffing. He took a big drink from one of his water bottles; then took over when the CSM called the company to attention.

"This next exercise is a key part in helping us select people for promotion," Capt Conkey explained. "It is one of the methods we use to select the best people, and to avoid favouritism. For those of you who don't know how we select people for promotion, this is how we try to keep things fair in this unit. We compile lists from various sources, of cadets in rank order of preference. One of those sources is this Leadership Evaluation Exercise. During this you will be assessed by seven different staff members, so, even if you have made enemies of one or two, you should get a fair hearing."

Capt Conkey then held up a piece of paper. "The second source is a thing called a Personal Qualities Report. At the end of camp each corporal will fill one out on each cadet in their section. Each sergeant will fill one out on each cadet in their platoon. Each CUO will fill one out on every cadet in their platoon. They have a marking scheme and can be added together and then averaged. So, even if you clash with one superior, you should still do alright. If you have clashed with all of them, then I suggest the problem is not with them but with you."

"The CSM and officers also fill these out on any cadet who has come to their notice for some special reason, good or bad."

With that Capt Conkey glanced at Graham, whose heart sank. Capt Conkey went on. "When we get the lists, we compare them. I also add attendance from the roll book. I don't care how good you are. If you are not a reliable attender, you are useless and I won't promote you. I would rather have an average corporal who is there, than a good one who is absent."

That also made Graham's hopes sink. Into his mind came the weekend when he had gone camping. *I haven't done myself much good,* he thought sadly.

Capt Conkey continued, "At the end of the year, after the Passing-Out Parade, we decide as a staff and select people to go on the promotion courses in December. What you need to do today is to try your hardest. If you are a bit shy, then make the effort to push yourself forward in these activities. How you perform during camp is very important in our selection."

Having explained it all Capt Conkey then separated all the corporals and lance corporals. They were grouped into sections to compete against each other.

"It would not be fair otherwise," Capt Conkey explained. "The story for this exercise is that your section are commandos behind enemy lines and have raided an enemy HQ. There has been a furious battle and you have captured some top-secret equipment. You have just pulled back and regrouped and must now withdraw. However, during the fight the corporal and 2ic went missing. They had the radio, maps, and compasses. So the section is now leaderless but must organise itself to make its way to the coast where a submarine will pick you up. Because you have no compass you have to follow the creek."

Having explained the exercise the first squad of corporals was sent off down the creek. By then the drizzle had stopped, for which Graham was thankful as he was starting to feel cold. Because there was a time separation between each squad there was plenty of time to talk and think. Graham ignored the jokes and conversation and seriously considered promotion in the Cadets.

I like this army stuff. I can do it easily. If I set my mind to it I am sure I can do it really well, he thought. *But can I now overcome the obstacle of my own past?*

Gwen gave him more food for thought by asking CSM Grey, who had been left to supervise them, how many corporals the unit needed.

"Sixteen," CSM Grey replied. "Three in each of the four rifle platoons, plus the four in HQ; the Q Cpl, the Signals Cpl, Intelligence Cpl and Medic Cpl."

Graham mulled over the figures. There were about 90 lance corporals and cadets. Sixteen of these would be promoted. *About one in four or five; two people from each section roughly,* he deduced. That got him seriously worried. He looked around at his own section and pondered who his rivals were. *Gwen for sure. And possibly Crane. And certainly LCpl Bannister.*

It was depressing. He was sure he was better than Morris and Harriet but that was all. The knowledge that he was facing stiff competition steeled him to try as hard as he could. When it was their turn, he at once tried to take control. To his chagrin, the others paid more attention to Gwen.

Graham ended up as the 'machine gunner' (although they had no LMGs, they still practiced the patrol formations and organization). In this position he walked along close behind Gwen. Crane went Scout. The others followed as Riflemen.

The first 'Stand' was merely a discussion. They were seated and told by Sgt Crossley that one of them had been badly wounded by a helicopter gunship. They had to decide what to do. The options were to try to carry him on a stretcher, hide him and hope he wasn't found (even though the enemy were in pursuit and had tracker dogs), or shoot him (because he knew their plans and secrets and might betray them under interrogation).

Graham opted for carrying the person. Crane said shoot him. Gwen supported Graham. Sgt Crossley watched and made notes on a Check Sheet. He then told them to make the stretcher. As they had been taught how to do this

The next 'Stand' required a physical response. The section patrolled along the creek bed until a 'shot' was called.

"Contact Front!" yelled Crane.

The squad reacted more or less as they had been taught. Graham didn't quibble. As machine gunner he raced up onto the steep bank on his left, went to ground in a washout behind a bush and 'returned fire'. Gwen organised the others into line and carried out an attack. Only as he went to ground did it cross Graham's mind that the dead leaves he was lying on looked very similar to the ones the big snake had been sliding across. Anxiously he glanced around, then shrugged. He had forgotten about snakes as he was focused on doing well.

Stand 3 was a theoretical problem: they had come to a minefield which they could not detour around, and they could hear the bloodhounds on their trail. CUO Madden was the assessor. This time Graham made sure he was the first to speak and he was satisfied his idea was sound: crawl slowly and scoop the sand aside to find the mines to clear a narrow path. Morris and Crane strongly disagreed and insisted that they should drop logs or throw rocks. Quite a heated argument developed in which Harriet took no part.

The section was then sent patrolling along the creek bed. This part of the creek had a steep bank beside it on the left. This was topped by short grass, a few bushes, and scattered trees. On the right was a low sandy ridge covered in trees, bushes, and weeds. As they moved along there was movement on the ridge up to the left. Capt Conkey and CSM Grey moved into view. They were standing talking and waved the section on.

There will be a problem here for sure, Graham thought. He resolved to try his best.

There was. Crane signalled 'halt', then 'enemy'. Gwen motioned to deploy under cover and went forward to look. Graham crouched and searched the bank to his left. He knew Capt Conkey and the CSM were watching, and it made him very anxious.

I really need to do well here, he told himself. But how?

Gwen came back and whispered to them, "There is a body lying in the open just past the end of this sand ridge. It has a map beside it. We need the map so we will search the area and then get it."

"Do you think there is a hidden sniper and the body is just bait?" Graham asked. They had been shown how to deal with the problem.

Gwen nodded. "Yes, I do. I want the machine gun up on the bank there; two of you. Harry, you and Crane will then search the trees on the right. Morris, you go with Graham."

Morris shook his head, "No. We should go round to the left."

He began to dispute with Gwen. As the argument developed Graham was aware that Capt Conkey and CSM Grey had walked closer to listen. He stood up.

"Stop arguing Morris. Teamwork is what counts now. Do what Gwen says. Come with me."

Without waiting to see if Morris followed, he set off up the bank at a run. On top he went on over and then turned right and went down to a crawl. To his relief, Morris did follow. They made their way forward to some trees which gave cover. From there they could see right along the creek and also out across the open country.

As he crawled into position, Graham again realised he had not been worried about snakes. His focus was on impressing Capt Conkey. With another shrug he moved to be ready.

Crane and Harriet moved as a pair, directed by Gwen. They circled around to the right through the trees and came in from the rear. The tactic paid off. A sniper was lurking in the trees, and they caught him from behind.

Capt Conkey nodded his approval. "Well done 4 Section," he said. "That was the best so far; and the quickest. You can move on along the creek to the next stand."

Graham was pleased but still anxious. Had he shown leadership; or just been an obedient pawn?

Stand 5 was a prisoner; an OPFOR 'soldier' who suddenly stepped out of the trees with his hands up. Crane called 'Bang!' and pretended to shoot him. It was CUO Broughton. He then strongly lectured them on the morality of murdering prisoners, on the moral weakness it caused, and on the value of prisoners. They discussed this; then went on along the creek.

The next Stand was a discussion. They had come to a deep creek with crocodiles in it. The enemy patrols were not far behind and they had to cross the creek. There was a narrow footbridge, but it was guarded by a slack enemy sentry who was seated at their end of the bridge with his back to them. He was cooking a meal and his rifle was leaning against a tree. What were they to do?

CUO Grant was the assessor. That put Graham under pressure again. He tried hard to contribute without making silly comments. Crane wanted to knife the sentry and throw him to the crocs. Morris suggested knocking him out and leaving him. Gwen added tie him up.

Graham shook his head. "The corporal who put the soldier here would wonder where he went. If we start a fight there may be noise, or blood or whatever. What we should do is just take him prisoner and take him and all his gear with us, then tie him up and leave him later."

"Eat his food too," Crane added.

That got a laugh. CUO Grant said nothing but took notes till their five minutes was up. He then said that Graham's suggestion was the best and told them to keep going along the creek.

As they moved on, Crane passed close to Graham. "Bloody little sniveller! Still crawling to the bloody officers!" he hissed.

The dart hurt but Graham gritted his teeth and made no reply.

The section moved on till it came to the concrete causeway where the gravel road crossed the creek. Lt Standish and Lt McEwen were there. Lt McEwen took their section. The problem was a theoretical one: the section had reached the beach and there was a boat to take them out to a waiting submarine. However the boat was too small and the sea was getting rough. If they all went, they risked sinking. Worse still, the bloodhounds could be heard close behind them. Someone had to be left behind.

First, they were required to do as secret ballot vote on who they would leave behind from the section. The names were written on pieces of paper and handed to Lt McEwen. Graham decided that Morris was the one he would leave. That done they discussed the options. During this, Crane and Morris both said that they would leave Graham behind. Crane was particularly hostile and the criticism really cut.

That was the last stand. Lt McEwen told them to return to camp and to prepare to go for a shower. Graham went last, wondering if he had done well or badly. The exercise had been interesting but stressful and left him feeling saddened by the rivalry and hurtful comments.

Their bivouac area was only 200 metres away. Cpl Grenfell was waiting and soon had them organised. As soon as Sgt Masters and CUO Grant arrived the platoon was loaded on the truck and Rover with their dirty washing, towels, clean clothes, and webbing. A 20-minute drive had them back at Camp Gedling.

This time the place was almost deserted. They were told that both 15 ACU and St Michaels were out 'in the field'. As before they were hurried through the showers as soon as 1 Pl had finished. By the time 3 Pl arrived on the truck 2 Pl had finished and were moving to eat. Mess parade was conducted the same way, a platoon at a time with CSM Grey controlling the moves.

While standing in the queue, Graham looked around and wondered where Warrant Officer Howley was. He had hoped to see him during the Leadership Evaluation Exercise and was disappointed not to see him now. Feeling unsure of himself, he went and ate his meal as quickly as he could, then sat waiting for the truck. Despite being with the platoon, he felt quite lonely and isolated. Watching the others joke and chat caused him what he knew were twinges of envy.

As soon as a platoon had showered and eaten, it was trucked back to the camp. By the time they arrived back it was dark. As he climbed down from the truck, Graham wondered if his hutchie had been cut down again but to his relief it had not been.

It was another free night. Graham hung up his washing and went to help Cpl Grenfell and Sgt Masters light a platoon campfire down in the sandy bed of Speed Creek. This led to another very stressful incident.

While walking along the sandy bed of the creek among the tree trunks and logs, Graham decided he needed to do a pee. As the nearest latrine was at least a hundred metres away up on the flat ground, he decided to just go behind a tree. As there were other cadets also looking for firewood, some of them girls, he switched off his torch and walked quickly away from them into the darkness downstream.

Seeing a clump lantana ahead he decided that would be a suitable bit of cover for privacy, so he headed for it. But as he walked around to the far side, he heard voices and saw the red glow of a cigarette.

Damn! Somebody there, he thought.

The soft, dry sand had muffled the sound of his boots so he was quite close by then, but he sensed immediately that whoever it was, was up to mischief. This was immediately made clear when a male voice swore and then a torch clicked on, and its beam swung around to shine full in his face.

Derek White's voice sounded from behind the blinding glare. "Who's that? Oh it's you, Kirk. Go away."

Graham stopped and tried to shield his eyes from the light. As he did, a second torch was clicked on and as it was also swung towards him it lit up part of the scene and reinforced his first impression: three or four people, and quite clearly for a second he saw a small bottle with a label lit up in the beam.

Whisky or rum! He thought, his identification coming from having seen such bottles at home. *They are drinking alcohol!*

And if Derek White was one of them then there might also be drugs. A wave of cold shock swept through Graham, and he shook his head. This was in a completely different level from the usual couple of smokers. But what to do?

Then another cadet spoke and Graham recognised Cpl Moore from 4 PL. "Piss off, Kirk! And don't you tell on us."

Derek White added to this, "Yeah, keep your mouth shut. You dob and we will bash ya!"

Graham didn't argue. A combination of fear and prudence got him turned around and hurrying away immediately. As he strode off with the torch beams still on him, he heard Moore again call, "Don't you run to the officers and tell or you'll regret it. Keep your mouth shut shitface!"

The torches clicked off and left Graham half blind. He slowed so as not to trip on a log. He found his heart was hammering and his emotions boiled with a mixture of anger and anxiety. His first reaction was to go and tell the officers but then, to his shame, he felt afraid. But he also still needed to do a pee, so he swerved and headed across to the far side of the creek bed. Once he was certain he was well away from anyone he stopped behind the trunk of a big tree and relieved himself. To his shame, he found he was panting and trembling.

But what to do?

His inclination warred with his courage (or lack of it) and with the general Australian cultural contempt for 'dobbers'. Even hesitating made him feel ashamed but the more he thought about it the more he felt afraid to do anything. He tried to rationalise it by telling himself that Derek White and his mates were like that, that they did it at school and probably did it every night at camp. But it all left him feeling bad about himself.

And will I be able to prove it, or will it be my word against theirs and then a bashing when we are back at school? he thought.

So in the end, and to his shame, he did nothing. Instead he used his torch to find more firewood and then returned to the fire. That made it worse as he had to speak to Sgt Masters and Cpl Grenfell but could not bring himself to dob.

The fire was going by then and when Cpl Moore, Derek White, and Dru all appeared out of the darkness and walked past giving him hard looks he felt even worse. But they had obviously stopped drinking and, he guessed, hidden the evidence.

So for most of the evening Graham sat feeling contempt for himself and shame. He silently watched and listened to the antics, jokes and stories of the others but did not join in, not wanting to stir up more rivalry or ill-will. Peter and Stephen joined him for a while and that cheered him up a little and he was careful to hide his feelings from them.

What Graham did note, and which also worried him, was Crane, Brooke, and White following Angela and Rita around, flirting with them. Later they all walked off along the creek bed into the night.

I wonder where they are going? And to do what? he thought.

It was easy to guess and made him feel disgusted; mostly with himself for being a hypocrite. He knew he was randy and jealous, and he had continual flashbacks to being with Amelia.

Later, back in the platoon area, Crane and Rita came walking out of the darkness. Crane met Graham by accident. Crane stopped and looked guilty. Graham was tempted to ask where they had been but held his tongue. In the event he did not need to.

Crane snarled at him, "Don't you say anything Kirk, or else."

"Or else what?" Graham snapped back. Somewhat to his surprise he found he wasn't at all frightened of Crane. "Don't worry Crane, it is your conscience. I'm not a dobber."

But it was a dilemma. If Crane and Rita really had been up to mischief then rumours would spread through the unit, then the schools. That would harm the reputation of the unit. For the first time Graham realised he really cared about the cadet unit and its reputation. Still tormented by not telling the officers about the alcohol, he dropped into sleep with a troubled mind.

The following morning Graham received another jolt. On the morning parade Capt Conkey thanked them for their good behaviour the previous evening. That made Graham bite his lip and glance at Rita.

Capt Conkey then explained that two sections were short of a section 2ic; 4 Section because LCpl Bannister was still in hospital; and 7 Section because the 2ic had not come to camp.

"To remedy this we are going to promote two cadets to lance corporal. Would the following cadets please fall out: Cadet Costigan from 7 Section and Cadet Copeland from 4 Section."

As soon as he had heard that two lance corporals were to be promoted, Graham's hopes had gone up, even though he knew it was unlikely he would be one. Still, it hurt to be passed over. He was jealous, and he knew it. And that rankled too.

I will win a stripe yet, he vowed.

Chapter 37

RESOLVE

During the next two days, a new ambition crystallised in Graham's mind. The catalyst for this was CUO Grant. Graham now admired the CUO enormously, although he would not admit to himself that it was hero worship. CUO Grant seemed to be everything he wanted to be: capable, strong, the leader. He exuded that indefinable something that Graham decided was an aura of confidence allied to a natural power of command.

And he's very handsome, he admitted, though only to himself, and then only reluctantly; not wanting to admit to anything that might be construed as homosexual tendencies. *He has a way with the girls too,* he noted enviously, watching from a distance as the CUO joked with Sheila Sherry.

I want to be like him. I want to be a Cadet Under-Officer, Graham decided. This ambition firmed into a strong resolve with extra-ordinary speed once he had thought of it.

That got his mind working again. *What are my chances? Can I overcome my bad reputation?* he wondered.

The figures were daunting. There were about 120 cadets of all ranks in the unit; but only four of them were CUOs.

About 1:30. That is less than one per platoon!

That was a dismaying thought. He brooded on this for a while but rather than being daunted he was challenged.

I will give it my best shot, he resolved.

The decision made Graham flung himself into training with all his heart. No more smart-alec joking or playing the fool. Now it was serious work.

The first step is to get on the promotion course for corporal at the end of the year, he told himself.

His changed attitude was quickly noticed by both his peers and his superiors. Crane and Morris both openly taunted him.

Crane sneered. "Bloody crawler! You are just snivelling for a stripe!"

The jibes stung but Graham managed to smile and hide his hurt. In spite of the teasing, he worked as hard as he could. Luckil,y the training helped. To him it was very interesting. For most of Day 6 they were trained on the use of the Steyr rifle. The instruction was done by four corporals from the 31st Battalion, the Townsville based Army Reserve infantry unit. Two of the NCOs were also adult staff in the Heatley cadet unit so understood well how to train cadets.

Graham's application to the rifle lessons was intense. He paid careful attention to the demonstrations and explanations and then practiced. If the instructor said to do it once, he did it three times. By the end of six lessons he had reached such a level of skill that he was starting to feel comfortably familiar with the weapon, to the extent of automatically placing his hand in the correct places. Several times the instructor, Cpl Barker, complimented him on doing it well.

That boosted Graham's spirits, but then he had his feelings hurt. During the break between lessons, Graham leaned his rifle against a tree.

CUO Grant called out, "Cadet Kirk, don't ever lean your rifle against a tree. A piece of bark could slip into the barrel. Then, if you fired a live bullet, the barrel could burst; explode in your face and blind you."

"Yes sir." Graham burned with mortification. His deepest desire now was to do it all right, to be a good soldier.

During Period 8 in the afternoon, the weapons were cleaned and stored in strong boxes in a vehicle. In Period 9 they prepared for a night patrol exercise, filling water bottles, packing jackets and checking torches and so on. Graham was relieved to note that Cpl Grenfell was coming with the section. To hide the plaster cast on his arm, it had been covered with some camouflage cloth.

During Period 10 they were driven to another training area.

As he climbed onto the truck, Graham felt happier and healthier than he could ever remember. It was a lovely cool evening with a glorious red sunset. The other cadets were also in a good mood. Even Crane and Morris let up on the teasing.

They were driven out along the gravel road to the bitumen road. Here the truck turned right and went south for 2 km to where a concrete bridge crossed another dry sandy creek the size of Speed Creek. The sign said GRANITE CREEK. As soon as he debussed, Graham took out his map and located the place.

1 Pl was already there, seated beside the road at a point where a vehicle track wound off west through open bush and grassland. The vehicles turned around and went back to get 3 Pl. 4 Pl and HQ had already been deployed into the area to act as the Control Group and Opposing Force for the exercise. Before the truck returned, Lt Hamilton arrived in his Rover with the evening meal. CSM Grey organised them to eat.

The meal was eaten sitting in the short grass as the sun sank behind a distinctive conical hill to the west. Capt Conkey called the CUOs and Sergeants over and briefed them and they then walked off along the vehicle track.

Once all had eaten, including 3 Pl, Capt Conkey and CSM Grey ordered the corporals to bring their sections and to follow him. By then it was getting dark. The sections filed off in numerical order in a long single file. Capt Conkey made them stop at the barbed wire fence on the other side of the road while he demonstrated by the light of a torch how an infantryman crawled under a fence; on his back with boots first at an angle, using his rifle to hold the bottom strand away from himself as he wriggled under. He then made them all roll under the fence.

They walked through knee high grass up a long gentle slope on the eastern side of the main road. Ahead was a long hill named Hill 398 after its spot height on the map. Graham assumed they were going to climb it but when they reached the break of slope at its base and about 200 metres from the road Capt Conkey halted them and made them sit behind their section commanders. This had them facing west, back towards the bitumen road.

He then briefed them for ‘Exercise Border Crossing’. The story was that they were in a mythical Middle Eastern country called ‘Rumdrunkia’ and were ‘Freedom Fighters’ from the neighbouring country, Badumba. They were using Rumdrunkia as a base to mount raids back into their own country.

Capt Conkey got them to use their torches to study the map and pointed out the main topographical features: the highway, the ‘Border Fence’, Granite Creek, Speed Creek, Target Hill, and Hill 430. The exercise area was about a kilometre from one side to the other. Winding across it were several small dry creeks, one of which was nicknamed ‘Wriggly Creek’.

“You are going to sneak across the border to carry out a series of special missions," Capt Conkey explained. "Each section will have a separate objective. You are all to go by different routes. For security sake in case you get captured and interrogated by the Badumba Secret Police, you are only going to be told your first leg. Once you get there, and give the correct password, you will be sent on to the next leg."

He then gave them a full set of Patrol Orders. Even though they were delivered to the section corporals Graham wrote most of it down himself, in spite of Crane's sneering jibes. The idea of the exercise really excited him. It would be a real challenge.

We have to sneak across the border past the guards, avoid the patrols and enemy spies to get to an objective, then back to safety, he thought.

Next, bright green cloth flashes were issued as 'lives', to be surrendered one at a time if they were caught by the opposing patrols.

"If you lose both you stay with them as prisoners until the end of the exercise," Capt Conkey explained.

Oh, we don't want that sort of shame, Graham thought. He resolved to try his hardest.

The exercise lived up to his expectations. He thoroughly enjoyed it. The sections were sent off separately. 4 Section set off at 2000hrs and walked slowly down in single file to the 'Border'. Two Land Rovers with spotlights were patrolling back and forth along the Main Road and there were foot patrols on the other side of the second barbed wire fence beyond them, so it took some skill to time it right, to crawl under the first fence; hide in the ditch beside the road to avoid a patrol; crawl under the second fence and then ghost across and into the trees beyond. They were helped by another section which ran into a patrol up to their left just as they went to cross.

Only later did it occur to Graham that he had not been thinking about snakes the whole time.

For the next three hours, the section crept, walked, and battled through the dark bush. They were sent from a 'Camel Salesman' at 'Two Buckets Junction' in Wriggly Creek to a 'Date Seller' further down the creek; to a 'woodcutter' who had a campfire at the junction of Speed Creek and Granite Creek.

To Graham's pleasure, this turned out to be Warrant Officer Howley. He gave them a glowing 'Cyalume' stick which he said was a Uranium fuel rod for making nuclear weapons which they were to take back to

Rumdrunkia. He then sent them to a 'Fisherman' who had a fire 700 metres down the bed of Speed Creek. Here they met Cpl Coralie Bates' 3 Section going the other way.

On the return trip, they twice had to lie in the grass to avoid patrols. One of these was led by Cpl Moore, and when he heard Moore's voice Graham experienced sharp feeling of shame and regret at not having told the officers about the alcohol. There was also a strong sense of satisfaction at outwitting Moore and his section of 'Senior' cadets.

Several times the section snuck past Check Points they were not supposed to visit. There were frequent sounds of clashes in the night as other sections ran into enemy patrols but 4 Section managed to avoid them all and arrived back at the bitumen road 20 minutes before the finish time for the exercise.

Graham's opinion of Cpl Grenfell went up even more. *He is very good,* he thought. *His navigation was spot on and he was always cool and in control, even with his arm in a sling.*

At the RV was the truck and Lt Maclaren's Rover. Cpl Sherry's section was already there so Graham sought out Peter and happily compared notes. Cpl Collin Whyte's 7 Section arrived next, and Stephen joined them. Over the next half hour three other sections came in. Capt Conkey kept checking on the radio. At 2245hrs he ordered them all to move back to the start point.

This entailed walking for a kilometre along the bitumen road. Morris and Harriet grumbled mightily about sore feet and blisters. Graham ignored them. He felt on top of the world.

That was a great exercise! I really enjoyed that, he told himself.

On arrival at the RV they were seated in sections. The CUOs, Sergeants, and Control Group joined them. CSM Grey did a careful check of numbers with the platoon sergeants. When he was satisfied all were present, Capt Conkey debriefed them and congratulated them on a very successful exercise. Then the officers began ferrying the company back to camp in the vehicles.

3 Pl went first in the truck. 2 Pl was then loaded into three Rovers. Graham made sure he went in Warrant Officer Howley's Land Cruiser. Warrant Officer Howley saw him and smiled.

"How's it going, young fella?"

"Great sir! That was a really good exercise."

"Did you get through without being caught?"

"Yes sir, we did," Graham replied with pride.

Only four sections out of nine had managed that. Seven sections had made it to their Objectives and back. Two, Cpl Hunter's and Cpl Telford's, had been caught twice and 'wiped out'.

"Good. Well done!" Warrant Officer Howley replied.

He then climbed into the driver's seat and started up. Cpl Grenfell sat next to him, and they talked about the exercise all the way back to camp. Graham sat in the back and listened avidly to every word.

It was nearly midnight when they arrived back. Even so they were allowed to brew a cup of hot drink if they wished, before being put to bed. This did not include the CUOs, Sgts, and Cpls, who were rostered to guard the vehicle with the weapons in it, two on at all times, for an hour each.

Day 7 was even more interesting for Graham. It was another of those experiences which were windows on another world. After the usual check parade, breakfast, inspection, company parade, etc, they were lined up in platoon groups and seated in the shade. At 0800hrs a convoy of six army trucks drove in and stopped. Platoons were loaded aboard, each truck having an adult staff member in the back with the cadets to supervise them for safety.

The convoy included the three Rovers and their own truck. To Graham's eyes, the convoy looked big and impressive as it drove out along the gravel road. It made him feel part of something important and worthwhile and gave him a yearning to do more. He recognised it as the same emotion he had experienced when he had watched the senior cadets head off for an exercise; a strong desire to be part of it, to be in the thick of things.

The convoy drove out to the bitumen road, turned right and went south for a kilometre, then turned left onto another gravel road which led into the army's High Range Training Area. They crossed Granite Creek and were unloaded at a dry, dusty place Graham learned was called Horne Dam. Nearby was an airstrip.

Here the trucks left them and went back to pick up 15 ACU. The company was briefed, then split into four groups. For the next three hours they were 'Bull ringed' from one activity to another. The most popular was an inspection of a tracked armoured personnel carrier, followed by a ride in it. There were three APCs there and these really impressed Graham with their apparent power. He climbed all over one, fascinated by the technicalities of it. The crew explained everything with good natured tolerance; then set out to show off by driving up apparently unclimbable creek banks. It was all dust, rumbling bumps and roaring diesels for fifteen minutes.

Most of the cadets were reluctant to get out and move on. The second Stand was a safety lecture by the Ammunition Technical Officers about types of ammunition and bombs. The thrust of the lesson was safety, not to touch or try to tamper with any ordnance that they found or that someone had stolen. Graham found that fascinating as well. He was particularly impressed by the style and confidence of the bomb disposal men.

Stand 3 was a display of different weapons and items of equipment with a section of regular soldiers to demonstrate and explain it all. Graham itched to touch and handle it all and studied the regulars with open admiration.

These blokes are real soldiers, he thought. *I wonder if I would like to be a soldier?* It was an idea he had already considered but now it had more substance.

Stand 4 was a display by military engineers. Graham had heard and read about sappers but had never paid them much attention. His thoughts had been focused on what he considered to be the 'warlike', 'fighting' troops. After watching the squad of sappers from 18 Combat Engineer Squadron for half an hour, he had completely changed his mind. Here was a group as skilled and warlike as anyone could ever desire! Assault demolitions, mine warfare, assault river crossings, tunnel searches, plus all the building tasks of roads, airfields, bridges and so on.

At 1100hrs the convoy of trucks arrived again. It unloaded St Michaels College Cadet Unit. Graham studied them carefully and agreed with Cpl Grenfell's assessment, "A disorganised rabble."

The Cairns company was loaded onto the same trucks and set off up into the hills. As they did, a Hercules transport plane roared in to land on the airstrip. Helicopters could be seen in the distance. It was all very military and interesting. Graham barely noticed the heat and the dust, indeed relished them as they gave him the feeling of being part of the regular army exercise they were driving through.

They drove up a steep mountain road and came to a road junction where a check point manned by very dirty, tired looking Military Police. These stopped them and Graham had time to study their uniforms and equipment. He was particularly interested in their automatic pistols. After a while the convoy was allowed to go on. Ten minutes later, they were unloaded in the bush. 15 ACU were waiting there and climbed onto the trucks.

This time the company was taken to watch an artillery battery firing. The guns were all deployed over hundreds of metres and were under camouflage nets. Everyone was issued hearing protection and, after a safety brief, moved to watch. While a regular officer was giving them an explanation, one of the guns fired. Even though it was a hundred metres off Graham jumped in fright, along with almost everyone else. The suddenness of the shock wave was nothing at all like the noise guns made on the movies or TV!

Each section of cadets was led up to a gun by a regular soldier and allowed to watch from the rear while a fire mission was fired. The sheer power and violence of it all was a sobering eye-opener. So also was the skilled teamwork and comradeship of the regular gunners. Graham studied them closely, fascinated and jealous. They looked like they belonged, and he knew he wanted to belong too.

He also noted that CUO Grant looked very similar to the younger regular officers, the same style and confidence. A fit looking young captain met the OOCs and CUOs and took them to the Command Post. That made Graham even more determined to become a CUO. The sergeants were all given the opportunity to help load a gun, and then to fire it. Graham stood enviously at the back, fingers in his ears to hold in the ear protection.

Whoompf!

For a split second he glimpsed the shell in flight. "Incredible!" he cried. It would travel 35 km in a few seconds. It was certainly impressive. *And deadly!*

After the visit to the artillery, they were shuttled a platoon at a time to another range a few kilometres away. Here they were given a sandwich lunch and tested by regular soldiers on their 'Test of Elementary Training' on the Steyr. If they passed, they were grouped into 'Details' and sent forward to fire the weapon.

To Graham's satisfaction, Warrant Officer Howley was one of the coaches standing on the firing mound. As the ten cadets halted, Warrant Officer Howley saw him.

He walked along to him and said to the regular corporal next to Graham, "I'll take this one, thanks Corp."

The corporal nodded. "Yeah, righto sir," he replied. Graham was simultaneously pleased and flustered.

Under Warrant Officer Howley's eagle eye Graham sweated through the shoot. His mind raced as he tried to remember everything.

I don't want to make a mistake with him watching, he thought anxiously.

He didn't. He fired 20 rounds and found it a quite thrilling experience. He also found there was something intensely satisfying in squeezing off each shot. The glint of the sun on the brass cartridge cases, the smell of the hot gun oil and burnt cordite, the feel of the weapon, all impressed themselves on his memory. After the weapons were unloaded and cleared safe, they were told to move forward to change the targets.

As Graham walked forward the hundred paces, Warrant Officer Howley walked beside him. "That was good weapon handling, young Kirk. And from the look of it your shooting is pretty good too."

Graham puffed with pleasure. The target had a close group, nearly every shot within a 10-centimetre circle.

"I like this rifle sir. It is a good weapon," he said.

"It is. How are you enjoying the day?"

"Fascinating sir," Graham replied.

"Enjoying the camp?"

"Yes sir. I love it," Graham replied honestly.

"Good. I've heard you are doing well. Keep it up. I've got a lot of faith in you," Warrant Officer Howley said.

"Thanks sir," Graham replied.

He was touched and embarrassed. The man had every right to hate him and give him hell but instead was going out of his way to help. It was a lot to think about.

After the shoot the cadets cleaned the rifles and then were trucked back down the mountains to their camp. It was 1700hrs by then. As soon as they arrived, they were issued with One-man 24-hour Cadet Ration Packs and told to eat.

The Ration Pack was also a whole new learning experience. Graham happily studied all the contents as he cooked his tea. He felt very happy. The only thing disturbing his enjoyment was the niggling thought that the camp was nearly over.

Only a few days to go, he thought with regret.

When he considered recent events, he was amazed at how his life had changed in the last few weeks. From despising army cadets as military morons he was now intensely proud to be one.

After tea they were given orders for a night defence exercise and then deployed to protect their part of the company perimeter. They did a practice 'Stand to' as it got dark, with everything packed, including their hutchies. In their orders they had been warned that St Michael's unit might be going to try to raid them. Graham hoped they would.

As he lay next to Gwen facing out along the vehicle access, track patrols from 4 Pl and HQ moved out. These had radios and were going to provide early warning of any enemy approaching. Graham watched them enviously. He wished passionately that he was going out with them. The rumour was that some of the senior cadets were going to locate the St Michael's camp and to raid it. Now that would be fun!

When it was completely dark the platoon 'stood down' so that there was only one sentry post per platoon. This was located near where Graham and Gwen were positioned. He was on duty for the first hour but then woke Morris to take over. As soon as he was sure Morris was on duty, Graham unrolled his sleeping bag and slid into it.

He was asleep within minutes.

Chapter 38

SINGLED OUT

Only ten minutes passed after Graham dropped off to sleep before CUO Grant came up quietly from behind the sentries. Graham was woken by the movement and listened in as the CUO passed on information to the two on guard.

"HQ have just received a radio report from our patrol watching the highway. They say that an army Land Rover has stopped there and that people have got out and are walking this way. They estimate eight enemy."

"St Michael's is it sir?" Graham asked.

"Got to be. 130ACU went home today and 15ACU and 122 Mackay are up on High Range," CUO Grant said. "Whoever they are, they must be coming to raid us. The platoon will be standing-to. So be alert."

He moved back into the darkness and Graham heard him wake Cpl Grenfell and talk quietly to him. Soon afterwards Cpl Grenfell came around, waking everyone up and checking they were ready. Graham grinned in the darkness. This was better, a bit of action! He slid out of bed and pulled on his webbing. Because it was a tactical exercise he had been sleeping fully dressed and with his boots on, so he was ready in a few seconds.

Time crept past. Ants crawled over them. A night bird hooted and flapped away. Sgt Masters came around with another message: the patrol over at the turnoff to their first bivouac area had reported four enemy passing along the road.

"Only four? Where did the others go?" Graham asked.

"Probably split up to hit us from different directions," Sgt Masters suggested.

He moved quietly away. Cpl Grenfell came and stationed himself close behind them. Soon afterwards CUO Grant did the same. Graham strained his eyes to peer into the night. Capt Conkey joined CUO Grant. They whispered for a moment; then Capt Conkey ghosted up beside Graham and crouched down.

"They are coming in along the track now," Capt Conkey whispered. "Here, have a look through this."

He passed an object to Graham. It was the Infra-Red night sight. Graham gripped it and raised it to his right eye, then pressed the button to activate it. The bush sprang into view in an eerie green glow. Moving through it, and clearly visible about 50 paces off, were the four raiders.

"Heading for One Platoon sir," he whispered.

Capt Conkey took the sight; peered through it, grunted and ghosted off across the dirt track to the left into the patch of mulga scrub occupied by 1 PL. Graham strained his eyes and ears to try to keep track of the raiders. To his annoyance, he heard the murmur of voices over in the 1 PL area.

"Halt!" called a voice over in 1 PL.

There was a scuttling noise then a voice yelled 'Bang!' and then the flash of torches. Voices shouted. CUO Broughton's voice yelled above the din as he attempted to control his people. There was the sound of running and two dark figures went to ground ten metres in front of Graham and Gwen. By now Graham was alive with excitement. His heart was pounding so hard he had trouble hearing. He lifted the stick he was using as a pretend rifle and aimed it.

Were the enemy advancing? Yes, they were!

He licked his lips and waited till the first one was almost close enough to touch. "Halt!"

"Shit!" the raider cried in fright. He yelled and jumped to his feet a second after Graham shouted 'Bang!'

The raider ran back as other cadets also started 'shooting'. Cpl Grenfell yelled to stop others from firing and Graham clearly heard CUO Grant order 5 Section not to fire unless probed. Silence settled as the raiders pulled back.

Ten minutes later they tried again, this time over along the bank of Speed Creek on 1 Platoon's left. Again silence settled, to be broken by a probe which came in against 6 Section and which rolled on around to 3 Platoon's area to the right. For fifteen minutes the night was alive with action.

It was nearly 2200hrs by then. CUO Grant came along to check. He informed them that another friendly recon patrol, which had been sent to the west to watch the vehicle track which ran beside the dismantled

Greenvale Railway, reported a vehicle had passed them and turned down the gravel road towards the company.

As the vehicle did not come into view along the gravel road, it had to be assumed that it had stopped somewhere between the railway and the company position. This kept everyone on their toes, in expectation of more probes.

So far none of the raiders had managed to penetrate the perimeter. Silence settled and the night began to drag. It grew steadily colder. Cadets started to grumble or drop off to sleep. CUO Grant, Sgt Masters and Cpl Grenfell came along frequently to keep them awake and alert.

Half an hour passed. Suddenly there were shouts and lights half a kilometre off at the turnoff to the first bivouac area.

"That must be one of our patrols in contact with the raiders," Graham surmised.

The action died down and silence resumed. Cpl Grenfell came along to relay a message from Coy HQ: the contact out at the road had been our HQ patrol there ambushing the raiders. They had hit them and sent them running off in surprise.

"But stay alert. That was only one group of four. There is a second somewhere around; and probably a third from that vehicle that came along the railway," Cpl Grenfell cautioned.

Just after 2300hrs another report came in. The friendly patrol led by CUO Hansen, which was in ambush beside the gravel road at a dry creek crossing half a kilometre to the west had ambushed five enemy. The sound of this 'battle' was audible in the company area and made Graham grin with delight. CUO Hansen reported the enemy had run off into the night in confusion.

Soon after that Sgt Cleland's patrol, which had been watching the enemy vehicle out at the main road, reported they had attacked it. They had waited till an enemy raiding party had returned to the vehicle and were standing talking to the officers there, then attacked. Our patrol had then withdrawn back into the night to an RV.

It all sounded very successful. Capt Conkey and CSM Grey came around to check, warning that at least one enemy patrol was still out.

"None of their raids has succeeded yet so their pride will be badly hurt. I expect them to make another effort so stay alert," he said.

"Yes sir," Graham replied.

"I wish I could go to the toilet," Gwen muttered.

"You can if you like. Out you go. Just don't be alarmed if the enemy raiders catch you with your pants down," Graham replied with a chuckle.

"That's what I'm worried about," Gwen replied gloomily. "I think I'll organise a dunny patrol of girls."

She rose and went off to see Cpl Grenfell. Ten minutes later, Cpl Grenfell joined Graham. "Five sheilas are heading down to the latrine. Don't shoot them by mistake."

He remained with Graham till the girls returned. By then it was after midnight. Now tiredness and cold took the shine off their enthusiasm. Capt Conkey decided to 'Stand Down', each platoon to have only section sentry posts. That was no help to Graham because, according to the roster, he was on duty from 0001 to 0200hrs. He shrugged. So what? He wasn't tired and wanted to be awake in case there was more action.

The company settled down. Time passed slowly. It was very dark, with no moon. At 0100hrs Gwen woke Crane, who took over from her. Another radio report came from the main road. The enemy Rover there had driven off back towards Camp Gedling. That only left the patrol which had come in along the railway.

Soon after that the moon came up, a half-moon which cast long shadows as it rose. Graham was glad to see it as it made it much easier to keep watch.

Then 0200hrs arrived at last. Graham rose stiffly and went to rouse Morris. While he was doing this, he heard voices over at Coy HQ and saw a torch shining on a map. Capt Conkey, Warrant Officer Howley and some of the officers were discussing something. CSM Grey came looking for CUO Grant who went to join the officers. Graham was curious but knew he could not just go and butt in. Instead he got Morris out of his sleeping bag, with some difficulty, and ensured he was on duty. Once that was done, Graham unrolled his own sleeping bag.

He had only just lain down when someone came walking over to him. It was CUO Grant. He knelt down.

"Cadet Kirk, are you awake?"

"Yes sir."

"You are wanted at HQ," CUO Grant said.

Mystified and worried Graham examined his guilty conscience. But no obvious lapse came to mind, so he rose, swung on his webbing, and followed the CUO over to where the officers were meeting. As he arrived, Warrant Officer Howley looked up, his face very serious in the torchlight.

"Ah good! Here's my offsider. I'll just brief him and get going sir," Warrant Officer Howley said, looking from Graham to Capt Conkey.

My offsider! Graham could not believe his ears. He stood uncertainly. "Sir?"

"This is the plot, Cadet Kirk. CUO Hansen's patrol, which is here," he pointed to the creek crossing half a kilometre to the west, "have reported they can hear someone shouting to the south of them somewhere along Speed Creek. We think it might be that patrol from St Michael's in trouble. We are going out to check." He indicated CSM Grey and Sgt Strutton.

Graham nodded. He was thrilled but puzzled. "Yes sir," he answered.

"Grab your webbing. Make sure your water bottles are full and that you have your torch," Warrant Officer Howley said.

"Got my webbing on sir. I'm ready to go," Graham replied.

"Good lad! okay, let's move," Warrant Officer Howley replied.

He stood and led the way across to the CP where Sgt Strutton collected a radio. Graham looked into the camouflaged CP with interest. The Signals Cpl and Intelligence Cpl were sitting there with a large map in front of them. A shaded light hung over the table on which were two radios, code books, signals log and notes.

As soon as the radio was checked and on net, Warrant Officer Howley led the patrol on through 3 PL area, speaking to CUO Madden on the way. In the moonlight, visibility was quite good and they walked very fast in single file, following a cattle pad along the top of the creek bank. Warrant Officer Howley used a torch for speed and safety. The others followed him. As they strode along, Warrant Officer Howley said to Graham, who was immediately behind him, "I suppose you are wondering why I have singled you out for this?"

"Yes sir."

"Well, the OC doesn't want to use the platoon commanders or platoon sergeants if there is a likelihood of another raid, and all the seniors except a few from HQ are out on patrol and won't be in till dawn. As well, I reckon you are the fittest cadet in the whole unit and a good navigator at night and we might need that."

"Yes sir." Graham was very pleased. The compliments glowed like a warm, golden flame deep inside him.

Warrant Officer Howley set a cracking pace. Within five minutes they were at the junction of the small sandy creek and Speed Creek. Beyond that they followed the dry sandy bed of Speed Creek as there was a rough little hill on their left. There was a real dapple of shadows down in the creek bed from the moon shining through the numerous trees which grew along both banks and in the bed of the creek. There was a shallow trickle of water, but they splashed across it with no difficulty.

Suddenly, Warrant Officer Howley stopped. "Hush! Listen!"

They did. Clearly, but faintly, Graham heard a cry.

"Further down the creek, sir. Someone calling out alright," he said.

"Not a curlew?" Warrant Officer Howley asked.

"No sir, definitely a person. There it is again," Graham answered.

CSM Grey nodded. "Someone calling for help," he said.

Warrant Officer Howley started walking. "Let's move!"

The group continued down the creek, moving at such a fast walk that Graham was soon sweating and gasping. The sound of shouting grew more and more distinct.

"Definitely someone in trouble," CSM Grey said.

"Yes," Warrant Officer Howley replied. He stopped and cupped his hands. "Coooeeee! Coooeeee!"

"Help! Help! Over here!" called a voice further along the creek.

Warrant Officer Howley broke into a run. The others followed, labouring along on the soft sand. After a hundred paces Graham was gasping and felt ready to drop but pushed himself to keep going.

A torch flickered in the blackness under the trees. "Oh thank God!" a voice cried as they raced up to it.

Two senior cadets from St Michael's, a sergeant and a corporal, were standing in the darkness. Warrant Officer Howley shone his torch on them.

"Who are you? What is the problem?"

"Snake bite sir," cried the sergeant in an almost hysterical voice.

"Where? Who?"

"Not us. Not here. Back there somewhere," the sergeant replied. "We... we tried to find you. We've been up and down this creek for an hour."

"For an hour! When did the snake bite happen?" Warrant Officer Howley snapped.

Graham felt his stomach tighten up and his heart go cold. An hour! A snake bite! If it was a Taipan the kid was done for.

"About 0100, sir," replied the sergeant, his voice almost a sob.

Warrant Officer Howley checked his watch. "0225. Good God almighty! Why didn't you radio?"

"We haven't got one sir," the sergeant replied.

"Haven't got one! Your unit sent you off on an exercise like this without one! Never mind. Sgt Strutton, call HQ and warn them. We need that vehicle and a stretcher. Get them as close to this Grid reference as they can. Now sergeant, take us to the victim."

The sergeant hung his head. "I'm not sure where he is now sir."

In the torch light Graham noted Warrant Officer Howley's lips compress into a grim line. "Okay son, calm down. Is he in the creek? And is there someone with him?"

"No sir. He is up in the bush. He has two cadets with him. We left them to try to find you. We knew your company was in the creek somewhere," the sergeant replied.

Warrant Officer Howley shook his head. "In the bush! Bloody hell! Which side of the creek?"

This time the sergeant broke into a sob. "I don't know, sir. We went up and down so many times I lost track."

"Right lad, calm down. Can you show us on the map where you think they might be?" Warrant Officer Howley said quietly, placing a comforting hand on the distressed boy's arm.

"No sir. We were lost. We got hit by an ambush and ran into the bush. Then we didn't know where we were," the sergeant confessed, misery and humiliation in every line of his face.

Graham now spoke. "Sir, they might have been hit by CUO Hansen's patrol over towards the old railway."

"Could be," Warrant Officer Howley agreed. He turned to the sergeant. "Which way did your vehicle come to drop you off- along the highway or along the old railway?"

"Old railway sir," replied the distressed sergeant.

Warrant Officer Howley nodded. "Good. Now, after you ran into our patrol did you cross this creek?"

"Yes," replied the sergeant.

"East of the creek then?" Graham suggested.

"Could be," Warrant Officer Howley agreed. He turned back to the sergeant. "Have they got torches?"

"Yes sir. And we lit a fire."

"A fire! Good lad. CSM! Run up that bank and look. Cadet Kirk, go the other way," Warrant Officer Howley rapped, pointing right and left as he did.

Graham didn't wait. He sprinted into the shadows towards the left bank of the creek. As he went, he heard Warrant Officer Howley say, "Any luck with that radio, CQ?"

"No sir. I had them a few minutes ago but can't get them now."

"Try to call one of the patrols. They might be able to relay," Warrant Officer Howley said.

Hearing that caused Graham another spasm of apprehension as he ran. He dodged through a line of trees, splashed his way across the shallow stream and scrambled up the grassy eastern bank to the top. Ahead of him was a gentle ridge. He ran up this, his eyes working well enough in the starlight to see rocks and logs. Within three minutes he was on top of a rocky knoll. Almost at once he spotted the glow of a fire among the trees off to the southwest.

"Here!" he shouted. "Warrant Officer Howley!" he bellowed. "I can see a fire."

His shout was answered and within a minute the others had joined him. Warrant Officer Howley clapped him on the shoulder.

"Good lad! CQ, have you got contact on that radio yet?"

"No sir. Can't get anyone," Sgt Strutton replied.

Warrant Officer Howley muttered; then pulled out his map and torch. "Where do you reckon we are?"

The question seemed to be directed at Graham who stood next to him. He bent and peered at the map, then pointed. "Here sir, on the end of this spur running down from Hill 376 to Speed Creek."

"Yes, that's what I think too," Warrant Officer Howley agreed.

He studied the map for a minute. "It is about a kilometre back to camp. CSM, I want you and Cadet Kirk to run back. Run, got it? Five minutes that should take you. Ten at the most. In twenty minutes I want a vehicle across Speed Creek here."

He marked CSM Grey's map with a pencil. "We will go on and get the casualty and carry him to the creek. Now get going. Have Capt Conkey phone the ambulance."

"Yes sir," CSM Grey replied. He and Graham turned and set off at a run back down the way they had come.

Running in the sand of the creek bed was the hardest part. They tried to run along the bank but soon gave it up as the western end of Hill 376 reached the creek in a tangle of rough little gullies. Within minutes it was apparent that Graham was the fitter.

Between gaps for breath CSM Grey called, "Go on ahead of me Cadet Kirk."

"No sir. Capt Conkey said we should never do that in this situation," Graham gasped in reply.

"He also said not to run in case we also have an accident!" CSM Grey replied. Almost as soon as he said it, he fell. "Aaah! Ouch! Blast! Twisted my bloody ankle," he cried.

Graham helped him up. By now he was feeling sick with dread. Every second might count! The cadet was dying of snake bite. Should he leave CSM Grey?

CSM Grey settled that for him, "Go on! Run! I will follow. You can come back and find me. It can't be much more than five hundred metres."

Graham nodded and ran on. CSM Grey hobbled rapidly in his wake but was soon left behind. Graham had never run through the bush at night on his own. As he ran, all sorts of little fears flitted across his mind: being bitten by a snake himself; wild pigs; wild cattle; falling and hurting himself.

He was also amazed at just how well his eyes worked in the dark. *I must have good night vision,* he surmised.

After a few hundred paces he slowed to find a track up the bank through the tangle of lantana. As he did, some instinct warned him. He stopped in his tracks and froze. A faint rustling noise made him click on his pencil torch. What he saw made his blood run cold with fear and shock. One of the dark lines across the track was not the shadow of a branch. It was a large brown snake with a flattish black head, and it was only two paces in front of him. The reptile was as thick as his arm and at least two metres long. It had drawn its body back into the striking 'S', and as Graham stared at it in horror he saw its tiny forked tongue flicker.

It is ready to strike. Don't move! his mind told him. For a few heartbeats fear held him frozen. Then he shook his head and felt exasperated. *Bloody thing! I must get the message to camp. I must back off and go around it,* he reasoned.

But it took an effort of will. What helped him was hearing CSM Grey hobbling towards him. The snake heard him too and became agitated, waving its head slowly from side to side. Graham took a deep breath and slowly moved his left foot back. The snake did not strike, so he moved his right foot as well. All the while he kept the torch on it, ready to spring if it lunged. The snake's eyes glittered a deadly red which fascinated him.

Another step back, then another. *Safe! He can't reach me now.*

Graham breathed easier. The snake lowered itself and started to slide away. Graham called out, "Watch out CSM, there's a bloody great big snake here."

CSM Grey limped up to join him. "Holy Moses! Look at the size of it!" he cried.

To Graham's intense relief the snake slid off into a pile of flood debris in the creek bed.

"I nearly stepped on the bastard," Graham explained.

"Bloody lucky you didn't. We don't want two snake bites in one night. Now get going!"

Graham needed no urging. He ran on. Now he kept the torch aimed at the cattle pad as he followed it up onto the flat between the two creeks. It was some comfort, but he doubted if he would see a snake in time at the speed he was travelling. He was also vaguely aware that he was more concerned about getting help than worrying about his own safety.

Up on top of the bank he came out into open savannah woodland. The ground was flat and there was a cattle pad to follow. *The bivouac is just along here,* he thought anxiously, his eyes probing the starlit darkness.

He was right. The faint glow of a light showed a few hundred metres ahead. Within three minutes Graham reached the company position. A lantern was burning in the centre and Capt Conkey and the officers sat on boxes and logs around it. Graham blurted out his story.

Capt Conkey didn't waste a moment. "Lt Hamilton, Sandra, get going." He turned to the other officers. "Jill, radio Range Control and tell them to call an ambulance. Mel, drive out to the main road and meet it and guide it in."

Uninvited, Graham ran to Lt Hamilton's Rover with the medic, Cpl Kelly. As he did, CSM Grey came limping into camp. They did not wait for him as he slumped onto the log. By the time Graham was aboard the Rover, its engine was going and its headlights were on. Lt McEwen was in the front.

As he swung the Rover around, Lt Hamilton called, "Which way? Where do I go?"

Graham hauled out his map and torch. "Go left across Speed Creek sir," he replied.

The Rover accelerated along the dirt track. In the headlights Graham saw Crane and Morris at the 4 Section sentry post. He had quite forgotten about the exercise. Lt Hamilton drove fast. They roared out to the gravel road, swung left and raced down across the concrete causeway. Graham bent to study his map.

A minute later they reached the dry creek where CUO Hansen's patrol was in position. No-one was visible and they didn't stop.

As they raced up out of the creek, Graham said, "Go left here sir and go due south beside Speed Creek."

Lt Hamilton did as he was told. The line of trees in the bed of Speed Creek gave them a guide. It was quickly apparent that Lt Hamilton was a very good driver as they drove fast through the bush. The moonlight helped as they could see outside the cone of the headlights. They dodged trees and ant hills, bumped over several small logs and numerous rocks. Within five minutes they reached a small creek which wound across the plain to join Speed Creek.

"Here sir," Graham instructed.

Lt Hamilton turned the Rover to face the creek and applied the brakes. He climbed out, leaving the engine and headlights on. Graham scrambled out as well. There was no sign of anyone.

"They probably aren't here yet sir. I'll go and look," Graham said.

"Not on your own. I'll come with you. Sandra, if they turn up toot the horn," Lt Hamilton replied.

Graham did not wait. He set off at the run down into the creek bed, impelled by a terrible sense of urgency. This time he used his torch. Almost at once, he was re-assured to find the tracks he and the others had made in the sand. He recognised the spot. They were within a hundred metres of the place where they had met the sergeant and corporal.

Hearing Lt Hamilton and Cpl Kelly coming Graham kept on running. He followed the tracks up the other side of the creek and onto the low ridge. Almost at once the flicker of a torch showed. Graham heaved a sigh of relief and yelled. Warrant Officer Howley shouted back. Graham, Lt Hamilton and Cpl Kelly ran across the rough ground to join the group.

They had the casualty on an improvised stretcher. Warrant Officer Howley, Sgt Strutton and four St Michael's cadets were carrying it. The sergeant and corporal were among them, helping to carry, one each side. All were panting with exertion.

"How is he?" Lt Hamilton asked Warrant Officer Howley as he took the corner of the stretcher from Sgt Strutton.

"In a bad way, unconscious and breathing is getting irregular. So is his pulse. Thanks young Kirk," this last to Graham, who took the stretcher pole from him.

The sergeant and corporal took over from the two cadets who moved to the sides. The group stumbled on over the rough ground to the top of the creek bank. By then Graham was panting and perspiring and his fingers were already feeling strained.

"Okay, take it easy down this bank," Warrant Officer Howley cautioned. "Hold the lower end high as you go down so the casualty doesn't slide off."

They started down the steep creek bank but almost immediately the sergeant slipped and they came to a standstill in a cloud of dust.

"Too bloody slow!" Lt Hamilton cried. "Lift him onto my shoulders, quick!"

Warrant Officer Howley grabbed the unconscious cadet and heaved him onto the officer's shoulders. Lt Hamilton grunted, shifted the balance, then strode down the bank into the trees. Graham ran ahead to shine his torch on vines and logs. The glow of the Rover's lights made a wonderful welcoming navigation guide. They splashed across the shallow stream and Graham helped steady the OOC as he staggered in the soft sand.

At the other bank, Warrant Officer Howley and Graham both grabbed Lt Hamilton's shirt and belt and helped him to stagger up the steep slope. He then strode to the vehicle. Cpl Kelly ran ahead and set up the army stretcher in the back and climbed in. Within a minute the casualty was on the stretcher and Lt Hamilton in the driving seat.

"Don't wait for us, get going! Do the First Aid while you travel," Warrant Officer Howley ordered.

Lt Hamilton swung the vehicle around and raced off through the bush as fast as he safely could. Graham stood and watched it go, his heart thumping with the exertion and relief. He suddenly felt utterly drained.

Warrant Officer Howley clapped him on the back. "Bloody good effort son! Twenty-five minutes. It's just on 0300 now. Well done! Now, where is the CSM?"

Graham related the story of the run. He was still puffing and sweating. Then shivering and reaction set in. All the while Warrant Officer Howley's words rang in his mind: My Offsider! Singled out! Well done! Bloody good effort son!

Son! He called me son! marvelled Graham. *And that after what I did to his daughter!*

Warrant Officer Howley made them all have a big drink then said, "Come on, let's get back to camp."

He then led the way along the creek bank in the Rover's tracks. On the way they picked up CUO Hansen's patrol. At that point the sergeant realised where he was.

"Sir, the vehicle which brought us is just up the road at a cattle grid," he said.

Warrant Officer Howley ordered CUO Hansen to send a corporal and two cadets to find the vehicle and to bring it to camp.

"You four stay with us," he said to the St Michael's cadets.

They continued walking, following the gravel road and arriving back at camp at 0320hrs. Here they were allowed to sit and brew a coffee. Graham sat himself down and listened to the talk, all the while his mind on the Rover that was racing through the night.

God, I hope they make it in time! he thought.

Chapter 39

COMPETITION

It was nearly 0400hrs before Graham returned to his section. He discovered that CUO Grant and Cpl Telford were the only people awake.

"Capt Conkey ended the exercise and sent everyone to bed except a piquet of CUOs and NCOs," CUO Grant explained. "So what's the story? What went on?"

Graham related the outline of the story. He thought it politic to minimise his own part in it for fear of more teasing.

But CUO Grant was plainly curious. "Why did Warrant Officer Howley single you out?"

"Because he met me on morning runs and he knew I was very fit. We used to run together before school," Graham replied.

This sounded a bit lame, so he outlined the incident on the Esplanade involving the St Monica's girls.

"Fair enough. You'd better to get to bed. We are still doing a practice 'Stand to' at First Light. You might get an hour's sleep," CUO Grant said.

Graham was glad to do that. He slid into his sleeping bag fully dressed and with his boots on. Having made himself as comfortable as he could, he tried to will himself to sleep. In this he was unsuccessful. Instead, he found his thoughts replaying the events of the night.

Twenty minutes later a Rover came driving in from the gravel road. It was from St Michael's. Graham saw an immensely fat officer waddle over to the lantern and would have loved to be able to listen in. After about fifteen minutes, the fat officer loaded the St Michael's cadets into the vehicle and drove off.

No sooner had it departed than another Rover drove in. It was Lt Hamilton. Curiosity drove Graham to get up and walk over to HQ. Capt Conkey and Lt Standish were still awake, and Warrant Officer Howley appeared at the same time as Graham. Both looked at Graham but made no comment on his presence. Lt Hamilton had LCpl Bannister with him as well as Lt McEwen and Cpl Kelly.

"He was still alive when we got to hospital. We met the ambulance just out of Townsville and followed it to help with his details at the hospital," Lt Hamilton said.

Capt Conkey nodded. "Do they think he will live?" he asked.

"Yes. They put him straight into intensive care," Lt Hamilton replied.

"Who was he? What's his name?" Capt Conkey asked.

"Cadet Snodgrass," Lt Hamilton replied.

Lt Maclaren came sleepily out of the darkness and the facts had to be related a second time. Graham listened to the conversation for a while; then went back to his bed. He lay down and again tried to get to sleep and this time was successful.

Within fifteen minutes he wished he hadn't been. No sooner had he started to dream than he was shaken awake by Cpl Grenfell.

"Get up. Pack up. No Noise. No torches. Then Stand to," Cpl Grenfell said.

By 0530hrs the company was completely packed and lay behind their packs with their boots and webbing on, ready as Capt Conkey put it, 'to march or fight.' CUO Grant and Sgt Masters came silently round several times to check that everyone was doing the right thing. After them came Capt Conkey, CSM Grey and Warrant Officer Howley.

Warrant Officer Howley bent down and whispered to him, "How are you feeling, young Kirk?"

"Fine sir. Bit tired."

Warrant Officer Howley patted his shoulder and moved silently on. Graham was very glad it was dark, imagining the flak from jealous cadets if they had seen the gesture. He shook his head in admiration at both Capt Conkey and Warrant Officer Howley.

How do they keep going? he wondered.

The 'Stand to' went on till it was fully light at 0550hrs. Just before they stood down the night patrols came filing in out of the bush. The senior cadets looked very tired and dirty but were immensely pleased with themselves. The thing that struck Graham most about them was how similar they looked to the Heatley patrol he had seen on Day 1: the same air of pride, competence and teamwork.

Next year that will be me, he thought.

'Stand down' was called and then the CSM called the platoons in for Check Parade. During this Graham was sent out to be sentry at the turnoff from the gravel road. Being the sentry guarding the camp was another experience Graham enjoyed. He wasn't entirely sure what to do if he saw someone, but he sat behind a bush hoping that St Michael's would attack.

But nothing of the sort happened. At 0635hrs Cpl Grenfell sent Harriet out to take over from him. Graham set off back towards the platoon. As he did, he noted a group over at the 4 Pl area.

What's going on over there? He wondered. It looked like the officers and CSM and when he saw Cpl Moore start emptying his kitbag onto his groundsheet a horrible sinking sensation began to settle in Graham's stomach. *That looks like a kit search. If they find any alcohol Moore will blame me!*

But the group were too far away to see any detail but the body language and set faces indicated it was not a happy gathering.

Poor old Capt Conkey! He doesn't deserve that sort of grief, Graham thought.

Feeling quite apprehensive, he returned to the platoon and quickly ate, shaved, and packed up. He was just finishing when the platoon was ordered to place their kitbags and packs in a line near the truck. While they were doing this, Graham's suspicions were confirmed. The rumour was that Cpl Moore had been found with whiskey in his kit and had been removed from command of his section and sent to HQ.

Gwen made the first comment. "Good! He should be demoted. We don't need leaders who sneak and cheat and don't keep their promises."

Stephen nodded agreement and asked the cadet from 3 PL who was retailing the story who was taking over Moore's section. "Or is it being disbanded?"

"Not sure," the cadet replied.

"A bad day for that section," Stephen commented, "Today being the Section Competition."

Graham could only agree but he was too anxious about any possible consequences involving him. It quite took the shine off the previous night's achievement.

At 0730hrs CUO Grant sent the corporals to collect their sentries. Sgt Masters organised work parties to fill in the latrines and to pick up any litter. That done the platoon was lined up. To CUO Grant's obvious annoyance 1 PL moved first. They went trudging past in a long line, offering smart comments about which platoon was the best as they did.

While they were doing this, a Land Rover drove in. In it were the OC of St Michael's and one of his OOCs. Graham saw them speaking to Capt Conkey and their own staff. The word was passed around that the cadet bitten by the snake was alive and out of danger. That was a great relief to Graham.

"Slack buggers," Sgt Masters said to CUO Grant. "They should have been better organised; and their patrol should have had a radio."

CUO Grant grunted. "Yes. Right, let's get moving."

By 0800hrs 2 PL was moving. They carried only webbing. For the first kilometre they walked in single file up a long, gentle slope through open bush to a line of low hills. Their route took them over the low saddle between Hill 376 and Hill 397 and once again Graham was amazed at the vast vista of empty bush and isolated hills that spread ahead of them. Once again, he had sharp memories of that first night.

They came to the fence near where Graham had tracked 9 Section on the first night and rolled under it. Thinking of that gave him mixed feelings. That event had made him some bad enemies and he still suffered twinges in his right thigh.

I suppose Moore and his cronies will have it in for me now, he mused.

From there and down another long, gentle slope dotted with ironbarks. *This is where that lost patrol was last night,* Graham realised.

He studied the ground with interest. It all looked very different in daylight; not nearly as rough. He looked for the remains of the fire but did not see it. The platoon members were apparently unaware of the facts, and he did not feel like telling them so walked on in silence.

After another ten minutes walking, they came to Granite Creek about 500 metres east of the junction with Speed Creek. At this point a vehicle track crossed and the creek bed had been gouged out by sand miners.

Up on the other bank, on a gently sloping area among an extensive stand of ironbarks, they found Capt Conkey, Warrant Officer Howley and CSM Grey waiting. They had driven around in a Rover. 2 PL was directed to another clump of ironbarks on a low rise fifty metres from the vehicle track. 1 PL was on their left at the track, which Graham now realised wound out through the trees to the bitumen road at the point where they had started Exercise 'Border Crossing'. When 3 PL arrived, they were placed on their right. Section areas were pointed out and packs and kitbags collected from the truck.

The cross-country march had only been 2.5 km but had tired some of the smaller cadets. Morris and Harriet moaned about chafing and blisters. Graham had thoroughly enjoyed it. Even to his inexperienced eyes the platoons were now starting to work like teams and he was glad to belong to 2 PL.

And Cpl Grenfell is a bloody good section commander. The best in the company, he decided.

CUO Grant called a Pl O Group and the cadets were allowed to set up camp while this was done. Graham soon had his hutchie erected and sat down on his pack to clean his gear. As he did, he was aware of an undercurrent which he was sure concerned his activities the night before. The mood he sensed was a mixture of jealousy and respect.

Cpl Grenfell returned from the Pl O Group and called them all together to give his own orders.

This was for a patrol exercise which was combined with a section competition. While the section commanders gave orders Capt Conkey briefed the staff, CUOs, Sgts and Control Group. These collected stores from the vehicles and dispersed into the bush in a dozen different directions. As they did Graham noted Cpl Moore helping HQ set up a new CP hutchie. Luckily Moore did not appear to notice him, but it was food for anxious thought.

There was then a pause while the cadets waited for the course to be set up. During this Cpl Grenfell sat the section in a group and revised section formations, how to use a compass, safety precautions with the rifle, first aid and badges of rank. Several work parties were sent to start digging latrines.

By 1000hrs everything was ready. Several sick cadets, including LCpl Bannister, were left to guard the camp. Capt Conkey and CSM Grey took half the company each and led them off to their start points. 4 Section was walked for another kilometre through the bush to where the dry creek nicknamed 'Wriggly Creek' joined Speed Creek at the base of Hill 430. Here they were seated in the shade by Sgt Strutton. He then called them over one at a time and asked them questions on Survival: how to find water, how to make a solar still, how to test plants for poison and so on.

Graham had no trouble with these as had learned enough in the Scouts to make a reasonable attempt. Sgt Strutton had a mark sheet and noted down each cadet's score. He then sent them on up the bed of Speed Creek for 500m. Here, to Graham's pleasure, they met Warrant Officer Howley. He asked them to solve a variety of pioneering problems.

Once again, Graham's scouting training paid off. He was able to tie the four knots requested. He also knew how to calculate the height of a tree (by pencil at arm's length and paces), how to measure the width of a creek (equal triangles, *My old mate Pythagoras that Mr Ritter is always carrying on about,* he thought wryly).

Warrant Officer Howley was impressed. "That is bloody good Cadet Kirk. You have got full marks. Keep it up."

Feeling pleased with himself, Graham went on to the designated waiting area 50 paces along in the shade of a tree. When all the section were there, they walked up the creek bed to the junction with Granite Creek. Here Sgt Crossley asked them general military knowledge questions. These were on the topics Cpl Grenfell had revised: section formations, badges of rank and so on, so Graham did well.

Their next leg took them almost back to camp. Here CSM Grey had a Drill Stand. The section had to perform a set sequence of drill movements with the section commander giving the orders. Graham had difficulty with the rifle drill but coped well enough with the foot drill, the turns and marching.

Lt Maclaren took them next for safe weapon handling. This was done at their new camp site. Each cadet in turn was handed a Steyr and empty magazine and had to perform the correct drills. Graham found this stand easy and got full marks. They were sent on over the low rise for a hundred metres to where CUO Broughton and Sgt Macalistair gave them a navigation test. Once again this was done individually, with the scores being reduced to a section average. Graham found it easy: taking compass bearings, setting the compass for night marching, finding grid references on the map.

The next stand was Lt Standish and Lt McEwen. This was First Aid. From there they went down to Wriggly Creek only a few hundred metres from where it passed under the bitumen road. Here CUO Madden and Sgt Mitrovitch tested their fieldcraft. By then it was lunch time so they sat in the shade at 'Two Buckets Junction' (so named because two old buckets hung from the branches of a tree) and ate. The food was again Ration Pack.

By then Graham was feeling both glad and sad. The section had settled down as a group and he felt he really belonged to it. He was also sure he was doing a good job. To counterbalance that was the knowledge that the camp would end the next day. In his heart of hearts Graham wanted it to go on for ever.

After lunch they were sent to patrol down Wriggly Creek. The creek was only about five paces wide with a dry sandy bottom. The banks were low but steep and lined with trees and bushes. Trouble erupted from these when two members of Control Group: (Sgt Brown and Cpl Holbrook), pretended to shoot at them from under cover. Cpl Grenfell quickly organised the section for an attack. This time Graham was one of the riflemen. He threw himself into the 'Fire and Movement' with fierce delight and energy.

Only as he raced forward from one piece of cover to another did Graham note Capt Conkey and CSM Grey watching from up on the bank. That impelled him to try even harder. He dived for cover so hard he bruised his knees and skinned his left hand. Sweat poured down his face and salt stung his eyes, but he carried on, firing, then running forward on command.

On the re-org he became the First Scout. This was a real challenge, which had an anti-climax. They came to Lt Hamilton and a radio test. One at a time they had to assemble, test and talk on an army radio. Then they continued the patrol. This time Graham's vigilance paid off.

At a sharp bend he spotted two 'enemy', apparently arguing about where they were over a map. Quickly Graham signalled the section under cover and called Cpl Grenfell up. Cpl Grenfell did a quick recce and gave rapid orders. The machine gun group (Gwen and Harriet) crawled up a small washout to cover on top of the bank on the right. The remainder of the section lined up on either side of Cpl Grenfell. When all was ready he called on the two enemy to surrender. Instead they grabbed their weapons and ran for cover. The section attacked.

"Well done, the best so far," was CUO Grant's comment as they re-formed to continue. Feeling very pleased with themselves they continued on, Graham still the scout.

Mines, trip wires and odd items he detected. Then he noted boot prints going up a steep cattle pad into the lantana on top of the bank on their left. He signalled halt and crept up to look. About twenty metres further along the creek he detected a hat among the bushes: an ambush!

With his heart beating rapidly with excitement, he made his way back down to report to Cpl Grenfell. Cpl Grenfell went up to have a look; then organised them to do a flank attack. The section backtracked for 50 paces to a bend in the creek; then went up a small washout to emerge among a thicket of small trees on the hill slope behind the ambushers. These were now clear to see and were identified as CUO Hansen and Sgt Cleland from 4 PL.

The pair were quite unaware they had been seen and kept peering down through the lantana into the creek, wondering when the section would come walking along. Cpl Grenfell waved the section to stand up and they walked slowly forward in extended line. Only when they were twenty-five metres away did CUO Hansen hear them. He turned to look, and the expression of surprise was so comical Graham laughed aloud as they broke into a run.

CUO Hansen was embarrassed at being caught so badly but had the good grace to tell them they were the only section which had detected the ambush instead of being caught in it. That made Graham feel very proud of his scouting.

This was the last 'Stand'. After walking along the creek for another hundred metres, they returned to their start point at Speed Creek. Sgt Strutton told them to move directly back to camp.

It did not work out that way. After moving only a hundred metres they were 'fired on' by 3 Section. An impromptu 'battle' began. This drew in 5 Section, who had just finished at CUO Hansen's stand on their right. This forced Cpl Bates to withdraw rapidly, until 2 Section was met. The cadets knew the exercise was over but the thrill of a 'Cowboy and Indian' battle got them going. In sheer high spirits they attacked, defended, rallied, and attacked again.

As the 'battle' reached the edge of the extensive mulga thicket on the flat, CUO Grant, Sgt Masters, and 6 Section came running in from their right. CUO Grant at once took firm control and began to manoeuvre the sections to drive back the 1 PL sections. These were outnumbered and, without their CUO, lacked the control of 2 PL.

By then it was late in the afternoon. The sun was low in the west. CUO Grant organised the whole platoon into one long extended line and began leap-frogging the sections forward. 1 PL was driven from the field, even after Cpl Sherry's section arrived. By then the camp area was in sight. Graham saw Capt Conkey, Warrant Officer Howley and the OOCs watching. As they made no attempt to stop the 'battle', CUO Grant kept attacking. During this attack Graham's admiration for his CUO rose even further.

I definitely want to be a platoon commander, he thought.

By then 3 PL had arrived back in the camp and they hastily tried to defend it by stacking packs and using logs and jerry cans for cover. CUO Madden and Sgt Mitrovitch came running up from behind, trying to get around them to get to their own platoon. This led to a chase by 6 Section, which ended when they, in turn, ran into 4 PL, which launched a flank attack. The 'battle' ended in a glorious free for all before Capt Conkey called a halt.

By then Graham was beside himself with excitement. He was laughing and panting for breath and thought it was the greatest fun.

"We won! Wiped you mob off the board!" he told Stephen as he attacked past him.

The company was called in and seated in section lines to do a roll check. Once that was over Capt Conkey briefed them on the evening and then dismissed them. CSM Grey then nominated platoons to provide work parties to dig latrines. 4 Section was told by Sgt Masters to set to work. Graham was ordered to help dig the male latrine but did not mind.

But that led to the next unexpected drama. "Where do I go, sergeant?" he queried.

Sgt Masters pointed along a cattle pad that led into the thick stand of stunted mulga-like trees behind 3 Platoon. "Follow that track. It goes straight to it. I think there are already tools there. I'll send Crane and Evans to join you."

"Sergeant."

Graham stood up and started walking. He did not really mind. He was still relishing the events of the last few days. Nobody paid any attention to him as he walked along the well-worn cattle pad. A minute later he was out of sight of the camp and was looking around for the latrine site.

It was 50 paces further along, in a small clearing of bare sand and clay amid the lantana and thick scrub. There was already a cadet there digging but as soon as he saw him Graham stopped walking. It was Moore.

Moore glanced back over his shoulder and Graham at once saw that he had been weeping. The dust on his face was streaked with tears. As soon as he saw Graham, Moore's face changed. Anger flared and then escalated to rage. Flinging aside the shovel he spun round.

"You, you bastard! You've cost me my stripes!" he shouted.

Graham stopped walking and bristled at the accusation. "I did not! I haven't told anyone," he retorted.

"You did, you mongrel! You dobbed and now Capt Conkey says he is going to demote me. It's your fault!" Moore screamed.

"I didn't!" Graham replied, angered by the false accusation. "Someone else must have told."

"Liar! Bastard!" Moore screamed. Before Graham could react, Moore launched himself into an attack.

Graham did not want to fight. *I am just starting to get out of the bad books. A fight will do me no good at all,* his racing mind told him, even as he staggered back and tried to fend off Moore's angry punches.

He tried to say again that he had not told anyone, but Moore was too upset to listen and he ran in and shoved and punched at Graham.

Graham was caught off balance and tried to move away but tripped over the pile of sand beside the half-dug latrine. Before he could recover, Moore had hit him again and knocked him flat on his back.

"Stop! Stop! It wasn't me!" Graham cried.

But Moore would not listen or stop. He began to kick at Graham as he rolled on the dirt. Savage blows took him in the kidneys, the back, the upper arm and the back of the head. The kicks by Moore's army boots really hurt and one of them took him in the side of the face as he tried to roll away, loosening several teeth. The shock of being attacked began to turn to fear. The kicking was being delivered with such ferocity Graham began to fear that he would suffer serious injury.

In desperation, he rolled away and tried to get to his feet. Moore rushed after him and landed several more kicks, one in the side and another near his left knee. That really hurt and added to Graham's anxiety. But he was also now reacting to the injustice of the attacks and his temper began to rapidly rise. Instead of trying to shield himself from the blows, he curled up and kicked back, driving Moore away.

Then Moore stepped into the latrine and fell backwards. That gave Graham a chance to roll over and get to his feet. By then he was hurting all over and his anger was coming to the boil. But there was still a niggling caution warning him not to get into a fight. Stepping back he took stock of his hurts and bruises and prepared to defend himself.

Moore, still enraged, came rushing at him, his fists flailing. Graham put his own fists up as he had been trained to do but just used them to block the hail of blows rained at his head and upper body. He was able to stop most of them, but a few got past his guard and hit him. And they hurt.

And it was obvious Moore was not a trained boxer. Graham saw that Moore's left hand was well down and away when he was punching with his right. The temptation was too good an opportunity to miss and by then he felt he was justified in hitting back. There was Moore's unguarded jaw.

Whack!

Graham drove his right in hard. Moore went tumbling back and fell to the ground. As he did, he let out a sharp cry of pain and then began swearing. Graham stepped back, still hoping to reason with him and end the fight.

As Moore scrambled to his feet, Graham called to him, "Stop it Moore! Stop it! I did not tell anyone! Stop!"

Now he was deeply worried about consequences. *I have punched a corporal! Capt Conkey could chuck me out for that,* he thought.

But Moore was now not only wild with rage, his pride had been hurt. He came rushing in again, swinging wild punches and screaming that he would kill him. Graham parried most of the blows but again a few got through. One hit his left lower face and loosed more teeth and he tasted blood.

Through Graham's mind flashed an image of him fighting Larsen at school. It seemed somehow surreal, like the replay of an old movie. Time seemed to slow down. There was Larsen's-Moore's unguarded stomach right in front of him. Graham reacted with a trained response. He stepped closer and swung his left in a short, hard jab into Moore's stomach.

Moore grunted sharply in pain. His head appeared in front of Graham as he doubled forward. Graham followed up with a solid right cross which smacked the left side of Moore's jaw. Moore just went down, sprawling back on the bare sand.

Graham stepped back to prepare to stop another assault but saw that Moore was scrabbling to get away. As Moore scrambled to his feet,

Graham saw that there was fear in the other boy's eyes and that he was not going to launch another attack.

"Now stop it!" Graham snarled, poised ready for another bout. "I didn't dob. I did not tell anyone. Someone else did. So leave me alone."

Moore glared at him and swore and then spun on his heels and hurried away. The retreat was so sudden that Graham was caught by surprise. For a moment he was tempted to run after him. But then the realisation sank in that he had won. For a few more seconds he stood ready to fight and then he lowered his fists and stood there breathing heavily.

As Moore vanished out of sight, Graham blinked to clear sweat from his eyes and he took a few deep breaths before doing a quick inventory of his hurts. He also looked around, surprised that nobody had come to investigate the yelling and noises. But all was quiet.

I suppose he will go and get his cronies and they will find an opportunity to bash me, he thought. How to keep out of that situation became his next concern but then he shrugged. *No. Better that they do beat me. That will get them into more trouble and I might not get chucked out.*

To his own surprise Graham found he did not care if Moore came back with his mates.

I will fight the lot of them, he resolved.

Chapter 40

DIRECTION

Finding that he had lots of little aches and pains but nothing obviously injured or broken, Graham went over to where a pick lay on the ground. Taking it up he began to furiously break up the hard clay down in the latrine.

Ten minutes later Crane and Morris appeared, Crane carrying a jerry can and Morris a washbasin and toilet paper.

"You finished yet?" Crane asked, peering into the hole.

"No. You have a go and dig out that soil," Graham replied.

He was astonished that neither knew about the fight and apparently did not see any marks on him to indicate anything had happened.

Surely Moore has told people by now? Graham wondered.

More minutes went by and still there was no obvious alarm or action. Graham concentrated on digging, working off his pent-up emotions while bracing himself for the dreaded summons. Several cadets came to check if they could use the latrine, but it was obvious they knew nothing.

There had still been no angry NCO telling him to go to the OC by the time they had finished the latrine. Graham was amazed. Still feeling intense trepidation, he picked up the pick and followed the other two back along the cattle pad. As he came out of the thicket, he looked hard at the cadets in 3 Platoon but even his usual enemies: Pigsy and Derek White, just curled their lips at him.

They don't know either!

Graham re-joined 2 Platoon and spent a few minutes washing his face and cleaning up. Still no serious consequences. He looked towards HQ and got a glimpse of Moore. He was sitting in his hutchie, and when he saw Graham looking he quickly looked away.

And then it came to Graham as clear as if Moore had held up a sign. *He hasn't told anyone!* he thought. *He's not game to tell his mates that I beat him in a fight, and he isn't game to tell any of the rank or the officers!*

That revelation caused Graham to let out a huge sigh. *Maybe I will get away with it?* he decided.

And he was still anxious and wary. But he also felt more confident and satisfied. Even so he was glad of a chance to sit on his own for a while as his bruises began to hurt. Pondering what he was going to do in the future and with his life he quietly sucked the blood from his loose teeth and decided he would aim at promotion in the cadets and think seriously about being a soldier.

Maybe even an officer.

The evening program was for a company campfire, at which each section was expected to perform as part of the section competition. To get ready Cpl Grenfell called the section together.

As they gathered, he said, "Where the hell is Cadet Crane?"

Graham looked around and saw Crane and Brooke talking to Angela and Rita. He pointed. "Over in Five Section chatting up the chicks."

Cpl Grenfell scowled and yelled out to Crane to join them. Crane did this with obvious poor grace. As he did, Graham could not help wondering if Crane had been trying to organise something else for the evening. Now that the camp had reached its last night there was a lot of socializing going on, much of it 'boy-girl'. He was not immune from it himself and wished he had a girlfriend he could be with that evening.

Once the section was all there, they practiced a skit for 15 minutes. Graham and Morris were then told to complete rigging a Hessian screen around the latrine. Graham knew he was being singled out but just shrugged. He and Morris went over to the HQ area to find the stores. To Graham's relief, there was no sign of Moore, but then he realised he did not care.

On returning past HQ after screening the latrine, Graham was intrigued to see Capt Conkey giving an O Group to the CUOs, HQ and Control Group.

The word quickly spread. Lt Hamilton, during a water run to Camp Gedling, had overheard the 15 ACU cadets discussing a raid on them that night.

Crane sneered. "Bloody noddies! They've got the wrong night," he said with a laugh.

"Good time to get us though, while we are all sitting around a campfire," Graham answered.

Harriet frowned. "Won't Captain Conkey stop them and get angry?" she asked.

Graham glanced over to where Capt Conkey was speaking to the OOCs and noted the fact that he was grinning and in a very good mood.

"No. From the look of it he's looking forward to it. I can see the light of battle in his eye," he replied.

Crane sneered again. "Well you'd know, being his bum boy," he taunted.

Graham flared with anger but before he could speak Gwen lashed out, "Shut up, Crane! Keep your filthy comments and insults to yourself. I object to that sort of talk!"

The argument between the two saved Graham from having to react. He shook his head in disgust and sat down to cook his tea.

Dusk set in quickly. As it got dark, two patrols, each of four cadets, went out. Both patrols were carrying radios. One, led by Sgt Brown, went out to the bitumen road near the Granite Creek Bridge. The other, led by Sgt Crossly, went south to the junction of Wriggly Creek and Speed Creek. When Graham asked why they were going that way Cpl Grenfell explained that 15 ACU had most of its cadets on exercise out towards Keelbottom Creek, which was in that direction.

Capt Conkey also organised a close piquet at the point where the vehicle track entered the bivouac area. That done the company got on with the campfire.

This was held in the bed of Granite Creek a hundred metres away. The sections filed down to the campfire with sleeping bags and blankets.

The fire was lit in a large sandy hollow. The sections were seated in order on the slope of the sandy bank under the trees. It was very comfortable and almost everyone appeared to be in a good mood. Graham sat down near the back of the section. By then he was feeling quite sore and ill from the beating, but it seemed that nobody had noticed anything, so he just acted as though he did not have a care in the world. Both Gwen and Harriet were there. Next to him sat Angela and Rita, but they ignored him and talked to Crane and Morris, or to the boys in 6 Section on their left.

CSM Grey acted as MC, assisted by CUO Grant and Lt Hamilton.

When all were seated Capt Conkey spoke a few words of thanks and then declared the concert open. Graham had been to plenty of campfires at Scout camps and had been unimpressed at the idea of the Army Cadets doing anything so childish. He was now pleasantly surprised. The jokes, skits and play acting were similar but much funnier and far better performed.

For the next two hours act followed act in quick succession. Each section in turn had to perform. Between acts different groups or individuals told jokes, sang, or put on acts. Graham found himself laughing uproariously and thoroughly enjoying himself. 4 Section put on a skit titled 'The Trained Elephant'. Graham and Morris were put under a blanket as the 'elephant'. Cpl Grenfell did the talking. They had to count with their feet, walk in step and out of step, step over people without stepping on anyone (the remainder of the section the first time and volunteers from the audience the second). On the second occasion, Morris, who was the back end of the elephant, emptied a water bottle over Cadet Doyle. This was acclaimed with shouts of laughter by the crowd.

The section sat down, glad to have the ordeal over. Act followed act: CUO Madden doing 'The Bear and the Rabbit'; CUO Grant and two sergeants doing the 'world's ugliest man'; 1 Section with 'Bomber over Berlin'; 2 Section doing 'The bobsled team'; 3 Section singing a song; Capt Conkey and Lt Maclaren doing 'The two retired Brigadiers' and so on. By then Graham was in stitches and, despite feeling sick and sore, thoroughly enjoying himself.

By then the sections were all intermixed, cadets having moved to sit next to friends. Peter and Stephen came to sit with Graham and that made him feel even better. As he sat there, a flow of emotions assailed him. To see all the happy, laughing faces in the firelight made him very glad he was there. But the knowledge that it was the last day of camp added a tinge of sadness. Seeing various boys and girls sitting close together and obviously in love evoked a deep feeling of longing, loneliness, and loss.

It was the boy-girl situation which provided the next drama. Capt Conkey had made it very clear he had no objection to a bit of genuine romance, as long as it was all open and above board. But when the campfire was over and they trooped back up the hill to the bivouac area, the word spread that there was trouble brewing.

Graham was a witness to some of this when he, Peter, and Stephen made their way to where Lt Hamilton was operating the canteen. Lt Maclaren came out of the darkness from the direction of Wriggly Creek with Crane, Morris, Angela, and a girl named Lisa from 8 Section in tow.

They were too far off for Graham to overhear the whole conversation, but it was obvious that they were in trouble.

What he did hear was Crane's loud protestation that, "We weren't doing anything, sir. We were only talking."

This gave Graham a moment of malicious glee, which he then recognised for what it was and regretted. Later, when they had been ordered to bed, there were hints of another drama. The rumours drifted from hutchie to hutchie: Capt Conkey was on the warpath because both Rita and Cpl Brooke were missing.

Silly buggers, Graham thought. *Why can't they wait one more day till camp is over?*

Which he realised was also unfair, knowing that, if Rita made advances to him he would have been sorely tempted. He lay back in the darkness in his hutchie, massaging his bruises and pondered the events of the last few weeks. Thoughts of Amelia got him sad and horny, tinged by concern as he had trouble remembering her face.

In the end Cpl Brooke and Rita were found by Lt Hamilton 'only talking' in a dry gully out towards the road. By then Capt Conkey was livid, and his anger was obvious to the whole company, even when his words were not audible. It seemed to end the camp on a sour note which annoyed Graham.

Capt Conkey gives up a lot of his spare time to make all this happen. It isn't fair to throw it back in his face, he told himself.

This helped fortify his own resolution to continue to be a good cadet. He dropped off to sleep fantasising about being a CUO, rescuing a girl from some group of desperate enemies.

* * *

Reveille was, as usual, at 0600hrs. Check parade and breakfast followed. As soon as that was over, they were ordered to strike camp. Graham found that depressing. The camp was nearly over; only hours to go. Sadly he rolled up his bedding and packed. While they worked the patrols came back in, tired but pleased with themselves, having located and annoyed St Michael's all night.

By 0730hrs all the hutchies were down, and the platoons were moving to place their kitbags and packs in neat lines beside the vehicle track. Water bottles were filled and the cadets were moved to sit in their sections in the shade of a large ironbark.

Graham was not the only one who was a bit down. Crane was in a very surly mood and Angela and Rita were both waspish. Cpl Brooke and Cpl Moore could both be seen working hard under Sgt Strutton's supervision, packing and loading boxes on the truck.

The morning was given over to an Orienteering Exercise. This was conducted as a treasure hunt, the results to count for the section competition. They were briefed by Capt Conkey and each section had a CUO or Sgt from another platoon attached to it to ensure there was no cheating. 4 Section found itself under CSM Grey's eye.

All of the clues were in codes. Capt Conkey gave them an Instruction sheet explaining the codes, plus a page of Trigram codes, where a group of three letters represented a word or sentence. He also explained that teamwork was the key. The first coded clue was then read out.

Gwen grasped the essence of it at once. She took over from Cpl Grenfell within a few minutes. "Look, there are eleven different codes. There are six of us. That means we each try two methods. We don't all sit around like a bunch of bubble-heads while Cpl Grenfell works his way through each method in turn."

She then allocated them each two codes. "Morris, you do Spelling normally but grouping the letters in Trigrams, plus Spelling backwards and grouping in Trigrams. Harriet, you do the Morse Code and Naval flags. Crane, you do the Trigram Codesheet and 'Pig Pen' code. Graham, you do Transposing letters and grouping in Trigrams, and Random alternate letters in Trigrams. Cpl Grenfell, you do the Codewheel for when the letters have been moved along to right or left and I will do the two types of numeral codes thing. Now, everyone work at once."

Graham took out his notebook and quickly copied the message. He then tried both methods. In the first he swapped each pair of letters and looked to see if recognizable words were forming. They didn't so he tried swapping every second letter. Crane and Morris were inclined to just sit and grumble but Gwen got stuck into them.

"Don't let us down you two. Make an effort. Just because you got into trouble last night you don't have to sulk today."

"I'm not sulking," Crane snarled, but he started working.

The first clue was written backwards, and Morris soon worked out the method. Gwen took over and finished it. They showed the message to CSM Grey and raced off.

This set the pattern. With Gwen driving and urging them at each place they quickly worked out which method of coding had been used. 4 Section very quickly drew ahead of the others. The only other sections which offered them serious competition were HQ and 1 Section. Peter was the brains and driving force of 1 Section. After a while the competition developed into a race between them, each section in turn leap-frogging the other for first place.

Capt Conkey walked along with the leading sections and this placed another level of stress to the competition. Graham thoroughly enjoyed it. Within three hours they had completed the course which led them over to Two Buckets Junction, down Wriggly Creek and back up Speed Creek, then zig-zagging across the flat on compass courses to end up back at camp. In the end 4 Section won by only a few metres, with 1 Section coming second and Coralie Bates' 3 Section in third place. HQ came fourth, but was 1st of the 'senior' sections.

Capt Conkey had the company seated when all sections were back in and he congratulated Cpl Grenfell and distributed prizes to the top three sections. He then spoke to them about the camp, congratulating most of them on doing very well, and on their good behaviour. As he said this he looked at Graham.

The platoons were then ordered to load their kitbags in the truck and to clean their areas. As Graham went to place his kitbag on the truck Sgt Masters said to him, "Not you Cadet Kirk. You are to report to Warrant Officer Howley with your gear."

Graham did so and found Stephen there as well. "You two are the Rear Party," Warrant Officer Howley explained. "You won't be going back today with the company. You will go back with me in two days' time. Don't worry, your parents know all about this. Put your gear in my Land Cruiser."

The friends did as they were told, Graham with a light heart and Stephen with some grumbles. They were then directed to rejoin their platoons for the clean-up. Graham had expected to have to fill in the latrines and was pleased to see that Crane, Cpl Brooke and Moore were given this task for the boys and Angela and Rita for the girls.

By 1200hrs the area had been cleaned up. One after another the platoons set off along the vehicle track. They trudged along in a long line carrying their packs, their boots stirring up the dust. It was unseasonably hot, and they looked very tired and glad to be going home. A few comments were cast at Stephen and Graham when it was realised they were not walking out.

After all the troops were gone Capt Conkey and CSM Grey inspected the area. Graham and Stephen were sent to pick up some rubbish missed in the clean-up. When Capt Conkey was satisfied the area was clean they climbed into the vehicles and drove out to the bitumen road where the company now sat in platoon groups eating lunch.

As they sat there, two coaches and two Land Rovers drove past towards Townsville. It was St Michael's unit on their way home. There were catcalls, rude comments and a variety of jibes and insults exchanged.

"We'll get you Cairns mob next year," they threatened.

"That'll be the day!" was the reply.

Good, Graham thought. *That is a challenge to look forward to.*

Soon afterwards three coaches arrived for the unit. The gear and cadets were loaded aboard, the Bus Roll ticked off by Lt McEwen, and the CSM did a final head count. Satisfied they weren't leaving anyone in the bush, Capt Conkey sent them on their way home. Graham waved to Peter.

"See you in a few days."

As the coaches headed off, Capt Conkey turned to Graham and Stephen. "Well you two, I am pleased with both of you. You behaved and your work was good. Keep it up. And thank you for doing this extra work. Have a good holiday and I will see you back at school."

He then drove off. Graham and Stephen climbed into Warrant Officer Howley's Land Cruiser and they followed, with the truck behind them. As they pulled out, Graham looked out at the bare, dry bush and felt a real twinge of regret and nostalgia.

"That was a great camp. I really enjoyed it," he told Stephen.

They drove down to Townsville and were quartered at Lavarack Barracks for the next two days. During this time they worked with Warrant Officer Howley, who mucked in with them in even the dirtiest jobs, to scrub, polish, dust, roll and re-pack all the stores. It was hard work, but Graham still found it enjoyable and interesting. Being in the largest army base in North Queensland also gave him a good chance to observe the regular army and that got him again seriously thinking about whether being a soldier might be a good career plan.

When all the stores were cleaned and returned, they drove back to Cairns, arriving mid-afternoon on the 14th day since they had left. It had been a long two weeks for Graham, but he sensed that they were of vital importance to him as they had provided him with a new direction in life.

When Warrant Officer Howley dropped him off at home he took the time to report to Graham's mother in glowing terms.

"A real worker and a good man in a crisis. You should be proud of him," he said.

He then shook Graham's hand and said, "You have done a mighty job. Keep going the way you are and you will do very well. I'm proud of you. Well done!"

The praise made Graham's eyes go a bit watery and he had to speak gruffly in response. By then he viewed Warrant Officer Howley as the greatest man he had ever met.

If I can be like him, I will be happy, he told himself.

Later, in private, he mulled over the entire experience. Out of this came a vow to keep on trying, to make himself worthy of the trust and effort Capt Conkey and Warrant Officer Howley had placed in him.

The second week of the holidays were a non-event. Most of the time Graham spent making model ships or playing 'Battleships' with Peter. When Graham went back to school after the holidays the teachers were amazed at how well he behaved and how hard he worked and they said so to Capt Conkey. Graham kept working hard. He not only behaved he went out of his way to volunteer for all sorts of school activities and extra jobs. Graham made sure he attended every Cadet activity and tried his hardest.

The weeks then slipped by. The pay-off came in November when the unit had its annual Passing-Out Parade. The ceremonial parade was held on the school oval in front of the entire school and hundreds of parents and family on a fine Wednesday afternoon. To begin with it was just a standard parade as they had rehearsed, and Graham stood stiff and proud in the front rank of 2 Platoon.

But then, during the inspection by an army colonel, the parade was thrown into confusion and disarray when a radio-controlled model aircraft, a replica of the famous Red Baron's World War 1 Fokker Triplane, was flown overhead and then buzzed right through the ranks causing some cadets to throw themselves flat and sending other cadets and the VIPs dodging and running.

Graham stubbornly stood his ground and was struck by the model's wing, causing it to cartwheel and crash. He knew at once whose model it was. It belonged to Willy Williams, the Year 8 'mad professor' who was also an air cadet.[2] The incident really annoyed Graham but he quickly recovered his composure as the parade was re-formed.

After the inspection came the 'March Past' and 'Advance in Review Order' and a speech. Following that was the presentation of prizes and Graham stiffened in hope and anxiety. Peter won the prize for Best Cadet for the year. Graham, to his own surprise, won the 'Most Improved Cadet' prize. As he marched out to receive it, he saw Warrant Officer Howley watching from the crowd. Their eyes met and the Warrant Officer nodded and winked.

There was more to come. 4 Section got 'Best Junior Section'. Graham moved out with the other section members, and as he stood with them having the colonel shake their hands and photos taken, he noticed his mother in the audience. She was beaming and he could not resist returning her smile. It seemed to bathe him in a warm glow.

And beside her were Kylie, grinning from ear to ear and Margaret. Her eyes met his and she gave a hesitant smile which he just as shyly returned. Even from 50 metres away he saw her happiness and that made him feel good too.

After the parade the list of candidates for the December promotion courses was put up. Reading that caused Graham a nervous flutter. Anxiously he scanned the list as he was jostled by dozens of curious cadets. It read:

Cadet Under-Officers Course:
WO2 Grey
Sgt Macalistair
Sgt Mitrovitch
Sgt Masters

[2] Read *Air Cadet* by C. R. Cummings

Warrant Officers Course
Sgt Cleland

Sergeants Course
Cpl Sherry
Cpl Grenfell
Cpl Yin Foo
Cpl Whyte
Cpl Bates (CQ)
Cpl Gayney
Cpl Yeldham

Corporals Course
Bannister
Brooke !
Bell (Good, Stephen made it!)
Bronsky (Even better, Pete as well)
Copeland (well, Gwen is very good)
Costigan
Crane (bloody hell)
Davies (Another pretty blonde!)
Doyle (bloody 'Dimbo' !)
Green
Griffin
Harris
Kirk

I made it! Graham told himself in wonder.

It seemed too good to be true and there was the lurking fear that it was a ghastly mistake. But it wasn't. In December Graham headed off with the others to do a 10-day Corporals Course at the Bunyip River Army Camp west of Townsville. Also on the course, and in the same section, was Cadet Nigel Snodgrass from St Michael's. The pair became firm friends, but also rivals.

Graham passed out 4th from a course of 120. Peter was top corporal. Stephen came 7th. At the Graduation Parade were both Capt Conkey and

Warrant Officer Howley. They congratulated their cadets for doing so well. In particular Warrant Officer Howley praised Graham.

"Good work, young Kirk. Keep it up son. I'm real proud of you. You are turning into a very good soldier. Keep going the way you are and you will be a winner."

Graham could only nod he was so choked up with emotion. For the rest of his life he treasured that moment. Warrant Officer Howley remained his role model and hero for the rest of his life, even after he had long surpassed him in both rank and military experience.

"He was a mighty man. He saved me and gave me direction. Thank you."

Enjoy more C.R. Cummings stories

The Air Cadets

The Navy Cadets

The Army Cadets

www.ingramcontent.com/pod-product-compliance
Lightning Source LLC
LaVergne TN
LVHW030907080826
845145LV00010B/2797